Scott Wellinger

CRASH

a Warren Dennihan novel

CRASH

A Warren Dennihan Novel
By Scott Wellinger

World Wide Publishing Group
New York   Los Angeles   London   Toronto
www.WWPGroupInc.com

Dedicated to my family. They live by the credo *you cannot build a big enough mess which cannot be fixed with a little extra love and support.*

PROLOGUE

THE NIGHT HAD DRAWN DOWN LIKE A THICK BLANKET OVER THE small New England town, tucked in the mountains of southern New Hampshire. A cloudless, late summer sky made the bright stars the only form of illumination, which were little more than pinholes of light off in a distant universe. The pine forest which shot up from the fertile ground gave off a rich perfume reminiscent of Christmas, which was less than half a year to come. Above the tree-line, the natural rock formation known as *The Old Man on the Mountain* was a slight, silhouetted backdrop bidding the tourists a final goodnight whilst he slept. The narrow, windy roads meandering through the hills below that watchful cliff north of Boston, Massachusetts, were fortified with guardrails and graveled pulloffs to accommodate the looky-loo tourist vehicles. The fall foliage leaf-peepers were still a month or so away, but the hiking and camping season was still in full swing. The heavy traffic from the visitors trying to get a last trip in before the arrival of colder nights, was nonexistent in the hours after dusk. The hikers, campers, and naturalists had long since ventured home for the night or abandoned their parked vehicles on one of the pulloffs on the side of the road, as they made camp somewhere in the darkened forest.

The *Old Man* was the sentry for several communities below his perch on the White Mountains; the county and township of Wayland, New Hampshire was by far the most affluent. The old and new money was drawn from the financial hub of Boston in the form of large salaries. The town flourished as the commuters preferred to spend their ample earnings in the sanctity and "tax-free" state of New Hampshire over the Metropolis of Boston which fed them to the South. Another form of income for Wayland is the tourism, though the affluent of the community continue to be torn in that while the outsiders boosted the economy, they trampled over their turf. The visitors should be felt yet not seen. The people of money from Wayland did appreciate the financial relief from the tourism, which was their dilemma in refraining from ousting their numerous intruders. While there is no sales tax on goods in New Hampshire, there is a nine percent tax on the prepared food served. Tourists eat out, contributing to the town's revenue. Restaurants are aplenty in Wayland, filled with a wait by those who don't live in the area permanently.

The winters were the most difficult for the citizens of Wayland in avoiding the onslaught of outsiders. The skiers would come from the flatlands by the SUV load and deface their great State. No matter the season, invaders inevitably made way toward the Old Man and the natural wonders he stood sentry over. The affluent of the community spent their time and income away from the flatlanders at the Wayland Country Club. Golf was just one activity taken in there, and in truth many claimed to play more often than they had a tee-time for. The sanctuary was more for camaraderie and companionship than the activities the club promoted. A place for the wealthy to rub elbows with others of their kind in the same area.

This particular night, those with money were keen to show off just how much they had and were willing to part with. The Gala and Charity event that was taking place in the pavilion was under way, all of the who's-who in place and opening wallets for the silent auction, though whom or what charity would be receiving these sums was anybody's guess. While the sprinklers were misting water over the lush back-nine of the manicured golf course, which could be seen out of the large windows, elegant gowns and tuxedos flattered the bodies of the occupants in the club. Live, light jazz music and the mumbled conversations of the local power couples mingling under the giant chandelier could be heard faintly in the distance, while the rest of the community went about their Saturday night. The well-to-do's had the evening festivities, freeing their assistants and staffers to have theirs.

Arelia Diaz had made her plans weeks prior, when she learned that she would have a rare night off. She was a live-in maid for one of the rich and beautiful, though she called herself a caretaker, and was looking forward to blowing off some built-up steam with a night of dancing with her girlfriends.

The initial response from her friends at her invitation for a night out on the town was a jealous decline, until they too were informed that they would have the night off. Her friends in the area were also in the employ of other event attendees and would also have the night free from; babysitting, nannying, serving, cleaning, maintaining, cooking, or the myriad other tasks their employers were too important to perform. A night of dinner; gossiping over the comings and goings of their respective power families, and certainly dancing would be just the cure for the tedium that ailed them. Only one friend, Marina could not make it. She was told that she would have to take care of a child, though her employer didn't have any children.

Arelia Diaz, a mid-thirties Brazilian woman, left her own family back in Recife to make a better life for herself and said family. A large portion of her income was sent back to Brazil to lift the station of her once poor family in Recife, keeping just what she needed to live on for herself. Other than her gaggle of female friends, she was alone in the United States. She had no spouse or children, which was the mainspring for many nights of tear-soaked cheeks and a saturated pillow. The oldest of four daughters, she saw limited opportunities in her native village and networked into an immigrant sub-community tucked into the American northeast almost ten years prior. Alone but not alone, she was content in managing a dream household, though it was not her own.

Miss Diaz did not consider herself to be what the Americans called a *cougar*, she was too young to be considered for the part, though she was going to be on the prowl this night. All women had needs, this was a rare opportunity, and she was going to make the most of it. She painted on a pair of the most expensive jeans she could afford, her ample bosom bursted out of the front of her new, sparkling, black-yet-shear blouse, exposing her black push-up bra, and donned a pair of high heels which lifted her four inches higher than her usual five-foot-three inch frame. With her raven hair done (in what was coincidentally called a Brazilian Blowout), and her makeup applied to accentuate her big, beautiful brown eyes, she would be turning some heads. She still had what it took to bag any man she wanted, despite her lack of practice.

She would not be bringing anyone back to her suite at her employer's palatial home, this was not allowed, nor did she have any intention of staying with an interested gentleman. Her duties would resume bright and early in the morning. Her employers would likely be as moody as usual, as demanding as usual. Maybe they would even be a little hungover, though they would never in a million years admit that to the help.   The agenda for the night would be dinner, *Forró* dancing, and a copious amount of flirting. Unfortunately the line would have to be drawn at flirting.

She was given an older, red, Honda *Civic* to use for her daily errands, which she was using while on her way downtown to meet her girlfriends. It was a small yet able car, in spite of the age, much like Arelia believed herself to be. She had plenty of life left, this was just a means to an end. A way to go back to Brazil with enough money saved to provide for a family back home and the new one she would make, and for their families after she was gone.

Diaz was used to the car and all of the idiosyncrasies that came along with it. She loved the limited freedom that the car provided her, but she loved the stereo system the most. In the ten years of being the caretaker, she was never allowed to listen to her music loud enough to be heard by anyone in any part of the house. Nor was she allowed to use headphones as she was always on call. Always. Failure to hear, much less respond to a call from the main house would mean an immediate end to the life she had built here and the inability to send money back to Brazil. Relegated to vehicular sonic therapy, she would blast her beats as loud as the car stereo and tiny speakers could muster.

She had the windows down, feeling the night air through her already blown raven locks of hair. The outside sounds were competing between the crickets, the sounds of the Country Club in the distance, and Arelia belting out the Portuguese lyrics over the loud music of her favorite band *Falamansa,* at the top of her lungs.

> *"Se um dia alguém mandou*
> *Ser o que sou e o que gostar*
> *Não sei quem sou e vou mudar*
> *Pra ser aquilo que eu sempre quis*
> *E se acaso você diz*

Que sonha um dia em ser feliz
Vê se fala sério"

She was blissfully unaware that this would be her final concert.

As she rounded a sweeping blind turn on Wayland Country Club Road, the singing and car-dancing was immediately interrupted by the harsh LED, high-beam headlamps glaring into her eyes from seemingly nowhere, yet everywhere. She knew nothing of candlepower light measurements, but the retina-burning headlamps blinding her surely could have illuminated Fenway Park. Diaz could not see anything, much less navigate the rolling left turn. She could not see the lever protruding off of the steering column to flash her own high-beams at the offensive driver coming towards her. Nor could she get her bearings on the road. Arelia was desperate to see a yellow line. A white line. Anything to pinpoint if she was in a lane. There were no vibrations from the warning grating on the side of the road, because there wasn't any grating on the side of the road. No reflectors, not that she would have been able to see anything being reflected in the already blinding light. She would have welcomed the grazing of a guardrail, just so she could sort out where she was in both time and space. Everything was happening so fast. Brakes were unused. The stereo remained at full, deafening decibels. There was no time to turn it down. No time to think. No time to sweat. Was there somewhere she could pull off? But that question did not register in the time it took her to sail off the road.

The little-Civic-that-could missed the end of a guardrail, grabbed the bit of gravel just off of the pavement, bulleted her through the small graveled pulloff area. The car continued, severing a maple tree that was contemplating the changing leaf colors, continuing on to impact the base of a large rock formation. The car came to an immediate halt from the forty-plus miles per hour it was traveling just seconds prior. The rear of the car was the last to learn of the immediate stop being insisted upon by the fixed and rooted boulder. The rear-end of the Honda had no choice but to follow the rest of the cars' lead after jetting into the air, the rear tire spinning as it tried to continue beyond the mess. It failed.

The sound of the dance music halted, replaced by the sound of the mangling of metal and the pulverizing of bone. The jagged metal sliced through flesh which added to the cacophony of horrific sounds. The macabre series of sounds lasted but a beat, but the devastation would be permanent.

Nothing would be continuing beyond the crash. Not the maple tree, not poor Arelia Diaz formerly of Recife, Brazil and more recently of Wayland, New Hampshire. Where her body existed in the cab, where she was car-dancing to her favorite band, singing as loud as her beautiful lungs could project, was a sick sculpture of metal, plastic, glass, rubber and human organs. The front of the car no longer existed. It was impossible to discern car from body, where the red paint from the Honda started, through all the blood, and the end of the former occupant. Her lifeless face rested, burning on the steaming engine that now occupied space in the back seat; searing what was left of her beautiful features, her head and neck was being pressed toward the truck of the Civic.

The offending headlights stared onto the wreckage for a time, determining what was already known. The lights crept slowly toward the destruction, attached to the black vehicle that was camouflaged by the dark of night. They would abandon the devastation they had caused. The upbeat, accordion-based dance music and singing, followed by the horrifying reverberations of the crash were no more. The sounds were replaced by the ticking of the cooling and destroyed engine; the sizzling of flesh against it; the acceleration of the fleeing murderous vehicle; and crickets.

1

UGLY. THE IMAGE APPEARING BACK AT HIM IN THE MAKESHIFT mirror was ugly. No other word could summarize the reflection and the atmosphere surrounding it; his every thought and emotion. The stainless steel metal above the all-in-one, Willoughby sink-toilet reflected pure ugliness. The image itself superimposed upon the backdrop of the institutional beige walls, the florescent lighting, the grey concrete floor.

Jacob Grantes had never been considered a hunk, nor an Adonis by any account. He was not a physical specimen for which to lust. He had never been compared to the likes of George Clooney but he had been somewhat attractive, smart, confident. His six foot one inch frame, his square jaw, his sea-green eyes were some of the features that admirers had named when defending him as 'a catch'. The image that had once stared back at him, however, had disappeared, morphing into the figure that was reflected back at him in the polished steel. He splashed water on his face, one push button on the faucet at a time, yet no matter how much water he applied, how much he washed, and how much he scrubbed his face, he could not cleanse the ugliness inside or out.

Grantes, inmate #437261, had been a guest at the Wayland County House of Corrections for the past six months, having been denied bail. He had not been in trouble with the law prior to the events leading him to this very moment, which made the denial pending trial quite unusual. Jacob was accustomed to living in a large home with his family and the picket fence, which made the current accommodations all the more intolerable. His cell was an eight by twelve foot concrete room with a double bunk, a small desk and a sink-toilet which he had to share with his celly. The space was tight and the nerves were stretched even tighter. Twenty hours per day were spent in this tiny space. Best friends could be put together in such a way and it would not take long to become mortal enemies. To make matters worse, the door to the cells lacked bars; a solid door, which allowed little air flow, with a narrow, horizontal slot at waist-high for food trays to be passed through, or to be handcuffed prior to exiting. The small, vertical window was convenient only for the Correctional Officers who had to execute head counts. This solid metal door was manufactured to make the most loud, god-awful clanks and noises when opened and closed. Studies had been done on this; millions spent, to craft an audible assault on inmates in an effort to make them uncomfortable, on edge, and contemplating the actions that had led them to their current place of residence.

The CO had awoken Grantes with a loud, mechanical unlatching, the grinding of metal as his cell door was sliding open at 5:30 AM.

"Grantes. You got 15 minutes to shit, shower 'n shave. Court. You'll get chow on the ride over."

"Yeah," he said between splashes of water on his face.

His grumbled reply indicated his malcontent, as this was to be a real shit day. It was to be a different kind of shit day, but a shit day all the same. All other days had the exact same schedule; filled with misery, meetings with so-called counselors, and a myriad of conversations with fellow inmates all of whom proclaim to be innocent or screwed by their lawyer. This day would be a shit day of a different color but a shade he knew quite well. Jacob Grantes had previously spent most of his adult life immersed in the muck and mire of the legal system, only on the other side of it. As a defense attorney, he knew exactly what this day would entail. The splashing of water on his face would make none of it go away.

"Jesus Christ, can you shut the fuck up? What time is it, bro?"

The shout came from a lump in the sheets, covering the body laying on the top bunk in his cell. Grantes' celly had a very low tolerance for anything beyond sleeping away his bid. This is known in prison as a bed-bid, and he is not the only one trying desperately to dream away the time.

"It's early. Sorry. I have court today. But it looks like you'll have the cell to yourself for the day," Jacob said to his cellmate in an effort spin a positive light on the early morning disruption to his much-needed beauty sleep.

"Goody." He said this without removing the covers which made him appear as though he was levitating five feet above a filthy concrete floor.

"You'll be able to shit in peace at least. I wish you'd spent a little time out of the cell so I could crap without an audience."

"You really gonna shower?"

"Yeah, I'm getting my shower bag ready now." Each inmate fashioned together a bag of toiletries to cart to the open shower area. Everything in the area was wet, as were the products after using them, requiring the cosmetics to be taken out of the bag to dry and then refilled before each visit to the showers.

"That means that the door is gonna open and close a couple more times. Why you gonna shower anyways? Gonna be front and center with a jumpsuit and shackles anyway, clean ain't gonna matter."

"They'll let me change into a suit."

"Ha - you're funny. You're an idiot, but you're funny. Where are you gonna get a suit asshole?"

"I came here in a suit. My lawyer will have another one if they won't let me have that one out of property."

"You're gonna be in a holding tank, good luck getting one of the courthouse COs to let you change. Lazy assholes might have to do extra work," he said. "Whats today anyway?"

"February fif—"

"— the case moron. What part of the case is it?"

"Oh. Discovery and motions. It's when — "

" — I know what it is. Fifteen minutes tops bro. They're not lettin' you change into a fuckin' suit. Two bus rides and a day in the tank for fifteen minutes. Have fun."

"Shithouse lawyers," Grantes mumbled aloud. It amazed him how much legal knowledge inmates had. Especially those with high recidivism. Grantes's cellmate had a very vast and intimate knowledge of the law from a certain prospective. He was, therefore, known throughout the prison as a good shithouse lawyer. During the short rec-times, inmates would leave there cells and seek out the shithouse lawyer for legal advise about their specific case. His services were never free yet many would line up to pay for his legal knowledge.

His celly was of course aware that Jacob was a real lawyer, which only caused that many more passionate discussions. One incident a few weeks prior, Grantes was accused of stealing his business because an inmate on the first tier chose to seek his actual legal expertise rather than his cellmate's. Jacob was no fighter and gave him the ramen he was paid for his legal services in order to keep the peace.

Jacob was determined to be in a suit for his appearance in court today. He was forced to wear a jumpsuit every day, all day, and he was tired of it. The entire ugly situation. As he left to go to the showers, he tried to convince not only his celly that he would be afforded the change of clothes, but also himself.

"We'll see."

2

JACOB GRANTES AND HIS BEST FRIEND RYAN WELLS HAD
started a law practice together fifteen years prior. They had, over time,
cornered the bustling criminal and legal market of nowheresville. The small
southern New Hampshire town of Barstone, in Wayland County, was
considered to be the other side of the tracks by the more affluent locals. Those
elevated locals being the residents of the affluent town of Wayland, which was
literally just across the train tracks of the commuter rail which took commuters
into Boston, Massachusetts. The clichéd delineation was real. The constituents
of Wayland Township made it quite clear to all of the inhabitants of Barstone,
and really anywhere else for that matter but less vocally, that they were not
welcome. The elected Sheriff of Wayland County, his office located in the
town of Wayland by design, was well aware of what would happen if the petty
crimes and riffraff of Barstone were to bleed into the backyards of the wealthy
community only a nine-iron away. And so the two towns within the same
county coexisted; the town with the same name of the county reaped all the
rewards, while the slums went about being the outcasts.

The law office of Grantes, Wells & Associates was strategically located in
Barstone, on the border of the two towns. They needed the criminal element
to pay their salaries, and therefore the business from the Barstonians, and the
partners wanted the much more civilized legal filings of Wayland. The two
townships utilized the same courthouse as they were in the same county. Life
was never boring for the two attorneys. Defending the proprietors of a Meth
Lab in Barstone one day; defending a restraining order filed by scorned trophy-
wife against an unfaithful husband in a messy fourth divorce on the next.

The *Associates* in the name of the firm was a mistruth. An embellishment
to look bigger and more established. JG, as he was called, and Ryan were the
only partners, the only lawyers, and there were no others seeking partnership.
None would be sought out either as they were not seeking any new blood for

15

such an arrangement. The associates consisted of their part-time private investigator, Warren Dennihan; and their full-time secretary in Ryan's wife, Angie. Warren had his own thriving business in Boston, with his own partner, and was subcontracted by the New Hampshire law firm whenever an investigator was needed. He was rarely, if ever, in the Barstone office. Angie was in the office every business day, much to Ryan's chagrin, and she had almost no legal knowledge. What she lacked in legal prowess, she made up for in organization and efficiency. She was invaluable and JG had said in the past, in plain language to Ryan, that whatever problem he had with the arrangement, to get over it.

The arrangement had been Ryan's doing in the first place. He had hired Angie Grummond, as was her name at the time, without consulting JG on the spot at the first interview. Rather than ask the prospective employee out on a date upon their first meeting, which was ultimately what Ryan wanted to do, he decided to hire her instead. The would-be sexual harassment suit in waiting didn't last long, as they were officially an item by the time she was finished her training. JG didn't mind as much as he had initially let on, not even annoyed if truth be told. The headache of starting a firm was a larger migraine than that of an office romance. Besides, Ryan had been JG's best friend since law school, almost for as long as he could remember, and he had never seen his friend so happy.

The startup capital for the small firm came from the money bestowed to Jacob via his surrogate family. His in-laws had been more than good to him, they had filled a hole left in him by the passing of his natural parents. His wife, Anna, had come from money and while she had married for love, her parents could think of no reason for them to struggle financially. Anna's parents had made the idle threats to rescind the money once they learned that Ryan was to be made full partner from the outset, but all concerned knew the threats were empty. Their apprehension came from genuine concern as they saw their son-in-law, Jacob, as the much more talented of the two-lawyer partnership. With Jacob viewed as having a much higher potential than his friend, especially since he had no money invested in the venture, they felt Ryan was there for the ride instead of the build.

Ryan was not a bad lawyer. He was no Alan Dershowitz either. He was talented but he was also a free-spirit. Wells would get caught up in the spirit of the law rather than the black letter. He took flyers. Rather than take on more legitimate claims, he often went to the hoop with little on evidence and heavy on the liberal sentiment. He would often take on the lost cause that was rejected by JG; acknowledging that he might win some, but he would lose more. Ryan was an idealist. His interest and passion for the law was in the good it could do. He actually thought the lady with the scales was indeed blind. He still does to this day.

JG had depended on Ryan to bring in fees not necessarily wins. Billable hours were billable hours, each generating income. Winning of course would draw the big cases, but with a location in Barstone, New Hampshire, who was he kidding? The business would come from the petty drug cases, larcenies, B&Es, DUIs, assaults, and the ilk from people who couldn't afford to be choosy when it came to a criminal defense. They knew they were going to prison with a public defender, at least with the hippie they had a chance.

JG had the wins, Ryan had the passion. But that was all in the past. What JG needed from his friend and partner now was a win. A big win. Ryan was going to defend him when and if this case went to the hoop. Today was discovery motions. The *I'll show you mine and you show me yours* part of the case. Today they would see what the State of New Hampshire had, and if this case was going to trial. If so, Grantes needed Ryan to win the case of his life. For Jacob's life.

3

"All RISE. PLEASE COME TO ORDER, COURT IS NOW IN SESSION.
The honorable Judge McCaglia presiding." The bailiff shouted with much too
much in the way of volume. There were few people in the fourth session of the
Wayland County Superior courtroom. It was entirely unnecessary to shout at
that level, but Grantes decided that the loud volume coordinated nicely with
the loud color of the neon, hazard-orange prison jumpsuit he was wearing.

He had asked the Correctional Officer, politely mind you, if he could
change into a suit that his lawyer had brought for him to wear to court. The
CO guarding the prison property room hadn't even entertained the idea of
fetching inmate #437261's suit from the cage. "No fuckin' way," were his
exact thoughts on the subject. Jacob had reckoned that this would be a
possibility when he called his attorney from prison, which is why he'd asked
Ryan to pick one out and bring an extra one he had on the rack in his office at
the firm. If truth be told, he preferred the one from the office, the suit he'd
been hauled off to prison in was probably quite wrinkly at this point. Now in
the tank below the courthouse, he repeatedly asked the jailhouse CO about
seeing his lawyer and changing into a suit. He even bargained to leave on the
shackles, but the request didn't warrant any response. He repeated the
question in case the officer didn't hear him. The CO had heard the request
because he gave the sternest of looks upon hearing it a second, third, fourth,
and fifth time. In each instance the guard gave no response. Ryan then got
involved but the plea to the Deputy Sheriff was in vain. The officer said he
didn't like the hippie lawyer in the linen suit, and never liked any inmate ever.
He was appointed to rid the county of these unwanteds, and this

nonconformist was working to free them. Chalk one up for the political right, getting one over on the liberal left.

"You may be seated," said the judge. She was the moderately attractive Judge Grace McCaglia. Wearing the usual black robe, matching black hair that may have been colored specifically to do so, and mystic blue eyes that could virtually see through a person. She confidently presided with a no-nonsense efficiency that would make Ryan's wife Angie proud.

In her late forties, she had accomplished more than most attorneys had in the course of their entire career, in a fraction of the time. In the *Live Free or Die* State of New Hampshire; there were rumors of political favoritism, affirmative action, and sleeping her way into a judgeship. Any explanation was more plausible than that she'd earned her position. These whispers did not go unnoticed which is why she once prosecuted as an Assistant District Attorney and now presided as a judge strictly but fairly. There would not be any second-guessing her rulings. She would not allow anyone to be justified in criticizing her for not being the right person for the bench.

"Where are we in the matter of the State of New Hampshire v Grantes?"

"Where are Anna and Brady is the better question." JG whispered into Ryan's ear as they sat in their seats at the defendant's table. He looked around the room but with few people in it, it was quite clear that his wife and son were not present.

"No idea. Three messages without a response this morning. Maybe they gave her a hard time about a four year old in the courtroom?"

Ryan finished whispering the response as he stood to address the judge to answer her question.

"We would like to request a continuance, your honor."

"On what grounds? This has been ongoing for six months, time is ticking here sir."

"We are still in discovery, judge."

"I must be confused. This *IS* the discovery hearing, is it not?"

"We've not received any of the ADA's documents, Judge. How can I file a motion or motions to exclude evidence or dismiss all charges without notice of said evidence?"

"Dismiss? Mister Wells, a Grand Jury was convened and subsequent to Rule 8, they found probable cause to sustain an indictment. The 90-day threshold was met. Do you want to weigh in here counselor?"

She swiveled her chair to her right so she could face the prosecuting Assistant District Attorney. 'Weigh in' was a poor choice of words and she immediately realized it.

Pierce La Fontagne was an enormous man. Fat. He was an unhealthy glutton that could blame whatever or whomever he wanted with regard to his obesity, but it was a fact that he tipped the scales at over four hundred-fifty pounds. He was always disheveled and just as disorganized. How he'd lasted as an ADA was a mystery, but his nickname was not so mysterious. They called him Jabba, after the enormous creature in *Star Wars*, behind his back. And he knew it. He spoke with as slow a purpose as his metabolism.

"We have … Ah … Given the defense … Ah … And have enough to provide the people to move … Ah … Forward with the case, Judge. We … Ah … Don't need much, but we do need a little more time." The fat on his neck jiggled when he spoke. He never looked up to face the judge when he spoke to her, as he shuffled his papers in the disorganized mess he had created at the prosecutor's table. Besides his disorganization, not making eye contact when speaking infuriated her. She felt it was a sign of disrespect.

"Does that mean you are ready or not? Kind of late in the game aren't we, counselor? You had enough to sustain the charges, do you have what you need to move forward or don't you?"

"Ah … We feel confident that the current evidence will prove our case beyond the threshold of reasonable doubt."

"I can tell." She had to pause to control her anger. She was a professional to her very core. She swiveled back toward the defendant.

"Mister Wells?"

"I'm happy for ADA La Fontagne that he feels so strongly about his case. If there is so much overwhelming evidence in moving forward against my client, why haven't I received it?"

"Again I'm confused," she said turning back to the ADA. "How about it? Did you send the material to the defense or didn't you?"

"I … Ah … Believe—"

"—Do you have the discovery documents with you now?"

"Ah … Yes."

"Excellent. Problem solved. Hand them across the aisle to the defense. Now. Speedy trial gentlemen. The defendant has the right to one, he is remanded and sitting in prison awaiting the disposition of this trial. Continueance? I would think his lawyer would be more adamant about moving this forward. He pleaded not guilty. ADA La Fontagne and the state requires a speedy trial, and frankly I demand it so I don't get backlogged. Six months gentlemen. This has been going long enough, wouldn't you both agree? We move ahead forthwith." Efficiency experts could learn a thing or two from Judge McCaglia.

"I agree that six months is a long time, your honor. Especially for my client, who was only remanded due to an imminent threat justification, which we will get to in a minute with the motion you have before you."

Ryan had filed to have the issue of bail revisited. Jabba had used a justification arguement that Jacob Grantes was an immediate danger to society and should be remanded as to allay any danger to the community. Additionally, she was clearly disgruntled with the prosecutor today, which he hoped to use to his and therefore his client's advantage.

"But with all due respect, judge, I do not agree with the a forthwith," Ryan continued. "In order to provide a proper defense against the charges, I need to ensure that the burden of proof and all pertaining evidence is met and provided to me by the prosecution. The ADA has just told you and I, after some equivocating I might add, that they now have all the evidence they plan to use when and if this goes to trial. I need time to assemble all the counter-evidence and exclusion motions supporting our claim against the charges, and that proving that my client is innocent."

JG nodded his approval. His friend and partner was doing well. Unlike television and movies in Hollywood, the State cannot come out of nowhere in the last minute of a trial with a damning piece of evidence. It was now time for the prosecution to put up or shut up and Ryan had just spoken legalese saying so.

21

"Whether you agree with my ruling or not, Mister Wells, is not my concern. You heard the ADA, he's moving forward, and unless you're going to change a plea to GUILTY, we're moving forward."

"With or without my continuance, Your Honor?" Ryan pressed.

The judge shook her head. "Just out of curiosity, how long would you need?"

"We request ninety days."

"Three months for discovery that was just given to you and prep for trial? You are joking right? Nice try." She turned back to the ADA. "I don't have a green sheet in front of me. Is there a deal being offered?"

"We ... Ah ... Haven't—"

"Get it together, Mister La Fontagne." She again shook her head in apparent disgust. "Is there anything else you would like to state before I rule on this?"

"Ah ... No Your Honor. I would just like to ... Ah ... Reiterate that — "

"—No need to reiterate anything, I heard you the first time. As much as it pains me, you've got thirty days." She turned toward the clerk to dictate. "Let's set a date for pretrial and jury selection at or about one month from today."

"Your Honor with that being settled, I would like to revisit the issue of bail. The motion should be before you," Ryan said.

He was hoping that since things had not exactly gone his way thus far, Judge McCaglia would throw him, and more importantly JG, a bone on the motion to revisit the issue of bail. Her disapproval about the performance of the presiding ADA could only help the cause.

"That has already been denied. I denied it six months ago. Is there anything new to bring forth where I would reconsider?"

"He is a prominent attorney in the area, Judge. He has a family, is a husband and father. He is the sole breadwinner. This has created an enormous hardship. His driver's license has been reinstated at this point, but we would surrender it again in lieu of incarceration if the State is still concerned that he is an imminent threat. But if we are now talking another thirty days before jury selection for a trial, I see no reason to continue to remand him. He has been a model inmate, never been in trouble with the law prior to this case, and he has — "

"Save it Mister Wells. You have nothing new here. A woman is dead. The allegation is that she is dead because of your client. Drinking and Driving is serious and a blight on our society. When a child is in the car on top of this, allegedly, the crime is reprehensible. I continue to believe that he may be an imminent threat. The fact that he is a prominent figure in this community; and that he is an attorney; that has been before me and this court in the past; is not a reason for him to benefit. He cannot garner favor from a court that is supposed to judge his alleged crimes. Any defendant before me with these same allegations would get remanded, remain alcohol-free, surrender their license to drive a motor vehicle, and pending the outcome of the trial, matriculate a Substance Abuse Program. I'm sorry Mister Grantes, but you are to stay at the Wayland County House of Corrections pending trial. Stay in the Substance Abuse Program or there will be consequences, sir. As your attorney just stated it is only thirty more days."

She paused only for a moment while she briefly looked over the rest of the documents regarding this case in front of her.

"So unless there are any other motions, we will resume these proceedings in thirty days. No more delays gentlemen, either one of you. Court is adjourned."

The gavel was only tapped onto the sound block but it sounded as though it was slammed through to the other side by a sledgehammer.

4

THE TRUTH IS THAT THE HARDSHIP THE GRANTES FAMILY WAS facing was not at all financial. It was Jacob who was suffering the most, to be sure, but they were all unaccustomed to this torment. Spending six months in that horrible place was a battle of its own, however not being with his wife and four year old child was all but killing him. Brady was not supposed to be without his father. He hadn't been in his life up to that point and 'away on business' was the story that his wife had sold him. Anna was good about sparing the boy the truth, that his father was accused of manslaughter with special circumstances, and at least played the role of understanding wife until now. Anna had been distant in most recently. They had dealt with serious difficulty in the past, but this was a big ask. He promised himself to make it up to her. They would get through it. Their college romance had started blissfully and had some serious downs despite their intense love for one another. Their eventual vows to take each other through good times and bad had taken significant meaning both past and present.

Norman and Olivia Craig had done whatever they could to encourage the college romance of their only daughter, Anna. Jacob, not Jake or JG as others called him (his natural parents had taken the time and effort to pick a name for him, and it was rude to bastardize that effort, they'd said repeatedly), was decidedly the perfect match for their Anna. Especially with the boys she had brought home in previous courtships. True, Jacob's family didn't come from wealth, nor had they built any. The Granteses weren't new money, they were no money. The Craigs had faith that this legacy would change with Jacob. He had work ethic, was smart, and pre-law. Yes, this is what they had in mind for their girl and they would do whatever they could, financially or otherwise, to support Jacob's goals. As long as Anna was included in the equation.

Jacob was always humbly appreciative, respectful in declining the offers of money or the "just because" expensive gifts, but relented over time. Anna joined in on the pressure to accept these material tokens of affection for they were deemed as simple manifestations of parental approval. She viewed the entire subject as "only money". Of course it was only money to her, she had been privied to these same gestures and more over the course of her entire life. These gifts were just an extension of her expectations from her wealthy parents.

"You should just get used to it honey, they won't let up. They love you and they just want to show you how much. Besides, you deserve to live a certain lifestyle even if you don't know it yet," she said in one of their more memorable spats on the subject. There had been more discussions regarding this very subject, all of which she'd won with some version of the same statement.

Jacob's fight for financial independence with her was a broken alliance, however. He would say things like, "I'm used to doing things for myself, babe. It's not that I am unappreciative of it, but there's something honorable in building a life for ourselves, by ourselves. I feel like I'm forever indebted to them."

These declarations would fall on deaf ears and would either reluctantly fade or would be the impetus for a battle royale, depending on the value of the gesture and how much Jacob really wanted to press the issue. Eventually Jacob acquiesced, as he did each and every time. As the relationship developed, the lifestyle became de rigueur. He had lost every battle and the war as well. In truth, he had built up enormous debt and was very thankful for the financial help. Boston University was not cheap, Boston University School of Law even less so. The money, cars, apartments, the ability to go to Law School (only 11% of those applying to BU School of Law get accepted. The competition is stiff, but Mr. Craig was friends with someone on the Board of Trustees, or so he said).

"It's not bribery," Norman Craig explained. "I love Anna," he also said. It was to ensure that they had a strong foundation on which to build their life together. Of that, Jacob was sure.

Jacob's biological parents loved him with all of their hearts, albeit with fewer trinkets to show for it. Actually, there weren't any trinkets. Reginald and Elizabeth Grantes had to work and toil for every nickel of property or possession they owned, and even then the nickels didn't add up to anything of worth. They doled out hugs and kisses the way Norman Craig doled out money. Before the Craigs, Jacob had been a wealthy man. His parents attended or coached every athletic endeavor their only son struggled to perform. Neither parent had attended college but made it a priority for their son to get the education they did't have. They would not, could not, contribute financially. But they were motivating and supportive as best they could.

Young Grantes left upstate Vermont to attend Boston University and achieve his and his parent's goals for him. His parents remained there, driving south for visits or sending care packages of sweets to their starving student. They were pleased to learn that as of his sophomore year, their son would no longer struggle financially. The ends would more than meet. Unfortunately, in the end, they would never meet Anna.

✸✸✸✸✸✸

It was the start of Jacob's second semester, of his second year at BU. Reggie and Liz decided to drive down to Boston to visit their son, as they had done two other times in his tenor there. He had been home for Christmas break and every other sentence was, "Anna this" or "Anna that".

Jacob had been a social mingler in high school, never the most popular kid but was a welcome addition to any clique. He was better than averagely attractive. He was polite, and was familiar with many a female as well, in large part because of his standing in a plethora of social circles. He had many dates, with a few sporadically retained as official girlfriends over the years. He certainly didn't have any that he had prattled on about for days on end.

His freshman year had been new and exciting, but also the most difficult endeavor he had undertaken in his life up to then. There were precious few stories regarding the fairer sex as he said there wasn't any time. That was only half true. The other half was that going to University was not about settling down but about exploring, both academically and socially. It was novel that this Anna would commandeer so much of a conversation, which made necessary the trip to Boston.

Interstate 89 is a long, windy, treacherous highway running north-south over and around the Green Mountains, crisscrossing Vermont and into New Hampshire. This is one of two major highways in Vermont, and is the quickest way south to Boston, Massachusetts. The two lanes of patchy, frost-heaved road are tricky to negotiate any time of year; soft shoulders, ice, elevation changes, with notorious fog make it more so during bad weather.

January brings major snow storms almost every year, often dropping several feet of snow in a relatively few number of hours. This particular *Noreaster* should have postponed the trek south to Boston, the storm well-tracked and advised in advance. But in the Northeast, weather personnel and meteorologists, were wrong as often as correct. Though every attractive weather girl, on every channel, was forecasting the same snow advisory. The days had been requested off, however, cashing in vacation and/or personal time, so the show must go on. The trip was planned, and the senior Grantses would stick with that plan. And so on that January afternoon, Reg and Liz Grantes of Burlington, Vermont embarked on their journey south.

Jacob found it odd that his parents had not called him once they'd arrived in Boston. They'd had a reservation with a late check-in scheduled at the Buckingham Hotel on Commonwealth Avenue, as was customary when they visited. When he had not heard from them, the thought of the big storm resonated in the back of his mind. He almost immediately disregarded it, however; his father had driven in the snow his entire life, had taught him how to drive in the stuff. He called the prepaid cellphone they used only when traveling, as cell phones were not the rage with his parents. Neither contended to be that important where they needed to be available for a phone call at every hour of every day. He could not get through to the cell when he called. Their voicemail was not set up, of course. It was not until he called the hotel and informed that they had not checked in that he began to worry. More phone calls to their friends and to their places of work without a definitive answer to their whereabouts led to panic.

By 10:00 AM the following morning, panic became horrified shock. The Vermont State Police informed him by telephone that neither had survived a severe car crash. Neither had been alive when authorities had arrived at the scene.

"We hate to inform you over the phone," they said. "How very sorry we are," they also said. "Please come to Montpelier, Vermont to identify the bodies of your parents."

They had not made it out of their own state. The reports showed that the snowy weather conditions inhibited sight; mixed with the unplowed snow on top of black ice, with an unfamiliar rental vehicle that was not equipped with all-wheel drive, were some of the variables contributing to the disastrous formula. The guard rail was ill-placed, meaning that there wasn't one in place. A guard rail would have at a minimum kept the vehicle on the road. The lack of this safety measure did the opposite and did not keep them on said road. The rental vehicle launched off the elevated section of highway on Interstate 89, into the icy ravine below. The final element in their premature demise.

The aftershock of the catastrophe had left Jacob scarred both emotionally and financially. Anna and her parents were there to reassemble the pieces as best they could. The financial piece was easy. Norman took care of the massive debt in one phone call. Anna was there for the emotional part. This was not as easy. But they dealt with it.

Reginald and Elizabeth Grantes, formerly of Burlington, Vermont, had loved life. They cared not for money but for the happiness it could provide from joyous memories. They loved each other and they loved their son, and in that they were rich. Realistically, they were not. They lived paycheck to paycheck and didn't manage those very well at all. There were always events deemed too important to pass up, spending money earmarked for bills; spending in lieu of life insurance, savings, or a 401k. They were upside down on their mortgage in part because of the market, but primarily because of the repeated refinancing and remortgaging.

Without life insurance, in their terrible financial condition, and most recently with the cost of their final expenses, they had left their only son with an enormous financial burden. He was already in debt because of his educational loans and the catastrophe would make him more so without a house or substantial property to sell. And so at the ages of 58 and 56, Reggie and Liz respectively, had left their son broken and broke. Had it not been for the Craigs, he would have been broke for the rest of his life.

5

JG WAS ANXIOUSLY AWAITING THE ARRIVAL OF HIS LAWYER AT THE
table in one of the courthouse conference rooms after the hearing. He was
immediately escorted there after his brief legal fray in the fourth session
upstairs. Ryan had scheduled a meeting in advance with his client before
being bussed back to the prison, should he not make bail. Which to his
misfortune is exactly what happened. Ryan seemed to be taking a long time
doing whatever he was doing in the eyes of JG; leaving him alone in the dark,
windowless conference room with a court officer standing watch in the corner.
It was an awkward silence which made Ryan's absence seem even longer. He
was not in any hurry to get back to his cell, nor to his cellmate, but he was
overwrought with how his case was progressing thus far. Or not progressing,
which consumed his thoughts every minute of every day in prison.

The large wooden door opened with a start, ending the tension that had
been building in the small room, adding a different sort of unease. Ryan
moved quickly to a chair opposite his client, setting his leather briefcase down
on the oversized table between them.

"I'd like to be alone with my client please," he said over his left shoulder
to the officer.

"Sure thing. I'll be outside the door when you're finished."

Once the babysitter had left, the lawyer-client pretense was abandoned.
"Well, that didn't go very well." The hearing had not gone well, they both
knew it, and neither one would needed to sugarcoat it to pretend that it had.

"Ya think?"

"Look pal, we have them on the ropes, right where we want them," Ryan
said.

"Rope a dope, huh? Who's the dope? They're kicking our asses, Ry."

"Well, I don't know what I could have done differently in retrospect.
Thoughts? I mean what would the Great Jacob Grantes have done?"

30

JG's elbows were on the table, head in hands. He needed a lifeline. The sarcasm and mucking it up with his friend needed to cease. He was on the verge of breaking down.

"You did what you did, Ry. I mean you did what I would have done. That woman is a ball-buster."

"McCaglia has always been brutal, you knew that going in. You've been in front of her before. Hell, she kicked asses and took names as an ADA, she's doing the same now that she's on the bench. She has something to prove, always has, and she doesn't cut breaks unless she absolutely has to. And she doesn't have to here. We don't have anything going for us, and Jabba isn't chomping at the bit to cut a deal either."

"Exactly. So what *DO* we have we going for us?"

"I was just speaking with tons-of-fun upstairs after our hearing. That's what took so long. I've got the 'one and only green sheet' right here. This is the only deal he is offering, or is ever going to offer, he says. It's not a good one, I'll warn you."

He reached into his briefcase that he'd set on the table, removed the green court document that La Fontagne had given Ryan a few moments prior. It was conveniently on top and quickly slid directly in front of his jumpsuit-clad friend. A green sheet is a bargaining document with legalese and three vertical columns in the middle horizontal third. The form is on No Carbon Required (NCR) paper with three sheets; one for the ADA, one for the defense, and one for the judge. The first column is for the prosecutor, which offers a sentencing recommendation if the defense forgoes the expense of a trial. The middle column is the defense counter offer, which typically chips away at what the State wants. The final column on the right, is the deal formed between the two and goes to the judge. He or she reads the statutory minimums to ensure nobody is ponying up the courthouse, then usually rubber-stamps the deal. When all is said and done, all the judge wants is to clear their docket, keep justice moving just like everyone else. This is called a green sheet for the complicated reason in that the color of the document is a light green. Though it must be signed by all parties, it is only legally binding when and if a formal hearing takes place and agreed to on the record in front of a judge.

"He likes where he is," Ryan continued. "As you can see, the offer is Vehicular Manslaughter with special circumstances, OUI 1 with injury, leaving the scene. He drops the child endangerment, and puts a recommend of eight to ten on the VM, concurrent. Loss of licenses, two years after release on the drivers, law for life because we're talking felonies."

JG shook his head. "Not much of a deal."

"You'd get fifteen years on the VM alone at trial. Add in the OUI-with, leaving the scene, and depraved indifference would get you another ten-plus separately. Tack on the child endangerment charge if we go to the hoop, and you would not be able to see your kid without someone watching over your shoulder until he's legally an adult. Eight to ten, to run concurrent means with good time, two years off the minimum. You've been in for six months already, so you would be out in five and half. No child supervision, no probation. It's not good but it's the best we're gonna get I'm afraid."

The drivers license didn't make that much difference to JG. The loss of his ability to practice law could also be dealt with, he had money, thanks to his wife and in-laws, and he could always find something to occupy his days. Maybe he could teach. The five and a half years away from his family was intolerable. He could not lose his family for any longer than he already had. Supervised visits with Brady was unacceptable also but at least he would be able to see him other than through glass. These thoughts were going through his mind but he wasn't vocal about them, which caused a long pause. He continued to stare at the offer, lost in the ramifications if he agreed to what was written.

"What's going through your mind? Talk to me. There's nothing saying that you can't be behind the scenes at the firm, you just wouldn't be able to take cases when you get out."

"You think that is what's bothering me, Ry? How long have you known me? You really think that is what's hanging me up?"

"No, I don't. I'm just trying to help. But Jabba isn't going to budge. It's this or we go to the hoop. But you have given me nothing to work with on defense. We go to trial? I think unless we come up with something really damned compelling, you're going to go away for a long, long time."

"Have you been in touch with Anna yet? I'd like to discuss this with her."

"She isn't, nor was she, here today. No answer either. Voicemail is full. I'm really not sure where she is, but I'll keep trying." He pulled out some other documents from the briefcase, spreading out the pile on his side of the table. "What I would like to discuss is all of this circumstantial evidence and see if anything jogs your memory. Anything we can hammer away at. If we weaken anything he has, maybe the deal gets better. I doubt it, but maybe."

"We've been through this, I don't remember anything about that night. Well, other than Sully's anyway."

"Yeah well, we're going to go through it again anyway. You admitted to quote, 'being hammered' when the cops picked you up at your house. You were passed out by the way. Again, Brady was upstairs asleep and legally unsupervised because you were out of it."

"I can't believe I drove in that condition, much less with Brady in the car. Then left him on his own like that in the house? I just can't believe it."

"Thats what they're going with. I have a sworn statement from the bartender, Jenna, that you left Sully's between 8:00 and 8:15 PM. You also admitted to being at the bar in the back of the cruiser, which means you had to be really banged up. You, of all people, know better than to say anything to the police after you've been arrested. But anyway, you left and picked up Brady at the Destriers at 8:20 PM; the servant that was watching him told Chamille Destrier that she put him in his carseat in the back of the running car, that you never spoke or left the driver's seat. She said she found it odd behavior, but this is all third hand through Chamille because the servant doesn't speak English, apparently. Double hearsay. We can attack that at trial if need be. The police never spoke to this housekeeper lady directly to confirm or deny anything. Chamille was at the charity event next to your wife, so we strike the kid being in the car as hearsay. I think that is why the big-boy is dropping child endangerment to begin with, the kind soul. I don't think he can prove it."

"Yeah, what a sweetheart."

"Right. So you drove away and must have bounced off a tree, veering into the opposite lane where this poor woman happened to be coming right at you. She goes off the road and plays chicken with a big tree and an even bigger rock. She lost and you went home to sleep it off."

"It's not funny, Ry. Please don't make light of the fact that this woman was nearly decapitated by a smoking-hot engine. I feel awful."

"Sorry, just trying to add some levity. You're right. It's not funny. Anyway, they have matching paint from the tree, black sapphire pearl, and the scrape on your Volvo has wood and bark all through it. Exact. No real credible argument there, I'm afraid. Furthermore the rubber zig-zagging on Wayland Country Club Road matches the Michelin 235/60R18s on your ride. Cops investigated your tires, they've got you dead to rights there too."

"Match? *Cops* are matching this all up? Can we get experts to refute them? Volvos are a dime a dozen in New England, hell I have two of them."

"Lab techs. This isn't *CSI*, they didn't stop everything they were doing and get top experts from all over the country to fly in on the state's dime, no. But you don't have to be an expert to see that all of this doesn't look good. Picking apart their lab technicians with our expensive ones is not going to win over a jury, if that's what you're thinking."

"That's exactly what I am thinking. The techs are overworked, underpaid, they make mistakes — "

" —This is New Hampshire, JG. They are neither overworked, nor are they underpaid. These aren't MIT grads by any stretch but they don't have a whole lot to investigate, trust me. Just between you and me, I looked at your car, the road, the tree. You killed this poor woman. If you were anybody else — "

"—So what are we doing here then? I should take the deal and kiss my family goodbye. My life is over?"

"You're my best friend. I'm trying to mitigate your responsibility here. I'm trying to help. I don't know? Find a technicality. What we're doing here is trying to get the best deal we can."

"Great. Just great. You think five and half is the best I can do?"

"We haven't discussed the 911 call yet. Anonymous, but that's how they nailed you. How they knew to go to your house to grab you."

"What is there to discuss? You've already told me to take the deal, right?

Ryan paused. He shuffled the stack of papers containing all the condemning evidence. He really wasn't sure why he was against taking the deal but he was. He knew his friend, knew him better than any other male on the planet, and something was not right. Endangering the life of his only son, the one they had so much trouble conceiving, was not scanning. True, he had been drinking more in the months before the accident, but to get that blackout drunk was not something he would expect from his friend. He was mister safety. People disappointed. But not JG. Not Jacob Grantes. He had never disappointed. Not until now. "Look, I'm not telling you to take the deal. At least not yet. We finally have all the evidence that fat-body has compiled; so we put Deni on it and see what he comes up with. I mean, the cops didn't pick you up at your house until 9:45 PM, which gives you a huge window to get shattered in the comfort of your own home. If everything comes back the way it looks here, which admittedly is really fucking bad, then we pick away at the bartender and the illegal lady."

"Please leave the vic alone. Arelia, right? Jenna too."

"Look. Jenna is a sweet girl, we go there and knock a few back, have a few laughs, and she's always good to us. But she over-served you. She claims not, but obviously she screwed up and is covering her ass. As far as the victim … She's dead. Which is unfortunate. But she shouldn't have been in this country to be dead. She was illegal. I feel for her just like you do, but when it comes to my friend or someone who may or may not even pay taxes? I might be a 'hippie' but I look out for my own. We've kinda got a role reversal here, huh? You're usually the cutthroat."

"Prison changes people I guess. Usually for the worse, not more sympathetic. But it is what it is."

"Maybe. But if shit goes south, all the cards lead to what we have before us? We go after the ladies. The bartender has some responsibility here, and so does the vic. This *is* New Hampshire. We don't like drunk drivers but we don't like illegal aliens more."

"Not very politically correct of us, is it?"

"Unfortunately, like you said, it is what it is. Peace, love, and get a green card."

"Well lets hope it doesn't come to that. Just get Deni going because we don't have much time."

"I'm on it. I'm not going anywhere. You need anything?"

"Actually, yes."

35

"Name it."

"Find Anna."

6

RYAN WELLS WAS JG'S LONGEST AND CLOSEST PERSONAL FRIEND.
They had both grown up poor but not impoverished, had been instilled with a strong work ethic, and were the first in their respective families to go to college. They'd met at BU during freshman orientation and were all but inseparable since. Grantes had been a loyal friend in pulling Wells into the fold of the partnership and Ryan had been loyal in many other ways, including during the death of Jacob's parents. They were each the brother they'd never had.

The two were so alike in so many ways that they could have been biological brothers. Ryan was good looking, tall and had what was once an athletic build. They would both be forty this year and had previously made plans for both families to go on vacation together to celebrate. Until the incarceration, all had looked forward to the time away. The only major difference between them was professionally. They were both strong advocates, but the hippie would live in the shadow of his more talented, leaning to the right, brother.

As Ryan left the courthouse, he pulled his iPhone out of his long winter overcoat to call Warren Dennihan, the firm's ad hoc investigator.

"Deni, how are you?" He immediately regretted not using his bluetooth ear device to make the call as he juggled his briefcase, the phone, and his car keys to open his parked car.

"Same shit, different pile. What's up?" Warren Dennihan was a *Southie*, or from the district of South Boston and had the severe accent to prove it. Bad. Or 'wicked bad, guy'. It was almost like he spoke a different language, as *pahk tha cah in hah-vid yahd*, just doesn't quite describe how broken his English really is. He didn't pronounce *r's*, unless of course they were not in the word like *drawr* instead of draw. It was work to hold a conversation with him unless you were familiar with him or those from his neighborhood.

"I just finished up with JG's hearing. It didn't go well."

"I figured. I got my partner workin' my other shit, so how much time do I gotta clear up?"

"Ah shit," Ryan said. He dropped his phone while opening his car to get it started and warmed up. He had to retrieve it out of the snow but fortunately it still worked. With the new synthetic oils and the fact that he drove an Audi A6, he didn't need to get the car warmed up for performance reasons, but he couldn't get the winter-fighter to work on his cold body until the engine was pumping warm air at him.

"You ok?"

"Yeah, Yeah. I'm here. Just dropped something. So everything we talked about? That's what they've got. The whole shah-bang. We've gotta work on it."

"By we, ya mean me."

"It's been a tough morning, are you really gonna give me a hard time right now?"

"Always. Hey listen. I've been callin' WHOC, I know a few guys over there. Not much I can do to look after him in there. Its all political. He's a lawyer, so nobody trusts him, and he can't gang up. At least he knew not to PC, just take a beat'n like a man if thats what they wanna do."

"If it was going to happen, it would have happened by now."

"Not necessarily, but we can hope. How much longer?"

"That depends on you, Deni. Thirty days if this goes to the hoop. Trial will probably take about two weeks or so, after that depends on what we get. I was hoping we could get enough to kill a trial, maybe enough to get a deal. They are offering eight to ten, which means five and half when all is said and done."

"All depends on me? No pressure. Who's breakin' balls now?"

Ryan was still sitting in his car, which was starting to kick out the warm seventy-four degree air that was set on his digital thermostat on the in-dash computer. He still couldn't drive, however; the car had not yet picked up the signal for the phone and you cannot drive and talk on the phone in New Hampshire unless handsfree. "Hey where are you?"

"Around the corner from you, I'll be there in thirty secs or less."

"Good. This might be easier face to face. I have a ton of documents you should look at."

"Do you still drive the silver Audi?"

"Yes, of course. I love this — "

" — I'm behind ya."

"Holy crap. That was fast."

Deni parked his blacked-out Escalade and relocated to the passenger seat of Ryan's vehicle. This was the part that took the thirty-seconds. "Let's see it all," he said without explanation of how or why he was in the immediate area.

"So this is everything." He handed Warren the stack of evidential material from his briefcase, then continued. "I know we discussed it when this thing happened, and since, but something just isn't sitting right about this case. You think I'm nuts though don't you?"

"I don't think you're nuts, per se, but would you really go through all this bullsh for anybody but JG? I agree that somethin' ain't stirrin' the kool-aid, but you and I both know he did it. He was drinkin' like a fish for months before this all happened. I was thinkin' family trouble at the time, but who knows? That kid is his life, so I can't see him throwin' that away. But we all fuck up, doesn't have to be on purpose for it to do damage."

"So does that mean that you're on board? I gotta know that you're on this."

"Loyal as lab, huh? Yeah, me too. I'm in, and you know it. I just need somethin' to work with here, guy."

"Look I never ask how you do what you do, because I'm not sure I want to know, but we're going to need all you've got on this. We need to dig into; Jenna, the bartender we know from Sully's Tavern, the Destrier servant or au pair or whatever the hell she is, the 911 call is a bit wonky, and if all else fails — we make the vic the most despicable person who has ever illegally entered the borders of this country," Ryan said before pausing. "I was kind of hoping for a sliding scale on this one. I know you have to clear your calendar and this is going to take some time, but with me taking this case, I have all of his cases I have to work, and mine, and of course he isn't in the office taking cases so the firm is really financially tight right now and — "

" — Hey relax, kid. I can't dig up what ain't there, but I'm on it. As legit as possible anyway. As for the fee, don't worry about it. I owe him. He's been good to me over the years."

"So what are you thinking?"

"I've got a couple of ideas. Mostly hunches, but I know people."

"I know you know people, that's why you are so good at what you do. Anyone I know?"

"Stop kissin' my ass Ry. I wanna check out the bar first. Jenna."

"Business or pleasure?"

"Both."

"I've got another project that's just as important."

"I'm listenin'."

"Find Anna and Brady. They didn't show up at court today and she's not answering phones. It's weirding me out, and JG is really freaked out."

"Huh. That ain't like her."

"Tell me about it."

"Lets go over to the house. You drive."

"Right now? Deni, I've got — "

" —You said it's important. Was that fact or bullsh?"

"Fact."

"Then start drivin'."

7

"HE'S BACK. ALL DAY BRO, JUST LIKE I SAID. How'd it go?" Loder, inmate #437254 was Grantes's cellmate. A dichotomous character, Loder had an IQ in the basement and a temperament in the attic. He has also spent well-nigh his entire adult life in one prison or another, and therefore looked the part. He was large with crudely drawn tattoos, cocaine fingernails, and eyes that were continually moving when he was awake. He didn't look for trouble, but he seemed to find it, and knew what to do when those moving eyes found some. Fighting was in his wheelhouse and everyone including his cellmate knew it.

Grantes didn't want to get into any conversation, let alone one with his celly. After his long day; his fruitless motion to get out of prison; the fact that he was right back in his drab, concrete cell; that he had not been able to see his wife and kid were all working to tune his last nerve guitar-string tight. It looked like Loder was in a fighting mood to top it all off, which meant that any dialogue with the Neanderthal was going to end in high-order violence. A situation he wanted to avoid all the way around.

"Yeah well, you know how it goes. Long ride over, longer wait in the tank just to come right back." Grantes was by design vague with his fellow inmates, just as they were with him.

"Just like I said. So how did it go?" Loder asked again.

"I thought it was bad form to keep asking someone about court?"

"Then let me see your paperwork."

"Not gonna happen. I'm back here so chances are, you can take a stab at how it went."

"I'll take a stab at you, you fuckin' bug. I got no problem with the hole for a week if you wanna go to HSU."

"Calm down, Loder. It's been a long day, a longer six months, and I just want some piece and quiet. If that means I have to go to the Hospital Services Unit to get it, then so be it."

"Then let me see your paperwork so you can think."

"You know I'm not a skinner, so why do wanna see my paperwork?"

"Prove it."

"Look Loder, I'm not a skinner, I'm not a rat, and I'm back here, so you know I'm not PC. What do you say you just lay off?"

"You're a fuckin' lawyer, same as a rat to me fuck-stick."

"That's a hell of a stereotype."

"It's only a stereotype if it's wrong. Don't you lawyers call it profiling if I'm right?"

"You're quite the philosopher."

"And a rat is a rat, asshole."

"Lawyers can't rat," JG said. He really wanted to finish that last statement with — "you moron" — but he didn't. Instead he said, "We have an obligation to keep quiet, which you know."

"Not if you can prevent a crime. And I ain't your fuckin' client."

"You're right about that. But if I were your attorney, I would be an even richer man." *Shit.* He said it.

"I'm going to bleed every dollar outta you, asshole — "

" — I'm sorry. Sorry, sorry, sorry. It slipped out, I'm sorry. I just need to think. You don't really want to get lugged do you?"

"No cameras in here, bro," Loder said arms open. His body language indicated he wanted a fight.

"You liked your day alone that much, huh? A week in the hole for you; and I get hospitalized, and stuck with someone worse than you in another pod when I get out. Spare us both would you?"

"I liked it here alone. Got to rub one out. Took a shit in peace too, it was kinda nice." He was slowly calming down, and Grantes was thankful.

"Masterbation and defecation, what more could you ask for? I'm glad to hear you had a good time."

"I got parenting class tonight, so you got the cell to yourself after chow. You can think all ya want then. My mags are inside my Temperpedic if ya

42

wanna crank one out." By Temperpedic he meant the paper-thin mattress that wouldn't provide cushion to an overweight molecule. Skin mags were contraband, playboy and soft stuff was tolerated but Loder had the hard stuff. Why he wanted to look at women being penetrated was a mystery to Grantes. Why anyone who was facing the number of years his celly was, without having access to an actual female, would want to look at females in coitus he thought was torturous. But this was an olive branch and Grantes accepted it though he wasn't going to use it.

"I'll keep it in mind, thanks."

The knowledge that Loder was a parent frightened him. Somewhere, sometime between his many bids with the Department of Corrections, he'd managed to impregnate someone. *That poor woman*, he thought. It was either against her will or she had some serious self esteem issues to agree to getting onto a bed with Loder. *Maybe it wasn't a bed.* Either way it was repulsive to Grantes. Teaching Loder to be a parent may have been an idea best suited for the garbage. It wasn't even a good idea on paper. Loder would never see this child, at least that is what any decent person would hope. He hoped more vehemently that he could hold his own son. To see his wife. *Why had they not been at court today? Did she forget? That was very unlike her. Why couldn't Ryan reach her? She was never without her phone, ever.* All of these thoughts and questions were consuming him. And they began to drive him crazy.

Loder was still jawing about something, but Grantes wasn't listening. He was cracking up and any interaction with the shitbag standing just a few inches away from him would only succeed in eliminating his good time; ensuring he went to the infirmary, then solitary confinement, and finally onto a different pod where anger management would surely be on the agenda. Being lugged was not going to solve anything, it would only make matters worse. He was earning ten days off his eventual sentence per month in good time while he was on his current pod, designated for drug and alcohol related offenders. Being taken down to solitary confinement by the lug team would take all that good-time away.

Grantes had been down to the hole in his first week of incarceration, when he was on the new-man block. Everyone goes to new-man when first arriving at WCHOC, regardless of the offense, unless the inmate opts to enter into Protective Custody. PC, in the eyes of prison inmates, is for snitches, cops who get busted and have to do some time, child molesters, or some other type of chickenshit asshole that can't or won't go into Gen-Pop. Inmates in PC were segregated onto their own block and the COs did their best to make sure that PC inmates never crossed paths with any of the other Gen-Pops from the other blocks, though it did happen more often than occasionally. If a Gen-Pop inmate ran into a PC in the hall as they were transported to HSU or a class or Sunday Mass or for some other reason, that inmate was duty-bound to shiv the PC else run the risk of being makeshift-knifed themselves if anyone found out. The new-man block got every Gen-Pop inmate for the first thirty days of incarceration, thus the name. Murderers, check. Wife beaters, check. Masked armed robbery, check. Even those who simply violated probation. All blended together in a testosterone-infused concoction called new-man.

On Grantes' fourth day on new-man, a GD, or a Gangster Disciple, approached him about offering protection. He politely declined the offer and thought the matter closed. Later that day, he knew better when a rival gang-member from the AB, or Arian Brotherhood, approached him with the same offer of services. It turned out that he knew the second thug who had approached him. He had defended him once about tow years prior on a drug trafficking charge, which he had successfully reduced down to a simple possession. The AB knew this, which was why they had sent that particular thug with that particular offer. He again declined after reminiscing a bit, but thanked him. The conference had not gone unnoticed, creating further discourse between the two gangs, out of the many factions that were on the pod. The discourse went from foul language to high-order violence the likes of which he had not seen even in a movie or a video game. He was caught in the middle and was lucky to get out of it with just a cracked rib, which in relative terms meant that he went untouched. But the pain was just as agonizing as the twenty-three and a half hours a day he had to spend in the hole after the four days he spent in HSU. He never wished to return.

By good fortune he had avoided it for the night. Tomorrow would be another story, that would be yet another struggle, for yet another day. But he would get the chance to look over the legal documents that Ryan had copied for him, documents every inmate had the right to have in their possession, without prying eyes. While his celly was learning how to refrain from kicking the ever-loving shit out of his next of kin, he would strategize on the best way to get the hell out of this hell. Thus far, he was coming up with blanks in his recollection of the events leading him to this dark place, this dark time.

8

RYAN FINALLY UTILIZED HIS AUDI'S BLUETOOTH TECHNOLOGY
to call Anna's cell again. This time Warren was in the passenger seat, listening. They left the courthouse parking lot while they listened to the phone ringing over and over again through all ten speakers in the luxury automobile. The automated voice was telling them that the voicemail box was full in surround sound.

"Where is she?" Ryan asked Deni. Though he knew that his investigator likely had as much knowledge of her whereabouts as he did.

"Did you try the house line?"

"Duh. I didn't think of that, Deni. Of course I did. No answer."

"Listen, guy, don't give me attitude or I'll give you a beat'n. I'm just askin'."

"I'll try again, if you'd like."

"If it's not too much trouble."

He didn't respond to the jab, he just dialed. Rather, the car dialed. Again, there was no answer in audiophonic clarity. They continued for the rest of the short trip in silence, after some time turning right into the driveway which had not been cleared of the latest dusting of February snow.

"Who do they pay to plow the drive, Ry?"

"I don't know but I can find out."

"It didn't snow last night. It's been a couple days."

"What's your point?"

"My point is that have you ever known Anna to let snow pile up in her driveway?" He paused long enough for his question to register with Ryan, yet not long enough for him to respond. "A dusting and she has the plow guy come out. Two, three days? My point is I'm not lookin' forward to whats inside that house, I ain't gonna lie."

The all-wheel drive handled the rest of the driveway without an issue, and he put the car in park. He had to admit, though he didn't want to, that his investigator was correct. It appeared that there was something very wrong about the home. He left the car running, to keep it warm, as this was likely to be a short trip to the front door and back. He got out of the car and lost his balance as he slipped in the snow. His loafers were buried along with his butt and elbows.

"Shit. Ahhhhhh, fuck me."

Deni was belly laughing so hard he nearly fell over himself as he came around the front of the car.

"Oh man, thanks. I needed that. I don't know what we're gonna find in there, kid. My stomach is in knots — "

" — Ya know, you could help me up, donkey, instead of standing there laughing."

"Oh yeah. Sorry."

Warren helped him up, pulling him up with one arm. Ryan tried to drag him down but it didn't work. Deni was wiry yet ridiculously strong. The PI also had better shoes in order to find purchase on the slick drive. Once Ryan was on his feet, Deni looked up as if he was studying the sky for a bit, then moved toward the garage doors.

"Where are you going? You've been here before, front door is this way."

"Nothing is comin' outta the chimney. No heat either means nobody is home or whoever is in there, doesn't need heat."

"Come on, Deni. Don't say stuff like that. I've already got a bad feeling, you don't need to say that."

"Both cars are in the garage. Wait. It's the same car. They have two of the same car?"

"Yeah, XC90s. His and hers. You know JG, mister safety. Volvo makes the safest car, so he got one for each of them."

"I knew he had a Volvo, I didn't know they had two identical, his and her, VOLV-OHS. Little weird, no?"

Ryan didn't reply as he made his way toward the front door like a hockey coach without his skates. Once he arrived, he knocked and rang the bell while he looked into the vertical window just to the right of the huge wooden front door. Nothing. The house was dark and without movement.

"You got a spare key, Ry?" Deni approached the door, standing behind him.

"Yes, but not on me."

"Is it in your car?"

"No, it's at my house. Should we go get it? What do you think?"

"I woulda thought you would have it on you. It's not like we were comin' over here or anything."

"I wasn't expecting to come over here. But in retrospect — "

" —Is there any mail in their mailbox?" The mailbox was to the left of the door instead of by the road like most other houses in New Hampshire. Ryan opened the lid to look in. By the time he had removed the contents, Deni was opening the front door.

"Yeah, they have mail. Hey! ... Was the door unlocked?

"Sure. We'll go with that. The door was unlocked, Ry."

"Deni, breaking and entering is a crime. You used to be a Massachusetts State Police Detective. You know that picking that lock is a crime."

"Did you see me pick a lock? You comin' in or what?"

"This is not my day," Ryan said. He followed his friend inside carrying the mail. "Hello? Anybody home?"

"Stop yellin'. You know as well as I do that there's nobody home. But stamp the snow off your feet just in case. You know how Anna is."

"Yeah, yeah. Loafers are ruined anyway, I think. And there could be somebody home, think positive."

"Who wears loafers in the winter?"

"A lawyer who has a court appearance. I wasn't expecting this side trip."

"House is wicked cold and the dog ain't humpin' my leg. I'll bet your shiny car out there, nobody's here."

"So what does that mean? She forgot? Chances are she had some appointment today and she forgot. That's why she isn't home."

"She forgot her husband's court date and went to an appointment with the dog? Forgot to get the driveway plowed for a couple days? Who you trying to convince, kid? Look at this," Deni added. "The thermostat says sixty-two degrees. That sound like Anna to you? This is what a three million dollar home? They ain't worried about a fuckin' heat bill. It's set so the pipes won't

48

freeze, not so people don't freeze.   I'm not sure what it means except that nobody's home and hasn't been for a hot minute."

They made their way through the living room toward the kitchen.   Ryan deposited the mail on the countertop.   Warren opened the stainless steel fridge.   Nothing.   It was clean and empty like it was new off the showroom floor.

"Maybe she went grocery shopping."   Deni was ever the smart-ass.

He went over to his PI and looked over his shoulder into the refrigerator. "No, no, no, no, no, no. This is not good. This is really, really not good."

"Lets go upstairs and see what we can see.   But you're right, this ain't good. She's leavin' him. At the worse possible time, she's leavin' him."

"We don't know that, Deni. There could be another possibility."

"Like she's dead? Is that what you are hoping for?"

"No, of course not. I mean another, less dramatic possibility."

"What color is the sky in your world, Ry? I know you're a hippie and all, but you must smoke some incredible weed. Do you grow your own or do you have a dealer? You don't take the dog and clean out the fridge if your comin' back.   And if you kill someone, do you help yourself to the cold-cuts before takin' off?"

"Stop yelling at me. And why now? Six months this has been going on, why now?"

"Nobody's been here for a while," Deni said.   "When was the last time you spoke to her? Face to face?"

He couldn't remember, so he avoided the answer.   "There has to be another explanation. Maybe they sold the house and moved."

Deni was walking toward the stairs to climb them toward the bedrooms. "Seems like JG woulda mentioned it though, don't ya think? I didn't see a 'FOR SALE' sign or 'SALE PENDING' out by the road. And it's probably just a coincidence that she isn't answering her phone, right? Or any phone, for that matter? And that she wasn't in court today?"

Ryan followed Deni up the stairs and immediately went through Brady's bedroom door like he was charging through it. Not a single toy.

Deni squatted down behind him in a catcher position in the middle of the room. The bed was there, and a bureau but that was it. He looked to his left and right.   The left wall was painted to look like Fenway Park's Green Monster, the right wall was an enormous aerial photo/painting of Gillette Stadium.

Ryan was starting to lose his composure.   His generally positive outlook on life was waning.   He went into the bathroom attached to Brady's room and started going through the child's drawers and cabinets.

"The drawers and medicine cabinet are empty in the bathroom, Deni. Thats it, I'm calling her cell again," he said as popped his head out the bathroom door and into the child's large bedroom.   Deni wasn't there any longer.   Ryan looked at himself in the vanity mirror as he made the phone call, though his concentration at the moment was not on his appearance.

"Go ahead.   I'm sure she'll answer this time."   His friend was shouting from the master bedroom.

Ryan returned to listening to his phone.   "It's ringing now."

"It sure is."   Deni had made his way back to Ryan in Brady's bedroom and was peering into the bathroom.   The ringing phone was in Deni's hand. The investigator held it out to show him the screen, Ryan's face and phone number were on the smartphone.   "Should I answer it?"

"What?"   Ryan asked as he turned to see the phone.   Ryan's iPhone was still up to his ear.

"She left it on the dresser in the walk-in closet."

"Oh, dear god, no."   Ryan looked at his touchscreen smartphone again to shut it off, realizing that the phone was wet.   He felt his cheek and it was soaked as well.   Tears were rolling down his face and dripped off of his chin. "What am I going to tell JG?"

"I don't know.   Nothin' to tell him yet, for sure.   According to you anyway."

He sat down on the toilet without a look.   Fortunately the lid was already down.   "Not now, Deni.   Please don't fuck with me right now."

"Sorry pal.   It took you a while to get here, but you're with me now, right? She's gone.   She left him and took the kid."

"What the hell are we gonna do, Deni?"

"First we need a drink, and I know just the place.   Get it together, kid, you're drivin'."

9

SULLY'S TAVERN WAS A SWANKY JOINT THAT ATTRACTED A mixed crowd. The bar and eatery was located in the downtown area of Barstone, New Hampshire, just off of interstate 93. While Sully's now attracted an affluent clientele, the establishment was located in a rougher neighborhood which suited its previous incarnation. The bar was conveniently located for those employed at Grantes, Wells & Associates, which was across the street. The appointments were as expensive-looking as the hand-crafted drink concoctions served there. The dark interior still had traces from the previous incarnation as a dive-joint, Irish bar. The stainless steel and plush, artsy booths and lighting were added to the pre-existing dark wood to give it a unique design of Old World pub meets trendy meat-market. The employees were all attractive women, save for a few of the hired muscle and kitchen help. These females were encouraged to be scantily clad, whatever clothing they did choose to wear needed to be black. The concept worked, the place was always busy with patrons from both sides of the tracks no matter the time of day.

Warren arrived alone after being dropped off by Ryan, who was too distraught to be seen in public. He'd been here countless times before to meet either the lawyers who hired him on an ad-hoc basis or a client. They would celebrate the cases they'd won in court at Sully's, and commiserate in the defeats. There were many reasons to walk down and across the street; a break in any case or the conclusion of one, good or bad, would inevitably end up at 'the office' as they had nicknamed it. Sometimes Deni would need clarification when they called him to meet at the office. *THE office, or Sully's?* The three had been imbibing there more frequently in the months before JG's arrest, which is why Deni had a difficult time bringing himself to patronize it since.

The place was always busy.   It was now the unofficial happy hour, however, so the place was an absolute zoo. Technically in New Hampshire, a bar can't advertise a happy hour without being fined or closed.   Illegally discounted prices, however, or getting one free after buying one was business as usual after 5:00 PM at Sully's. Deni was recognized at the door through the masses, being allowed through, and made his way toward the front bar.

"Hey handsome, what's your pleasure?" the buxom bartender said. As with all the staff, she was very affable. Another reason for the consistent level of business.

"I need to see Jenna."

"Don't they all. I can make you feel just as good, hun. Whiskey drinker if I remember right.   Right?"   If she was frustrated that this transaction was taking too long with a full bar, she didn't show it.

"Right. Irish. Make it a double and I still need to see Jenna."

"Coming up. But she's pretty busy right now, sweetie."

"I didn't ask ya if my timing was spot-on, I asked for you to get me the Whiskey and Jenna."

"Easy tiger."   She handed him his drink.   "The bar in the back, but you gotta pay me first."   She eyed him up and down as he grossly overtipped in cash and walked toward the large room in the back with a second bar.   She was staring a little too long for the next customer in line behind him who was belligerently ordering his libations to deaf ears.

Deni walked back toward the ancillary bar, having to gumby his way through the loitering crowds of people which were shouting to one another over the music. Once he arrived, he spotted his target busily making elaborate cocktails at a packed bar.   All the barstools were taken, plus three and four deep in places, where patrons were vying for her attention.   Other female servers were buzzing to and from the bar delivering trays full of drinks to the high tables and booths.   He stopped one of the young ladies abruptly but standing in her way but before he could utter a word, like lightning, she said, "I'll be right with you luv. As you can see I'm a busy girl, but I'll be back. I promise."

Before she could leave, he gently but firmly grabbed her bare arm. "I just need to speak with Jenna, it's important. Can anyone relieve her for a few?"

She wasn't shocked by the physical contact, but it was quite apparent that she was annoyed by it. This happened many times because the staff was both friendly and provocatively dressed. Deni had seen it many times before. There was a protocol for handling the countless gropers. A massive bouncer had arrived at the scene as if by magic, leaping into action like an angered panther. He grabbed Warren's shoulder with his monstrous paw, covering it in its entirety.

"Hands off — "

Deni, all in one motion; put his drink down on the offended server's tray, removed the hand off of his shoulder by twisting it, contorting the monster so the limb wouldn't be snapped off his large body. The man was down on his knees before the Whiskey had time to slosh back and forth in the glass. He did not let go of the bouncer when he addressed him, recollecting his drink.

"I was just askin' if I could have a word with Jenna. No harm, no foul. If I let go of your arm, are you gonna be calm, or are you gonna be hurt for-real?"

The bouncer's ego was more damaged than his wrist. So far. The question was whether his bruised ego was going to affect any more of his appendages. He took only a moment for the mammoth to decide.

"If you let me up, I can cover for her for a couple minutes. You can use the office, but can you make it quick? We're really busy here man."

Deni let him go. Right away he was rubbing his wrist and wincing. "What is that? Karate or something?"

"Or something."

The bustling bar went silent as patrons and staff alike took in the show. The bouncer went behind the bar to relieve her. When she came around to him, she didn't look happy. The bar was slowly returning to normal. Which meant really damned busy.

"Why'd you hurt him? You're half his size."

"He started it." He finished his drink and put the empty glass on another tray that was passing them.

"Lets make this quick," she yelled over the crowd as she headed toward the office.

"It'll take as long as it takes."

53

"You know the poor bastard is going to want to know what you did to him. The least you could do is show him sometime. I'm sure he's embarrassed. He was just trying to protect us."

"Boyfriend?"

"No. But it doesn't mean you need to use that MMA stuff on him." They arrived at the office. She looked better in the bright, fluorescent office light than she had in the dim lighting, which was strategically set to near dark in an effort to assist in picking up mates in the bar. Even in the bright light, Jenna was a stunning woman. Her flaxen hair was pulled back to reveal jade eyes that weakened knees. She was wearing a black bustier, which looked more like an expensive lingerie top, pushing her ample breasts up to her neck. The very short black skirt accentuated her firm buttocks and hips. The knee-high boots lifted her small body, ensuring that patrons could see her when she was behind the bar.

"So what's up tough-guy? You could have just sat at the bar like a normal person instead of beating people up. It's hard to believe you used to be a cop." She had waited on him many times and been the recipient of his flirtations just as many times. In short, they'd met.

"The bar is kinda loud, and we need to have a serious talk."

"You're supposed to be some kind of a sleuth, you can't tell its not a good time?" She sat down hard in an office chair, crossing her legs. The ornate piping at the top of her thigh-high, black stocking was revealed.

"I like the garter belt."

"You brought me in here to flirt? Jesus, you almost ripped Chris's arm off so you could have a go at me in private? You're unbelievable."

"Sorry, force of habit. I came to talk to you about JG. Jacob. What do you call him, Jay? He has so many nicknames."

"Oh my god, Jake. Yeah, I call him Jake. Is he okay?"

"Yeah, no change. He's in the same spot. You look wicked good by the way."

"Deni. Focus. Stop leering and get it together. I wear this crap because I have to. I'm nice to you because I have to, not because I like you that way. So now please tell me what is this about?"

"Hey, calm down. I'm a guy. When a girl who looks like you is in front of me? Its like a reflex. I genuinely am here to talk about the night of the charity event. That night. The night Jake was here."

"Great. That again? You already know the cops came and talked to me. I only poured the guy two Stone IPAs. That's it. I gave them a copy of the receipt and everything. You've seen him sling those things back. He loves them. He gets a phone call, he goes to the bathroom, and bails. I would never have let him leave here as bombed as they say he was. I would do anything for Jake, so believe me, I had no idea he was that shattered."

"You would do anything for him? Is that part of the job too?"

"Go fuck yourself. You know what I mean. I didn't over-serve him and I can prove it. I had to prove it to save my job."

"You and I both know that less than half the drinks I have in here get put on a tab. Receipts can be doctored. How many did he actually have? Honestly."

"I don't have to take this shit from you. You might be able to push other people around but not me. Do you think I want to do this, wear this for a living? I went to school to teach kids. I love kids. Do you know what that pays? Dick. So I have to babysit big kids who can't handle their liquor."

"Were you babysitting Jake that night? He must have been pretty wrecked."

"Bad choice of words," she said.

"You know what I mean."

"I'm telling you he wasn't though. I'm being straight with you. I told the cops the same thing. It was busy that night, as it is every night. The big spenders from Wayland weren't in because they were all headed to the event, but the Barstone crowd was here in full force. I was supposed to go to the event as well, I managed to get an invite through Jake, ironically. I was working alone when he got the phone call and asked for his check. It was busy but I know what I poured him. When he went to the bathroom, I switched out my drawer for the girl that replaced me so I could go home and freshen up for the charity event. I never saw him leave, but he did because after I came out of the office when my drawer was counted, he was already gone and somebody else was in his seat. He had two beers. Full stop. End of story." She began to tear up.

"You seem wicked sure. To me, though, it all looks suspect. There is no way he got more drinks from someone else? Shots? Did you two do one together? Sometimes you do that with us. He ran a woman off the fuckin' road, Jenna. He was blitzed. Shattered to the point that he can't remember anything after leaving this very bar. He had Brady in the car. You say you love kids, you could have helped him kill his kid, Jenna. Talk to me here."

She was crying so hard at that point that she was having difficulty breathing. "You don't think I beat myself up about that every day? Feel guilty? Maybe he drank somewhere else before here. Or after. I don't know but I know damn-well what he had here. From me or anybody else. He had two from me, and then he left."

"If that's true then why do you feel guilty? Seems like you didn't do anything wrong, so why would you feel guilty about anything?"

"I don't know what you want me to say, Deni."

"Start with the truth and we can move on from there."

"I *am* telling you the truth. I don't know how to say it any other way. If this is an old interrogation trick you need a refresher, because you've lost your touch. If you can't tell that I am telling the truth then the issue is you, not me."

"The whole truth. From the beginning. There's somethin' you're not telling me, and that could be the thing thats not sitting right with me. Two beers don't do this. Two beers don't cause this much havoc." He tried to look into her eyes; but those big, beautiful, green eyes were looking at her lap, and drizzling like small waterfalls.

10

"HEY HONEY I'M HOME ... WHERE ARE YOU?"   Jacob yelled to his wife as he entered the house from the side door to the garage.

"In the kitchen babe. You're home early," Anna said.

He took off his suit jacket and shoes, putting them in the entryway closet. "Your message said you wanted to actually see me before bed time tonight, so here I - hey, what is all of this?"

He made his way to the large kitchen and smaller, less formal dining room.   The small, round table was set formally, however; with candles, fine china, and an open, breathing bottle of 1997 *Josephs Phelps Insignia*, Cabernet Sauvignon from Napa Valley.   It was Jacob's favorite.   It was ridiculously expensive, but he felt it was worth every penny.

"I haven't seen you, truly seen you, other than the bedroom for a while. I thought a nice dinner at home and an actual conversation — not just 'we have to get pregnant' sex in the middle of the night when you get home — might be good for a change. You like?" She looked fantastic. Her natural, slightly strawberry-blonde hair always looked nice; but she had it highlighted and loosely curled, flowing over her shoulders.   Her slate-blue eyes, bright and beautiful as ever, sparkled in the candlelight. Anna was wearing a formfitting tank dress with her cooking apron covering it.   The apron showed not stain, detritus, or held indication that she'd been hard at work performing magic over the stove top. She was a beautiful woman. Always had been.   Stop traffic stunning.   She now posed in front of Jacob in the dim lighting which silhouetted her lean, athletic body. He thought himself the luckiest man on the planet.

"Wow. Yes, I like."

She unbuttoned his necktie, "Welcome home."

He could smell her sweet perfume as he lowered his head, kissed her lips.

"Slow down there speed-racer. We'll get there, I'd like to get through dinner first. Like I said, you know, have a conversation. It's almost ready." She turned to retreat into the kitchen. "Nice suit by the way, is it new?"

He grabbed her waist, pulling her back to him. "Yes, and it is about to get wrinkled in a ball on the floor."

"Stop. I went through a lot of trouble. While you're pulling off my apron is sexy....Oh boy is it really sexy, I really do want to talk for a change."

"So talk. And make it dirty." He was gently nibbling on her ear, which was her weakness.

"Aaaaaaaaah....All this work for nothing. You are so not making this easy."

He smoothly lifted her on top of the small table, slid the china to the only available space, taking note of the open bottle of vintage wine, but only in passing.

"You should know by now babe, I'm very easy."

After their lovemaking, they spooned naked on the couch in the nearby living room. Their heavy breaths slowed into the afterglow. They maintained a great sex life since their first time together. It had gotten better over time, never boring like they had heard their friends warn. They had mixed it up; passionate, animalistic, makeup. All good. Great, in point of fact. The silent post-coitus purring was broken by Anna.

"I hope dinner is salvageable, I'll bet you've worked up an appetite."

"I'm starving but I don't have any desire to move."

"One of us is going to have to move to get you your wine."

"I'm happy where I am."

"Did you stop by Sully's on the way home? Insignia is your favorite. A '97. It was hard to find and its open."

"I'll drink it, if it didn't break when we were on the table. I just want to be here for a while. This is nice."

"Mmmm. It is. We aren't going to have many more quiet nights like this." She moved his hand to her stomach, hand over his, interlocked. "It is still rather early, and we've had so many false starts, but the doc likes our chances this time."

He slid the other elbow to prop himself up, looking into her beautiful, glowing face. "Really? Is that what she said? When did you go? Why didn't you tell me?"

"Like I said, we've had way too many setbacks to let you get excited for nothing."

"We're in this together, babe. You should have let me know when you knew. I feel terrible that you had to worry with this alone. How long?"

"Just a couple of months, but she said there doesn't seem to be any 'chromosomal anomalies' this time. This is the furthest we have made it so she's confident."

"Please don't get mad, but should we get our hopes up? I don't want to go through any of that business again. For your sake."

"Are you saying that you don't want kids now, Jacob? We talked about this and I - "

" — Ssshhhhh. No, No. I am not saying that. You know I want to have kids with you, I know you know that. I just saw a piece of you die every time you lost it. Its like a knife in my heart every time I see you hurt. I love you, I don't want to get our hopes up for a big let down again. Its too far to fall, thats all I'm saying."

She kissed him on the mouth, rolling on top of him. "You're going to be a dad, so get used to it pal."

"I'm gonna be a dad?"

"You are going to be the greatest dad. It's going to be perfect this time you'll see. Now lets have dinner. Did we break the plates?"

✳✳✳✳✳✳

Shooting up from his bed, he just missed hitting his head on the bottom of the top bunk. Grantes stared at the dreary walls so close to him. His cellmate was above him, snoring, presumably having his own dreams. They had worked so hard for everything they had built, he and Anna, and it was steadily being disassembled. He did not yet know why Anna had not been at the courthouse that morning, nor did he know why she was not answering the phone at the prearranged times he attempted to call her. But Grantes was wide awake, forced to linger over the events of the day and the dream. Sleep would not return to him.

11

WARREN DENNIHAN WAS AN ENIGMATIC MAN WITH COUNTLESS connections that he had made throughout the many incarnations of his life and careers. He was Boston born and bred, having grown up in a rough neighborhood of crooks and wannabe gangsters in South Boston. *Southie* is a borough with a very bad rap; but it is well deserved, as it's an exclusively Irish, self-isolated community, and has an inordinate number of crimes which continue to be largely unsolved.

As kids, Warren and his neighborhood friends would boost car radios for extra cash, and in some cases the entire car surrounding it. He learned when he was quite young, however, that those petty crimes were cause for added attention from authorities. And these small indiscretions were ones the bigger crime syndicates didn't appreciate. They didn't give a shit what he and his friends did as long as they didn't shit where they ate. They could have anything they wanted as long as they stayed clear of the neighborhood, that was for higher up the food chain. The big dogs ate alone.

He would get his offers to join those higher orders a few years later, but managed to steer clear of that life. In the meantime, the cops pretty much left him alone. His thefts, gun possessions, and what-not were Mickey Mouse compared to the organized crime, murders, armed robberies, drugs, hookers, money laundering, and extortion, to name the top few of the rackets. The Police were too busy.

Deni managed to have his juvenile record expunged, but retained contact and respect from all the associates, family, and friends from his old neighborhood. There was an unspoken contract between them; they would continue to be useful resources, as they had been countless times, while he stayed clear of the crime in his old stomping grounds. He had become, of all things, a cop. They harbored no ill-will when he found work outside of Southie, good for him. They held their collective breath when they learned that he went into the academy, but after a few conversations he was able to maneuver through his maneuvers.

The Police Academy accepted him despite coming from Southie. More likely, he was accepted because of it. Early on they had asked him if he wanted to become an undercover detective in that part of Boston. He literally laughed out loud at them when the subject was first broached. He knew everyone down there, they knew he went into the academy, not even the most idiotic of the idiots would let him get involved in a crime with them.

Once they realized their mistake, which took the bureaucrats until nearly the end of his training, he was relegated to state highway duty. As punishment for getting one over on them, he sat in a cruiser all day catching speeders traveling east and west on the Massachusetts Turnpike, Interstate 90. He saw no value in that job whatsoever. He was a tax collector. He spent each shift filling the state coffers with money collected from the issuance of tickets and fines. These poor commuters were already taxed to use that stretch of road in the form of exorbitantly high tolls. The Pike would be backed up for miles in either direction, in part because of those toll booths, each and every day. Whenever a small bit of traffic would open up, commuters would try to take advantage by speeding up to make up for the lost time. A cluster of vehicles would travel ten or fifteen miles per hour over the limit, and Trooper Dennihan would be there to punish them. He felt dirty.

It took a couple of years, but he would in the end manage to make Detective Junior Grade in Boston. The honeymoon ended quickly, however. The political bullshit ran high in the big city. The job was not about how well you performed, how well you detected and cleared cases, it was about how good you looked doing it. It was about the same time—a few years after making grade—that young kids with college degrees in criminology or some such nonsense were being aggressively courted and taking over for the 'uneducated' veterans. He had seemingly just gotten into the detective squad and he was already being forced out.

So he decided to take on a few side jobs the last year before he left the Staties. He worked part-time for a local private investigator, which was highly frowned upon, but he didn't care. With all that he knew, all the shady deals not on the books by his fellow troopers, he was safe from any internal exposure. He would never have revealed any of those secrets or deals, but they didn't know that, which further ingratiated him to the corrupt. They would also eventually prove useful.

Deni continued to make a few bucks as a Mixed Martial Arts fighter. He had been a scrapper all of his life, starting from his old neighborhood, why not get paid for it? He didn't relish hurting people, but sometimes people needed a good beating. And it wasn't like he was going against unwilling participants. If he didn't hurt them, he was going to be hurt. He won more than he lost but he didn't want to go on the circuit like his younger pal Kenny Florian. Deni filled in on an ad-hoc basis on several undercards. He still practiced his Brazilian Jiu-Jitsu daily in Kenny's Brookline gym, not only for the exercise and for the occasional fight in the cage, but for his current line of work. As a Mass State Trooper, it had come in handy more times than he could count.

As a private investigator, he was extremely successful because of his work ethic, street smarts, contacts, and most definitely his toughness. Though he was wiry, he was as strong and intimidating as they come. He was covered in tattoos from collarbone to thighs, completing his bad-boy image, though he had built credit with a diverse group of people. Journalists, crooks, and cops alike could see him coming from a mile away. Some would run while others were eager for the visit.

Warren had met a couple of attorneys from southern New Hampshire on a case during his moonlighting days, and had occasionally been on the payroll, on a case-by-case basis, since. They had helped to extricate him from the legal excrement that was piled shoulder-high from time to time in his past, and he had reciprocated, getting them out of jams. They were his friends, in some cases closer than his childhood buddies, and he trusted them with his life. And now, JG was counting on him for his.

✳✳✳✳✳✳

Interstate 495 is a circuitous route around the main artery of 93, which runs south through Boston. Southbound commuters looking to circumvent the heavy traffic into the city, use 495 to steer west of the metropolis.   Fifteen miles west of the city is exactly where Warren needed to be.   This is called the Metro-west area of Boston and he is virtually at the junction of the Mass Pike and 495.   The New England Emergency Services Information headquarters, or NEESI, was in all likelihood plunked there for lack of better place to locate it.

NEESI is the center for the communication, coordination, and storage of all 911 emergency phone calls.   Each public phone company, cable bundler, and cell phone carrier must satisfy a minimum set of requirements for the handling and management of emergency phone calls.   Though AT&T was instrumental in the invention of 911 with the FCC in 1968, the carriers no longer handle the calls themselves like they used to, as all calls are connected to a regional administrator.   There is a live person, of course, nobody wants to speak with an automated computer on the other end of the phone when they are in dire need, but that live person is not likely to be close to you.   They relay the information to local authorities who respond locally.   For New England States, the FCC regulates NEESI for all the emergency phone calls, which is located in Newton, Massachusetts for some reason.   Also home of Doug Flutie and Fig Newtons.

In 2011, the Federal Government made it illegal to broadcast; publish; or make public any 911 phone call in an effort to encourage anonymous tipsters, without fear of reprisal.   What most people don't know is that every call can be traced using technology like GPS and geolocators for all VIOP lines.   So while the spy movies show the ability to trace these calls may be somewhat true, laws are in place to protect the callers.

Warren was aware that he had no legal right to investigate the anonymous 911 call which reported a drunk driver, who ran a woman off the road in southern New Hampshire, that late summer night.   He was also aware the woman that he was going to try to persuade to give him this illegal access, was his former scorned lover.

"You got fat," Althea said.

"Hello to you too.   I'll take the high road.   You look good."   The truth was she had always been super-curvy, and she had gotten more so since last he had seen her.   She was not built to be model thin, nor was she that day.   Althea was also super-crazy.

"I knew you would come back to me, less than a year after you dump me and your back already. Well, you're not going to get back in that easy, Mr. Man."

"If I was crawlin' back, I wouldn't do it at your work Althea."

"Yeah I know, I'm squeezing your plums. Where's your sense of humor? You only call when you want something, so what do you want."

Her office was nondescript with all sorts of techie gadgets and screens. She sat down behind her desk, leaving Deni to stand before her with hat in hand. As if.

"I called you yesterday to tell you what I need, so how long are you gonna try and make me squirm? I drove all the way down here because you said you might be able to do something for me, if not 'totally hook me up'. Are you gonna help me out or not?"

He was not normally attracted to voluptuous women, preferring the more athletically built. He took painstaking care of his body, other than his alcohol habit. He was lean and muscular, and he was attracted to women who were as well. But there was something about this crazy chick that kept him intrigued, and yet drove him nuts at the same time. Crazy was what he was attracted to. He had a thing for psychos.

"Keep quiet and close my door. You're gonna get me fired. You said I look good, right?"

"Yeah, you look good, Al."

"I love it when you call me Al. Can I squeeze your plums for real? We can just lock the door — "

" — Maybe some other time. I'm here for the 911 call, that's all. I thought I made that clear yesterday when I - "

"—I got the message yesterday, asshole. I was just hoping to see you. I look good though right? Come over to this side of the desk and tell me that."

"Where are all the big spools of tape spinning with all the phone calls on them like they show on TV?"

"It's a good thing you're pretty, because TV is killing your brain. Read a book or something, this is the digital age. Its all on computers. Binary. Ones and zeros."

"It's the digital age and your talkin' to me about books. Funny. Anyway, this cat and mouse game is fun and everything, Al, but JG is dependin' on me here, so are you gonna play games or help me out? It didn't work out between us but that doesn't mean you should punish my friends. You remember JG right? The lawyer guy in New Hampshire? We had dinner with him and his wife that time."

"I remember.   It's gotta be cold in here for all the computer equipment, why don't you come over here and warm me up?"

"*Althea.*"

"It's on my computer. You have to come over to my side of the desk if you want your information. Your choice. Do you want it or not?"

He went around her desk and was looking over her shoulder at both of her large monitors.

"Don't get any ideas, lover-boy."

He rolled his eyes behind her back. "So what are we looking at? I'm old school. I have trouble with my iPhone."

" I know just listen."

She played the recording with a click of a mouse.

EMS: "911, this call is recorded,
            what is your emergency?"

CALLER: "There is a bad accident
            on Wayland Country Club
            Road, by the big bend. It
            looks bad."

The female caller's voice didn't seem nervous, nor shrieking like that of someone who had just witnessed a horrific accident. She could have been ordering a pizza.

Warren was looking at the screen on the left which was indicating the various sound bars, they rose and fell based upon the specific pitch, bass, treble, decibels, dynamics, and the like. What struck him was that the bars for the caller were not rising very much, any of them. The caller was basically monotone, though the voices were coming out of some fancy speakers he had never heard of called Magicos.

EMS: "Are you hurt miss?"

CALLER: "No, no, I'm not involved.
            I just saw it happen."

EMS: "How many cars are involved, miss?

CALLER: "One. Well, two. The car that is totaled and the one that took off."

EMS: "Emergency personel are on the way. Did you see the other vehicle? The one that left the scene?"

CALLER: "Of course. It was a black Volvo XC90 SUV. New Hampshire plates." She then recited the number matter of factly.

EMS: "Did you see which direction the Volvo went?"

CALLER::   "There is only one direction that the thing could have gone." This was the first time that the caller had any emotion in her voice.

EMS: "OK, can you see the victim?"

CALLER: "I can see where the victim is supposed to be. Like I said it's bad. She's dead."

EMS: "Did you get her pulse? Do you have medical training? Are you certain she is dead?"

CALLER: "I'm not going anywhere near that car. But there is no way she could have survived that crash.

EMS: "OK. What is your name and where are you at the sight? There will be someone on the scene within a few seconds."

CALLER: click.

"The caller was way too calm. Don't you think? You must hear a million of these calls," Deni said as he straightened, standing fully erect.

"You hear all kinds, but yeah she was totally calm. Especially when she knew the woman was dead."

"How did she know she was dead? She never went near the car. I saw pictures of the wreck, and I admit that it looked really bad. But still."

"The wreck must have been bad enough where she just knew."

"If she saw the whole thing happen, like she says, there was always a chance she could have been alive. I mean, she had no way of knowing without going up to the car that the woman was decapitated."

"Maybe she didn't want to see all the blood and guts."

"I don't think so. Have you ever driven by a wreck on the side of the road? Slows traffic to a stop because everybody has to see the damage. Everybody wants to see, or to help, or be a hero. She knew the woman was dead. Wait a sec."

"What? You have that look. That totally, super sexy look you get when you think you figured something out that nobody else knows," Althea said. Her eyes were taking him in again.

"How did she know it was a *she*?"

"The caller?"

"Yeah, the caller. Who else? She said the woman was dead. Played it off like nobody could have possibly survived the crash and wasn't going anywhere near the car. But she knew it was a chick. Play it again."

Althea played the call again after a few clicks of her mouse. After the second run-through, she said, "Interesting, but what does that prove?"

"Well nothing, but it's weird right?"

"I think you're desperate to help your friend and you're reaching."

He looked onto the right screen where the caller's phone number and location was pulled up. He began to write it down when Althea stopped him.

"Hey you can't do that. I'm sorry, but my neck is out just letting you *listen* to the call. The cops can get it with a warrant, but it's anonymous, so they aren't likely to get authorization. Additionally, it's from a burner phone."

"Additionally? Who says that?"

"Smart people."

"Whatever. Anyways, you said that phone number is from a burner? Who bought it, who is it registered to?"

"I can't tell you even if I knew."

"Whattaya mean? You don't know? All this equipment and you aren't tellin' me shit." He was playing to her sense of IT superiority. She was an information junky and her skills with technology were extraordinary. Whatever NEESI was paying her, her talents were wasted.

"It's an *unregistered* burner phone. It's still legal to go out and buy a disposable phone without putting any of your personal information on it, especially if you pay in cash. Drug dealers would be out of business if they couldn't do that. You can't trace a phone that gets thrown away and that isn't connected to the dealer in the first place."

"Come on Al. You don't find this weird? Mysterious lady, who buys a burner phone, an unregistered burner phone like you just said, sees the whole thing but doesn't help? She never even goes near the car but knows it is a woman, and conveniently makes JG's vehicle and plate number?"

"It's not that odd. I'm sorry, but people are paranoid. Especially in New Hampshire. Live Free or Die, right? They think the Government is tapping their phones, tracking their movements so they get untraceable phones. She wants to be a good Samaritan, but she can't stand blood. Maybe she saw more than she needed to from a distance, and that is how she knew it was a female. It's all explainable. I know you want to help, but this call isn't gonna be the way to do it, I'm afraid."

"Will you give me a copy of the call? And the phone number. And who sold it to her?"

"Ugh. You are going to be the death of me. It's illegal and can't be used in court, so why do you need it?"

"I have a hunch. And I'm desperate, like you said. Come on, Al. I know you wanna."

She paused for ten-seconds, then pulled out a pink memory stick that said *Susan B. Komen* on it in small print. She had already had it inserted into the USB drive. She handed it to him and said, "You owe me dinner. Not just Wendy's but like, an actual date."

"You got it."

"Verizon."

"What?"

"Verizon is the carrier, so my bet is that this Samaritan bought it at a Verizon store or kiosk."

"Thanks. You look great by the way," Deni said as he dashed out of her office.

"Call me."

12

THE 'CORRECTIONS' PORTION OF THE NAME WAYLAND COUNTY
House of Corrections was designated such, in large part, because of the programs it offered the inmates the institution housed. The programs included trades like culinary, print pressing; or counseling programs like parenting, substance abuse, and anger management. Considering the prison's unemployment and recidivism rates, only those who had a sense of humor or were defending their jobs could argue that these programs had any positive affect whatsoever. Federal money was doled out by the fistful to the States who opted to build institutions with these programs to curb rising incarceration rates. WCHOC was one of these county run, federally funded, maximum security institutions.

The Sheriff mandated that these program rosters remain full at all times in order to fleece the Federal Government for every dollar he could. If an inmate didn't have a high school diploma or equivalent, they got a GED whether they earned it or not. Federal monies came into the prison for every equivalency test passed. Cha-ching. If the inmate didn't have a job lined up upon his release, they earned a trade, but only one of the two trades offered. Cha-ching. And if any portion of the alleged or convicted crime involved substance abuse, the inmate received counseling for it. Cha-ching. Keep those tax dollars flowing, the system is working fine in Wayland County.

Grantes had received higher degrees from prestigious schools, was a successful attorney, and a business owner. He had not yet been convicted, but he was being housed in the Sheriff's institution. The Sheriff wasn't maximizing any federal tax dollars on Grantes' back, and so he was perplexed as to what to do with him. Attaining a GED was moot, he had a trade, and his own business, therefore no money could be garnered from any of these programs. Grantes was a father, and was alleged to have operated a vehicle under the influence of alcohol, so he would be made to take parenting classes and alcohol abuse treatment. Inmate #437261 was going to earn his keep one way or another.

The federal money was contingent upon the prison adhering to federal incarceration guidelines; such as twenty hour lock-ins, and the size of the cell that two men would spend locked into said cell. With four total hours for recreational time dispersed in intervals throughout the day, *rec time* meant; showering, eating, lawyer visits, seeing the nurse, exercise, phone calls, and any programs that were assigned. Grantes was mandated to be enrolled in three hours of programming, which meant he had one hour per day to eat, exercise, shower, call someone on his pre-approval sheet, and get an aspirin if he had a headache. His sanity was not part of his 'rehabilitation' JG reckoned.

His every day was scheduled exactly the same. A routine was deemed an important element in correcting behavior. Grantes started every day with the loud clang of the opening of the metal door to his cell at 6:00 AM for chow, closing again with the same sound at 6:10 with him back inside of it. The door would open and close many more times throughout the day so he could; go to parenting class, lock-in, substance group therapy, lock-in, 11:00 AM for lunch chow, lock-in, self-help, lock-in, SAP (Spousal Advocate Program), lock-in, 5:00 PM chow, lock-in, one hour of rec to do whatever he had to do like shower or call Anna, then lock-in again until 6:00 AM the next day where he would do it all over again.

His parenting class was a counselor-led group with a preset agenda and course workbook. Grantes hadn't the faintest idea whom had written the course workbook, but he did surmise that it was written for those whom had difficulty with reading and writing in the English language.

Alphonse, the parenting counselor, was a megalomaniac, African-American man who was clearly not in the top of his field, and despised calling upon Grantes in class. He avoided the inmate at all costs as he had been embarrassed by him in the past. This suited Grantes just fine. Every so often, however, Alphonse would be forced to include the inmate in the discussion to avoid the appearance of favoritism, but always did so with trepidation. Alphonse would speak to the group while standing in the front of the seated half-circle to further assert his dominance over the flock.

"…. and wouldn't you agree, Mr. Grantes?" Alphonse said at the end of a monotonous monologue.

"Most likely not, but I can't say for certain as I wasn't really paying attention to you."

"We were discussing the likelihood that children of criminals tend to become criminals themselves. I was inquiring as to your thoughts, as you seemed to be lost in your own thoughts. Also, as an attorney, or former attorney, whichever the case may be, you are in a unique position to agree with that assessment."

"Cheery, that. You must be a glass-is-half-full kinda guy. I haven't been convicted of anything, so I'm still an attorney. As far as the discussion, you're trying to sound smart but I'm not buying. No, I do not agree. If the father is in prison, he would have little, if any, influence over his — "

" — If you were to look at — "

" — I wasn't finished. You asked my opinion then you interrupted me, which is disingenuous. 'A man expects his son to be as good a man as he *meant* to be' - Franklin Clark. I am sure you knew that."

"No, I didn't know that. But I prefer the Bible which says — "

" — 'He who brings up, not he who begets, is the father.' There. Thats from the bible. Now do you feel better? It isn't genetic, its environmental. And even that is just a statistic. You are statistically more apt to become a criminal if you live in an area where there is high crime, but that doesn't automatically mean that if you live in say, Barstone, that you are going to be here at one point or another. What are you trying to feed these people? Hopelessness?"

"I was trying to illustrate that they need to break the cycle of crime."

"I know what you are trying to do, Alphonse. You assume that because these guys are here, that their fathers were criminals also. You're only interested in kicking a man when he's already at his lowest point. It's not enough that he is here, in this horrible place. No, he has to be made to wonder how his kids are doing in his absence; only to be told that it doesn't matter one bit, because his kid is going to wind up here anyway. And he will probably have to listen to you tell him the same bullshit story you're spilling out right now. You must feel great at the end of your day."

"I don't appreciate your tone, inmate. The fact is that unless you are willing to change your behavior, the cycle will continue." He was losing the group of men, losing his stature as the authority figure of the group. He embarked in this dialogue to open up a non-participating inmate, a quiet one, but he was getting embarrassed. Again.

"You want us, oh wait, that last comment was to me directly wasn't it? You want me to change into what you consider to be a good parent. No parent is perfect, even you. Besides, how do any of us know that you're not a junkbox, or that your kid is? Is your kid some deviant destined to be here? You spend a lot of your life here, so what does that mean? What would you say to your kid if he were sitting here? That in all likelihood his kid, your grandson, is going to be sitting here no matter what he does?"

"Maybe we should move onto the exercises in your workbooks." He turned to everyone else in the group. "Open your workbooks and quietly complete the next two exercises." He lowered to say in Grantes' ear, "Another outburst like that one and I will have you lugged for insolence and inciting a riot."

"The trouble is, Alphonse, you called on me. You don't like me and you don't like my opinions. You think you know me because of my circumstance, but you don't know me or anybody else here. And you won't unless you speak to us like we're human. We aren't animals in a zoo. If you want respect, you'll have to give some."

"You can't win, Grantes. You will never win. Not in this place, and not over me. No matter what you do or what you say, I get to walk out that door at five o'clock. And you'll stay here to rot. Society doesn't want you, so they send you here. This is your life and you better get used to it."

Instead of concentrating on the workbook, as he was instructed, Grantes thought back to when he first became a parent. He remembered it like it was yesterday, though he was four years removed.

✳✳✳✳✳✳

The large flatscreen was tuned to football, as it was every Sunday during every NFL season, with the surround sound blaring. Anna was standing in front of the couch with her oversized #12 New England Patriots jersey, filling it out more like a linebacker than the quarterback the uniform represented. She was nine months pregnant, and while she couldn't experience this football season the way she had in the past, she was enjoying listening to the helmets smash, bones crunch, feeling the hits as the bass kicked with a high fidelity that would make George Lucas proud.

"Baby, can you pleeeeeeaaaaase explain to me why they have such a hard time playing against Miami? The Dolphins suck, they always suck and yet we play like shit against them every time." Anna said 'we' like she was on the roster.

From the kitchen JG shouted back to her. Neither one of them was able to hear the other with the sounds of football turned up so loud. He was putting the finishing touches on a platter of boneless chicken wings.

"I honestly don't know, hun. The Pats always have to make things interesting. They can't just decisively beat the crap out of them, they have to keep you guessing." He walked back into the entertainment room with the large platter in one hand, and a bottle of Stone IPA in the other. His wife was standing in the middle of the room with her eyes glued to the enormous TV.

"Thanks babe. These better be spicy. They say spice helps induce labor and I'm ready for him to be out." She took the entire platter out of his hand, leaving him only the beer. He sat down in the recliner to her left.

"They're tossed in *Sriracha*, they are going to be spicy. Is that vat of ranch dressing going to be enough for you?"

"Fuck you, I'm hungry. I'll trade you. You carry your son around for a while and see how it feels." She was shoveling the wings into her mouth without looking away from the game. He was laughing despite being left to go hungry. He struggled to understand exactly what she'd just said between the mouthful of food and volume, but he was able to glean the gist.

"You look amazing in that jersey. Who needs 3-D when I've got that big #12 popping towards me?"

"Get off that couch, I'm gonna kick your ass. It's a good thing you are the most attractive shithead I have ever seen." She turned her face but not her eyes as she leaned down to kiss her husband. The kiss smeared hot sauce all over his face, matching hers. She licked the sauce off her thumb before grabbing another wing with her dripping hand.

"How are they, good? I like mine."

"Delicious. You are a master chef — Oh honey, I'm sorry. Do you want one?

"Ha. No, you eat them. You look like you're enjoying yourself. I think the whole thing is a wive's tale anyway; but if you think spicy chicken will help, I'm here for you."

"Thank you. I love you."

"I love you too, although you might be bigger than the blimp that is floating over Gillette Stadium right now." And he did love her, with all of his being.

"When I get back to fighting weight, we are gonna wrestle, and not the naked kind, my friend. Now shut up so I can watch the game, we're on the 20."

They remained silent for a couple of minutes. Jacob found it odd that there was no reaction when the Patriots had to settle for a field goal, even more odd that she muted the TV right before the kick. Muting the television during a football game was forbidden.

"Babe, how many beers have you had?"

"I just started my third, why? You said it didn't bother you if I had a couple even though you can't. Are you gonna start in on me — "

" — Shut up, I don't care about that. It's go-time."

"Go-time?" He was slow on the uptake.

"The wings worked, *go-time* you fool."

"Oh. Oh God, lets go."

"Call the hospital on the way, they need to have the game on when I get there. I'm serious."

"Yeah, yeah hun. Let's just get over there and we will worry about the game when we get there. They're gonna think we're nuts." He grabbed the prepared baby bag and his wife, stuffed both into the car. "No shit, the spicy wings did work," he said to himself as he made his way around the car to pack himself into the driver's seat.

✳✳✳✳✳✳

The walk back to Grantes's cell was not long in terms of distance, but it was long in that it took a lot of time and was always an adventure. The rooms that held all the programming were in a separate area of the prison. He would make bets with himself, taking the over/under on how many times he would be pat-down or asked to see his ID. Just for some kind of fun. He thought the entire charade was inefficient, but soon realized that it was less about efficiency and more about the appearance of insurmountable security. Much like the security in airports. The armed guards at Logan and every other airport, the TSA personnel, the police, and security teams were all in place to create an atmosphere of impenetrable order. To make people think they were safer, else nobody would fly. Prisons were the same. The pat-downs and ID checks were to make the inmates think it impossible to misbehave, when in fact misbehavior was rampant.

He stopped by the COs desk when he returned to the pod. The desk which was known as the *bubble* because an inmate was not allowed within the imaginary forcefield around the desk, much like the game that kids play. Grantes asked if he could get some extra rec time so that he could use the library, but of course the request was denied. No reason was given. He had a couple of hours before the next evolution in his reprogramming and wanted to investigate some case law instead of being unproductive in his cell.

As the solid door loudly slid open, the acrid smell of burning paper and smoke billowed out at him. Loder yelled at him to close the door, as if he had control over it. His celly was smoking what appeared to be a cigarette, which was contraband. Grantes was trying to decide whether to go into the cell or stay out of it, when the door started to close. He went in.

"What the hell are you doing? You're gonna get us both lugged," JG said.

"Chew-ports, bro. I'm making smokes. You want one?"

"No. And it's not fantastic that I'm gonna be just as screwed as you when you get caught. Jesus-H, that stuff smells terrible. You're putting me in a spot here, Loder."

"You're not gonna snitch. But you are gonna block that window and keep flushing the toilet."

"The COs aren't gonna buy that one of us is taking a shit. It smells awful but it smells like burnt-awful, not shit-awful."

"Just shut up and keep flushing."

"How the hell do you make cigarettes in here anyway? You fly in some tobacco? It's not like they let you receive that in the mail."

"The COs chew tobacco."

"What? And they just give it to you?"

"No, one of the guys in the pod cleans at night, so he saves their spit cups. I dry it out and then roll it up in paper I rip out of the library books. See? Who says readin' ain't useful."

"That is absolutely disgusting. Fucking gross. And I don't think this is what they're striving for with the library books. No wonder half the books I try to read are missing pages." He watched and flushed again when a thought crossed his mind. "Hey, how do you light those things, they don't allow us to have fire, let alone a lighter where we can make our own."

"Two batteries and a bread tie."

"You're shitting me."

"Nope."

"Loder, if you would just use your powers for good instead of evil, you could make something of yourself."

"My genius only works in here. Besides, other guys are just as smart if not smarter. Prison is full of MacGyver-types, I saw a guy the other day trying to sell speakers for the radio."

"Which brings us to back to the cigarettes. You either gotta sell them all today before cell searches tonight, or you have to cop to it if they find them. I'm having a hard enough time fighting off the charges I have, let alone pick up more. I'm not gonna snitch, but I won't cop to it either."

"Fair enough. For a lawyer, you ain't half bad Grantes."

"Gee, thanks."

Unfortunately, Loder, #437254, was very likely to be caught. Cell searches were at least daily, sometimes more if the COs were suspicious of a certain inmate. But the real danger was in the other smokers on the pod. The COs would find them in someone's cell during a search, and that someone would cut a deal to get out of the additional charge, and the additional time that the charge would bring. One of the worst things a man can be in prison is a snitch, but it happened every day. Someone would rat to save their skin, and everyone would know. A guy can't fart in prison without the entire prison population knowing. The rat would be hunted and beaten without mercy, take a trip to HSU, then spend the remainder of his stay in Protective Custody. Once you checked in there, you had better hope that you never run into another inmate on this stay or the next. Word gets around. A PC is the absolute worst thing an institutional man can be, just above a rat, and then a skinner although it's close. The prison protects a PC, hence the name, as much as possible by segregating them. But then, for some absurd reason, they give them a special color jumpsuit so they stand out a mile away. That is why they get themselves cornered by another inmate, and why those guys get killed. It was the duty of every professional inmate to beat down a PC'd inmate when running into them between pods. It didn't matter if they were known or not, anyone with a PC jumpsuit was beaten down. God help the inmate who passed up the opportunity to send a PC to HSU. If anyone found out, the abstinent inmate would get the beating meant for the PC in spades.

Cigarettes were just one of the many commodities traded on the pods. The prison was not the NYSE, but the methods for successful trade negotiations were just as intricate. Economics courses could be taught on the supply and demand formulae used to compile price analysis and forecasting for the prison exchange system. Every day; pharmaceuticals, narcotics, hooch, smokes, hardcore mags, and the like were smuggled or manufactured in prison. If the inmate was a known quantity, hot as they're called, he has a seemingly inculpable cohort store and distribute the contraband. The value of the commodity is based upon availability, risk, and going rate of sale on the outside. Payment is then made in one of a myriad of methods.

One such method is in the form of outside trade. A phone call is made to someone who is on the pre-approved phone list on the outside, as calls can go out but never come in. All calls are recorded which makes necessary a highly elaborate code for communicating logistics, dollar amount, the recipient, their contact information, et cetera. The outside person then makes the appropriate calls and connections, the money transferred. The inmate then calls back his contact on the outside at a designated time to ensure that all funds have been exchanged, where it is then given to a baby-momma to hold, use, or send back to the prison in form of a money order through the mail to be deposited into another inmate's account.

The prison store, or canteen, is set up for inmates to buy various items from that account. Everything from sneakers and clothing, to radios and foodstuffs are sold at up to three hundred percent over the three hundred percent markup a retailer sells them for on the street. This is yet another way the prison makes money on the backs of the downtrodden.

Canteen is another way goods and services are exchanged because, without cash, canteen items are the same as cash. The value of each item is like money in the bank, or the pocket if prisoners were allowed to have pockets.

Prisoners can pay bills from their account, not just buy canteen items. Child support, alimony, and court fines are also the usual reasons for an inmate to send out a money order from a case manager. Once that money order leaves the prison, it is as good as laundered.

Grantes wanted no part of this system, no part of the cigarette distribution company currently being run out of his cell. The triangle trade was very lucrative for the professional inmate, which Grantes did not consider himself to be. His extra rec time was denied and he was, therefore, relegated to the lock-in with his celly. He couldn't tell anyone, nor could he escape. So he waited for his next dose of therapy or reprogramming, repeatedly flushing the toilet, all the while his mind raced about the past.

✳✳✳✳✳✳

The funeral of Norman Craig was a lavish affair. Jacob thought it gauche to have such extravagance for an event as somber. The enormous church to which his in-laws gave astronomical sums of money, though rarely (if ever) attended, was packed beyond capacity. The crowd spilled out onto the front lawn, onto the street, and down the block. The death of an Investment, Insurance, and Banking Mogul such as Craig Investment Group, CIG, brought the finest people out of the woodwork. Hundreds of America's biggest players (and some of the World's) had come out to pay their final respects. Jacob wondered how many were Norman's friends, and how many were sycophants. When Sheikh Hamdan of Dubai was in attendance, it made Jacob wonder just how rich Norman was.

Craig's battle with esophageal cancer was a short one. Jacob had thought that his father in-law could overcome any obstacle, that there was nothing in the world that could best him. This particular ailment, however, was terminal in statistically every case, regardless of wealth or power. What began as a sore throat, for which true movers and shakers have no time, became five months of torturous misery. For the family, the defeat was pronounced almost overnight. For the epitome of a mainstay, both familial and in commerce, it was an excruciating reminder that there are some things even the most influential can't control.

The pillar that was Norman Craig would never get to meet his grandson. Jacob and Anna had tried to bring him a grandchild for years while Norman was alive, without success. There'd been some pregnancies but none had lived outside the uterus. When Brady finally became a reality, Jacob suggested that he be named after his deceased grandfather. The idea was immediately shot down, Anna would not hear of it, and Olivia—Brady's would-be grandmother—was in exile then. After her father's death, Anna became isolated from her mother. What exactly had happened between them in the days that followed Norman's passing wouldn't be discovered until much later, but the mere mention of his name, or Olivia's for that matter, was deemed too painful, and would cause volcanic tirades.

Mrs. Craig was presumed alive and well, her whereabouts however, were unknown. She was financially one of the most secure and was most likely spending it in her golden years.

Jacob missed her terribly. The passing of his own parents, the death of his father in-law, and the isolation from Olivia was heartbreaking.

Olivia had disappeared and had been unheard of until a letter arrived at the law office years later.

❋❋❋❋❋❋

JG had taken a few weeks off after Brady was born. Ryan had covered the workload happily, keeping his partner apprised or seeking his advice only in the most dire of circumstances.

Upon his return to the office, amidst the immense stack of messages, to-do's, and mail; Angie had set aside an urgent, certified letter. It was a large, thick manilla envelope devoid of a return address.

"Welcome back, JG. We have several well-wishes, gifts, a ton of mail for you to go through, and this one marked 'urgent and confidential'. No return address and came by currier, so I was curious about it. I almost opened it but thought better of it. If it's rigged with a device, I want no part of it. What mysterious person did you piss off? Do you want some coffee, by the way?"

"Thanks Ang. Yes on the coffee, but if we could take it down a notch please until I get caught up that would be great. Maybe you should switch to decaf."

"Ha ha. It's just good to have you back, and we have so much to go over, and I am curious about the package. I left it on top of your pile."

"Ang. Please, huh? It's like trying to take a sip of water through a fire hose with you right now. I'll be in my office." He closed the door behind him only to have it opened again thirty-seconds later.

"Here is your coffee. Sorry to come at you right when you walked in the door."

"Thanks, Ang. Sorry to tear into you. I'm not getting any sleep. I love that little guy but he never sleeps. Is that normal? Everybody says its normal, but not sleeping for this long doesn't seem normal to me."

"He never sleeps?"

"Well sometimes, but not for very long stretches."

"Yeah, that's normal."

He was behind his desk, took a sip of his coffee which, truthfully, Angie fixed better than his wife. "I gotta be honest with you, it was tough to leave the house today. My head is not really in it."

"I don't blame you. I'll hold your calls and leave you to it."

"Ang?"

"Yes."

"Thanks for all your help in holding it all together over here. I couldn't have spent all that time with Anna and Brady without you and Ry. I appreciate it."

"Anytime. You know that," she said as she closed the door behind her.

They were likely just as exhausted as he was. They had each been putting in fifteen plus hours per day, six days a week while he was taking maternity leave. They had lives of their own, albeit together, and had set them aside for the good of the firm. They needed the income more than JG did. But any critique about Ryan sliding into a free partnership could be quieted, he had worked his ass off.

JG decided to inspect the mysterious package first. It was on the top of his pile anyway. The document sized envelope was uber-sealed, requiring him having to rip apart the outer envelope to retrieve the contents. No bomb. No anthrax. The thick stack of documents were typed, the top sheet a congratulations of the birth of his son, Brady. Whomever it was knew him and knew him well enough to know he was now a father. On the double, he rescanned the envelope, but still no clues.

The dawn broke in the next few paragraphs on the first page. The sender spoke about how sad it was that she could not be there for the birth of her only grandson. How she wanted more than anything to be a part of all of their lives. She apologized for being persona non grata, for her part in it anyway. She begged for continued anonymity and wished to take the opportunity to share the reasons she had been alienated. She further hoped that after laying all her cards on the table, that some sort of forgiveness and reunion would take place in the foreseeable future.

"She must be dying. Why else is she getting her house in order?" he said to himself. He went on to read the rest of the documents, which told of the day the earth shattered and swallowed Olivia Craig.

******

The meeting with Cecil Brand, the Craig family finance manager and board member of CIG, took place less than a week after Norman Craig had passed on. The meeting that took place after Craig's death was not unexpected but the result was very much so. Brand was a slight, weaselly looking gentleman. Frail-thin, beady eyes behind oversized oval glasses which rested on an aquiline nose; Cecil was as irksome to look at as his voice was to hear. Olivia and Anna would have to deal with him in order to sort out the nuances of Norman's will.

"I'm sorry we have to meet under these circumstances, Olivia. Anna, it's been too long," Cecil said.

"Your condolences are appreciated as are your years of service to my husband and our family," Olivia said. "My daughter and I, if it is not too much trouble or crass Cecil, would like to take care of the business at hand without fetter, so that we may be free to grieve."

"Yes, of course. Once I've explained everything, you both will simply need to sign the documents. You don't even need to read them if you would prefer, though I see Anna has dived right into them."

Each of the women had been given a small binder of documents as they took their seats. Olivia had not so much as looked at hers.

"I'm sorry, Cecil, was I not supposed to read these? There has to be seventy-five or a hundred pages here," Anna said.

"Well, the Craig Estates and holdings are extensive and complicated. Given how vast and diversified his assets are, it has been painstaking work to sort it all out. Much less to organize it in one small binder. I've been responsible for his personal financial well-being for years and I assure you that — "

" — My father was an investment mogul, I'm sure he was able to manage his own checkbook just fine."

"Anna, there is no need to be hostile toward Cecil. He was just trying to make a complicated situation less so, isn't that right Mister Brand?" Olivia was ever the diplomat.

"Yes. Quite right and well said. So as I was saying, he was extraordinarily wealthy and while this may look complicated, since the numbers are so large, there should be no need to quibble over a few dollars, pounds, or euros."

"You mean Norman *and* Olivia's, don't you? You said 'he was wealthy' but you meant *they*, correct?"

"I apologize for her, Cecil. She has taken her father's death very hard. Though he was home so rarely, Norman and Anna were very close."

"Please don't apologize for me, Mom, like I'm not in the room. Cecil, I'm sorry. I don't really want to be here. Daddy gave me everything I've ever wanted and I hate that he's gone. I loved him very much, as I'm sure you can imagine. Mom worked just as hard as he did, she just did it at home. So all of this is hers. I'm not sure why it takes all of these documents to explain and to be signed since it's already hers."

"Right. Well, that was a bit insensitive of me. I'm sure this is a very trying time for both of you. It certainly is for me. The reason for the lengthy legal documentation before you, is that it is far more complicated than just signing everything over to Olivia. There are many more beneficiaries."

"I'm getting a headache. How can there be many beneficiaries to Daddy's *personal* finances? CIG, of course, but personal should just be Mom, me, and maybe Jacob."

"Yes, well, if you look in the appendices in the back of the binder you have, you will see that it is not quite as simple as all of that, I am sad to say. There are vast sums, spread out all over the world, and — "

" —Hold on please. Who are all of these people? I've never heard of any of these people. Aveda something or other, and — "

" —As I said, your father was quite wealthy and wanted to ensure that certain people of his acquaintance were well taken care of with the various homes, portfolios, trusts, accounts and stock holdings." Cecil was speaking to Anna, who had been questioning him much more than he'd obviously hoped, and was now looking at Olivia for some help.

"What say we just have him tell us what monies and things are directly bequeathed to us, Anna? You don't want to be here any more than I do, so let poor Cecil just cut to the chase and we can sign whatever it is we must. How would that be?"

"Well, no I don't want to be here at all. But since I am, and since the man whom has been entrusted to manage yours and Daddy's money seems to be giving us the run-around about that money, I think I would like him to take the time to explain. So please, Cecil, please explain it to me. Since you need my signature, which you're not going to get until I get some answers. How would *that* be?"

Cecil was cornered, and the weasel didn't like to be cornered, but he was nothing even close to a fighter. He had backed out of every fight he had ever been involved in. And this was turning into an all-out brawl.

"There is the contingent of future heirs, so those are listed," he said after some thought.

"What am I stupid? I can see that. But everyone on the beneficiary list has money set aside for future heirs. So, for the last time and before I call an attorney, Mister Brand, who are all of these people? In English. No more run-around, no more vagaries. Answers or I call a lawyer."

He looked to Olivia, who was looking at her lap. "Maybe you and your mother would be more comfortable using my conference room, to uh....collect yourselves."

"You know who these people are, Mom?"

"Maybe we should take some time to, as Cecil put it, collect ourselves."

The two women were shown into a side, private conference room off of Brand's office. Once they were inside, he closed the door and bravely ran away from the situation. Olivia gracefully took a seat at the end of the conference table. Anna remained standing.

"Okay Mom, what gives? Who are these people and why doesn't anyone want to tell me?"

"Please have a seat dear so we can discuss this rationally and civilly."

"I'm fine where I am."

"Stop being stubborn and please sit down so I can explain."

"Explain what, Mom? Did Daddy have some distant relatives that I didn't know about? I know about Uncle Robert but Daddy despised him, and he's gay so future heirs is kind of a stretch. I don't see his name in here anyway."

"Would you like some water or something, dear?"

"Mom. Quit stalling."

"Your father was a complicated man. Generous but complicated."

"So these are charity cases? No wonder they have exotic names."

"No, no. They aren't charity cases, dear, they are …. your half-siblings."

"My what? My half-siblings?" She did sit down just then. Hard.

"Your father traveled all over the world on business, sometimes he stayed extensively — "

" —Hold on, hold on, hold on. Hold-the-fuck-on. Stop for a minute. Are you trying to tell me that Daddy had other families?"

"Well, not in so many words, but he was the father to other people yes."

"Like a father? Or he donated sperm?"

"I don't believe that I follow you, dear."

"Forget it. It doesn't even matter. Was this before he was married to you? No, wait, that doesn't make any sense, you two married after college, right? Tell me *that's* true."

"Of course it's true. So no, not before we were married."

"And you knew about this?"

"Yes."

"How long? How old are they? How long have you known?"

"I was suspicious for some time, years ago. I found out what was going on many years ago. Fairly early on, in fact."

"What the fuck, Mom?"

"Please calm down dear. There is no need for vulgar language."

"You just told me that my father was a lying, cheating motherfucker, and you're worried about my language?"

"Please calm down."

"So Dad. Norman. Was touring the fucking world, spreading his seed like a landscaper, and you let him?"

"I didn't let him, he did it. I chose to keep our family intact."

"So my life is a big scam. My entire life. You allowed me to think we were a happy family. To bring Jacob into our happy family, which it turns out is just a big joke? I thought we were the luckiest people on earth, Mom. We had money, we were happy, we loved each other. A big fucking lie. It was all for show?"

"It isn't a scam, nor a lie, dear. It's not as if I had a career. I did it to protect you. To protect us."

"Oh, fuck that, Mom. It's betrayal. I love Jacob with all of my heart, but do you think for one minute that if I found out that he was cheating on me that I would stick around?"

There were a few moments of silence, which seemed like an eternity, as Anna tried to keep her composure, tried not to weep. She had to be strong. She was losing the battle, however. Tears rolled down her cheeks, her hands were trembling. Any attempt to touch Anna, was rebuffed.

Olivia said after a time, "What was I supposed to do?"

"What do you do? What do you mean what do you do?" She stood up, bent over to within an inch of Olivia. "You take me and you leave the son-of-a-bitch. You don't take shit then ask for another helping. You pick up whatever dignity you have, and with your child you leave. You take him for every dollar that he's worth. You leave him penniless, that's what you do." She stood upright again, wiped her tears on her shirtsleeves. Spittle had formed on the sides of her mouth. "Jacob will know nothing about this. You betrayed me, and you betrayed him too."

"So you do see why I kept the secret?"

"Am I really your daughter?"

"What Anna? Of course you are my daughter, how can you say that?"

"I can't believe we have the same genes."

"Anna, I love you. Please sit down so we can talk about this."

"You love me? Love is not lying to someone. Love means you don't betray. You don't really love me, and you cannot expect me to love someone who has done what you've done."

"Stop it, Anna. What are you saying?"

"What am I saying? Here is what I'm saying. I'm saying that you clearly do not know what love means. I'm saying that you decided to cover this all up and betray those people you say you love. I'm saying you are as guilty as he is, that you made your choice and now you have to live with it. I'm saying that you make whatever excuses you need to, continue to cover up whatever you need to, but you disappear. You stay away from me and you stay away from Jacob. Live with that." Anna walked out of the conference room and never looked back.

******

Mrs. Craig wrote that she would do anything to take it all back. Do anything to get her family back. She would do it all differently. All of it.

If only she could have back what she was so desperate to save from the beginning.

She wrote how much she longed to see her only daughter and grandson. She assured Jacob that she loved him with all her heart though she had never met him. Her heart was breaking in exile, but there was nothing she could do about that. This was not her choice, only that she was being punished for a choice she'd once made.

'Please keep this between us, Jacob. I just wanted you to know what happened and how I feel about you, and of course Anna. It has been too long and life is too short. I wanted you to know why I had to move away and why I remain there. I sincerely hope that someday you can find it in your heart to forgive me and that we will be able to reunite. I would love to meet my grandson. In the meantime, please take care of him and yourselves. Love always, Olivia.'

13

THE RESIDENCE OF ROMAN AND CHAMILLE DESTRIER WAS A sprawling English Manorial-style home, if you could call a building that large a home. There were many wealthy homes in Wayland, each trying to be more majestic than the next. The Destrier estate, however, was the most stately north of Newport, Rhode Island, even besting Tom Brady and Gisele Bundchen's 14,000 square-foot mega-mansion in Brookline, Massachusetts. In fact, the Destrier estate was fashioned after a mansion owned by the Vanderbilts, then later the Dukes, known as *Rough Point* in Newport, Rhode Island. There was nothing rough about it. It was set far back from the main road and gate, consisting of the main house, a guest house, housing for the help, and even a house for the boat located on the man-made pond.

Roman Destrier was bred from an upper-middle class family. He was an up and coming young financial mind when Norman Craig recruited him from Duke University (which is where Roman fell in love with *Rough Point,* which was owned more recently by James Buchanan Duke, the benefactor of Duke University). Roman began his career with CIG under Norman's tutelage, moving on to head his own financial division, and in the end his own conglomerate.

Chamille had gone to Wellesley College where she'd met Anna at a social event for future business women which took place at Boston University. They became fast friends. Chamille made the trip up to New Hampshire on several occasions. She too was from money, and of course the Craigs approved of Anna's friendship with her. Norman would introduce Chamille to the hot young talent he was grooming, Roman Destrier.

Soon after they married, Roman was heading his own international finance division for CIG, which made him wealthy, but never home. He would stay at one of their numerous homes, flats, or an exclusive hotel somewhere on the globe, but not often in New Hampshire. Once he left CIG, the situation became worse as they were married in name only.

Chamille saw her husband with such rare occasion she would forget what he looked or sounded like. They rarely spoke, and when they did it was as if they were strangers.

Chamille was bored in her corner of New England. With hired help doing any and all daily household duties, she involved herself in everyone else's life, chiefly Anna's. Chamille knew Roman strayed with other women, no man can go without being intimate for as long as she and her husband did. She had to make appointments with her own husband through one of his female personal assistants to make trips to meet him somewhere on the planet. She was bitter and lonely but at least she was rich. Immensely so.

Ryan put the car in park after stopping at the Destrier front gate, his driver window steadily receding into the door. He pushed the button on the security system to gain access, or speak to someone who could. The voice on the other side of the mechanism spoke in Queen's English.

"Good Morning. How may I help?

"Ryan Wells to see Chamille Destrier."

"Very good. Do you have an appointment, sir?"

"No, I don't. If you could please just let her know I am here."

"I beg pardon, but she is quite busy. May I be of some assistance in scheduling an appointment for a future call?"

"She knows me. If you could please just tell her that I'm here, I only need a couple minutes of her time."

"I'm not quite certain that she is currently on the grounds Mister Wells. I could confirm, but it may take a bit of time. Are you able to hold, or should we reschedule?"

"I'll wait."

"Very good, sir."

He waited for ten minutes but it seemed like ten weeks. The window was still down so he could hear the gentlemen when he came back on the line. He was freezing even with the heat blasting. He contemplated hitting the call button on the machine again, but kept telling himself, "twenty more seconds. If the guy doesn't come back in twenty-seconds, then I'll push the button". But twenty-seconds came and went and he would tell himself the same thing all over again. Had the fruity Englishman forgotten about him?

"Mister Wells, are you still there?"

"Yes, still here."

"Missus Destrier will see you. Please follow the drive to the roundabout. Park to the side, if you please, by the car park. I shall meet you at the main door."

"Thank you." After his window was back up, he said to himself, "What a production." The drive, as it was called, was really a long road which was lined with tall, thin, perfectly shaped, isosceles triangular trees of unknown name or origin; evenly spaced every fifteen yards, on both sides. The car park was a small, covered parking area. He parked his car where he was told, and was about to lock it when he thought better of it. The car was in the safest place on the planet. His new Audi was nice, but it was not the Bentley nor the Maserati he was parked between. It was winter. *These cars should not be exposed to the salted, frost-heaved roads of New Hampshire*, he thought.

A dark-skinned man met him at the door. It was the same person that matched the voice from the gate. "Mister Wells. Welcome. Please follow me to the sitting room, Missus Destrier will be with you at her earliest convenience. May I get you a refreshment of some sort?

"Do you know how to make an Alabama Mudslinger?"

"I'm sure we have someone on staff who could make that for you, sir."

"Forget it. If you don't know how to make it then don't bother. Thanks anyway." He didn't really want one, didn't even know what was in it, if truth be told. Everything was just so stuffy. He thought of the most outlandish beverage he could think of at that morning hour, just to get a laugh or a reaction from the stiff. He failed.

"Very good, sir. Please wait here."

He sat on one of the two matching, very white, very plush sofas. In looking around the room, he predicted that the knick-knacks were worth more than everything he and Angie owned, in total. Who would think that all of this was located in southern New Hampshire? If a person had this kind of money, who would decide to live in the cold Northeast? "Wow, who knew?"

"Who knew what, Ryan?"

"Chamille. Nothing, nothing. I was just talking to myself." She wore long, flowing chestnut hair, deep-brown eyes and porcelain yet tanned skin. Hollywood had come to New Hampshire. She reminded Ryan of Angelina Jolie, though he wondered which was more wealthy.

92

"Thank you for seeing me on such short notice, I hope I am not disturbing you this morning."

"No bother, though I am a bit surprised to see you. Pleasantly so, but still."

"Yeah, ten in the morning unannounced is probably impolite in your circles. But this is important."

"Well then, by all means." She sat on the other white sofa, opposite his but not before removing her suit jacket, revealing her transparent, lace camisole. That was all she was wearing on her upper body, which meant there was nothing left to the imagination. Her plastic surgeon was clearly top-tier. "Were you offered a refreshment? I have Arnold Palmers on the way, would you like one?"

"I'm not sure what that is, but sure," he said. He was thankful for the distraction as the tray of lemonade and iced tea was delivered. If she noticed his leers, she didn't show it.

"So, what is so urgent Ryan?"

"When was the last time you've seen Anna?"

"Anna?"

"Anna Grantes, your best friend."

"Anna Grantes is my best friend? I was unaware, but it has been some time. Why, did she say that I am her best friend?"

"Come on now, Chamille. You two are practically inseparable. You did the charity event together this year."

"Yes, she is a very good friend, but a *best* friend? I'm not sure. What is this about?"

"She's missing. Her and Brady."

"Oh my. What do you mean missing?"

"Do you know where they are?"

"You mean other than her home?"

"They are not home, else I wouldn't be here. When was the last time you spoke to her?"

"About a week or so ago, I suppose. On the phone. I would have to check on the exact day. Maybe she took a trip with her son. You know, to get away from all the chaos. I was thinking of doing the same. Winter can be so dreary here." She leaned to take a sip of her concoction, her spaghetti strap fell down off her shoulder. It was only one of two very small strings holding up her top.

"Do you know where she would go? She emptied the house."

"Wow. That does seem ominous, doesn't it? Have you contacted the authorities?"

"I wasn't sure how long she's been gone, so I couldn't file a missing persons until I know. Plus all of her and the kid's stuff is gone, which makes it look like she left of her own volition. Nothing illegal about that. But with this trial, it's the worst possible time for her to, uh, take a vacation. As you put it."

"I'm not so sure she's been happy as of late."

"Of course not. I'm sure it has been very difficult with JG in prison."

"Before that. Are you faithful to your wife, Ryan?"

"What? Yes, why?"

"That's sexy. Ever been tempted?"

"What does this have to do with Anna and Brady being missing?"

"I was talking about you. And me. But mostly you."

"Listen, Chamille, I've heard the rumors. I don't know if they're true, and it's none of my business. But if your marriage is one of convenience, that is yours to carry. There is not going to be a you and me other than friendship. I love my wife, she loves me. We might not be rich, and we are probably very boring. I'm not even sure how we fit into some of the same social circles, to be honest, but I'm not here socially. I'm here because my friend is about to lose his life, his freedom. And now it seems he's lost his family as well."

"Nice speech. Kind of sexy."

"Can we focus on why she was unhappy before JG went into prison? Why you think that anyway? Please?"

"She was always looking for someone to look after Brady. More so than usual. She seemed preoccupied."

"Didn't they have a babysitter? Why call on you? You don't have any kids, correct?"

"No children, no. I don't want to ruin my body with having to go through pregnancy. The thought of adoption crosses my mind occasionally, but then passes."

"So why did they use you?"

"I'm not so sure they were using their childcare anymore. I certainly didn't take care of the child, one of my staffers is really great with children. She used to be an au pair with another family. I'm friendly with Anna, she needed help one day, and it continued beyond that one time."

"Was she involved in some project or something?"

"I really don't know. She just needed someone to watch Brady quite a lot. She would disappear for a while, much like now I suppose."

"You say you haven't spoken with her in about a week, would she just takeoff for a week or so, leave Brady with you?"

"No, of course not, just for a few days sometimes. Since JG has been …. Unavailable. Maybe she took Brady this time because she was going to be gone longer."

"So I'm back where I started. Where did she go and why? The other times."

"And I've already answered you. And I'm afraid that I'm out of time to speak with you."

"I'm sorry to have taken up your time, but if I could just speak with the maid or au pair or whatever for a few minutes, I will be on my way."

"I'm afraid I won't be able to help you there either. She no longer works for me."

"What? She doesn't work here anymore? Why?"

"I'm not sure that she was interested in all of this excitement."

"As usual I have no idea what you are talking about."

"It seems I am boring you as much as you are me. Good day, Ryan."

As if listening for his queue, the Englishman entered to put an end to the question and non-answer period. "Nigel will show you out. In the future, it is considered polite to have an appointment when calling on someone. Ten in the morning is still considered an inconvenient time," Chamille said as she left the large sitting room.

Ryan could not help but review the entire interaction in his mind, repeatedly, as he returned to his car and drove out past the main gate. *What the fuck just happened?*

14

AFTER THE FIRST WEEK IN THE INVESTIGATION HAD PASSED,
Ryan had asked Warren to meet him at Sully's Tavern to discuss the
progress, or lack of it. There were twenty-one more days left before the
trial and they needed a break. They needed some evidence to counter
all the charges that would prove to be the end of JG. Unless Ryan had it
wrong, they still had none. It was time to regroup.

Deni was more than happy to meet there. He wanted to see Jenna
again, maybe mend a fence, and without a doubt to flirt. He had
arrived twenty minutes early, knowing that the 3:00 PM meet time would
be a good time to see her, as it was before the start of the happy-hour
crowd. He found a spot at the front bar, where there were just a few
customers, which was unusual. Jenna looked great, which, on the other
hand, was very usual.

Ryan was running late. He had called just before Warren's
entrance, which gave him all the time he needed to chat up the beauty.
She would be finished for the day soon, but not before being literally
trapped behind the bar conversing with him. He made his way to the
bar where he was all but alone with her.

"You again. What now?" Jenna said.

"Is it me or have service standards fallen a bit? I'm meeting
someone here and they're runnin' late. Can I get an Irish Whiskey?"

"Do you have a preference?"

The top shelf alcohol was on the top shelf, of course, but at Sully's it
was so the male patrons could get a good look at the posteriors of those
serving it. Maybe that was why the stuff was so bloody expensive.

"Redbreast 12 year. Please."

"Going expensive today, what's the occasion? Good news with
Jake?"

She made her way up a small ladder, reaching for the bottle located
on one of the high, glass shelves. Whether it was her normal posture or

she was so accustomed to posing for those that ordered expensive drinks, her butt was positioned for viewing. Deni was leering and he was not ashamed of it.

"More money means a bigger tip for you, right? I came to make peace, or to get a piece. Or both."

She came back down behind the bar and poured his drink. "Very funny. Here you go. I get off soon so if you can settle up with me before, that'd be great."

"Yeah, I was hoping you could join us when you get done. I'll buy, of course."

"Another interrogation? I think I'll pass, thanks."

"No interrogation, just a chat with me and Ry. Friendly. We used to be friendly when we came in here."

"Friendly. Not familiar, Deni. I'm not going to sleep with you. EVER. It's never going to happen no matter how many expensive drinks you buy or how many times you stare at my ass and chest. You think I don't know why people make me reach up for the good stuff?"

"I'm not tryin' to fight here, Jenna. You are a smoke show, we both know that, but all I want is to just sit and talk with ya. I'm not askin' for your hand in marriage, I'm askin' you to sit and have a drink with Ryan and me. No threesome, unless you're into it."

"All right asshole, but it'll cost you."

"The threesome?"

"I'm regretting this already. Now pay me before I cash out."

He handed her the money, which was three times too much.

"Keep the change."

"That's a good start on the apology, thanks. Now go find a booth."

Ryan came into the bar and hurriedly made his way to Warren, who was making his way toward a booth with what was left of his drink.

"Hey, thanks for coming over. Sorry I'm late. I just can't keep up with everything at the office without JG. I'm swamped."

"Course I'd be here. Time is creepin' away on us here, kid."

"I need to grab a drink and warm up, it's freezing outside."

"You walk over?"

"The office is down the street, Deni. I'm not going to find another parking spot closer than the one I have." They sat down in a high-backed, round booth on the opposing ends of the horseshoe. "What are you drinking, Scotch or your usual Whiskey?"

"Irish Whiskey and I'm going exclusive today. Redbreast. Wanna try it? It's good."

"I'll stick with Scotch, thanks. Since you're so high-end today, I'll go big also. Truth is, I need a drink and we need a break."

"Go big or go home."

The server arrived, also scantily clad, showing more leg than chest which was hard to do without being naked. "Afternoon, boys. I see one of you has already started, so what can I get you? Happy Hour hasn't started yet but I can see about getting you appetizers at half off. Or is it all liquid today?"

"Lagavulin for me, and my friend here is drinking Redbreast."

"OKAY. I'll make sure to keep an eye on you boys."

"Keep 'em comin'," Deni said. "If you see us low, don't inquire, just assume and pour."

She winked at him in understanding and made way toward the bar.

As the server left to fetch the expensive liquors, Jenna arrived with her filled martini glass already in hand. Deni slid over to the middle of the booth, leaving his spot for her on the end. She had changed into a tight, long-sleeved sweater to cover her black work garb.

"That was fast," Deni said. "What are you drinkin'?"

"You made quite the impression your last time here, Deni. The guy you nearly beat up is counting my drawer for me. I'm drinking a Cucumber Tea-ni with Belvedere. I told you, you were going to pay."

"Do I even want to ask what's in it?"

"Belvedere vodka, Yellow Chartreuse, Sencha green tea syrup, fresh cucumbers, and a little lemon. Want a sip?"

"No thanks, and I'm sorry I asked. With all that stuff in it though, how can you taste the alcohol? What is the point of buyin' good booze if you ain't gonna taste it anyway?"

"The point is that you cornered me the other day, made me uncomfortable, and you're extending an olive branch, which is going to cost you. That is the point. And I don't want a hangover. Any more questions?"

"Yes, but nothing to do with booze."

The server arrived with the expensive libations, giving the gents more winks and smiles. Ryan was thankful for the interruption as he was feeling a bit awkward watching the other two at the table verbally spar.

"What happened the last time you were here, Deni?" Ryan asked.

"It was nothin', Ry. No big deal." To Jenna, "Tell the big man that I said thanks for helpin' out."

"I will. It will have to be soon though, my days here are numbered." She immediately regretted the last statement. It was obvious on her face that she had revealed more than she had wanted to. *Maybe expensive martinis are like a truth serum*, he thought.

"Oh yeah? Gettin' outta Dodge?"

"I'm not sure what you mean, but yes I'm leaving here. With all the events as of late, and our last talk. I'm not getting any younger and I don't want to be shaking my ass, slinging drinks for the rest of my life. Maybe I'll go back to school."

"Your last talk? I'm sorry to be behind in this conversation but what happened the last time you two were here?" Ryan clearly hated the fact that he was so lost.

"Warren kindly pointed out the last time he was here that the reason that Jake is in this fix, is because I over-served him. I didn't. But I do feel responsible for some reason."

"Well, good for you, Jenna. It's gonna be tough to give up all the money you make here though, yeah? The place is always packed, so you must do pretty well. It seems sorta all-of-a-sudden to me."

"I thought you said that you weren't going to interrogate me again, Deni? I've been thinking about leaving Sully's for quite a while. I've come into some money, and I have some money saved. I told you before, I want to teach. I love kids, not big kids. I don't want to be doing this at forty, even if they allowed me to. The girls Sully is hiring lately are younger and bustier and have more 'junk in the trunk' by the day."

"You don't even look close to forty, you're beautiful, and you can thank your surgeon for me. He did and an amazing job. I'd like to shake his hand." Stick the jab, then flirt. That was Deni's plan.

Ryan sat idly by, watching the sparring. He was growing tired of the game after a long day at work and an even longer week. He thought the two of them would strategize, the reason for the meeting, but it was obvious that his friend had a hunch and was going with it. Ryan was just the there for the ride at the moment; he was so far behind the curve, he couldn't even play good-cop. He was going to be the audience while sipping, letting Deni work his magic, even if the audience could see the magic trick a mile away.

"Funny. You're quite the joke-teller. I'm all-real Mr. Funny Guy. I have to take this shit all day, but I'm not working, so if this is the way the conversation is going to go, then thanks for the drink and I'll be leaving now."

"I'm sorry, I didn't mean to offend you. I thought I was giving you a compliment," Deni said.

"It's that type of chauvinistic bullshit that's getting out of hand. The unofficial uniform keeps getting smaller and smaller here, which the veterans like me keep going along with because if we don't, we lose shifts to the new girls. The smaller the outfit and the more we show, the guys think they can touch and be lewd, especially when they're all boozed up. Women come here because it's swanky and there are plenty of geared-up men with money. I've been fed up for a while, this is the final straw."

There was something else that was going on, Warren knew it. He had made a living being able to read people, and while she was sincere in what she was saying it was not the complete truth. He wanted more light on JG's last night here, something wasn't right and he wanted to get to the bottom of it. This meeting for social drinking was just an excuse to get there, only he wasn't getting anywhere. The eager server came back over toward the booth but before she had arrived, Ryan had nodded that they wanted another round. It was an unnecessary nod, as she knew what to do.

"So with all the rubbin' and grindin', your dance card must be full."

"Fuck You, Deni. What's your deal? I don't date the guys that come in here and you know it. How many times have you tried? A million?"

"What about JG, er, uh, Jake?"

"What about him?"

"You tell me. I've seen the way you look at him. And you're right, nobody gets those kinda looks from you. You blame yourself for his present situation, that's why you're sittin' here. Whether that guilt is justified or not is what I'm tryin' to find out. That guilt is the real reason you are leavin' this bar, I think."

The new round of drinks arrived. Jenna's drink looked similar but not exactly the same color. This interruption was unwelcomed by Deni as the pause gave Jenna just enough time to regroup.

"I was close with Jake, Brady, and his wife. I babysat for them. To say that what happened hasn't affected me would be a lie."

Ryan interjected, "I thought Chamille Destrier's housekeeper was Brady's babysitter?"

"I'm not sure what you mean, but I picked Brady up from Jake's wife all the time."

"Did you ever pick him up at Chamille's estate?" It became Ryan's turn to interrogate.

"No, I don't thinks so."

"You would definitely know if you had been to that place. It's a palatial mansion owned by her best friend."

"Then, no I haven't. Brady was always with Jake or his wife when I picked him up."

Deni said, "Anna. His wife's name is Anna. You keep saying 'Jake's wife' but her name is Anna. And she's missing. She took the boy and left."

"What? Where did she go?"

"The definition of missing is we don't know. But you didn't ask why? You asked where, but not why. Is that because you know why?" Deni felt he'd hit the jackpot.

"I know what *she* thinks," Jenna said after a long pause and long pull from her first Cucumber Tea-ni, draining it.

"What does she think?"

"That Jake and I were having an affair. That we were in love."

"Is she right?"

"Do I love him? Yes. Do I love that little boy? Yes. But he's married, and I don't know if Jake loves me."

"Oh my God. How long were you two seeing each other?" Ryan asked. He couldn't just sit there anymore. "I feel like I've just been punched in the stomach."

"I just said, we weren't. I said I know what she *thinks*. I only saw him here. Well, at first I only saw him here. Then I started to see him around town here and there. I started to babysit because his wife was doing more stuff outside the house, or at night, or whatever, and he started coming in here more and more …. What can I say? I fell in love with him. But I never did anything about it."

"How do you know what she thinks? Did you get to know her also? Did you talk with her regularly?" Ryan was no longer a spectator, he needed answers.

While Ryan was back on the warpath, Warren swallowed the last of his newest whiskey, waved his hand ordering another round, which was already on the way. It was now happy hour and the bar was busy, but the server spied him easily as if she had eyes in the back of her head.

"After that time maybe a year and half or so ago in the park, I think she was suspicious. Then I would run into her, or see her in the distance looking at me trying to be sneaky. Phone calls started after that. That's how I know what she thinks," Jenna said.

Ryan looked at Deni then back at Jenna. "I'm a little slow, I think. It may be that I'm half in the bag, but I need someone to start from the beginning. Phone calls? The park? I am officially lost."

She looked around the table, slugged back the rest of her second martini and told her version of the story.

＊＊＊＊＊＊

"Careful of the swings, Brady." Jacob was yelling toward his son. At three years old, his motor skills, among his others, were advanced. And motor he did. The little man was fast.

Brady loved going to the park. He liked playing in the sand well enough; he liked the merry-go-round more, as long as the bigger kids weren't spinning on it at mach-3. But what Brady loved the most was the swing set.

The recreational park was an expansive property that was annexed by the town of Wayland, but as it was located directly behind the Wayland Country Club, the plot was generously and gorgeously maintained by the landscapers and the maintenance crew of the exclusive club. The sandbox was filled with the soft, white sand that filled the bunkers of the golf course, which made it much more fun to be in. The slides and amusement equipment always looked freshly painted, gleamed like stainless steel kitchen appliances, or was replaced for new. The tennis courts were not as top shelf as in the club, but were used by the high school for tournaments as they were far nicer than the school's. The skate park within the park was rid of the graffiti that decorated it on a regular basis, which made it less hip but well groomed. The jogger and bike path meandered around the man-made body of water and grass that was like a soft, green carpet. The warm, late spring sun was the only accoutrement not controlled by the wealthy club. The less fortunate could go to the recreational park and fantasize about being an affluent member of society while they stared out at their benefactors from a distance.

As per usual, Brady was getting too close to the older kids playing on the swings. They were competing with each other to see which had the acumen to swing high enough to launch themselves over the top of the crossbar to the other side, and presumably around again. He was fascinated, not realizing the danger he was in if he were to be struck by the feet of one of the swingers.

"We'll go on the swings a little later after the big kids are finished, little man," Jacob said as he lifted his son from under his armpits. He tossed him into the air a few times, which was another activity he thoroughly enjoyed.

"Higher. Higher," Brady said. He laughed and egged on his father for more. This was distracting him as he was being moved away from the swings.

A female jogger was approaching them on the jogging and bike path. She was removing her earbuds which was blaring the latest Christina Aguilera dance tune.

"Hey there, hunks."

Jake set his son down when he realized it was Jenna who had now stopped and was trying to catch her breath. She was fashionably dressed for either jogging or Yoga, and looked ravishing despite her exertions. She wore her hair back in a long ponytail; a pink jog bra, accentuating her ample top, gray capris spandex pants which started from her hips which exposed her rock-hard abs, buttocks, and shapely legs.

"Uh, hey Jenna. How are you? Fancy meeting you here. Nice sneakers."

"Nice running into you guys. Ha ha. This handsome guy keeping you busy? Chip off the old block, he has your eyes."

"He keeps me busy for sure. Brady, can you say hello to Jenna please?"

"Hi."

"Just the boys out playing today?" She was speaking to Jake but Brady answered.

"Yep."

"You mean yes, right Brady?"

"Yes."

"My wife is in a meeting at the club." He pointed toward the distant clubhouse. "She's coordinating the big charity event again this year, so we have been on our own a lot in the last couple of weeks."

"Oh yeah? Do I get an invite?"

"You want to hang out with us?"

"Of course, but I meant the event, silly. I need an excuse to squeeze into a slinky dress. I bet you clean up in a tux, you're always in suits when I see you. This is a nice change."

He was dressed in a Foo Fighters t-shirt and jogging pants, though he would be doing no jogging on that day.

"I can see about an invitation for you, plus one. I'll ask the wife. As for me, no tux I'm afraid. Brady and I will be on our own that night too, most likely."

"Bummer. I would have liked to see you in a tux. But if you need a babysitter, just let me know. Seriously, I love kids."

"Hitting the pavement today?"

"You know it. The miles keep the body fit and trim." She posed for him, accentuating her phenomenal figure.

"Well it's working. Maybe a little overtime. Maybe I should start running again."

"You look great to me, but it's a date. We can set it up next time I see you at Sully's. Keep me in mind for babysitting also." She began to jog in place, placing one of her earbuds back into her ear. "Well, I gotta run. Ha ha again. I need to keep that heart-rate up, though it did just skip a beat. Bye boys." She replaced her other earbud and continued her run down the path. When she had covered fifteen yards, she turned back around, and ran backwards while taking in a last look. When she had gotten her fill, she righted herself, continuing her jog while leaving Jacob and Brady staring at her ponytail swinging from side to side.

"Bye," Brady said with a wave.

"That might be trouble, little man."

"Who was that?" asked a voice behind them.

Jacob turned with a start to see his wife next to him. "Oh hey, Anna."

"Mommy."

"Who was that?" she said again.

"Oh, just a bartender at Sully's Tavern. Jenna. You're out of your meeting early."

"So that's why you spend so much time and money at that bar." She lifted Brady up into her arms, who then gave his mother a big hug. "Yes, I got out as early as I could so I could spend as much time as possible with my guys. I think this year's event is going to consume even more time than we had originally discussed."

"Its good for you. You need to get out and use your talents, babe."

"It seems like it might be good for you too. I agree with you by the way."

"Great. What? You agree with what?" He leaned in to kiss his wife, but she stopped him by using her free hand to grab his chin.

"She is trouble," she said. She stared into his eyes.

He thought it an inopportune time to tell his wife that he had found a new babysitter for their son.

******

"So that was the first time that I had seen Jake outside the bar," Jenna said. She sat back in the booth, reminiscing like it was yesterday. "I saw her coming from a mile away, which is why I took off. She didn't like me from the start."

"She? You mean Anna? Why can't you say her name?" Deni stared at her, waiting for an answer. He never received one.

"How do you know that?" Ryan said. He was starting to treat her differently. Like a home-wrecker.

"Like I said, I saw her. I hadn't met her at that point but I knew who she was. I'd seen a picture on Jake's phone, the three of them. She was staring me down from afar. I just knew, so I took off. Also, Jake told me the next time he came into the bar what she said. He said that running together and the babysitting offer sounded great but it might make his wife feel uncomfortable. I told him that I understood but that it might make her feel better if we were to get to know one another. That I should meet her. Ya know, introduce myself."

"So you couldn't leave well enough alone. You couldn't take no for an answer? You had to keep pressing?" Ryan was getting more agitated by the minute.

"He agreed. He thought it was a good idea. He brought her and Brady in and had lunch in that booth right over there soon after." She pointed to an identical booth in another corner in the same room, then continued.

"I offered to babysit again right in front of her because I was told that she was going to be busy with the event committee. She said that she would think about it and back to me, but either way she would get me a free invitation. She kept pressing to get the name of my nonexistent boyfriend to add to the invitation. I repeatedly told her that I didn't have a boyfriend to which she kept saying stuff like she 'didn't believe that a beautiful girl like me didn't have at least one man on the hook, but she could fix me up with someone if I wanted'. After that I saw her when I would pick up Brady. She was never friendly. And I saw Jake all the time. If I wasn't running with him, I was babysitting for him. Or he came to see me here."

"What do you mean 'never friendly'? She gave you her kid 'all the time'," Deni said.

"Let's put it this way, if looks could kill, I would have been a chalk outline at a murder scene whenever she laid eyes on me. I get the feeling that the child care thing was mostly Jake's idea. Then the phone calls started."

Yet another round of drinks arrived. During the telling of the jogging story they had multiple libations, the three of them were getting well-lubed. Warren was maintaining the best; while Jenna was loose and chatty, Ryan was getting angrier by the Scotch.

"What did you expect? You were moving in on her family. These are my best friends and while I'm not a violent person, I'm tempted to commit a felonious act right here in this bar."

"Is that what I was doing Ryan? Do you honestly think I would intentionally do anything to hurt them? I fell in love, God forgive me." She began to cry. She was trying with all her might not to lose control in her place of work, but emotion combined with alcohol overcame.

Ryan's anger began to dissipate in slight, and he was struggling with his movement toward sympathy. Warren, ever calloused, appeared indifferent and remaining unbiased in the investigation. A technique he was well accustomed to. He pushed on despite her tears.

"So let me see if I have this straight. You didn't want to hurt him or his family, but you moved in on them like you were stormin' Normandy. With your looks and charm, you invaded not only the marriage but formed a relationship with their kid. I don't understand how you don't see that as a problem. His wife hates you, but you don't give a shit because that works in your favor. Actually, I take that back, maybe you did give a shit. You realize he's not going to leave his wife, and you care so much that you get him cocked at the bar, and give him his keys. Only you omit some of the drinks, or you doctor the check so it looks like all is on the up and up. He goes off and instead of getting killed himself, he kills some poor lady, but you're not done yet. You're still pissed about all of the phone calls and evil looks. So you figure two can play at that game. So you call her. Or you say or do something to Anna which makes her take Brady and vanish. You scared her so she took her son and ran for safety. Or you vanish her and the kid yourself. Is that how you did it? You off 'em and bury 'em someplace and make it look like they moved out? This is what you wanted from the start, her and kid out of the way, no?. You're not crazy in love, toots, you're cookin' a pet rabbit in a pot on the stove kinda crazy, lady. Tell me I ain't right."

That was all Jenna could take. The alcohol and the verbal attack was beyond what she could bear. She bolted from the booth, covering her mouth as she cried her way out of the bar.

"I think that was my answer, Ry. So I think we got the story. Now how do we help our boy?"

"Honestly, if we could prove any of what you just said, or heard her say? Not much."

"Whattaya mean? She just basically said that she got him all banged up and that she is a nutty, jealous bitch. She wanted the family and the picket fence and she couldn't stand the fact that she couldn't get it. So she went after the wife and kid. Reasonable doubt. It's a story."

"That and the fact that he still got in his car, picked up Brady and ran somebody off the road. Correct me if I'm wrong here, but she didn't *say* that any of what you just said is what actually happened. You don't think she killed Anna and Brady, do you?"

Deni shrugged in lieu of an answer.

"Well, I don't think so. And even if she did, it's after the fact. It has nothing to do with the crime at hand. If it is true that she overserved him, which is a big if, and if we could get proof, because she certainly isn't going to go on the record and admit it, *might* be mitigating. But at the end of the day, he still did it. He still drove drunk with his son in the backseat. I say we add it to the fact that this poor lady shouldn't have been in the country to be on the road in the first place and call it the 'perfect storm of OUIs'. It was all of the above that created this whole conflagration."

"What if we had proof? Get a few years off?"

"I must be drunk. I just told you, maybe. But I don't think so. It's worth a try. But we don't have any proof. So what's your point?"

"Look up in the corners, Ry. Cameras. Closed Circuit TV cameras for security. Maybe it prevents a bartender from stealing, maybe not. But I bet he had more than two beers."

"That was how long ago, Deni? Never gonna happen. In all likelihood, it has been long recorded over by now. If it was significant, the ADA would have it into evidence already."

"It's worth a try. Besides I've got a feeling about this. Plus the 911 mystery."

"Yeah what happened with that?"

"I don't have a name. But who buys a throwaway phone and doesn't provide a name or information on it? Drug dealers and people who don't wanna be traced. Nobody legit that's for sure. Janey Do-Good, doin' a solid on a burner phone, is botherin' me. So I got the kiosk in a mall up Nashua way that sold it to her. Cash of course. The cameras here give me an idea of how to see who bought it. The kiosk must'a had cameras too."

"Again, Deni, I hate to be a glass is half-empty kinda guy, but this was over six months ago. That tape has probably long gone by now."

"You say half-empty or half-full, I say there's always room for whiskey. My contact says that CCTV isn't tape anymore. It is all binary. Digital. Ones and zeroes. There is this thing called a cloud, stores like millions and millions of stuff. Nobody needs to worry about storage space anymore, so everything is saved."

"I have another mystery which you can solve then, Mister 'Room for Whiskey'. The Destrier servant, or au pair, or whatever. She disappeared. She was the one who babysat Brady the night of the accident, she was the one who put him in the back seat of the car without a word. She is gone too."

"I thought Busty Galore just said that she was the babysitter, before she ran off."

"You're getting drunk too, huh? Deni, she just told you that she was going to the charity event. Remember? Slinky dress …. Not gonna miss it?"

"Oh yeah, right. She was feeding him drinks and was on her way out to go change and then go. Did she ever go? Maybe there is more to her than slinky dresses and slingin' drinks."

"Maybe, but too many people are disappearing, don't you think? Anna and Brady, the maid? It's unsettling," Ryan admitted.

"Add to that a female voice on a 911 call, a burner phone, and possible infidelity. At a minimum Anna thought there was. Maybe the wrong person was killed."

"OK. I'm definitely buzzed, if not completely drunk. Where does that leave us? Our working theory is that Anna leaves with Brady because she is getting muscled by the bartender about having an affair with JG? That Jenna intentionally got him all banged up to kill him because she couldn't have him? But he didn't die, so she threatens to make it right by killing Anna and the boy. Speaking of which, what about Brady? JG was going to pick up Brady, what did he ever do?" Ryan was in the weeds. He was fighting through the fog, trying to keep up with all the various revelations.

"I don't know all the specifics yet, but I think it was Jenna on the 911 call. She followed him outta here that night. Now I follow up with the cameras here and the kiosk where the phone was sold. I go see if I can find this housekeeper or whatever and put a trace on Anna and Brady, if they're still alive. All that in three weeks. I'd ask for the tape tonight but I'm cocked."

"If you go to the Destriers, be warned that Chamille is rich but she is also completely nuts. Bored, horny, and nuts."

"Good. So am I."

15

WARREN WAS CONCERNED, TO SAY THE VERY LEAST. He was hungover and concerned. He was trying to piece together a thought, any thought, through the fog of the previous evening. Nothing was clear except for the thumping pain in his brain and the thick wool sweater he must have eaten at some point the previous night. The meeting with Ryan over a vat of premium Irish Whiskey had left him with more questions than he had answers at present. A situation which he needed to correct. He was also left with the question of why he had spent so much money on alcohol that was supposed to reduce, if not eliminate hangovers, only to have a terrible one.

The biggest of all the concerns in his haze was why people in this case were disappearing. He'd worked many cases throughout the years, people vanished when things were too heated around them, or they were dead and buried in an undisclosed location. In every case there was something to hide. The parties who disappeared never intentionally left a forwarding address; however, there were always clues left behind which could lead to them being found, in one state or another. Anna and Brady were gone. That much was clear. He would need to get back over to the house for a more thorough inspection, for a clue as to where and why. The maid was gone too. Odd, that. Maybe she was afraid of Immigration coming down on her? Or maybe she was six feet under as well. The Destriers had resources to protect her, of that he was sure. So why was that protection deemed insufficient? He would have to go talk to the rich, crazy lady.

This case was supposed to be a drunken crash that led to an unfortunate death. He was going to try to help his friend by finding some evidence that said it was less his fault, but under every rock he turned over there was another oddity which created more questions. It was turning out that this crash might not be his fault at all. Nobody had forced the beer to his lips, to be sure. But while he was drunk, he was a pawn in a game which JG didn't know he was a part of. A game in which possibly he was the one that was supposed to be dead on the side of the road.

Finding Anna was a priority. She would shed some light on this Jenna thing. If she was alive. She would help him right? Hell hath no fury …. So maybe not. But why would she leave now? Six months after the accident and the arrest, she decides to leave? He wondered what had changed. Jenna. Had Jenna muscled Anna out of town in one way or another? Why? And why now?

He decided to go over the house again, to find a clue as to JG's family's whereabouts. The psyche of an inmate is simultaneously fragile and volatile. Warren knew this all too well from his time as a trooper. A prisoner's mind wanders night and day, having all the time in the world to think and rethink every detail, of every happenstance.

Once the decision was made, he rolled out of bed and fought off an inhuman bout of vertigo. He shook off the cobwebs as best he could, then padded into the kitchen to make coffee. The shower helped, but with coffee finally ready, that helped more. By the time the Escalade was warmed up and he was backing out of his short driveway, he was as right as rain. Which was funny because it was raining. Freezing rain.

Though the weather was bad, the drive wouldn't take long. It never took long from his house in New Hampshire. He grew up on the South end of Boston, a rough neighborhood which was no comparison to his neighborhood in Barstone. He could afford better, but he liked the fringe. It was close to JG and Ryan's law practice, so when he worked with them, or needed to be in New Hampshire, he stayed there. When he worked in Boston, he stayed at his three-decker in Southie.

He stayed in South Boston with less frequency as of late. His neighborhood was being gentrified, his community was being forced out. Movies and television shows were being shot there. Property values were relatively low for Boston but on the rise. The yuppies had moved in and more were taking over. The Young Urban Professionals had started to buy up the three-decker properties, converting them into upscale apartments which current residents couldn't afford. These new property owners and the upscale tenants now occupying them demanded more police to keep these residences safe. These more affluent homeowners and tenants also had a taste for finer dining, clothing, and the ilk. This brought businesses that the locals were unaccustomed to, didn't necessarily want, nor could they afford. Slowly but surely, the locals were being pushed out and Southie was becoming less like Southie.

The drive and lock-picking took a grand total of eighteen minutes. Upon his entry, he noticed that nothing had been touched since his last walk-through. Who moves but leaves all the furniture? Those that want to vanish in a hurry, he told himself. Or not to be seen leaving. But why now? After six months? The nagging question without answer was eating at him.

He toured the house again, going through drawers, closets and found nothing. She was thorough, he had to give Anna that. Or Jenna if she was the one who'd been here to throw off investigators. He went through the kitchen and out into the garage.

"I must be seeing double," he said to himself. Appearing before him were the two identical black Volvo SUVs. "His and hers, how cute." He walked around the first vehicle closest to the kitchen door. It was spotless. Hanging from the rafters on a piece of string was a pink tennis ball at the end of it, touching the windshield. Deni had seen this trick before; designed to give the driver a perfect reference point to drive into the garage with greater ease, leaving enough room around it. The pink tennis ball led him to believe that the vehicle closest to the house was Anna's. Chivalry isn't quite dead. He checked the driver door to see if it was locked. It would make little difference if it was, but it was not.

He opened the door and peered inside. It was immaculate. The soft, tan leather smelled new. Nothing in the console. The child carseat was in the back. He tried to get into the driver seat to reach across and check the glove box but the seat was far too close to the steering wheel for him to fit. He felt for a lever under the seat to move it back but there wasn't one. He then found the numbered, electronic buttons which adjusted the seat in every position, on the side facing the door. He pushed one of the numbers.

Everything moved. The driver seat moved back to a comfortable position, lumbar support included. The steering wheel moved into a different position, the rear and side-view mirrors adjusted for the new seat position as well. *Presets*, he thought. He pushed the number one on the panel, which moved everything back to the original position, where everything was compact. He was being crushed like the trash compactor on Star Wars only without the liquid sludge. He quickly pressed the number two before the movement was complete, which relocated everything back into the comfortable position. The other preset numbers did nothing.

He next opened the glove box, which was barren except for the owner's manual. No insurance card nor registration. The vehicle was picked clean. She either kept a very clean car or it was cleaned for a purpose. He leaned back to see if there was anything in the back that was forgotten. That too was clean. Wherever she was traveling in the days before her departure, he thought, she didn't go by car. That car anyway. Or it was professionally detailed.

He gave up on Anna's rig and moved over to what he assumed was JG's side of the garage. No hanging tennis ball, pink or otherwise. He checked to see if this one was unlocked. It was also. He attempted to climb in and was crushed as he was in the first SUV. Surprised and uncomfortable, he pushed the number two button to move the seat but nothing moved. He pressed number one and all the movement began as it had in Anna's. He was again comfortable yet the thought struck him that made him ill at ease. Both cars were set for a shorter person.

He looked into the back of this vehicle to see a child carseat. On the floor was the refuse of a child. The ejected DVD in the player was *Despicable Me* and various action figures were peering out of the pocket on the back of the front passenger seat.

Baffled, he opened the glovebox and found that this Volvo was indeed registered to Jacob Grantes. He extracted himself from the SUV to inspect the exterior. This was the car that was involved in the crash. The damage remained ever-present along with the dirt and grime.

If ever there were two opposites, these once identical XC90s illustrated the definition. What confused Deni was, except for the outer damage, all evidence led to opposing owners. JG's vehicle indicated that it belonged to Anna, and vice versa. Both vehicles were adjusted for a shorter person, presumably Anna. The presets, however, indicated the correct SUV was on the appropriate side of the garage. The number one and number two presets coincided with the predominant driver.

Warren drew out his iPhone from his pocket, pressing the screen to call Ryan.

"What's up Deni? I'm due back in court any minute."

"Nice greeting, how are you?

"Hungover and busy, you?"

"Hungover and confused. How tall is Anna?"

"Five foot six or seven, I think. Why?"

"JG is like six feet, right?"

"Yeah, six-one. Get to the point."

"Anna and JG had identical rides."

"You must be hungover. We went over this already. After his parents were in a fatal car crash he always insisted on safety. He found the safest SUV on the market when Brady was born, and bought two of them. So what?"

"Anna drove both cars."

"Again, so what? They were married. I'm a little slow, what are you driving at?"

"I'm not sure what I'm driving at, mister bad-pun. Except the last person to drive each one of these vehicles was Anna. And that adds yet another question to the growing list of 'em."

16

RYAN WAS ALWAYS A BUSY MAN, BUT IN THOSE DAYS HE WAS out straight. He truly was, or at least that is what he told himself. This was the excuse for not going to see JG in prison. He was busy with cases, keeping the practice running; court appearances were aplenty along with constructing a logical defense in JG's case, which seemed to an increasing extent like an insurmountable task. That is why he kept away.   It was not because he had no good news at all, nor the whereabouts of his vanished wife and child.

Try as he might, he could no longer avoid JG. Ryan's cell phone, work phone, and house phone were all incessantly ringing from the same institution. Angie was told by her husband that she was not to accept any call when that number popped up on the caller ID, under any circumstances. His best friend was trying to get in touch with him to find out what was happening. He knew JG wasn't getting through to his wife, that number was disconnected. That was in all likelihood driving him insane. Not to get an answer from his best friend and lawyer was probably making him psychotic. It was not fair of Ryan, but he just couldn't face him.

Until now. He could avoid it no longer. Revelations had come about and it was now time to divulge them.

Ryan was successful in procuring a private room at the prison in order for the two of them to speak at long last. He had told the Deputy Sheriff that there had been a death in the family and he had to tell his client. Privacy was essential. As if by miracle they had complied, setting aside not only the room but eliminated a time limit as well. The sole stipulation was that body searches take place. Inmate Grantes was used to them, Ryan was not.

Nerve racking minute after minute passed as he sat in the closet-like prison conference room waiting for his friend and client to arrive. When Grantes eventually did appear in the doorway, shackled at the wrists and ankles, Ryan was shocked at how disheveled he looked.

Uneasiness became guilt as the once striking eyes of his friend stared into his. Prison was aging him, the weeks without communication had done immense damage. That damage was evident not only in his appearance but how he was carrying himself as well. Grantes was a broken man, the blind could see it.

Once he was unshackled and the correctional officers had left the room, Ryan leaned toward his friend on the other side of the table. "Hey buddy. How are you holding up? You don't look so good."

"Gee, I wonder why?"

"I'm sorry I haven't come to visit you. I've been busy with the practice, your defense, my life. I'm sorry. I'm trying."

"Too busy to answer the fucking phone, Ry? Any phone? I'm sitting in a cell wondering what the hell is happening, and I can't get in touch with anyone. Nobody."

"Deni isn't answering his — "

" — Fuck you, Ryan. He isn't on my pin sheet and you're avoiding the fucking point. And me. Why?"

The phone system at the WCHOC had been outsourced to a private contract. That business made an immense profit off of people who are already at rock bottom. Phone calls are not allowed into an inmate. The prison set up a limited number of phone numbers per inmate which are designated on a pin sheet. The numbers on the sheet are then vetted to ensure that prisoners were not calling other wanted felons or those whom had restraining orders filed upon that inmate. Once the numbers are approved, the recipient of the outgoing phone call needed to activate that number by setting up an account. This required money. To add money to the account required a fee. Every call made out on the phone was assessed a connection fee. Each minute while on the phone cost money from the time the recipient picks up the phone. The entire enterprise was an expensive, elaborate scam endorsed by the county.

"I've been working on this case, with Deni, to try to bring you some good news," Ryan said.

"So you've been avoiding me because you don't have any. Is that it?"

"No, I don't. In Fact, that's why I am here in person instead of answering your phone call. I have some very troubling news."

"Anna? Brady? What happened?"

"What makes you say that?"

"The phone is either shut off or there's no money on it. We have money so I'm guessing that it's shut off. Either way it's not a good sign. There's a reason, and all I do is think about what it could be."

"What reasons have you come up with?"

"Reasons she's not putting money on the phone or that it's shut off? All I can come up with is that she's upset with me. It's obvious why, but I'm not sure why *now?* Anna's been here with me saying, 'it'll be all right, babe' and 'we'll get through this together,' for six months. Then she's a no-show at court and I can't get in touch with her on the phone and she doesn't come to visit. I keep thinking that there's another guy, but she wouldn't do that. She wouldn't do that, would she Ry?"

"No. Well, I don't think so."

"Then?"

"That's just it, I don't know. All I can tell you is what I suspect and what it looks like."

"Just out with it. What happened?"

"They're missing."

"Missing? What do you mean *missing?*"

"I filled out a missing persons report on Anna and Brady but no hits, which is what I sort of figured when I filed it. We went to the house and it looks like they moved out. Gone, vanished. She left all the furniture, both the cars. She took everything personal though like clothes, and Brady's toys, jewelry. But it's all gone. I've been checking the accounts you had, the money."

"Money, what do you mean the money?"

"Well, it looks like she has been getting her ducks in a row for a while. It appears that she's been using all of her Dad's old contacts and been syphoning money into accounts without your name on them. She was the executor on Brady's trust money, so she leveraged that as well. She left you with a house, a couple of cars, and our practice, but that's pretty much it. It may be that she had a nudge, getting pressure to leave. We don't know that part for sure, but we're working on it. Maybe she thought you wouldn't need a ton of money, given your current situation."

He let that information sink in for a few minutes. They sat in silence.

"We were, Deni and I, thinking that maybe something .... worse .... had become of them. So I looked into her finances. If she was .... no longer alive, there wouldn't have been all of this money syphoning. It's clear to us now that this was planned."

JG sat there in silence.

"What we need to do now is focus on a defense for you."

"But why now, Ry?"

"Because you are looking at a long time in prison, that is why."

"No, why did she leave now? No notice, no goodbye, no reason? I can't believe it. There has to be someone else."

"I know what you meant, but dwelling on it doesn't help you get out of prison. The other shoe will drop when you get the divorce paperwork. I don't know when that day will come, but I can only assume that it will."

"This is my wife and child, Ryan. What am I going to get out of prison to?"

"She may have left for someone else because she thinks that you already did."

"What the hell are you talking about?"

"Jenna. Talk to me about Jenna."

"Jenna? The Babysitter?"

"Yes. And I noticed you didn't say, 'Jenna, the bartender?' by the way. Which is what you probably should have said."

"Jenna was our babysitter and yes, she was also a bartender. Never mind what I 'should have said'. Is that what you think? That I had an affair with Jenna? Is that what Anna thinks? Is that what you told her?"

"I didn't tell her anything, JG. I'm late to the party and everyone is hammered. I'm just trying to catch up here. Deni and I talked with her. Jenna. We still can't find Anna and Brady."

"Yeah, so. What did she say?"

"She said enough. She said that she was in love with you and that besides being the babysitter, she went running with you. Often and alone. She didn't say that you two were balls-deep or anything, but then she really didn't have to did she?"

"Did she say that we had an affair?"

"In those words, no. But the way she — "

" —Because we didn't. In plain english, Ry, there was no affair."

"Well, did you know she is bat-shit crazy about you? And maybe just crazy altogether?"

119

"Maybe. Yeah, I knew. I know. Not about being completely nuts, but about me. Yeah."

"And you saw her everyday anyway?"

"Yes, but not for the reason you think."

"Does it matter what reason I think? I mean seriously. What should I think, buddy?"

"You should think that Anna was consumed with her charity event. You should think that she was distant and growing more so. She was going through something but not with me. She was out more than she was home. I didn't want to pry, or to be controlling, so I let her work out her shit. I spent time with a pretty girl, Ry. She was good to Brady, and if you were my true friend, you would know that I would never cheat on my wife."

"I am your friend. I will always be, no matter what. If you say it, I believe you. But the real question isn't what I think, it's what did Anna think?"

"So you think she suspected that I was having an affair all this time, and used my crash as an opportunity to leave me? That over the last six months she has been getting herself situated? At my worst is when she decided to do this? When I need her the most is when she abandons all we had?"

"I'm saying that I don't know for sure. At least so far. I think she may have suspected, but Jenna had been shoving it in her face. But that's not the point. The point is that she's gone and she took your son and the money. We're working on finding her, but that is something we are going to have to work on once you get out of here, together. But it can't consume you in the meantime. Getting you out of here is the number one priority. That *has* to be the number one priority."

"Easy for you to say."

"That was not easy, nor is anything else I have to say today."

"There's more? Jesus Christ, Ry. I don't think I can take any more bad news. Maybe you were right to stay away."

"We really don't have a defense for you thus far. We have less than a couple of weeks to go before the trial and we might be able to piece together some mitigating circumstances, but nothing open and shut."

"What have you come up with?"

"We know the 911 call came from a burner phone. We know it was a female caller that didn't want to be traced, because she paid for the phone in cash with no address or contact information. That burner phone was used for one call and one call only, *that* 911 call. The now infamous Jenna most likely served you way more than the two drinks she claims and put on your bill. Warren thinks that she was the one who bought the phone, followed you and called in the accident. As of today, I think maybe she is the one that maybe forced you and the lady off the road. Maybe she finally realized that you were never going to leave Anna, or that she was jealous of what you have, or had. And she is the reason that Anna has run off. You say that you didn't have an affair with her, but she may not have received that memo, and she snapped. We're working to piece together evidence to corroborate all of this theory, but make no mistake—this is all just theory. Smoke. Smoke and mirrors is what we have."

"Smoke and mirrors and I was still drunk and as a result still on the hook for the chain of events that took place once the OUI happened," JG said while nodding his head. He knew the legal ramifications of his statement.

"Correct. We'll try to get La Fontagne to go for a reduction, but I'm not confident."

"Lovely."

"At least you are off the hook for child endangerment. So once you're out you won't have to deal with someone supervising you with Brady."

"Which will be great if we can find him."

"Deni is on it. Sooner or later he'll find them."

"Why didn't the Destrier maid make any attempt to stop me from driving?"

"That's a good question. I would love to ask her, but she is in all probability deported or something. She's gone. Disappeared. She may not have known you were drunk anyway. Her initial statement, through Chamille Destrier, was that she never even spoke to you. That you never left the car."

"You're kidding."

"Nope. My guess is that the crash happens, cops start asking questions, and that brings light on the fact that the good housekeeper is illegal — not so good for the Destriers. So after babysitting for a few weeks, Camille gets rid of her. The entire thing is weird but we're digging. If she's around, or if Chamille knows where she is, we'll find out. She is cuckoo for coco puffs by the way."

"I know. She's gotten worse over the years," Grantes said. "So at this point we go for the vic, right. Did she have a legal driver's license? If so, how can an illegal immigrant get a valid license? It pains me, but it looks like that's our only option. Two wrongs don't make it right, but an OUI is better than going down with whole sha-bang."

"If that flies, then that gets you a reduced sentence and out of football numbers. That might be all we've got at this point, and it's a long shot. In the meantime; we see how many drinks you really had that night from the cameras, find the maid, and see why she didn't intervene. Then we see about the 911 call, and where that leads. Deni is pretty confident that Jenni is behind this entire thing though. He's like a dog with a bone."

"Swell."

Ryan left the conference room and the prison without mentioning the mystery surrounding the SUVs. Since Warren had mentioned it a few days ago, he had been thinking about what it could mean. Subsequent conversations with him had not shed any light on it. He was not sure why he didn't bring it up. If someone else drove the car, when? It had to be since the accident and not related to it. But if it had been untouched since and could be proven, then someone else had driven the car, not JG. But was that possible? *No, that didn't seem possible with all of the evidence*, he thought. Still...

17

IF RYAN WAS BUSY, WARREN WAS TO THE POINT OF BEING overwhelmed. He had many avenues to investigate and an impossibly short time to complete them. He needed to; acquire the surveillance video from Sully's, reconnoiter Jenna and her movements, track down who had purchased the burner phone, sort out the Volvo mystery, find the Destrier maid, and in his spare time put a trace on Anna and Brady. All in under two weeks. No sweat.

He went back to Sully's at 10:00 AM on a Monday, as was discussed between he and the owner as the best time to meet. It wasn't busy. It wasn't busy because it was an hour prior to opening for lunch service, not because it was a Monday, or that it was too early in the day for those that wanted an adult beverage. The front door was unlocked so Warren walked right in. A large man was behind the bar counting money from an open cash register. Over his shoulder and without a look, he said, "We're not open yet, we open in an hour." He continued to count without losing his place.

"Good 'cuz I need your full attention." Deni had arrived at the bar but did not sit down, he simply leaned on it with both elbows on the countertop.

When the large man turned to face the intruder, his annoyance softened once he determined whom was in need of his attention.

"It's Marty, right? Sully? We had an appointment. I don't think we've officially met but we spoke on the phone. I'm Warren Dennihan." He stuck his hand out over the bar-top toward the man behind it who was at least twice his size. Martin Sullivan who preferred to be called Sully or Marty made no move to reciprocate.

"Oh yeah. I forgot you were coming in today. You had some questions about Jenna over-serving somebody, right?"

"Well, yes, it's a little more complicated than that, but yes."

"Funny, we get that a lot. People can't handle their booze so it's the bar's fault they got in trouble. Nobody takes personal responsibility anymore, everybody wants to sue everybo — "

" —This isn't about you getting sued, this is about me getting information about what exactly happened on a night six months ago."

"Oh, now I see. This is about that lawyer who hit and run that woman. You should have said something when we were on the phone. I don't believe I can help you."

"Can't or won't?"

"Pick one. The cops came in already, asked a bunch of questions including which guests were in that night. Not good for business."

"It doesn't seem to me that it affected business at all, I come in all the time and the place is packed."

"Whatever. Look, I'm busy. Whattaya say we cut to the chase. You ask me a question, and I tell you I don't know. Maybe after a couple of go-arounds you finally figure out that a guy came in and got hammered; that I'm not going to say or do anything to get my ass or my business in a sling, then you leave. So go ahead and show yourself out."

"And I'm here to tell you, or show you if I have to, that I'm not leaving until I'm fully satisfied that I have all of the information I can get from you about that night. We can do this the nice and easy way, where you get on with opening up for the day, or we can do this the hard way where shit gets broke. Maybe even *you* get broke. You may be bigger, but I guarantee you're gonna know you've been in a fight."

"What do you want from me? I'm almost never here, and I am for sure never here at night. I come in every morning or so and count money or make change when a manager or supervisor needs a day off. Like today."

"I want a copy of the check from that night, just like the one you gave to the police. I want a copy of the security footage from the CCTV from that night. I want to know about Jenna, good employee or bad, anything in her personnel file. That, for starters, is what I want from you right now."

"Personnel file? What do you think this is? We don't have a Human Resources Department, man. If somebody fucks up, they get canned or we cut her shifts. Pretty simple. Besides, she doesn't work here anymore. She *was* a great kid until she decided not to show up ever again. No call, no show. Her phone's shut off too. Never even came to get her tips or her last paycheck."

"That sounds unusual. She said something about quitting the other night when we were in here, but not getting money that she is owed? That ain't right. Right?"

"Whattaya gonna do? She isn't the first to no-call, no-show; and despite my prayers, she ain't gonna be the last."

"We can come back to that. How about a copy of the check from that night."

"You got a warrant?"

"I'm not a cop, so no. But I used to be one, and I can make life difficult for you with a phone call or two. Still want to see a warrant?"

Sully looked around the bar, then at the floor as he thought about his options. He was beginning to understand that he didn't have any.

"What day did you want?"

Warren gave him the date of the charity event, the date of the crash and the approximate time that he was in. Around 7 to 8:00 PM.

"Do you know where the guy sat, or any other information? There are, like, a ton of checks to go through."

"I know you know which check it is. The cops have a copy and the prosecutor has one."

"Then why do you need to see it?"

Deni ignored the question. "He sat at the bar, Jenna served him. If it makes it easier, we can look at the CCTV footage first so you can see where he was sittin'."

"You want footage from six months ago? Ha. We keep that for two weeks, then the drive is recorded over with the new footage. If nothing happens, we don't save it."

"But something did happen. You remembered the event when I brought it up. The cops were in here. You mean to tell me that you didn't save that footage?"

"Maybe. I'll have to check. Maybe the cops have it. Did you ask them?"

"I know for a fact that they don't have it, because the prosecutor didn't include that in the evidence package they have against the guy I work for. So I guess you're gonna have to look."

"Let me make a phone call, maybe my General Manager knows where it is."

"You're not a real hands-on kinda owner, are you?"

"I've got other businesses. I can't do it all."

"I see that."

Marty-slash-Sully left to go into the office. He seemed to be in there for a long time while Deni was hanging around in the open but not opened restaurant and bar. He thought it odd that the owner would leave a stranger in his establishment with still uncounted money out in the open, expensive bottles of alcohol, and an unlocked front door. He also thought this guy was not much of an owner, not much of a businessman, and overall Deni was unimpressed by the overall intelligence of Marty. When he returned after a bit, the big man looked as if he was thoroughly confused, which Deni thought about right.

"I have good news and bad news. The good news is here is the receipt I printed out of MICROS, our sales system." The receipt didn't look like the one the prosecutor had. It had times and keystrokes on it, indicating when each of the two drinks were ordered and by whom. It was helpful but led to more questions. *If he really did only have the two beers, how is it possible that he was so cocked?* Deni thought while the owner was still speaking. "The bad news is that according to my GM, the footage was saved to a drive that is no longer in the office."

"What kinda game are you runnin' on me here, guy? You *had* the footage saved, but it's now conveniently missing?"

"You are more than welcome to come back to the office and look for yourself. My GM is on his way in. He isn't happy about it, since he closed last night and didn't get home until 4:00 AM. But he sounded concerned enough to make the trip."

"So help me, if this is a scam there are going to be beat'ns. Who else has access to the office, and wherever the drive was located in the office?"

"I honestly don't know. Like I said, I'm not usually here during hours of operation. I say we wait for him to arrive and we can all go in there together."

Marty finished opening the place while Deni waited. Attractive females were also arriving about that time, presumably to start their shifts. The bar was officially opening. A lunch crowd was beginning to come in as well. Some for an honest lunch, some for a liquid one. A tall, lanky gentlemen entered through the back door looking haggard and disheveled. He made no idle talk, no introductions; he plowed through any and all that tried to make contact with him. He Heismaned through the office door like if it didn't open, he would just go through it. Warren spied him from where he was sitting at the bar waiting, and made his way back to the office to join who he assumed was the General Manager. Sully was nowhere to be immediately seen.

When Deni arrived inside the office he saw that the owner was already in the office, having a conversation with his manager. They both looked at the investigator with extreme caution, unsure of what violence he was capable of. The manager had seen a small sampling first-hand once before.

"What's the verdict, gents?"

The skinny one chimed in first. "It was here, it's been here since the day after the accident happened. I mean the Barstone and Wayland communities aren't that big, so when something big happens, everybody hears about it. It made the news. I knew he was having drinks here before the accident, so I purposely saved it. It's not here. It's been in the same spot for six months and now it's not here. I was waiting for the police or somebody to want it, but nobody ever asked."

"Well somebody wanted it, since you're sayin' it's gone."

"Even so, it isn't here."

"So make me another copy. Go back and pull it up, or whatever you do to get it."

"Our system doesn't work that way. It records over itself to save hard drive space. If you don't save and store something specific within two weeks, it is gone. We saved it, but since that flash drive is gone, the information is gone. That's what I'm afraid to tell you, but that is what I'm telling you. The footage is gone."

"I have a friend that says that today all digital stuff is stored in a cloud, or on a cloud, or something about a cloud. Internet or something, right?"

"Well, that is kind of, sort of, true. Except we don't have ADT, or LifeShield, or somebody like that off-site managing our system. Ours is a cheapo, self-contained system that isn't connected to the internet or anything. So no cloud. That drive was what you needed, and it's gone."

"So what was on the footage? Did you see it?"

"Specifically? No. It was six months ago. It was a crowded bar."

"So nobody who works here knows what was on the drive that sat in this office for six months. And that drive, conveniently, is gone."

"It's not convenient, but yes it's gone."

"And so is Jenna. The girl who, according to this sheet of paper with the receipt on it, was the bartender who 'only served him two beers'. So you boys are tryin' to sell me on the fact that not only is the drive gone, but so is the employee? Both just disappeared?"

"You don't think Jenna took it do you? It's just a coincidence."

"Neither one of you are too smart, huh? There is no such thing as a coincidence. I came in a couple of weeks or so ago and had a chat with her. Then my lawyer friend and I came in the other night for a follow-up. She stormed outta here crying that night. Mister Marty or Sully or whatever here, says that she didn't show up, nor did she call, nor did she come to get her money that was owed to her since then. Now we find out that the footage, which in all likelihood shows that she over-served the guy that was in a car crash, a crash which left one person dead, is also missing. And neither of you are putting two and two together huh?"

"I admit, it does seem like they disappeared at the same time. Roughly."

"There are way too many things disappearing around here."

"Excuse me?" the tall man said, glancing at the stoic owner.

"Nothing. That is what I've got. A big fat fuckin' nothing," Deni said as he walked out of the office and out of Sully's Tavern.

******

Back in his car, Warren was angry. He wasn't ah-shucks-and-fiddlesticks angry, he was I-want-to-kill-something-with-my-bare-hands angry. This case had turned on its ear. This was no longer a situation where the stars had aligned and bad things happened to good people. This was something sinister. There was evil taking place. Someone had an agenda, and that agenda was to bury Jacob Grantes.

In Deni's business, he had investigated many cases where people covered their tracks to hide evidence. He was used to being smarter than those trying to cover-up their misdeeds. What he wasn't used to were the seemingly separate entities all conspiring to form a black hole that vaporized evidence. Why make something disappear unless there was something to hide. Were all of these bits going to the same place? Were all the people? Was there one big rock that, if uncovered, would provide; the maid, the 911 caller A.K.A Jenna, the CCTV footage, Anna and Brady? Cover-ups were one thing, this was something else.

Everywhere he turned, one more thing was added to the list of things he had to find. He was almost afraid to continue moving forward for fear of the next thing vanishing as well. Anger was helpful to him in certain situations, this was not one of them. He had to keep his cool. He was more determined than ever to uncover the truth behind the crash. JG had no memory of the night after leaving the bar, where he insisted, and the receipt provided proof, that he only had two beers. Now everything and everyone surrounding it had vanished. He had to pick away at his list, and do it fast. First on the list was the housekeeper.

He started the car and without allowing it to warm up, he headed toward the Destrier residence. Ryan had been there, but it was now his turn. He was in no mood for nut-jobs, but his threshold for much of anything at that moment was low. The servant was an important piece. She was the last person to see JG before the crash and was probably forced to disappear. Ryan had said there were separate living quarters for the Destrier help, he wanted to comb through that home. There, he would likely find the clue as to her whereabouts. In his experience, those from another country who had spent time, money, energy, and at great personal risk to get into this country, didn't just leave unless they were forced to in shackles. Once they had become accustomed to the land of dreams, they didn't just leave without a fight. Especially when those back in their native land were counting on the money being sent back there.

Warren Dennihan arrived at the Destrier Estate, he pushed the white button to open the iron gate in front of him. The place was secure, he thought, as the button didn't open the gate but instead produced a British voice.

"Good Morning. How may I help?"

Warren looked at his watch, confirming the time on his dash, assessing that it was technically still morning but only by three minutes.

"Open the gate."

129

"Do you have some business here, or an appointment, sir?"

"Yeah. Open the gate."

"If I might have your name sir, so I may check the calendar."

"Warren Open-tha-Gate. I'm sure I'm on the calendar. Seriously, open the gate."

"I'm afraid you will need to be more specific regarding your business here, sir."

Warren was already on fire, and he was getting more annoyed with the voice emanating from the security box outside the gate. More so with every word. He had always found the male British accent to be a combination of being uppity and gay. He realized it was not necessarily true that they all felt superior to Americans, nor that they were all homosexuals, but that voice bothered him just the same.

"I need to speak with either Roman or Chamille Destrier. It is an emergency. Open the gate."

"Do you have an appointment, Mister Warren?"

"How many emergencies have appointments? And it's not Mister Warren, It's just Warren. Now open the gate or I'm coming through it looking for you."

There was a brief pause before the accent said, "Please park your truck off in the service parking area, off to the side of the property, out of view." He said it in a way that suggested he was driving a disgusting garbage truck instead of an Escalade.

Then the gate opened.

Warren looked at the speaker next to the white button he had pushed, seeing a tiny camera which would normally go unnoticed he suspected. He smiled to himself and said, "Can't go anywhere without bein' on TV anymore. Let's see if this one disappeared."

Once inside the estate, down the long road lined with trees, he parked his car where he was told. Even the help had decent rides, he thought. He walked up to the door, a dark-skinned man was waiting for him.

He was welcomed, for lack of a better word, by the man whose voice he recognized from the speaker. "I do hope that your rather large automobile is parked out of sight."

"Easy there, guy. Don't get your turban in a twist."

"I beg your pardon. I demand to know what emergency has occurred to warrant such a presence without prior notice."

"What are you Indian? British accent kinda threw me off at the gate, there. Are you legal? Your papers in order?"

"I've had quite enough of your vulgar behaviour, I would like you to leave straight away."

"Its fine, Nigel. I believe I know what this is about." Chamille Destrier descended the wide, spiraled staircase behind her man-servant. More like gracefully floated down it. "You may leave us, but please have some beverages sent into the sitting room." She turned to Deni as she arrived at the bottom of the stairs. "Would a Bloody Mary be acceptable to you?"

Warren was not easily impressed, nor easily at a loss for a witty retort in any situation, but he was mesmerized by the tanned beauty that had floated toward him. "Sure." That was all he could come up with.

She was wearing a key lime green silk dress with what Warren gathered to be nothing underneath. Her dark eyes were demure, yet penetrated him as if assessing his soul. The dress had a high slit that revealed her long dark legs as she negotiated her way through the house to the sitting room. She already had the air of Angelina Jolie, the slit up the dress was too much. Yet her appearance was elegantly exotic.

Chamille had gently cupped Deni's elbow urging him toward the sitting room. "Right this way. We can take refreshment in comfort, I hope."

Gathering himself out of stunned silence, while taking in the luxury of the room, he managed to recover his wit and charm. "In this dump? I guess we'll have to make do. So where is Brad Pitt and the million African kids?" He plopped himself on the plush, white-silk sofa, spreading his arms along the back.

She laughed as though that was the first time she had ever been compared to Angelina. His guess is that she secretly wanted to be her. "He is very, very away." She sat in the matching sofa opposite him, crossing her exposed legs. "What brings your delightful personality into my otherwise dreary day? Jacob? Or is it Anna and Brady?"

The accoutrements for their Bloody Marys arrived via the servant on a large serving tray doubling as a lazy Susan. The clear vodka in one carafe was resting inside a bowl on a bed of crushed ice; the premixed tomato concoction was in another, separate vessel. Lining the rest of the setup were; celery, shrimp, olives, limes, lemons, chili powder, Tabasco, more ice, and empty crystal highball glasses.   The assemblage commandeered half of the glass coffee table between them.

"Ah yes. Here we are. That will be all. Thank you." The server who was not Nigel was dismissed.

"I'm here about the housekeeper that babysat Brady. The one that I am told has gone missing."

"That damned housekeeper is getting more action than I am, lately." She leaned forward to assemble a cocktail, the plunging neckline to her dress fell loose exposing her entire top, giving Warren a birds-eye view without fetter.   His first impression of her lack of undergarments under the silk dress was correct, she was indeed naked under the very thin garment.

"I hope you like it spicy, I know I do," she said.

"What is that a navel piercing?" The big, pink elephant in the room was not going to leave without being discussed. It was not Deni's style. Brash and in your face, that is Warren Dennihan.   He tried to look as though it was blasé, as if he was not thoroughly turned-on, but he was unsuccessful. The black widow had him in her web.

She pretended to be embarrassed, changed her position to eliminate his vantage point. She mocked a sheepish laugh.

"Hmmmmm.   You like to get right down to business, don't you? Here is your drink. You see, I can be servile if the mood strikes."

"Thanks.   Speaking of business, I really do need to find that maid that you fired. Time is kinda of the essence. I could also use any records you might have from that night, like a time card and what-not. I'd love to see her room too."   He took a sip of his drink, it was the best Bloody Mary he'd ever tasted.

She seductively ate a shrimp off of the rim of her cocktail, staring at her prey as she did so. "Are you always so aggressive?"

"I get what I want, if that's what you're askin'. I like to do things the easy way, but most people have to do things the hard way. I was kinda hoping that you being a smart, rich lady, that you would be above all that shit. I can see that you like to play games. You're bored, I get that. But I'm leavin' here with what I came to get, plain and simple.   But listen, if you wanna do this the hard way, I'm game."

"I am all for doing this the haaaahhd way," she said, imitating his thick Boston accent. "I always get what I want, also. It's just a matter of time.   You intrigue me.   You want something from me, and I know,

132

without a shadow of a doubt, that I want something from you. I don't get too many bad-boys kicking in my door. You scared poor Nigel, but you don't scare me. Quite the opposite in fact."

To Chamille, it was clear that Warren was ruggedly handsome, tall, and leanly muscular. His scars added to his bad-boy charm. He was also incredibly wrong and sinful for her, which made him perfect. Deni had known the type, albeit not so wealthy. He was good a reading people, and he could read her like a book.

She left her couch and sat on his lap, straddling him. He made no bid to protest. "I'll give you everything you want, after you give me every single thing that I want."

She unbuttoned his Oxford shirt, which he almost never wore, and pulled it down to his waist, which essentially handcuffed him. His exposed torso uncovered a tattoo-laden tapestry which would normally be hidden if he had worn a short-sleeved shirt. Her eyes filled as she took him in. Her smile grew, the art was adding to her wantonness.

"Oh, you *are* a bad-boy." She slid off his lap and grabbed his belt, helping him to his feet.

"This is probably a very bad idea, lady." He slipped out of the shirt that tethered his hands.

"Cammy. Call me Cammy." She kissed him hard on the mouth, then neck and chiseled chest.

Warren gently pushed her away from him, she stood staring at him less than an arm's length away. He clutched her dress at the bottom of the plunged neckline and in one quick pull, tore the thin, silky dress off of her body; then threw it on the floor in ruins, while she stood before him, naked.

The two of them didn't make love, they ravaged each other in hot, animalistic, carnal sex. They devoured one another without any sensual romance, but fucked each other in a raw, sweaty, lustful way. It was if it was a consensual rape. She dominated him, then he reciprocated. They were one another's personal plaything, using up the other until spent. And they spent each other over, and over again. They both found release multiple times until they were sweaty and exhausted like they had been marooned in the hot desert.

Depleted, thirsty, and dripping with sweat, they lay next to each other on the floor of the library, three rooms away from whence they started.   They both panted heavily, letting each other enjoy their respective euphoric states in silence.

After a lengthy period of time, he caught his breath while remaining naked on the floor. Next to him was the sweaty but otherwise perfect, tanned woman. Deni broke the silence. "Hey Cam."

"Yes?"

"I really do need all those things I mentioned earlier. Also can I get the video footage from the outside security gate from that night?"

"Don't ruin this moment, honey. I'm wet in every possible way and enjoying every second of it."

"Cam."

"If you do that to me again in a few minutes, I swear on everything that I love, I will do anything you want. Including sign this house over to you." She rolled over on top of him and began to kiss him again. "We have to do this again."

"Cam."

She continued to re-seduce him. A desperate ploy to continue their very adult activities.

"Cam."

"I know, I know." She got up off of the floor and padded naked into the recesses of the enormous mansion, almost in a huff.

Deni watched her leave, then return with a towel. She tossed it at him and stormed out of the room again. Nigel entered within seconds of her second departure with all of his various pieces of clothing that had been strewn from room to room during their activities. He stood staring at Warren, making the awkward moment that much more so. *Maybe he is gay*, Warren thought.

Nigel finally broke the silence. "MISSUS Destrier will meet you in the sitting room in a short time. I will bring you some water once you have dressed. Would you care for sparkling or flat?"

"Huh?"

"The water. Would you like it with bubbles or not, sir?"

"Not."

Nigel turned and left the room after setting the clothes on a reading table.

"You never said if you were legal."   Deni tried to salvage some dignity in the situation with humor. The truth was he didn't care where Nigel was from, nor if he was in the United States legally. He was just breaking Nigel's balls. He didn't like being the recessive person in any interaction. He had just been used and discarded like a disposable toy, he was not going to be made to feel that way by the help.

Once he started to dress, he realized why he was being stared at. The tattoos. He was used to them, and when he was clothed, even in a T-shirt and shorts, nobody was the wiser. But standing there naked, he could see where it would be a sight. Maybe even off-putting.

Other than the awkwardness between he and Nigel, he felt great. He was going to get what he had come for, and he had a great time in accomplishing the task. She was a nut-job, but nobody is perfect.

He made his way into the sitting room after he was fully attired. The Bloody Mary bar was replaced by a coffee tray. The last thing he needed was to be more dehydrated. He hoped that Nigel would keep his promise, and that water was in fact on the way. It was.

The assistant, after a long period, did enter the sitting room. "Apologies for the tardiness of your water. I was unavoidably detained in fetching it. It seems that Missus Destrier will not be able to revisit you today, as her, ehm, exertions this afternoon have exhausted her." He handed Deni a bottle of Tasmanian Rainwater, which he assumed was just expensive tap water that someone bottled. "She apologises for not being able to rejoin you, but wanted me to thank you for your, ehm, business. She said that she very much looks forward to future transactions with you." He placed a large envelope on the end of the giant, glass coffee table which literally had coffee set up on it. "These are yours to use with discretion. While all of Missus Destrier's relationships are important, and would never betray, I reckon that your relationship with her has been elevated rather apace, wouldn't you agree?"

"I'm not sure what you mean by that, guy, but I'm not the one hidin' her secrets and fetchin' her coffee." He picked up the envelope, peered inside. There were a few documents and computer memory stick. "Seems a little light on info here, Nige. Pardon the expression, but, what the fuck? Also I need you to show me where the house cleaner's room is, or was, or whatever."

"All the information that you seek is contained in that folder. I am to inform you that there will be no tour of the staff's quarters today, but should you seek to come back, Missus Destrier will with pleasure, ehm, see you again." He turned and opened his right arm as if to show him the way to the door. "Your presence here today has been and should remain discrete. If there is nothing further, the door is this way."

Back in his car, he emptied the contents of the envelope onto the front passenger seat. While he let his car warm up, he looked over the few documents that were before him. The first document had an address and directions on it that appeared to have been printed from GOOGLE Maps. In the margin was large, feminine handwriting,

"Her last known address, family I think. We must do it again, and I hope soon. Cam."

Below her name was a large lipstick kiss.

The address was in Brighton, Massachusetts, a borough of Boston. This area was well-known for college students as well as a significant Russian and Brazilian presence. The address was two hours south with traffic and Warren had other stops to make in New Hampshire. Brighton would have to wait a day or two.

******

The cell phone that was used to make the 911 phone call was sold at a Verizon kiosk that sat in the middle of a large mall off of Interstate 293 in Nashua, New Hampshire. It took some doing, but after a few phone calls to Verizon, he determined that the particular type of phone used was sold out of inventory at that location. Interstate 293 was a loop that diverted traffic off the main artery of Interstate 93. Inside that loop was a huge mall, located just off the highway.

Nashua was not far from Wayland, nor was it very far north of Boston, in distance. The amount of time the trip took depended upon traffic, to a large extent, which was a gamble at any hour. Many commuters worked in Boston but called Nashua home. New Hampshire houses were less expensive in comparison, the taxes were far less in the 'Live Free or Die' State, and the politics slanted much more to the right than the Commonwealth State to the South. The commuter rail, or purple line, made it that much more convenient for those that chose not to fight the traffic on the main artery.

The only downside to living in New Hampshire and working in Massachusetts, for those that choose a more suburban lifestyle, is the traffic. Getting into and out of the Hub of New England during rush hours made the commute a daily stress-test. Those that opposed taking the train did so because the stops were frequent, times could be a bit unreliable, and the parking structures were an open invitation for thieves. So those avoiding the train, also tried to avoid the heavy traffic times of rush hours, which became popular with many commuters, making those hours less clear. Most hours of the day on 93 were a headache, full-stop. And the loop of 293 was no picnic either.

Despite all of this, people still made the daily adventure south, because of the greater earning potential. Property values in New Hampshire started to rise, and therefore businesses began to adopt Boston pricing. Designer stores, factory outlets, and large malls all catered to the sophisticated metropolitan tastes in the sleeper towns of southern New Hampshire. So did the drug dealers, all of whom needed burner phones.

The kiosk in the mall was a legitimate business. Those shopping for a cell phone could purchase an iPhone, Blackberry, Samsung, Droid or the like, succumbing to the monthly service plans associated with all the data requirements those phones demand. Those looking for a phone that is untraceable, can buy those legally as well. There are a myriad of reasons to have a throwaway phone. Prepaying eliminates the required service fees or contracts, and the customer can simply pay as they go. Lack of credit, or bad credit, eliminates eligibility for said expensive monthly service plans, at any rate. Some consumers are not technologically savvy, therefore do not need all the bells and whistles of a smart-phone. Or they could be a drug dealer, call-girl, pimp or other felon that is on the run, and need to be untraceable which are less legitimate, all.

Warren walked around the kiosk twice without being asked by the nerdy kid behind the counter if he needed any help. The pimple-faced kid, with a very long black tie, a shirt three sizes too big, and pants below his ass-cheeks stood behind the counter, and was too busy typing away on his personal phone to offer anyone any help. The white man-boy could not have been twenty-one yet. He looked to be a cross between a nerd from the *Big Bang Theory* and a wannabe thug. The name tag he wore said his name was Slice, but that was not likely to be the name his mother had given him.

"How can I, like, help you? We have the latest and greatest of all the phones. The prices marked are negotiable if you commit to a two-year contract." The entirety of his spiel was performed without looking up from his smartphone after Deni's third trip around the kiosk.

"What if I don't wanna commit to a plan?" While doing laps around the kiosk, he was scoping out the cameras that were strategically placed to maximize coverage. He could see no blind spots where the security would fail to pick up anyone looking at the phones.

"Oh, so you want a prepaid. A go-phone."

"Yep."

"Well, we got lots of goes, bro. All depends on how many minutes you need." This kid was a bullshitter through and through. His dialect went from nerdy wannabe thug to a young punk gangsta. This little chameleon was a hustler in the making, a used car salesman had nothing on this kid, once his attention was finally garnered.

"Yeah well, I don't really need to make many calls with it."

"I see." He turned around and retrieved a phone, placed on the plexiglass counter between them. The phone was packaged in a hard, clear-plastic, sealed case. "You still burn minutes when your guys call you. Here is our cheapest burner, bro. How many you need?"

"None."

"Man, are you wasting my time?"

"I don't see anyone else in need of help, you do work here, right? I need to see who bought this phone." He handed the kid a piece of paper with the date and serial number of the phone used to make the 911 call."

"What is this? I can't just give you someone's information. I'll get fired." Punk and gangsta had left the building. "Also, I only have access to it if it's a Verizon phone and it was sold here, I don't have access to information about other — "

" — Lucky for you it was sold here, which means it's a Verizon prepaid phone."

"Look, I can get into a lot of trouble, man. People get those phones for a reason. If you have a problem with some dude who's movin' in on your territory, leave me out of it. Seriously."

Deni quickly snatched the kid's necktie, pulling his face to the glass counter which held the more expensive phones inside. "Let me put it another way. You *are* gonna do whatever it is you do in your little computer there, and you *are* going to tell me who bought that phone. You're not *going* to get in trouble. I *am* trouble, and I'm right here. *Man*."

"Alright, alright, alright." He was let go to begin typing and searching in his computer. In between searches, he tucked his tie into his shirt so his assailant wouldn't be able to use it to hurt him again.

"This is totally surreal."

"What?"

"It means — "

" —I know what it means, and it's overused. Just get to work kid."

He went back to work and when he was finished, he looked at Deni with a look of pure fear. He backed himself as far away from Warren as he could. "Ah, man. No name or address. The dude paid in cash. Please don't hurt me, there really isn't anything I can do. I'm sorry."

"You're gonna be if you don't get creative."

"Look it's not illegal, you know. You don't have to give your information on a prepaid. It could have been a gift. Look, they paid cash so that's the end of the road."

"You can give me a list of the phone calls made into and out of that phone."

"I could except there was only one. It was to 911. Go kill someone there."

Deni had forgotten that piece of information. "What about your cameras here?" He pointed at the cameras above them.

"What about them? Are you a cop or something? I mean, you can't just assault people even if you are the po-lice. Don't you have to have a warrant?" He looked around the mall for a passersby that might be able to help him. The would-be witnesses showed no interest and walked right on past. "Yeah you aren't a cop, but maybe I should call them. Or security. Or my manager."

"Why does everyone have to do things the hard way? Listen kid, all I want you to do is tell me who bought this phone. You can get the shit kicked out of you in front of security or your boss or whoever you want to call, but if you don't figure out a way to give me what I want, you are going to get *fucking* hurt. I mean hurt like you have never been before. I'll break both your arms so bad, you won't even be able to think about jerkin' off again. So stop jerkin' *me* off and get busy."

"I don't know if I can get it. Seriously. I don't wanna get hurt, but I don't think I can get it either. All the data is stored off-site and this phone was bought a long time ago, mister."

"What do you mean off-site. I was told by a friend of mine that all of these new fangled systems store all the information on a cloud or The Cloud or some internet thing."

"Yeah, your friend is right. That's what I mean by off-site. And that's what I mean by I can't get it. It's all password protected. They don't let people like me just have access to their security videos."

"Who has the password to get into it?"

"My boss. The manager. Good luck getting it out of him, but be my guest. If you beat him up though, I would love to watch."

"He won't give you the password over the phone if you call him?"

"No way. But if he was the one that set it, I might be able to figure out what his password is. He's a dog-lover and he has this sick man-crush on his little pug. It's gross."

"So you think his password is pug or pug related? Go ahead and try it."

He typed on the wireless keyboard with a grin on his face as he watched the computer screen in front of him.

"Ha, whattaya know? Fifth try," the kid said after twenty-seconds or so. "Lovepug. What a sicko."

"How did you get it? Never mind. So you are in? You got it?"

"Yeah, yeah. Hold on. This is really cool, by the way."

There were a couple of twenty-somethings that were browsing the phones, whether they were actually interested in making a purchase was anyone's guess, but they were completely ignored by Slice or whatever his name was.

"Got it," he said, at long last. "I just need something to store this onto."

Deni reached into his pocket and pulled out the memory stick that he had been given earlier by Cammy in the envelope. "If you store stuff on this, will it erase what is already on it?"

"You're not much of a computer guy are you?"

"You ain't outta the woods with that beat'n, kid."

"Sorry, sorry. No. As long is there enough space on it, it will just add it to the stuff already on it. Just give it to me and you can be on your way." He inserted the disk and was storing the footage within seconds. While he was waiting, he said, "You know it's funny, I thought you were looking for a dude. I think I remember this lady, she had all kinds of questions, kinda like you. Only she wasn't violent."

"What lady? *The* lady? What are you talking about? Let me see that."

Slice turned the screen so Deni could see the multiple angles. The kid pressed a button and it turned into a single view, a view of the person who bought the 911 burner phone.

"This lady. If it's the same one I'm thinking of." He looked at the sheet of paper that he had originally been given with the date and serial number on it. "Yeah, that's my associate number. I sold it to her. I thought it was funny at the time because she was so not the type to buy a burner phone, but she kept asking about it being traced and stuff."

He handed the memory stick and the paper to Deni when it was finished saving.

"Gotcha. I recognize her, too," Deni said. He grabbed it began to run toward the mall's exit.

"You're welcome. What an asshole. Not even a tip."

18

THE CITY OF BRIGHTON, MASSACHUSETTS IS NOTABLE
but not for the size, nor because it is a wealthy borough of Boston.
When tourists flock to a New England city, Brighton is not usually a
point of interest on their travel map. The exit, off of any of the major
arteries into the area, doesn't even warrant its own sign. The exit shares
a sign that reads: Allston/Brighton/Brookline. The tiny city within the city
is noteworthy because it sits between Boston University and Boston
College. It is also a haven for a large immigrant population from Russia
and the Eastern bloc, as well as Brazil.

The concentrated center for Russian Jews sits on the western side of
Brighton, where the Orthodoxes have lived for generations. Within the
enclave, are shoulder-to-shoulder, rundown townhouses where the
college students attending Boston College reside; those buildings being
converted to apartments which are owned by said Russian Hasidic Jews.
Some found it odd that the Jesuit College was nestled on the borders of
this community in Brighton and Chestnut Hill, which was another
concentration of a less orthodox, but a more affluent Jewish people.

On the opposing end of Brighton, in the East, sits another devoutly
religious community of Catholic Brazilians. This area is made up of the
same style of rundown apartment buildings. Those residents not only
live there without proper documentation, but generally live outside of
the number allowed by fire code, and without landlord approval. In
some cases, a dozen inhabitants would dwell in a single studio
apartment. One of the more legal of the inhabitants, or at least with the
best plausible paperwork, would score an apartment, which precipitated
the phone calls and letters to others who would, in the end, fill the
dwelling beyond legal capacity. They obviously don't do this for the
comfort but for the sustainability. Under-the-table salaries are low,
requiring many earners per apartment in order to afford it. And to be
able to send a substantial portion of their incomes back to their homes in
Brazil.

This Eastern part of Brighton is not a secret, the prideful inhabitants are brazen in flaunting their native flag throughout the community. It was in this concentrated area that the maid, Marina, formerly in the employ of the Destriers, now lived.

Warren made the trip down to Boston the afternoon following his tryst at the mansion, and the kiosk discovery in Nashua later in the day. He took care of a few things with his business partner and investigator that worked with him there that night, and slept in his three-decker in Southie. On Wednesday, he drove into Brighton on Commonwealth Avenue, which should have taken very little time if he could have taken a direct, traffic-free route. But in Boston, that was impossible. Unfortunately there was no direct route from Southie, with all the one-way streets and such. The traffic was as heavy as it always was. By the time he arrived at the address given to him by Cammy, he was sick of being in his car, sick of traffic, sick of looking for a parking space, and irritable was an understatement of his current mood. He was in no mood for the shrugging of shoulders and the feigning of language issues by the people who responded as he knocked on doors.

Apartment number two may have been the mailing address, but the hidden side door where Warren would find Marina after a number of attempts, was not the physical address. From what he could ascertain from the number of unmarked doors, all answered by non-English speaking people, Warren guessed that seven apartments made up apartment number two, on the 1600 block of Commonwealth Avenue.

"Marina?"

"Sim. é você a policia?" (Yes? Are you the police?)

"Uh. Shit. I thought you would speak English. No English?"

"Yes, a little. Who are you?" The short, thick woman gave him a skeptical look, wondering who the intruder was. Her eyes gave the impression that she had decided that he was not the police, yet the visitor before her was very unusual.

"I'm Warren Dennihan. Missus Destrier sent me. Camille." He hoped the lie would go unchecked. Cam had more or less given him the address after using him for sex, but she certainly hadn't sent him there. He was hoping to ease his way into the apartment, which was not happening.

"Eu não penso assim, eh, I don't think so. Go away, please," She said but made no effort to close the door. "She no send you, whoever you are, no trouble para mim."

"I'm here about Jacob Grantes. I need your help. Please."

"I cannot help. I very sorry. Nenhum problema para mim." With that, she decided to close the door, which she would have done had Deni not wedged his foot on the bottom of the door to prevent her.

"Did you know the woman who died in the crash? She was from Brazil also." It was a long shot, that the two women had met.

"Sim. Yes, she was my cousin. I very angry that she die, e, I no help man who kill her." Brazilians use familial terms like cousin differently than Americans. Warren was aware of these loose cultural differences but not the exact relation between the two, if in fact there was one. Certainly the two knew of or about one another, which was all he wanted to know.

"I'm sorry. I understand. But something is very wrong about what happened, which I think is why you were fired. That is what I want to talk to you about. Can I come in?"

"No. I meet you at café. Fifteen minute." She pointed toward a Brazilian coffee shop on the next block, behind him. "Você não pode entrar."

"Are you hiding something from me, Marina? If I go over there, are you going to meet me there, or are you gonna run away?"

"No, I meet you. I promise. Eu prometo. Fifteen minute."

"I'm not going to hurt you, we're just gonna talk. Don't run away, that is only going to make me mad."

"Sim, sim. I meet you."

The café was in fact an internet café. It was either Brazilian owned, or the owner was a marketing genius. Brazilian flags, soccer balls, and pictures of famous World Cup victories covered the walls, all while tanned beauties served coffee. If the locals had computers, they didn't use them. Every computer was being used while the small two-top tables were mostly free. Deni hadn't dashed right over from the maid's apartment, instead he waited for her to leave so he could follow her. He wasn't entirely sure she wasn't going to run, despite her promise. Once he was certain she was on her way to the café, he then jetted over as quick as he could get over there.

He arrived within seconds before her arrival, still panting in fact, from the run over from his car. She ordered a concoction in Portuguese, which he doubled and paid for. It turned out to be delicious. Once they found a suitable table, he started with some light conversation.

"What is this? It's phenomenal."

"Cafezinho."

"Yeah, you'll have to write that down for me."

She gave no response, nor did she make any attempt to write down the name of the espresso drink. She just stared at him in bewilderment.

"So how long have you worked, or, did you work for the Destriers?"

"Many year."

"Look, I know you don't really wanna talk to me, but this is important. Maybe I can help you get your job back. If you help me."

"Why I help you. Por que?"

"Because while Arelia's death was tragic, someone is hiding what really happened. The truth is not complete. If Jacob Grantes really did kill her, he will pay for it in prison. But if someone else helped him or had a hand in it, they should pay too, right? I think you know something. You know that something isn't right, and that's why you were fired."

"I fired because I not legal here."

"Is that what Cam, er, Missus Destrier told you?"

"She tell me nothing. Nigel do it."

"OK. What did Nigel say? Listen, I don't like him either, so feel free to talk shit."

"He tell me to pack my room and leave. If I make trouble, it will be bad for me. Eu não o quero ser ruim para mim. I cannot have trouble."

"So she paid you to go away because she knew you knew something, and were in no position to put up a stink?"

"Que?"

"Never mind. How much did she pay you?"

"She still pay me. Every week. Cash. I save so I go back to Brazil. Rich. I like here, but minha familia es home."

"Wait. She still pays you even though you don't work there anymore? You don't think that's wicked weird?"

"Week - ed?"

145

"Weird. Very weird. You don't think that paying you without work is very weird?"

"Sim. Yes. But I get money to no work, they tell me no question just hide. You here mean I must go home now."

"Who gives you the cash? How?"

"Nigel give me Sábados, eh, Saturday." She took a sip of her drink while looking out onto Market Street, which runs perpendicular to Commonwealth Avenue. She seemed very nervous.

"When were you told to go?"

"One night. They help me pack. But sometime they call me back to look after child."

"Who are they? Missus Destrier wasn't there that night. Right? Wasn't she at the charity event?"

"Sim. Nigel and other. Drive me here. Mister Destrier and Mrs. Destrier both go to party. Sra. Grantes pick up Brady, I go to bed. I wake up by Nigel say 'you go but we pay'. I cannot have trouble, so I go. Next day, I find out Arelia tem morreu. Is very sad for me. I surprise you find me. I want no troubles. Sometime I go back with Nigel, then he bring me here. You here is no good for me."

"Wait, you're all over the place. Sra. Grantes. That means missus, woman, right? Mother?" Deni was frantic in his digging for the memory stick out of his black, leather jacket. The memory stick that was given to him by Chamille Destrier, through Nigel.

"Sim, yes."

He got up from the table they were sitting at, grabbed Marina gently by the wrist, bringing her with him to an already occupied computer terminal. "That's why you're here in Brighton, why they're still paying you. That sneaky minx." He commandeered an extra, empty chair from a table next to the terminal, telling Marina to sit in it. He then handed the twenty-something guy using the computer forty dollars while pulling him out of his chair at the terminal.

"Hey que?" There was complete shock on his face and because of the surprise, posed little physical resistance at being ousted from his spot at the computer.

"Beat it, kid. Kick rocks." He turned to Marina and said, "How do you say go away in Brazilian?"

"Portuguese. People seja de Brazil. Speak Portuguese."

"Whatever. I don't need a lesson, I need this kid to fuck off."

146

She looked at the young man and said, "Você deve partir ou você está indo ser dano por este homem. Please."

The young man turned and walked to the coffee counter.

Warren plugged the memory stick into the USB port on the processing unit of the Acer computer. He hoped there wasn't going to be any compatibility issues on what was clearly and older model computer. He was no computer genius, any problems would require someone more tech savvy than he.

Fortunately, the bell that sounded when he inserted the wand indicated that at least it recognized the device. The window that popped up looked like a small TV, with remote control features lining the bottom of the image. He began to fast-forward the video footage from the Destrier security gate, by clicking the double-right arrow. He hadn't had to wait but a heartbeat before clicking the double-vertical lines. The image was paused in front of them.

He looked over to Marina and said, "Sra. Grantes. When she picked up Brady?"

"Sim. Of course. I tell you this, I no liar." She looked outright confused, not understanding what the image meant. Not that Deni really knew what it meant either.

"*You* aren't. But wasn't Missus Grantes supposed to be at the charity event, er, the party? Why was she picking up Brady when she was supposed be five miles away?

"Eu não compreendo. eu não sei. I don't know, senhor."

Just then, the disrespected twenty-something male was back with a wary, petite, female café manager in tow. She was there to bring some weight to the situation, despite her size, but anyone could see that her heart wasn't in it.

"Well ain't you the brave one? Bring a shorty over to fight your battles? Grow a pair of balls, guy." He stripped the two twenty dollar bills still in the adolescent's hand, pulled the memory stick out of the drive. "All yours chief." He looked at the manager who was speaking softly to Marina. "No sense of humor," he said to her as he pointed with his thumb at the kid. He handed the forty dollars to the manager with a wink.

✳✳✳✳✳✳

Deni's mind was turning as fast as the tires of his Escalade on the highway as he returned north. He was making progress, but what was he learning? If JG didn't pick up Brady, and Anna did, then what else in this story isn't accurate? Was Anna at the charity event at all? If Chamille was covering for her, why stop now? How was Jenna involved, other than serving him the alcohol in the first place? Were all of these women working together? That seemed far-fetched.

The fact that Anna was hiding something, and was hidden herself for that matter, was disconcerting to say the least. Jenna had disappeared with the CCTV footage. Why? He thought these women despised one another, at least that was the impression Jenna had given him. Maybe that's why JG was bellying up to the bar in the first place, he knew he didn't have to pick up Brady. So why does he think that he did? Why was everyone saying that he did? How did Brady get up to his room? Anna? Jenna? His mind wouldn't stop.

Warren had wanted to track down Jenna the moment he learned that she had taken off, now it seemed imperative. Time was running out for JG and there were far too many unanswered questions. He needed to find this girl, and make her fill in the missing pieces, conclusively, once and for all. He had doubts that she would be there, but he would again have to sift through her home for clues.

It was illegal to make phone calls on a cell phone while driving unless using a handsfree device. Warren didn't have such a gadget to his ear, though if he had the wherewithal, his Escalade probably had the capability for handsfree communication via bluetooth. Either way he wasn't using it, nor did he give a shit. He was calling a contact, a New Hampshire Statie he had known for many years.

He wanted the last known address for one Jennifer Beaumont, Jenna. His contact hated when Deni would call him, using him for these types of crusades. Though he complained, he always came through. The conversation was short, if not curt. There was no breaking of balls, no 'you can't keep doing this', he just gave his contact Jenna's name and what she looked like and the trooper spit back everything but her shoe size. Sometimes it paid to be a former cop. Fortified with her address and other information, he continued his drive to it.

She was a Barstonian. He parked in her driveway, the VW *Passat* that was registered to her, according to his contact, was not.

He knocked on her door with a set of three raps. One set. Then the second. After the ninth knock there was still no movement. No answer. Also no surprise. Plan B was really Plan A anyway. Time for the pins.

Personal shame was beginning to form at the loss of his touch at picking locks. It took him two full minutes to break into Jenna's place. Which was about as much time as he spent inside once the door was opened.

Upon his entrance, he had obtained all the information he had expected. He might as well have been a prospective renter, or homebuyer, or inspecting it to see about a security deposit. The place was empty. Empty empty. The garbage had been removed, so he wasn't able to rummage through it. She even took the ice cube trays.

"Who takes the ice cube trays?" he asked the empty room. "OK, Deni. Think this through old boy. She hates the job but makes great money at it. She says she is gonna leave so she can go back to school, or some shit. We break her balls a bit, she cries and takes off. At some point she has to go back to get the CCTV footage, then bails. She knows she has to leave town, cuz I'm onto her like a fat kid on cake. Where do you go? Family. Nah, this chick is smart. She ain't goin' somewhere obvious.

"So where did you go, Jenna? And why? You doin' this for Anna? By lookin' at this dump you lived pretty sparse. So all of a sudden you've got money. Cammy. That crazy nympho is payin' the bills. But why give me the maid and the video if she's involved?

"I gotta talk to Ryan. This is gettin' outta control." He closed the door behind him. The empty walls were not talking back, so it was not much of a conversation. He needed some light shed on this, at least another perspective. Ryan would help. He would have to.

He made a phone call to Ryan as he backed out of the driveway, again breaking the law. And again, he didn't give a shit.

19

PROGRESS, BE IT NOUN OR VERB, IS DEFINED AS 'ADVANCEMENT, *moving forward, development, growth or improvement in condition, space, or time'.* While JG was progressing in the forward movement of time, moving closer toward the trial, he was regressing physically and mentally. The regression was progressing, if you can call it that, with quick and drastic results.

A prisoner has nothing but time. Time to think, rethink, and dwell on every event that has ever taken place in his life. Be it significant or not is of no matter. Time is their enemy and so is their own brain. The insignificant becomes monumental once it festers over time. The thoughts eat away at the host like a cancer. An event that is already significant, metastasizes to the point of subjugating the host.

Grantes was no longer a confident yet mild-mannered attorney. He was an abandoned, caged animal. What had kept him going all of this time was the love of his wife and child. The many phone calls and letters he had received and sent had been his life blood. They were the white blood cells that were attacking those cancerous thoughts that destroyed men. The knowledge that he had Anna's love and support throughout his turmoil made the day to day abhorrence of incarceration tolerable. But barely. The absence of his family had decayed his driving force into nothingness.

The downward spiral began with the trivial event of being cut off in chow-line. Which was less about food than the cutter disrespecting the cuttee. The 5:00 PM dinner chow began like every other over the course of his six previous months. The cells open with the loud clang and the metal-against-metal squealing as the solid steel doors slide open, everyone on the pod lines up in their best, Bob Barker jumpsuit, ID pinned to the collar. Once the line is formed, inmates would sneak to rearrange themselves in that line, in order to eat with whom they like. The trays of food are handed to the men just before taking their seat in the order that they were lined up in. The wrong person cut in front of Grantes, on the wrong day, at the wrong time.

"What the fuck?" The outburst was not discreet. The cutter, it turned out, just wanted to eat with Grantes' cellmate, Loder (why was an entirely different question, nobody should have to eat with such a Neanderthal). Grantes was handed his plastic tray at the time of the outburst, which was the worker-bee inmate's mistake. The cover was quickly removed and the remainder of the untouched food was shot-putted at the offending inmate in front of him.

The correctional officers had watched this all unfold, expecting the disruption or worse after the vocal outburst, and immediately responded to eliminate the possibility of any retribution.

"Grantes. That's a seventy-two," said the CO. He made sure it was loud enough for the entire pod, both tiers, to hear. The officer came out from behind the bubble, pulled him out of chow line, and led him back to his cell. Supper was over for him.

A seventy-two is the number of consecutive hours to be locked into the cell without being let out. No rec time. No shower. Nothing but cell time for seventy-two straight hours. At least he wasn't lugged down to the hole. Yet. The toilet had definitely flushed, and he was circling the bowl, but he had not gone down the drain quite yet.

While locked in, he was consumed with thoughts regarding the whereabouts of his wife and son. Even more than usual since he learned of their disappearance. His trial was imminent, his family had vanished. Ryan had no news. Unless he took a deal, which would keep him where he was for the next five and a half years, he would be facing football numbers in the same prison once a verdict was in.

He wanted to speak to Anna. *Maybe about football,* he thought. He would lose his license to practice law. *Brady will make a great lawyer, someday. Where in the hell are they?* He was losing his mind.

The next event took place the following morning. It is hard to get into trouble while locked in your cell with no contact except with your celly, but he managed. The following morning, Grantes was not allowed to go to his mandatory AA meeting, because of his lock-in. Missing a meeting means a loss of rec according to the Sheriff's rules. This meant that a ticket would need to be served to him in his cell. This also meant that the first time he could come out of his cell after his seventy-two hour lock-in, he would not be allowed to. This was only day one of his

CRASH

three, so with all the meetings he would miss, he was going to get at least one additional day added to his lock-in, which would then lead to more unattended programming. Frustrated, he decided to sucker-punch his cellmate when the ticket was slid under his door by the CO. It was right in front of the officer, so there was no way to get away with it or to deny it.

Loder, inmate #437254, would not suffer one quick punch to the face, he would suffer twenty-seven more. At least that was the number written on his new charge of assault. He would now face another day in court, for another felonious act. He was able to beat his cellmate, hitting him as many times as he had, because the COs needed to get the lug team into the pod, the rest of the pod locked-in or on their knee, before the cell door would be opened. All things considered, they responded rather quickly. The Vegas-style camera coverage, covered every angle of the pod except for the inside of each cell. The twenty-eight total punches could not be proved or disproved, but Loder's face was all that was really needed to know that an assault had taken place.

The lug team, all six of them, invaded the cell (only two of them could actually fit inside the small cell, why they always bring six officers to diffuse these situations when all the other inmates were locked down, was a mystery to him), taking shots of their own until he submitted. He was beaten, shackled at the wrists and ankles, and lugged to solitary confinement.

The Hole is a long row of single cells juxtaposed along each side. If the two-man cells in the pods were considered tiny, the singles in The Hole were microscopic. Upon arrival, his ankles were unlocked. Grantes was then inserted into the cell, back to the door, while the slot in the solid door was unlocked and opened. He then backed up against the re-closed door so his wrist cuffs could be removed.

JG was given a one hour cool-down period before an officer in a white uniform shirt with a single metal bar on his collar arrived. The lieutenant was in a short-sleeved shirt and was jostling a huge set of keys on a ring while holding some documents. The food slash cuff-up slot was reopened, and a chair was then placed next to the door for him by a subordinate.

"Grantes. Come to the door so we can chat please." He said it without any detectable emotion. "If you are gonna be nice, I won't cuff you up.   If you reach through the slot we're gonna have problems. Understand?"

"Yes."

"All right, well, you've got yourself into a serious situation here," said the lieutenant.   He flicked the documents with his middle finger. "But you already know that don't you? You're a smart guy, a smart guy who just did something supremely stupid. Why? What's going on?"

Grantes knew to remain silent, and he did.

"Talk to me. I'm trying to help you. Loder is in HSU, broken jaw, broken orbital bone, he's pretty beat up. You did that to him. What did he do to you?"

Silence.

"Well, he must have done something. Or did you take it out on him for the ticket?"

Stoic reticence.

"You're not giving me much to work with here, you must want this charge. We can make the charge go away if you help me, help you."

"Out of the kindness of your heart, you want to erase this? What, I just go back to my cell? That'd look good."

"Oh, you *can* speak.   Maybe you go back up there, maybe you don't. Just tell me what happened."

"Off the record?"

"Nothing is ever off the record. You're an attorney, you know when you talk to the police all bets are off."

"You are not the police. You're a CO, a babysitter."

"I'm a lieutenant, wise-guy. The same rules apply, and I'm trying to help you."

"Then you're going to be having a one-way conversation."

"Hypothetically. Hypothetically, what happened?"

"Hypothetically, lock-ins mean missed meetings. Missed meetings mean more lock-ins. The Hole breaks the cycle. Hypothetically."

"Uh huh. Look …. Loder is a low-life. A professional inmate. He gets his face rearranged Picasso-style, I don't lose a bit of sleep.   But you're not a pro. You're a civilian, and you can help yourself here."

"I'm accused of vehicular manslaughter. The trial is a week or so away, solitary seems good to me."

"The Hole means no visits, two showers a week, and no rec. You don't want that, trust me. Let me help you out. How about a single cell back up on your pod?"

"For free? What do you want from me?"

"Information."

"About?"

"Anything. Just general information. I'll give you my card here, which will work from the phone on the pod, without being on your pin sheet. You see or hear something, you call that number and leave a message. Simple as that."

"So you want me to be a rat," Grantes said. It wasn't a question.

"I take care of this, you take care of us."

"There are no secrets in this place. Doesn't matter which pod you put me on. Besides, how long do you think I would last if you just put me back up there the same day I get lugged with no celly? I'd get a buck-fifty within my first hour. Or is that your plan?"

A buck-fifty is the term for what is given to a rat by another inmate. It refers to the one hundred fifty stitches it requires to sew up the slice made to the man's face. It is specifically done to the face so everyone who comes in contact with that inmate knows that he's a rat.

"You spend three days down here, for the sake of appearances. We give you a job up there so you basically have free-reign, contact visits whenever you want. Life could be really good. Everything stays in place when you come back after sentencing."

"What if I win?"

The lieutenant laughed but there was no humor in it. "There is no way you are not coming back here."

JG shrugged. "I'll give it some thought and get back to you. I'll leave a message."

"No, wise-guy. You'll decide right now. I'll make sure Loder doesn't want to testify, though he probably wouldn't anyway. Fuckin' criminal baffle me. The only code of ethics is inside these walls. Anyway, he'll be relocated to a different pod, so you won't even see him again. You tell me now what it's gonna be. If you accept, you go back up there in three days."

"If I get found out? What then?"

"We PC you."

"Protective Custody? How lovely."

154

"Then don't get found out."
"What a deal."

20

THE TRIAL WAS DRAWING EVER NEARER, THE TIME PROVIDED BY Judge McCaglia was nearing the end. With only a week and a half to go, there was still too much to learn, too much to do, and the minutes were ticking off on the proverbial bomb. Warren had called Ryan to set up another meeting, only it took a few days to arrange, and it was not at a bar this time. This was no time for a drunk, a hangover, or the like; time was a-wasting and this was a time for action. They just needed a direction. They needed a plan.

With Ryan's busy schedule, they would meet at the law office. Ryan was backed up on his other cases and was drowning in work. His now twenty-hour days were wearing on his relationship with his wife Angie as well. They saw each other at the office, but they had agreed a long time ago that work was work, and home was home.

Paperwork and assorted law books were stacked on top of file folders which were stacked on top of every hard surface. It looked like a scene from *hoarders*, with piles and piles of somehow-organized chaos. Ryan was diligent in his work behind one such pile on his desk but remained unseen.

"Ry? You in here?"

He stood up, revealing himself from the chin up behind his current heap. "Yeah, right here. Just move a pile and have a seat."

"I love what you've done with the place. Who's your designer?"

"Sorry, Deni. I'm swamped."

"I see. It looks like an Office Max threw up in here."

"Hey, stop breakin' balls. JG had cases, one of which is on appeal scheduled this week, on top of all of my work. I'm trying to keep this place going and help him get out of this jam at the same time. I get enough ball-breaking at home, I don't need the extra help. There's a system to all of this believe it or not."

"Yeah, I can tell. Get into JG mode, kid. I need help sortin' this out. You told me when we started this that I was supposed to find stuff to help lessen his sentence; dig up some dirt on the vic. I haven't even gotten into the vic yet because for every rock I turn over, all I get is more rocks. I haven't had the time, and my gut tells me it's a dead end anyway."

Ryan didn't respond. Deni made himself a seat before continuing. "Somethin' is wicked odd here, though. And I got way more questions than answers, with only ten days to go."

"I'm sorry I haven't been more helpful, but like I said — "

" —You got a computer under all this? It would be a lot easier to show you rather than have to explain. Besides that, I don't know what I'd be explaining. I have no idea how all this fits together, but it's wicked fucked up, Ry."

"Questions are good, Deni. Questions inject reasonable doubt. Reasonable doubt in a trial is our best friend. My computer is buried, here's my laptop. Give me a sec while it boots up."

When it booted up, the bells and whistles that indicated he had email were going off. Out of habit, he opened it and glanced at them. Most of them could wait, but one caught his eye.

"Huh. Deni, look at this."

He made his way around the debris, looked over Ryan's shoulder to see an email that said:

Subject: About Jacob Grantes. Urgent.

"You recognize the address, Ry?"

"No." He then opened the email, which revealed a long, complicated web address in the body of the email. "Should I open it? What if it's a virus, or a prank, or something?"

"Click it."

Ryan clicked on the blue, underlined address and a video panel appeared on his screen. After a few seconds of blank screen, a dark bar room appeared in black and white. It was busy with people moving about the small screen. It was virtually indecipherable what they were seeing. The picture was grainy in addition to the establishment being busy.

"Can you make it bigger? I can't see shit," Deni said.

157

Ryan maximized the video screen to fill his laptop screen. The picture was still grayscaled and blurry with distorted pixels, but the overall image was a little easier to interpret."

"That's Sully's isn't it?" Ryan was staring at the video in squinted disbelief.

"It sure is, kid. It's hard to tell but I think that's our boy sittin' at the bar."

They looked at each other and said at the same time, "The surveillance video."

"The missin' CCTV video," Deni added as if it needed to be said.

"It's not missing, Deni. It's right here." Ryan was still unaware that both Jenna and the video were in the wind.

"That's one of the things I was gonna talk to you about. Jenna took the video from Sully's and then vanished. She never went back. But here it is. Why did she steal it? If what she said was true, that she only served him two Stones, why run? And then here it is emailed to you? Why disappear with it and then send it to you? I'm even more confused."

"Jenna is gone?"

They were speaking while watching the video. The person who looked like JG, likely *was* JG, had just received a call on his cell phone which he answered. The phone call was short, he hung up and then left his bar stool.

"This is probably when Jenna said he left to go to the bathroom. And yes, she's gone, Ry. Cleaned out her place. Took the fuckin' ice cube trays. Who does that?"

"Whoa, whoa, whoa. Who's that?" Ryan pointed to a woman with her back to the camera. She had a white, adjustable cap on with a long ponytail pulled through the opening in the back. It was impossible to tell what color her hair was, as the picture was in black and white but it certainly seemed light in color. The petite woman was moving like greased lightning toward the empty bar stool, and the unattended beer on the bar top.

"Do we have another angle on that? I'd love to see this chicks face," Deni said.

"No this is it. What in holy hell? Did she just put something in his beer? Look, her hand goes right over it, but I can't tell."

"That's why you never leave your drink. If ya do, this is what happens. If ya don't wanna bring your drink to the head, you should at least put a coaster over it so it's harder to mess with on the sly," Deni explained.

Ryan rewound and played that section of the video over and over again, ignoring the life-tip. It was impossible to tell who the female was, or if she did in fact doctor the unattended beer. He hit pause at the exact moment her hand was over the pint glass before asking, "Is that Jenna? Hair color seems light for Jenna, but I don't see her behind the bar. She was working that night and this is when she said she was finished for the night. She headed over to the charity event from here, right?"

"Yeah, she did. But there's more to this than just that. Why would she send you the video of her juicin' his juice?"

"How do you know she sent this?"

"The owner and manager said that the disk that this video was stored on, was in the same spot in the office for six months. It was in a desk drawer or somethin'. Then, just when Jenna quits without notice, she shuts off her phone, moves, and the video is gone too. Who else has it? If she didn't send it, who did?"

"OK, fair enough. So let's say she sent it. If that is her in the video, why would she send it?"

Deni shrugged. "Either she is thumbin' her fuckin' nose at us, or that ain't her. She might be involved though, and dimin' out the person who did."

"Why would she 'dime' someone out?"

"She took off, which means she's scared, Ry. You heard her say she was leavin'. She came into money or somethin' and screwed. It doesn't look like her on video, but it's next to impossible to tell. Unless she wore a wig, or died her hair lighter, then died it back …. Which seems less likely. Plus … "

"Plus what, Deni?"

"Plus, Anna wasn't at the charity event that night. At least not all night. She picked up Brady from the Destriers, which means she couldn't be in two places at one time."

"Ho-ly shit. You're sure? No doubts?"

"I've got the video from the gate right here, and I found the maid who confirmed it. She said she told people, but nobody listened. They pushed her out because of what she could say. I think Cammy, er, Cam …. Chamille Destrier is involved."

"Jesus, you've been busy. Chamille Destrier; rich as all hell, Chamille Destrier, who I just heard you call Cammy by the way, is involved? How? Why? She's completely nuts, right?"

"I'm not sure exactly how, but she had to cover for Anna that night. There is no way the planner of the event leaves the big party without someone noticing unless she has cover. Cam was at the event, so the doser in this video wasn't her. And the maid. She got rid of the maid and sat on this gate footage. They're really good friends, right?"

"Yes, great friends for years. But that means that you think Anna is in this too," Ryan added.

"I don't like thinkin' that way but, ok, maybe she is. Two weird things with her besides her vanishing."

"She wasn't at the event all night like she said she was, that's one. Which is a pretty good trick, because I was there with Ang and we had no idea she wasn't there all night. I would have testified under oath, given her an alibi, if she would have asked or needed one."

"That woulda been good," Deni said.

"Yeah well, why would anybody accuse of her of anything? This seemed like a pretty simple case from the jump."

"Yeah well, it gets weirder, Ry."

"There was more? What am I missing?"

"She bought the burner phone."

"What? No way. She made the 911 call? Anna? I don't believe it." Ryan was shaking his head.

"I'm not sayin' she made the call, I'm sayin' she bought the phone. With cash. And she didn't activate any personal information when she activated the phone. Why go all the way to Nashua to buy an anonymous burner phone? There are plenty of places to buy one right here in Wayland."

"So what are we saying? I'm stunned here. What does all of this mean? One of these, or all of these ladies, dump something into his drink so he would drive off the road and kill himself? And instead he kills some poor Brazilian lady? Is that what we are saying? Are we saying that JG is *innocent* in all of this?"

"What I'm saying is that after seein' that email, that I think there is a strong possibility that someone dropped a Ruphie in JG's drink. He was given Rohypnol, if I had to guess. The date-rape drug. It kinda makes sense now that you look at it. He can't remember anything, it takes fifteen minutes or so to work, kinda puts it all in perspective. I'm saying that Anna calls him while he's at the bar, or somebody does, and says 'go home and put on a tux, muffin, Brady's covered. Come to the party.' Jenna, or somebody, waits for the poor prick to use the head and slips him the Mickey."

"I didn't think that it was legal to buy Rohypnol in the U.S., they took it off the market didn't they? Does it show up on a breathalyzer test?"

"It's not legal, but it's easy to get because it's still prescribed as a Valium substitute in countries like *Brazil*. And no, it doesn't show up on most tests. Nobody even thinks to test for it on guys, because nobody gives the date rape drug to a dude. At least usually."

"There's no way it's still in his system, and you can't tell from the video for sure. If that's even what happened. How do we prove it?"

Deni tapped Ryan on the shoulder. "I thought you said that reasonable doubt was our friend? We're runnin' out of time but I think we can shove this up that fat-fuck-prosecutor's ass. What are you thinkin'?" Deni was beginning to feel under-appreciated.

"I'm thinking that we don't have authentication, that we have no chain of evidence, and we don't know for sure that is what happened, and we most definitely can't prove it," Ryan said.

"She wasn't blessing the beer in the name of the Lord, Ry. She wasn't just waving her hand over it. She did something to the drink."

"Nevertheless, I'm thinking that I would like to have this conversation with Anna, or with Jenna, and find out if Chamille Destrier is financing this project and why. You're right, we don't have much time so where do we go from here?"

Deni shook his head. "If I go back to Cammy's, that's an all-day event and we don't have the time. Plus she'll just deny it. She's bored and this is probably just some kinda game for her. Jenna, we find Jenna."

"What about Anna? If she's mixed up in this, we're going to need to find her. Poor Brady."

"Yeah, I get it. Poor kid. We'll get to Anna at some point, but she has resources. She's gonna be tough to find. Jenna, she ain't got shit. She just came into money because somebody is payin' her bills, and she was the last to leave town so the trail is more fresh. I find her and maybe she rolls over on the others."

"OK, I'm with you," Ryan agreed. Sounds reasonable. You called the other day asking about the cars, what's up with that? You said Anna drove the SUV last?"

"Yeah, it looks that way. I still don't know where that fits in, but yeah. Did they impound the car to run tests on it, so she had to drive it home?"

"No, it was parked and the police ran their tests where it was. I'll double check, but I'm pretty sure that it didn't move."

"Then she drove it. After he did or somethin', but the seats were, like, on top of the steering wheel. She might be five-seven or what-not, but no six-one dude drove with the seat that close. The back seat was a mess like Brady had a play date back there. A DVD and the whole nine. The only thing missing was the bouncy room."

"So she used that SUV after the accident. Why? She had an identical one that wasn't in an accident."

"I'm not sure, Ry. That's why I called you. Why would you use a mangled ride, if you've got a fresh one that looks like it came off the showroom floor right next to it? If I get the chance I'll ask her. Here, take these videos, the receipt from Sully's, and the address of the maid." Deni handed the attorney all of the evidence he had in his possession. "One thing's for sure, buddy. In this day and age — everyone is on video, all the time. You can't escape it."

21

THE USUAL CONNECTIONS AND METHODS WEREN'T WORKING for Deni. Whomever was financing Jenna's clandestine operation and new home, was very good and had more resources than he could muster. Which said a lot. Deni knew a lot of people. And she most certainly had to have had help, he thought. She may have made a very good income from her tip jar, but to dump one life for another is expensive.

People move all the time. They hire movers, buy boxes, a moving truck, all of which costs money. People who move out of one area and into another need to switch bank accounts, get new jobs, and otherwise leave a trail for someone to follow. Should that someone be interested in following said trail, it wasn't usually this difficult. But Jenna hadn't left a single crumb.

She was alone and must have moved in the middle of the night. No friends to help her move, nobody to confide in, nobody to keep her new location a secret. He checked. All of her friends seemed to be as shocked by her sudden absence as Deni. Professional movers must have come in the middle of the night, quietly moved all of Jenna's belongings to her new location. But there was no sign of it and no record that any of the local moving companies had taken on the job. There weren't any tire marks left from a big moving truck, nor fibers from moving blankets, or scuff-marks on the walls from hand carts or furniture. The neighbors looked befuddled when asked about the move and would have sworn on a stack of bibles that the quiet bartender still lived there. She was apparently in the place one day, and without a sound or trace, was gone the next. Along with all of her belongings up to and including the ice cube trays.

Vanished.

The house she lived in was rented. The owner of the property said that she was paid through the end of the year. When asked if she always paid her rent in advance, the landlord said, "She said she would be traveling a lot for work and wanted to make sure the lease was taken care of."

Warren asked the landlord if he was aware the place was completely empty, that the place could easily be re-rented to someone else at that very moment. He replied, "I wasn't aware of it, but people can live anyway they wanted to, with furniture or not. It's illegal to double-dip on the rent, so I won't rent it out again until the lease is up. I'm fine with it. She's probably just traveling, like she said." In other words, he was no help whatsoever.

The Post Office had no change of address form on file, he had one of his contacts look into it for him. She therefore no longer needed to receive mail. People were admittedly using snail-mail with less frequency, going green or whatever. But no mail of any kind and no change of address? That was very hard to accomplish and very much intentional.

He looked into her finances extensively, diving in like a forensic accountant though he didn't have the degree. The VW Passat that should have been parked in her driveway was leased through Volkswagen Financial Services. The car was paid off in full the month prior. This was further evidence that there was planning involved. And money.

A look at her other bank accounts and credit reports divulged no leads either. She didn't apply for any new credit cards in planning her new life; no new apartment lease, no major purchases, no new bank account. Her old credit cards were paid off and closed. She had cash and she was well funded.

All of this digging took time. Phone calls were made, contacts returning those calls with anything but answers. Visits were made, which meant travel throughout New England. Time was ticking away. Days were used up with nothing to show for it other than added miles to an already limping Cadillac *Escalade*.

He had an idea who had the deep pockets, but he was still unsure why. The three women seemed an odd trio. Chamille and Anna had been friends for years, since college as the story went. Both women were rich, but Mrs. Destrier was ridiculously so. Anna's only plausible motive for being involved in this was that she thought her husband, JG, was unfaithful. The woman with whom he was believed to be having an affair was the third woman in this odd team, an affair which Jenna denied. Chamille Destrier was Anna's friend and would help her through this time, though her views on adultery were obviously a bit more enlightened. *So where does Jenna fit in? Did Anna and Cammy hatch this scheme, setting Jenna up to be the fall-guy? The patsy? If so, why were they financing her new life?* All of these thoughts were rattling about his brain, yet his gray-matter wasn't manifesting any answers.

Deni spent days on all of this, reviewing these questions again and again. There was less than a week left before the trial and he was in the dark. He would have to suck it up and pay Mrs. Destrier another visit. While the exercise would be fun, he didn't want to be played. He would have to go in there blind and hope she would be willing to spill her guts about what the hell was going on in this case. Was the original plan to kill JG, but the plan went haywire? Make it look like an accident, but the wrong person was in the wrong place at the wrong time? If Cammy was involved, why would she admit to this scheme? The rich bitch had lawyers, of that he was sure.

There's only one way to find out, he thought. He headed over to the Destrier Estate on a crisp, early Saturday morning. He was hoping to catch Chamille off-guard with the early hour, though he knew he would be made to wait until she'd had her coffee and was well awake. Nigel would make sure of it.

The gate was closed, of course, but the white button on the security system was there and waiting.

"Good Morning, sir. Are you aware that it is not yet 8:00 AM? A bit of an early time to call, yes?"

"I need to see Cam, er, Missus Destrier. It's an emergency."

"Yes, well, you seem to be experiencing many emergencies with regard to Missus Destrier as of late. You said as much the last time you were here, I believe, which was decidedly not an emergency."

"Just ask her if she'll see me. It really isn't up to you, Nige, is it?"

"I believe it bloody-well is, sir. It is my job to ensure that her schedule is kept and that undesirables are kept at bay." The nancy-boy's dander was up, Deni thought he like it.

"Why don't you ask her what she desires, Nige. You said yourself on my last trip here that I've been elevated or whatever. So go ask her how desirable I am."

"My name is Nigel, not whatever basterdisation you might come up with on a whim."

"Sorry, Nige. Just go and tell her that I need to see her again. You can stick around for the show if ya want."

"I'm not going to even dignify …. I cannot speak to her right now, nor would I even If I could. She is on holiday. She will be for some time. Now please go."

"It's not a holiday. Oh shit, you mean on vacation."

"And the dawn breaks. She is not here, nor will she be in the immediate or near future."

"Where'd she go?"

"I'm afraid I cannot say. Would you like to schedule an appointment for when she returns?"

"Uh, yeah, yeah. I would like to *shed-yule*," Deni said. "What date are we looking at for her return?"

"If you will leave me your contact information, I will be in touch with a date and time when she returns. I can queue you up at that time, though I'm afraid I cannot be more specific just now."

"Never mind. Hey, Nige?"

"Yes?"

"You better hope I never see you out on the streets."

"Very good, sir. You will do what you must, and I will do the same. Good day." With that, the other end went dead.

Deni sat at the gate for a while in thought, his warm Escalade idling. He'd finally gotten a rise out of the English bloke, which made him happy. But as far as the investigation was going, he was at a loss. That didn't make him happy. Anna, gone. Jenna, gone. Cammy, now gone.

Are they all in the same place? Probably sitting on a beach somewhere, at a bar with a straw roof, drinking some exotic drink together, having a laugh. Job well-done ladies. You didn't kill him, but you killed him.

22

THE MONDAY BEFORE THE TRIAL; RYAN AMASSED ALL OF HIS courage, compiled all the information Warren had uncovered, coming up with a succinct presentation, and headed to the WCHOC. With a week remaining before the big show, he needed to let his friend and client know where they were with his case. Most of what they had was supposition. Theory. Would it amount to reasonable doubt in the eyes of a jury? Not likely. Who would believe that a wealthy woman suspected her husband of sleeping around, conspiring to kill him with another and more wealthy friend and the woman her husband was caught cheating with, making it look like an accident? And in the execution of that plan, an innocent bystander was killed. This is the stuff in movies. Or books. This stuff didn't happen in stuffy Wayland, New Hampshire.

The case-law Ryan looked up concerning illegal immigrants obtaining driver's licenses, and the motor vehicle infractions surrounding it, was murky at best. Whether a person whom had questionable immigration status should be able to have a license was politically debatable, but if the driver had a valid license was the crux of the issue, they had a legal right to be on the road. In this case, Arelia Diaz did have a valid license. The Department of Motor Vehicles works their own agenda, with their own timetable. End of story. If it was proven that Jacob Grantes was indeed too impaired to drive, then who was on the road was of little consequence. If Diaz hadn't been on the road, another innocent would have been. Two wrongs didn't make a right. His actions were reckless. This was not an avenue for defense that they could win. In legal terms, it is Depraved Indifference, meaning if not but for his actions, a woman would still be alive—whether she was legally allowed to be on the road or not. It wouldn't even affect sentencing if, or likely when, he was convicted.

The usual security drill at the prison of x-raying the briefcase, the metal detectors, and pat-downs took place, only there was an unusual and excruciatingly long wait in the conference room. Ryan asked several times where his client was, had even called ahead so they could have JG waiting for him. Instead, it was Ryan who was waiting. And waiting. This was not the same long wait. Something was wrong. As the second hour approached, Ryan was freaking out. He was about to get up and complain for the umpteenth time, and likely ignored for the umpteenth time, when Grantes was pushed into the room.

"Oh, thank God you're ok. I was getting nervous. Nobody would tell me anything. I didn't think the prison was that big. What the hell is going on?"

"It's nice to see you, too. Been waiting long?"

"Yes, like two hours. It was pretty irritating, then upsetting because I thought something happened to you."

"You poor baby. I have to go through this shit every fucking day, Ry."

"Hey JG - let's not go there. I'm glad you're ok, ok? I'm here to tell you where we are and what we're going with. We're back in court on Monday, so we need to discuss our options. Which isn't good. Not horrible, but not very good either. You look like shit, no offense. You need anything?"

"I need many things, Ry." He sat back in his chair, drained.

"Like what? I'm here to help you in any way I can."

"I just got out of The Hole. I need a bath, some daylight, some exercise. What I need is to get the fuck out of here." He leaned back forward, putting his head in his hands. After a long pause, he continued. "Do have an Attorney of Record form, or a Client Agreement form on you?"

"Of course, why?"

"I need as many copies as you have."

Ryan dug into his briefcase, retrieving his only two copies. He also withdrew a manilla envelope pre-stamped with a red 'CONFIDENTIAL' on it. He then put the documents inside the envelope and handed it to JG. COs can't touch confidential material. Attorney/Client privilege is a sacrosanct right, even in prison.

"Grabbing a few new clients while you're here?"

"Just surviving, man."

"Anyway, we're going to put our best foot forward to get you out of here. Just hang in there."

"Am I getting out of here, Ry? I mean really? Give it to me straight."

"It's all smoke and mirrors, but yes, that is still the goal. We're going to prove that; yes, you were banged up, but that it wasn't your fault. New evidence shows that you were induced, and we prove that you did do all the things that you were accused of, but that you had help."

"I'm listening. Start from the beginning. Who helped and how?"

"We're going with your wife set all of this up, because she thought you were having an affair. She used her friend Chamille Destrier to help finance this entire project off the books, and Jenna is involved in this somehow also. We are going to say that the three of them conspired to, and this is where it gets tough for you to hear ....They conspired to kill you. They slipped you a drug, Rohypnol we're thinking—given the symptoms, and you'd drive off the road and kill yourself. Instead, you almost hit the woman who died, forcing her to veer off the road. You hit a tree but kept right on going and slept it off at home where the cops found you."

"A jury is going to wonder why my wife set up a plan to kill her own son along with me. I picked up Brady, he was in the back seat when all of this happened."

"No, he was not. We have proof that you never saw Brady that night. You, in fact, received a phone call telling you not to go get him at the bar before you were Ruphied. You don't remember that though, right?"

"No, not at all. I remember most of what happened at the bar, leaving was a blur."

"Yeah well, we have your cell records. We also have a video showing that somebody, probably Jenna, drugged you at Sully's, so it's no wonder you don't remember. Anna picked up Brady from Chamille Destrier's, and then dropped him off at your house so he was there when the police arrived."

"I thought she was at the charity event?"

"Chamille covered for her. Anna left and came back, nobody knew the difference."

"Hmm. If I was supposed to go off the road and kill myself, how was she going to explain Brady being home alone? This doesn't make sense, even to me."

"That's the point. Brady was never going to be in any danger. Jenna was the babysitter, right? She followed you out of the bar and was supposed to run you off the road but this Arelia Diaz mucked up the works. She said that she was going to the event, right? But she never did. I certainly don't remember seeing her there. Brady would have been home with Jenna. But instead, all hell breaks lose. They now have to scramble with a quick Plan B because you don't die. Some innocent bystander does.   This is proven because they tried to hide the housekeeper that knew you didn't pick the boy up. The 911 call diming you out was from a phone bought by Anna at a mall in Nashua. She probably gave it to Jenna to make the call, or made the call herself."

"I can't believe it. Jenna seemed so sweet. I thought she genuinely cared about Brady, she was so good with him."

"We spoke with her and she seemed really into you as well. But facts are facts. Remember, this wasn't about Brady, it was about you. She's gone. Anna's gone. Camille's gone. They're all gone. They're probably on a private island enjoying the shit out of themselves right about now. Anna, we believe, paid her to get close to you. The whole thing was fake."

"No way, Ry.   Now I know you're full of shit.   Anna has an extremely low threshold for cheating. Her dad was big cheater. He had multiple kids, with multiple women. I'm not supposed to know that, but I know. There is no way she set me up with someone to cheat with, and I didn't anyway. Jenna couldn't have had anything to do with this. At least she isn't working with Anna. No way in hell. I just don't believe it."

"She's gone, buddy.   She fled in the middle of the fucking night. Planned to leave, she told us about it. Me and Deni. She steals the CCTV footage from the bar where she works, which shows you getting drugged, then leaves without even picking up the money that is owed to her. She has cash and she's using it to stay hidden. Who do you think is financing her? Anna. Or Chamille. Or both. But any way you slice it, she looks guilty as sin."

"If she's missing, it's because she is dead. I'm telling you, there is no way that Anna partners up with a woman who she thinks that I had an affair with. I know the woman. She would kill her, maybe, but she is not going to buddy up with her. That's dead. No way."

"You know her so well, huh? She tried to kill you. Did you see that coming?"

"Because she thought I was cheating. I understand it. She is bat-shit crazy and wrong, but I understand it. Jenna I don't understand. Maybe she was played, like me. But I am telling you that you have it wrong if you think Anna and Jenna are in this together. I'll go along to see what we can do about getting me out of here, reasonable doubt is our best friend right now, but there is no way. I guarantee we're going to find a body. Sooner or later someone is going to uncover a body, and it is going to be poor Jenna."

"There's one last piece that we cannot figure out, for the life of us. We just don't know how it fits. It's small but it is bugging Deni, and it's also bugging me the more he harps on it. The SUV you used as a bumper-car off a tree hasn't moved since the police went over it when you were arrested. Documented, I checked and rechecked. But all the presets for the seats and mirrors were set up for Anna. Preset number two. For a short person, shorter than you anyway. If not Anna, who else would drive your car? Jenna?"

"So she drove the car last? Is that what you are saying?"

"Either she did, or Jenna, or someone shorter than you. But it seems more likely it was her. Jenna is taller than Anna by at least an inch,maybe two. Five-nine. Anna's SUV has all the same presets, only hers are set for number one. So she was the last to drive both vehicles. What if she picked up Brady in your SUV?"

"Then how did I get home?"

"I don't know, like I said, I can't figure it out. Deni's baffled as well. But, and I'm just spit-balling here, what if you drove Anna's SUV home? They match, how would you know the difference?"

"You don't think I would be able to tell my own vehicle over my wife's, Ryan?"

"I don't know. You were pretty out of it, and it's the exact same car. The presets are just a touch of a button. One button and everything including the radio station is set for you. Is it plausible? Can we use it in court? I don't know, but it's worth a try."

"So I don't get in any wreck, is what you are saying. I'm banged up but I make it home, alone, and pass out with my own son upstairs? I don't remember much from that night, no matter how much I rack my brain. So I would say sure, why not? She would have had to switch car keys also. She would have had to change them out between my leaving for work and then driving home after the bar. Presets alone aren't going to impress a jury."

"Good point. I just thought of all this right now, as we were talking, so I haven't discussed it with Deni yet, but I will. Look, I'm not going to sugar coat it. This what we're going with, in the hopes that a jury will buy it. But I wouldn't hold out too much hope that you walk away from this free and clear. Like I keep saying, it's still the goal. But a lady is dead and somebody has to pay for it. Deni's trying to locate the people we're claiming to be responsible for it, but without a little more than smoke and mirrors and a whole lot question marks, it's going to be tough to win. Finger-pointing is a long shot anyway, but without an actual person that the jury can see, to point at? The entire exercise becomes academic."

"I get it. I've done this before. I'm just not used to being on this end of things, though I'm getting there."

"Mull this all over and get your head around it before Monday. Reasonable doubt. That's all we got."

"Look, we have to sell it but it doesn't mean I have to believe it."

"Of course not, JG. But Jesus, it helps.

23

WHILE RYAN WAS TRYING TO LIFT THE SPIRITS OF HIS FRIEND and business partner, Warren was calling upon yet another one of his friends. This friend was of the female persuasion. Again. He needed access to computer skills that he did not possess. The website and email to Ryan with the CCTV footage of Sully's the night of the crash came from someplace. Someone either wanted to help JG out or send the investigation off-course. None of the people he had been looking for were coming to the surface. Anna. Camille. Jenna. His last-best hope was tracking down the web address. Deni knew that it could be done, he also knew he was not the person to do it. However he did know just the person, with just the skill set required for the job, which was just as important. Her phone was picked up on the second ring.

"Althea. It's Deni. Whattaya doin'?"

"No plans, why. Are you in Boston? I can barely hear you."

"I'm in the car, on my way to you."

"Now? It's 11:00 AM. I work nine to five, you know that. What is this? I don't see you for forever then you darken my doorstep twice in a month. What do you need this time?"

"Nothin'. I just wanna see you." He was not necessarily a smooth guy, but he was going to need to be smooth here.

"On a Monday morning out of the blue? Why am I not buying this? At any rate, a little warning would have been nice. I'm at work, and I look a mess."

"I doubt that."

"I work behind a computer all day, there's no reason to get dolled up."

"Bail outta work. We can spend the whole day together. I want to thank you for your help the other day."

"I feel a cold coming on. Do you remember where I live?"

"Yeah, you're in the same spot?"

"Same one. The complex in Natick. Give me a couple of hours and I'll get into something clingy."

"Cool."

The drive wouldn't take the two hours Althea was looking for, and he wasn't planning on giving them to her either. The trial was just around the corner and neither he nor Ryan were entirely satisfied with where the investigation was at this point. Too many pieces were still missing, too many people were missing. Everybody, in fact. He was flying south on the interstate to rectify this situation, never one to follow the rules, nor the speed limit.

Deni was back in Natick, Massachusetts in short order. Althea's apartment complex was exactly like a million others scattered about the Country, with virtually the same layout and made of virtually the same materials. The brick building was five floors high, nondescript with a large parking lot, outdoor swimming pool, which was set on the side of the building, hidden by a fence. It was nothing fancy, though it was just located in Natick. That and the name of the place gave justification for higher-than-market value pricing. 'The Bluff at the Edgewater' sounded the part, but wasn't in actuality.

Though she requested they meet at her illustrious apartment complex in two hours, he was on-location in a mere one hour and twenty-five minutes. Warren dilly-dallied. The knock on the door went unanswered after several attempts. He was about to retrieve his iPhone out of his pocket to call her when he heard the chain rattling on the other side of the door. She opened it in a huff as she stood before him soaking wet, wrapped in a thirsty towel. The ends of her hair strands had droplets clinging to them like dewfall.

"I said a couple of hours, I am nowhere near ready. I just got here myself a few minutes ago."

He didn't respond, he pushed through the open door which closed itself much like a hotel door. Althea's frustration melted away almost as soon as he walked through the door. She put on a big smile, her eyes big with excitement as well.

"Well at least give me a few minutes to put on my face and get dressed. What are we doing anyway? I don't know what to wear."

She padded down the short hallway to the same bedroom they'd both shared for many nights, once upon a time. She'd been in love with him back then and it was clear that her feelings for him hadn't changed. Althea had told him many times before that there was something about his rugged good looks and his ubermanliness. Even when he was a cop, he reeked of Southie bad-boy. His lean, muscular, tattoo-cloaked body turned her on the way no other had before or since.

"I thought we could get somethin' to eat, for starters. You hungry?"

"I could eat. Grab a seat on the couch, I'll be out in a few."

Deni had no intention of waiting in the living room. The smell of Indian or some other ethnic food was wafting in from another apartment, and was making him sick to his stomach. He wouldn't have waited on the couch anyway, but that was the excuse he was going to use to go into the bedroom. Smooth.

He knew his former lover's idea of getting dressed and the timeframe it would take to accomplish the feat. Given that the encounter wasn't planned, she would turn her entire wardrobe inside out until the perfect outfit was created. He didn't have the time, nor the patience.

He followed her into the bedroom, stopping at the threshold, leaning on the doorjamb.

"It stinks out there. How can you live next to these people?"

He startled her as she was drying her hair and body in the mirror, not noticing his presence on the threshold. She covered her naked body. She spoke to him with her back turned, but spying him in the mirror.

"Hey. A little privacy please. You've always complained about the neighbors and you've always dealt with it before. You're a tough guy, tough it out."

He walked into the room, approached behind her, and started to kiss her on the base of the neck from behind.

"Ah hell. We aren't going anywhere are we? This is a booty-call." She turned to face him, the towel dropped to the floor. They had been in this very room many a night before, she had spent many a night in it fantasizing about him since. When fortified with alcohol, she would call or text him to admit to just that.

"After," he said. He whispered in her ear, one hand on her lower back and the other pulling the wet hair from her eyes.

"Take your time," she whispered back.

Afterward, Althea was using Deni's right bicep as a pillow. Deni was staring at the ceiling, Althea was staring at him.

"Was that the only reason you pulled me out of work today? Or was there something else? She covered herself with the wrinkled sheet that was miraculously still on the bed, the way women who are suddenly embarrassed or uncomfortable will cover themselves. "I should have known when you called. You know I had a ton of stuff to do at work today."

"Are you complaining? You said call anytime."

"No, I'm not complaining. I just thought we were going on a real date. I was looking forward to it."

"What, for like, the hour after I called?"

"No, asshole. For, *like*, the entire time since we broke up."

"I'll take you out, we'll do somethin' fun. I'm just wicked busy with a case right now."

"Same case as the 911 call? Your friend?"

"Yeah. And I could use your advice. Well, your expertise."

"Ah-ha. I knew it. You needed my help, and why not get a piece of ass in the bargain? You are a complete asshole."

"I came for the help. You were naked, I got caught up. Just think of all the shit I will owe you when we do go out."

"You better know you're taking me someplace nice. Not *Legal Sea Foods* nice, someplace *really* nice. And don't even think about *Capital Grille,* either."

"What about *Abe and Louis*?"

"Getting closer, but I'm talking places like *Mistral,* or *Clio*, or *Radius*. I mean celebrity chef expensive. Somewhere Downtown. Someplace super expensive with wine and the works."

"Deal. Now can you look at my computer problem? We get this done and we can go have lunch someplace. And, no, it won't count as the date I owe you."

"Go wait in the living room while I get dressed. For real this time. Plug your nose or whatever, but I'll be out in a minute."

"A real minute? 'Cuz I really don't have a whole lotta—"

"—Just so you're aware that I'm aware, this is like extortion or something. Using sex for favors is illegal. As an ex-cop you should know this."

"Whatever. Turn me in."

******

Althea is a woman with many talents. Warren was thinking this as he was driving away from Natick, without having lunch as promised, but fortified with information. *She's wasting her gifts with computers*, he thought. Working in the IT department at NEESI was beneath her. He had no idea what skills were required of a truly great hacker, but was sure that Althea possessed them.

He explained that the email containing the CCTV footage from Sully's Tavern was crucial evidence; that just like the 911 call, the sender wished to remain anonymous, a detail in which he could not abide.

She understood his dilemma and was willing to help him, but was struggling with helping a drunk driver. She loved her bad-boy; but because of her work, she had heard and seen the devastation from so many drunk drivers that she was reluctant to help. Once it was explained, even if inaccurate, that he was drugged and set up, she sat down at her computer and hammered away at the keys.

"In theory, you can determine a physical address from an IP address. But it's not always that simple. If the person is emphatic about staying well-cloaked, they could spoof the IP address or may be behind a proxy. If they were that clever, it'll be much more difficult," she said.

"I don't know what any of that means. Can you give me the physical address or not?"

She explained that the email was like a footprint. And that all web addresses, and emails, leave these footprints. She further explained that when people use software to eliminate those footprints, you have to be able to decode and deactivate that software. She spouted off more of what he thought to be gibberish while she typed furiously on her computer.

At one point, while Deni helped himself to a drink from her kitchen, she said that she was inside the sending computer, or at least that is what he understood her to say. She was enjoying her work. He sat back down and watched her delve into someone's computer, maybe their life. If it was illegal, he didn't care. Nor did she, apparently.

After what turned out to be relatively short work, she sat back in her chair, turning toward him, grinning like the cat that swallowed the canary. She had his information. She was clever and they both knew it.

He now called Ryan from his Escalade, while he negotiated his way east on the Mass Pike.

"Ry, these bitches are startin' to piss me off. I think I found them though."

"What are you talking about, Deni? I've heard that tone in your voice before and you're scaring me. This is the second time today I've nearly had a heart attack. JG is — "

" — I'm on my way to the airport. I gotta catch a flight outta Logan as soon as I can."

"What? Slow down. We only have a week, *this* week. Where are you going?"

"I'm not taking a fuckin' vacation, guy. I'm going to Charleston."

"Wait, what? If you're in Boston, why are you flying to Charlestown?"

"NO. Not Charlestown, Charleston. South Carolina."

"You're accent makes that an easy mistake, Deni, don't get pissy. What's up in Charleston?"

"I found 'em. Those bitches are probably all laughin' and pushin' each other in the bushes, making fun of us. But I got 'em now. We caught 'em."

"I hope you do. Seriously. JG is cracking up. He spends his time in Solitary, then comes out and wants to take clients in prison. I laid out the plan and he didn't seem to care. I think he's giving up. We're losing him."

"One thing at a time, Ry. Let's get him outta prison before we commit him to a rubber room."

He then explained that he had a contact that helped him locate the address in South Carolina from the email sent to him. He left out whom the information had come from, which was not at all unusual. In fact, it was the norm and the firm's preference.

"Just keep in mind that the video was helpful. I'm not sure what game they're playing, but without that video we would still be in the dark. I'm not sure if they're sinners or saints."

"I'll keep you posted."

"Do that. And let me know if I can help."

Warren didn't reply, he just hung up. He sincerely hoped that the two hour flight would help to calm him down.

24

OF COURSE THE LAST AVAILABLE SEAT, ON THE FIRST FLIGHT OUT of Logan for Charleston, South Carolina, was in first-class. Even the Irish hate that bastard Murphy. And his laws. The outrageous price pulled on a nerve of Warren's and there were too few remaining. He was already heated and hoping the flight would dissipate his rage, but it was not to be. The first available flight was a red-eye that night, which would put him in Charleston in the early morning on Tuesday. And yet another nerve snapped when he came to the realization of just how far first-class had sunk. The airlines had not been stellar at hiding their cutbacks, for what he presumed were for financial reasons. Coach was little more than being packed in a cattle-car like rush hour on the subway. First-class was demoted to what was once just coach.

He was thankful that the drinks were still 'free', so he was determined to get his thirteen hundred dollars worth. Slowly, he began to relax as the alcohol numbed his few remaining nerve strands. There used to be a flight attendant dedicated to those who paid the high price to sit in first-class, but that must have been another cutback. The two working this flight were spread thinly throughout the entire plane, and given the hour of the flight, were hoping for it to be a relaxing one. Deni's repeated calls for more alcohol were met with looks of concern and frustration, but no other exchange.

Upon arrival in Charleston, he made his way to the car rental agencies. He had no luggage, so he made his way cheetah-quick from the jetway to the rental area. The clerk behind the counter informed him of 'very few cars left available', which meant he had to pay yet another surcharge. He got on a bus which transferred him to the Budget parking lot with only four cars left in it, or at least only four cars the employee there was going to show him. The four cars ranged from tiny tin-can to a Flintstone-mobile. After some discussion with the employee, the security guard at the parking lot, and the bus driver, he was brought back to the rental desk by the same bus. Discussion meaning he did a lot of yelling and the Budget employee, the security guard and the bus driver listened. The last nerve snapped.

When he arrived back at the rental desk in the terminal, Deni dragged the man behind the rental desk by the lapels, over the counter to the customer side.

"I need a real fuckin' car. Not a Prius, not a leaf, not a battery operated go-cart, I need a real car. Something that will get out of its own way. When I let go of you, don't even think about chargin' me any extra money, don't get on a phone and call a supervisor, no faces with some hemmin' n hawin'. I want you to put me back on that bus, and when I arrive back on that lot, there had better be a real car waiting. Nod like you understand, cuz if I have to come back here? The kinda day I've had? I'll probably kill you."

Southern hospitality had it's finest hour. His second visit to the rental parking lot was quicker, friendlier, and a black Dodge *Charger* was waiting for him. This was a car that could get out if its own way, it would just have to do it with a six cylinder engine versus an eight. The bus driver didn't stick around for an encore performance. Deni wasted no time getting into the car and driving away. He'd spent enough time in or between airports. The security gate was wide open before Deni approached it, the guard seemed to have had his fill as well.

The GPS on his phone directed him off of Interstate 95 and onto Route 17, which traversed the Ashley River draw bridge, through a nondescript and all but evacuated area, before he came upon the historic and beautiful downtown. The cobblestone streets were lined with shoulder-to-shoulder Georgian townhouses throughout the peninsula, block after block. These historic landmarks nestled in with Louis Vuitton-class storefronts, surrounded by ocean, parks, and restored Civil War cannons facing the coast. It was an absolutely gorgeous city, he thought. Every other building was a postcard, every third a modern retailer or restaurant in a historic building.

While the Bostonians egged on the American Civil War, with their antislavery movement, the first shots of it were fired on Fort Sumter right there in Charleston. Warren found it funny that this little war was also started in the North and would end here in the South; as he stared at a plaque stuck to the side of a cannon on Murray Boulevard, in White Point Gardens. The city was immaculately clean, which was unlike Boston. On the other end of the spectrum if truth be told. In fact, by comparison, Boston was a dumpster fire. The only thing they had in common was lack of parking.

He was forced to park in a metered spot with a two-hour maximum. Deni wondered if the meter-maids chalked the tires like they did in Boston, to penalize those who feed the meter. He also wondered how much was the going rate for a parking ticket in the South, but he knew he was going to find out. It was a rental anyway, he thought, try to find me.

The parking spot was a fair walk from where he wanted to stake out. The meters were along Murray Boulevard, which was fixed between the ocean and the park, he needed to be a few blocks inland. He would not be able to reconnoiter from the comfort and confines of his rental vehicle, he would have to sweat out the heat on foot. West of the gardens were all of the historic mansions overlooking the bay. Somewhere in that cobblestone maze was the address he sought.

Since he would be on foot, and he had no luggage, he was forced to buy some clothing from the shops. Only he had to wait for the shops to open. The trip was already breaking the bank, all being charged onto his soon to be maxed-out credit card. The overpriced couture in The Marketplace on King Street was the icing on the cake. His extravaganza ended with him sporting a Callaway Golf hat, Maui Jim sunglasses, a pink Lacoste alligator shirt (because the gorgeous saleswoman with her southern drawl said he looked hot in it), multicolored shorts from Benetton, and his tan shoes from Aldo. He hated the way he looked with all of his being, but he needed to be unrecognizable, and with this outfit he was. Deni would never in a thousand years be caught dead in what he was wearing, and yet he was. He reckoned he looked like a metrosexual tourist.

After his shopping spree, he walked through the maze of cobblestone streets between the historical mansion-turned-condos. Later, rather than sooner, he found the address with the help of the GPS on his iPhone. The ornate, wrought-iron gate was locked though he could see the gardened walkway beyond it. Set between two, four-storied townhouses, the flora was old-world gorgeous replete with ivy hugging the side of the buildings. The courtyard was painstakingly manicured and elegantly perfumed. He studied the property for a short while, though there was no movement.

"You must be my twelve o'clock." The woman behind him took him by surprise. She, too, had a sweet southern drawl. She was equally manicured, yet casual in her designer business dress. The forty-ish blonde eyed him from head to toe, while he was trying to assess the situation. The pause was almost to a point of awkwardness.

"I'm Faye. The realtor? I spotted you as I was walking down the street, only you're on the wrong side of it, sweetie. The unit for sale is on the other side of the street." She immediately stuck her hand out.

"Oh, right. I know …. I was just checkin' out the neighborhood."

"You're accent is …. Well I guess I didn't pick it up on the phone. It's very intense. Where y'all from?"

"My mom."

"Funny. Right this way, hun. You'll just love Rainbow Row. This property is bright yellow, and as we discussed on the phone, completely restored to keep it's historic beauty, yet updated. Not that it will need it, but any further renovating would require city approval because it is a historic landmark, as are all of these homes."

"Rainbow Row?" He didn't hear anything after Rainbow Row. He thought she was referring to his outfit, which was very colorful. "What are you sayin' lady?"

"All of these houses along East Bay Street are various pastel colors, it's known as Rainbow Row. We talked about this, hun. What'd you think I meant?"

"Oh. I thought you meant somethin' else."

The showing, and the woman would prove to be a pain in the ass. He had to extricate himself from the situation without suspicion while maintaining a surveillance position on the house across the street. There was no activity there as of yet, but there was also no telling what could happen while he was being dragged around what, in truth, was an amazing property. He took extra long pauses at the windows at the front of the house he was supposed to be interested in buying, so he could continue to investigate the inactivity on the other side of the street. Faye must have taken note, for after the third such pause she mentioned the view.

"If you're interested in the view, the estate has a three hundred sixty degree view from the well-appointed roof deck. Would you like to see it?" As if she didn't know.

"Absolutely."

"Usually I would save the best for last, but I can see that you are interested in the breathtaking scenery." They made their way up a wide staircase, opened the oak door onto a massive roof. She was right, the view was breathtaking.

To the East, a mostly unimpeded view of the Atlantic Ocean; only the roof of another historical mansion, the roof of the gazebo in the park, and the tree-line of the park itself marginally obstructed the any portion of the view. The trees and other horticulture made the deck oasis like a prized trophy hoisted toward the sky. Like a small heaven shot up toward that which it emulated.

To the North, the roofs of the estates on the other side of East Bay Street. Warren leaned on the marble rail facing his prey and was disappointed at the lack of observation he would be afforded from that vantage point. The courtyard on the other side of the gate was well hidden for privacy behind the canopy of trees. Only the bird's-eye view of the cobblestone in front of the residence could be studied from where he stood. He was about to turn away, and back to the annoying real estate woman to tell her that the tour was over; when in the panorama, he spied someone walking down the street, toward them on foot. He was some two hundred or so yards away and above, but even at that scalene angle he knew who it was. He would recognize the pedestrian anywhere.

"Well, ok Faye. Thank you very much. I've seen all that I need to, I have your number and we'll be in touch."

She must have responded, but he didn't hear it. He bolted back down the stairs, taking two and three at a time until reaching the bottom floor. If the front door had been locked he would have burst through it like the Kool-aid guy from the commercials. Fortunately it wasn't.

As he was rushing off the property, a bearded man he hadn't seen from above was just outside the door with a briefcase in his hand. This must have been Faye's real appointment. Deni almost ran him over but dodged him in the nick of time. "You're gonna love it, it's fuckin' beautiful."

Once he was beyond the bearded man, he slowed and began to catch his breath as the woman was approaching him not fifteen yards down the street and closing. He was blocking the entrance, the wrought-iron gate, and there was no place to go or hide.

He waved with his hand while he panted. "Hey Jenna."

25

INMATE GRANTES WAS ENJOYING HIS TIME BACK ON THE POD.
Enjoying may be bit of a stretch, but he wasn't in The Hole. Hell is relative. Whether in solitary or on the pod, he had ample time to think and rethink the events leading him to what was his current situation. And his mind was running riot. Fortified with the knowledge, even if just theory, that things concerning his case might possibly to work in his favor. He thought of all of the possibilities. Where once there was complete darkness, now there was at least some point of light off in the distance ahead. A penlight amidst a dark forest, but a light nonetheless. When a man is in prison, that man clings to any hope he can. That hope, however small, is what keeps him sane and alive.

There were questions on the block when he returned from his three days in solitary confinement. When an inmate caves in another's face, a mere three days in The Hole tends to pose some questions. None of them good. Was he a rat? Who did he know? Who did he blow? The Sheriff? All were plied to him, all went unanswered. Instead, he made illegal copies of the form given to him by Ryan and stuffed them under every steel door on the block. Both tiers.

They had given him a job on the block, one that gave him access to the counselor's office, which had a copy machine. That cleaning job, as disgusting as it was, also helped to occupy his days which freed him from being in his cell twenty hours a day. He had freedom to move about the pod, under the guise of having to clean it.

It was the Thursday before his trial, during afternoon rec time, that the Ellis alarm blared at near-deafening volume. That alarm dictated that if you were outside your cell, you were to get on a knee or your face. Somebody was getting lugged. A dozen COs and two German Shepherds poured into the pod like SS troops in full riot gear. Shouts of "get down on your face" and "get the fuck down" and "eat the floor asshole" were shouted over and over, and over the sound of the Ellis alarm. All inmates complied one way or another. The invasion took less than ten-seconds and those who were too frozen in shock to understand the commands were beaten until they figured it out. It was prison, for some it took a while, and some had to learn the hard way.

The officers knew whom they wanted in advance, but there would be a cleanup of fish big and small. Dirty urines had come back on twelve of the last eighteen sampled. Nine had been sampled on Wednesday morning, nine Wednesday night just like they had on every other day before. These last twelve dirties had come back testing positive for Seboxolan.

Seboxolan is an opioid, or more commonly called a narcotic. Big Pharma came up with a drug to cure those who are addicted to drugs. How nice of them. It's prescribed by doctors as an opiate blocker for patients who suffer from addiction to substances like heroine and crack. The fact that doctors who prescribe it often received kick-backs from the pharmaceutical companies who developed it, means that it is very often over prescribed. The drug was developed to deaden the receptors in the brain by filling it with a small amount of a mixed opiate. Those who are not on heroine or crack, can misuse Seboxolan as a primary opiate as it is not blocking another narcotic, but filled the receptors in the brain by overdosing them. The opitate gets into the blood stream faster by crushing and snorting it, rather than taking it in the proper pill form. These pills are snuck into the prison, usually in someone's rectum.

Twelve dirties within twenty-four hours meant that the Sheriff had a problem. The fact that the prison was rife with the drug was bad for him, bad for the prison, and bad for his Federal Funding. Twelve dirties meant a shakedown of massive proportions.

Anything that was in a cell was thrown out of it and into the main part of the pod, used for eating and rec time. Not before being stomped on, shredded, and dog-chewed, however. Anyone unwittingly walking onto the pod would think there was a riot. Both tiers were destroyed. Paper, clothing, wool insulation from the pillows and mattresses were floating in the air like feathers in wont for a place to land. Inmates were buried, face down under the detritus.

Fifty-nine of the one hundred twenty-two men on the pod were lugged that Wednesday. It was heard about and talked about all over the prison, not just on JG's block. That day would henceforth be called by the prisoners Seboxo-gate.

Charges and indictments were being handed out like playing cards, so Grantes' favorite buddy, the lieutenant, came a calling. The ruse that Grantes had a visitor was used to get him off the block, and became an hour-long interrogation.

"Where were you on this one Grantes?"

"On the block. You know that. You guys keep records of where I am at all hours of the day, don't you?"

"What are you a wise-guy now? Don't toy with me, I'm in no mood. I gave you a good deal, kept you from catching more charges. Now you play possum while drugs are rampant right under your nose?"

"Maybe they don't trust me yet."

"Maybe you should start making more of an effort. You dropped the ball big-time, inmate."

Grantes sat there in quiet thought at the last comment. The Lieutenant paced back and forth in the room while the supposed informant sat quietly watching him. It was like JG was a spectator at a tennis match.

"Well?" The lieutenant finally broke the silence.

"Well, what?"

"Well, what do you have to say for yourself?"

"I don't have anything to say. My piss is clean."

"Why didn't you use the phone number I gave you on the card to drop a dime?"

"I didn't need to. You busted the twelve for dirty urines and what, sixty more? What do you need me for?"

"Where did it come from? Who had it and distributed it? Did it go to other pods? That kind of intel. That's what I need from you. Right now."

"I can't say."

"What do you mean you can't say?"

"I mean that I am literally not allowed to say, even if I know. Which I'm not admitting to either."

"I can make your life a living hell here smart-guy. What kinda game are you playing?"

"I'm not playing any game. I *can't* because of privilege, and you can't hurt me because it's illegal under reciprocity."

"What the hell are you talking about, Grantes? You're not a lawyer anymore."

"I haven't been disbarred yet, number one. I'm innocent until proven guilty in our system, a concept this prison is unfamiliar with. Second, I have one hundred and twenty-two signed agreements which make them believe that I am their attorney. It is their belief that makes any of their statements protected under the constitution. Attorney/Client privilege. You must have heard of it. If I 'dropped a dime', as you call it, I *would* be disbarred. I'm sorry I couldn't be of any help to you."

"So you fucked me. Are you admitting to that? You are a useless piece of shit and I can't wait until you are here for good. Time is your enemy, asshole. Too bad for you, I'm not going anywhere."

"I'm not admitting to anything other than being caught up in the middle of a terrible situation. Seboxolan is no joke."

"No, it isn't. We don't have it on the Med Carts here, so we know nobody cheeked it. It had to have come in up someone's ass. When we find out who and when, I am going to make sure that the entire prison pop thinks we found out through you."

"Make me out to be a rat? Good luck with that. By the way, if I get shived; I'm suing the prison, the Sheriff, and you personally for the threat you just gave me."

"Get out of my face!"

"Go back to my clients? All one hundred twenty-two of them or just the sixty you busted?"

"Go back to your cell, asshole."

"Back to my single cell? Ouch. You're a real hard-ass, lieutenant." He got up and made his way to the conference room door. Another CO was there to cuff him, collect him, and bring him to his pod.

"You're ass is mine, Grantes. Sooner or later, I'm gonna nail your ass to the wall."

26

THE SHOCK ON JENNA'S FACE DISAPPEARED ABOUT AS QUICKLY as the big, shit-eating grin on Warren's. Which is to say, it took a hot minute. Both stood in the middle of the cobblestone street, speechless in the early afternoon sun. Deni was catching his breath, Jenna was stunned. Both stood and silently eyed one another.

She was wearing a light blue, high on the thigh sundress, and she looked as stunning as she was stunned. In her right hand was a large, brown paper bag with handles, which had a large logo from what Deni imagined was an expensive restaurant, Circa 1886, on the side. Her other hand was on her hip.

"I just happened to be in the neighborhood," Deni finally said. "Nice of you to bring me lunch. How'd you know I was starvin'? Where are they? Where are the rest of the girls? Across the street?"

"If I'd have known you were coming, I would have ordered you something," she said. After another brief stare-down, she added, "What other girls?"

"Come on now, Jen. The jig is up. I know what you and Chamille and Anna have been up to. It's all over. Now let's go inside so we can get outta the sun. I'm burnin' up."

"I don't think you're a cop anymore, are you Deni? You can't just barge your way inside someone's home. I'm certain you don't have a warrant in that very colorful outfit of yours."

"It's been a long couple of days, and I'm not in the mood to fuck around. It wasn't easy to find you, I'll give you that. You're a clever little bitch."

"And you're smarter than I gave you credit for, I'll give *you* that. Look, Deni, I don't know what you think you know, but from that last little comment, it's pretty clear you don't know a damn thing. Which is disappointing, quite frankly."

They reached the gate, she unlocked and opened it, and they walked into the courtyard together. Jenna made no attempt to keep him out.

"Who's place is this, yours? You had a come-up, huh?"

"You don't know? You came all this way? I thought you had it figured out? Wow, maybe you're not as smart as I gave you credit for."

The perfumed smell of the flora in the courtyard was intoxicating, or maybe it was Jenna. Maybe both. But if heaven had a smell, Warren thought that was it. But he needed to stay focused, needed to be ready for what was on the other side of that door. The three women had planned, and schemed to bring about the death of JG, and were successful in killing a woman. He was here to call them on it.

They went through the front door and the interior was elegant. There was no other way for him to describe it. The antique furniture was plentiful but not gaudy. The pastel colors of the painted walls reminded him of a picture he had once seen of a mansion in the Garden District of New Orleans. What the Destrier home was to New England, this place was to the Southeast.

Jenna had left him in the dust. In his taking in all the appointments, he had lost his bead on the girl. She was somewhere in the confines of the amazing home, while he stood there taking it all in. He heard voices, all feminine. Deni cautiously headed toward them. He was not allowed to carry a gun on the plane, so he didn't have one on his person. He wasn't sure if he needed one with a house full of rich women, but he sure wanted one just the same. Better to be safe than sorry, and sorry might mean dead. If they were getting ready to eat, there were probably knives. Physical strength was not going to be an issue one-on-one. Three women with sharp knives, however, might prove to be a bit of a struggle.

He zig-zagged into the mansion from the foyer through the parlor, a right past the sunroom which overlooked the garden in the courtyard. He took a left past a formal dining room, the voices getting closer. He could only discern two voices, but there may have been more. He smelled food, the contents of the paper bag must have been opened. Whatever it was, it smelled phenomenal. His stomach gurgled as he just then realized that he'd not eaten since early the day before and was ravenous. When he took another left into an enormous kitchen, he spotted Jenna. And an older woman.

The elderly woman was sitting at a small table off to the side, a low breakfast counter. She was very well maintained. So well put together in fact, that it was nearly impossible to pinpoint the lady's age. Not a reddish-blonde hair was out of place. Wrinkles about her face were either well-hidden or permanently removed, nor was there a wrinkle on her attire. Most of her body was hidden by the table, but her face and torso suggested she was slim. She was watching him with an elegant grace.

As he moved closer, he took a copper frying pan off the hook from where it was hanging to use as a weapon.

"Mister Dennihan. I'm embarrassed to say that I was not expecting you today. Won't you please come in, just the same."

"I'm embarrassed to say I don't know who you are." He looked over at Jenna, but she was looking at her feet, leaning against a counter closer to the massive kitchen.

"Of course. How rude of me, please for give me. I'm Olivia Craig. We've never met but I've heard quite a lot about you." There was more silence as Olivia let the information set in, it seemed to be taking a while for Deni to process the information. "Not what you were expecting?"

"Uh. No."

"I'm rather glad you're here, Mister Dennihan. I believe we need to catch up. Long overdue, I should think. You'll have no need for that pan, nobody here is going to harm you."

"What are we, old friends? What the …. What's going on here?" He got rid of the pan on the closest surface.

"Jennifer, maybe we should take lunch in the dining room. Would you be so kind as to set it up for us? There should be plenty for a third plate." She then turned to Warren and said, "Circa is not open for lunch, but I know the owners and the chef. He prepares us a beautiful lunch on occasion. You are in for a treat, the grilled quail and the foie gras au poivre are an absolute delight."

"I don't even know what you just said," Deni admitted.

"Mister—"

"—Call me Deni, or Warren. That 'Mister' shit is irritating. Now, would you please tell me what the fu …. eh …. sorry. What, *the hell*, is going on here?"

"Very well, Warren. You may call me Olivia. With that out of the way, Warren, would you please join us for lunch?"

"Olivia Craig. As in Anna's mother. The one who has been dead for — "

" — excuse me? I am clearly not dead. I am Anna's *estranged* mother. She will no longer have anything to do with me, but I am alive and well, thank you very much. I shall explain all of this over lunch, however. Right this way."

They moved into one of the rooms Deni had passed on the way into the house, a formal dining room. Jenna had put the finishing touches on the table, setting up a proper lunch from the takeout she'd fetched. A bottle was in her hand.

"Would you care for some?" The southern hospitality thing had worn off on Jenna, apparently. Or she had a new bartending gig. She poured Chateau de Beaucastel Chateauneuf du Pape Blanc into the proper Ridel glassware.

"If it has alcohol in it, make it a double."

"It's french white wine. 2004. We were going to pair it with our lunch. In other words, it's not Whiskey," Jenna said.

"Whatever, it'll do. Now will someone please tell me what's going on? JG, or Jake as you call him Jenna, is going to trial on Monday and you two are playin' games down here like southern bells. I can't tell if you're friend or fuckin' foe."

"Please calm down Warren, and refrain from cursing. We're here to help. We don't under normal circumstances break bread with mortal enemies. Do you?" Olivia was as dainty and elegant as every rumor he'd heard.

"Not normally, but people are funny, and these aren't normal circumstances are they? Where's your daughter?"

"We have been tracking her through her banks, with some help from Olivia's banking contacts," Jenna said.

"*We*? What, are you two a comedy team now? Or do you work for Olivia? Who else are you two tracking?"

"*We* have an arrangement, Deni. The specifics aren't important and are none of your business. Let's just say that Olivia has Jake's best interests in mind, as do I. And I trust her."

"Is that why you sent Ryan the video?"

"That is precisely why I asked Jennifer to, retrieve shall we say, the footage. She had firsthand knowledge that Jacob was not as inebriated as he was accused of being."

"And you contacted her, because you knew that something wasn't right?" He asked Olivia.

"I have been in contact with Jennifer for some time, yes. My daughter may have asked me to stay out of her life, but do you honestly think I would not keep watch over her? Over my son-in-law? Over my only grandson? My deceased husband was a man of means, bequeathing me a fortune. What good is any of it without family?"

"So Jenna …. You weren't working with Cam and Anna to try to kill JG?"

"Jesus no. Excuse me, Olivia. No. And who is *Cam?*"

"I think he is referring to Chamille Destrier, Anna's close friend. Is that right, Warren? How do you suppose Chamille is involved with this?"

"I thought you were watching from afar? I'm tryin' to piece this all together and you two are sittin' down here spyin' on everyone. I thought you had all the answers."

"Do you honestly think that if I had all the answers that I would sit idly by and watch this tragedy? I have watched with as close an eye as I am able. This is a family that I am not supposed to be a part of. You did know that, yes? Jennifer has sent me pictures of my grandson in secret, or has tried to as often as possible. I let Jacob know a long time ago that I didn't abandon my family. Anna forced me away because of her father's infidelities, and her belief that I was complicit in them. That knowledge has done so much damage to my daughter."

"And she thought Jenna here was bangin' …. excuse me …. *having an affair* with her husband. So she sees red, and plots with Cammy to kill JG. I find it a little bit weird that she chooses to be friends with a woman who is as loose as an alley-cat, but what do I know?"

"Yes, she thought that Jake and I were seeing each other, but she was distancing herself more and more. The entire thing is ironic. Not weird, Deni, ironic," Jenna said.

"What is this that I am eating? I am not sure if I like it because I am starving, or because it is some culinary masterpiece. It's wicked pretty, I'll give ya that."

"Since you didn't understand Olivia when she said it before, foie gras is duck liver. It's served on a rosemary and lemon biscuit with a blackberry …. You don't really care do you? Yes, it is a culinary masterpiece."

"So why are you two playing The Wizard of Oz down here, Olivia? All this behind the curtain stuff? Your daughter — "

" — Excuse me for interrupting you again. But before you go any further, Warren, I need to clarify that I will not help you in further destroying my daughter. My objective is to preserve my family. I will not see Anna incarcerated, nor can I tolerate Jacob being imprisoned."

"So where have you been for the past six months? JG has been rotting in a cell all this time, and it seems less likely that he belongs there. I guess it's better than being dead though."

"I couldn't extricate him from that dreadful prison, unfortunately, no matter how I tried. As for Anna, frankly, I have no excuses, nor do I have comment. I hesitated as long as possible in forwarding what little information I had that, compromises shall we say, my daughter."

"Maybe you can try to help in her defense at trial, lady, but she used Cammy as an alibi. And she called JG at the bar and told him not to pick up Brady. She drugged him and let him think that he endangered their son when he lived through the accident. He was supposed to die on that trip but another woman died instead."

"I find it incredibly hard to believe that she wanted Jacob dead."

"Believe what you want, Olivia, it happened. If it wasn't Jenna, then it was his wife. Your daughter."

"It seems hard to argue. I will say, Olivia, she did hate me. And she took it out on her husband and son. I can't help but feel somewhat responsible."

"That is nonsense, Jennifer. My daughter had problems, and while you certainly didn't help, you did nothing wrong and you most definitely didn't cause them. You've been an ally to me and for that I am grateful."

"Olivia, do you know where your daughter is?" Deni asked.

"Warren, I am willing to help clear Jacob of the charges against him. I think I have demonstrated that. But I repeat, I will not help you destroy my daughter. She may have problems, and she may need help, but I will not see her go to prison for the rest of her life. I still love her though she wants nothing to do with me. She is still my daughter."

"She's goin' down one way or another. You seem like a sweet old lady, but you got this all wrong. Do you want her dragging Brady along from place to place hiding from justice? She's on the run, and she's always gonna be on the run. She may have money and she may be able to get away with it for while, but in the end there will come a time where she *will* be caught. Brady has a right to be with his dad. Brady didn't do anything wrong, yet he's not going to be able to play with just any kid, go to just any school, because his mom is a fugitive. She's a bad lady and it ain't your fault, Olivia. But it *will* be your fault if Brady gets all messed up in the process. If you know where she is, you can put an end to it. He deserves a better life and he belongs with his dad."

Olivia began to tear up. She was as graceful and as sophisticated as she could be about her emotions, but she was losing the struggle for strength. She pushed the plate holding her culinary masterpiece away from her, untouched. Deni watched her for a few moments while she tried to regain her composure. He felt for her. He admired her. But he had a mission, which took precedence over all else.

Jenna was not so demure. She had once again lost control of her emotions, using the guise of clearing the lunch plates to excuse herself from the room. Deni now knew where her loyalties lied. Whatever arrangement she and Olivia had, he knew that Jenna would walk away from it if it meant helping Jake and Brady. In that, they were aligned. If the guilt trip on Olivia failed, he would have a strong backup plan.

"San Diego," Olivia whispered after a short time. She composed herself, dabbing the corners of her eyes, then looked into Warren's. "They are in San Diego, California."

"With Cammy?"

"I don't believe so, why do you ask?"

"You said, 'they'."

Jenna returned to the dining room and took her seat at the table. After draining her glass of expensive white wine, she replenished all three glasses. She seemed to be the only one measurably consuming it.

Deni said, "Cam helps your daughter, then me, then goes missing."

"She helped you because I told her to, Warren."

"Excuse me? *You* told her to help me?" Deni was taken aback to say the least.

"Yes. How do you suppose you came about the address of the missing Destrier staff-member, and the security footage from the gate?"

"I, uh, earned it."

"Yes, I'm sure you did. However, I have some rather embarrassing information about her, that she would like to never see the light of day. When Jennifer spoke of your interest in any involvement she may have had, I reached out to her. I told her she needed to provide you with any

195

information to help Jacob. I was unaware that she had anything to do with this except to provide childcare. And now you say she provided coverage for Anna at the event? I take it you believe she has more to do with this than that?"

He was still having trouble with the fact that he hadn't needed to sleep with Chamille in order to retrieve the information. That she was told to.

"I'm not sure anymore. But she did take off. I thought Jenna was involved too, but it looks like I was wrong about her also," Deni said.

"No offense, Warren, but it seems that while you may be good at your profession, you have missed the mark quite often in this case."

"And it's buggin' the …. It's really buggin' me." He took a long pull of his wine, though he didn't enjoy it as much as he reckoned he was supposed to. "Olivia, I'm gonna need an address in San Diego. I'm catchin' the next flight outta Charleston."

"Jennifer and I will go with you."

"No way. She's gonna be cornered, and cornered people do crazy things. It may get ugly."

"That is precisely why we are going to go, to bring some cool-headedness to this very upsetting situation. I will not see Anna get hurt. Brady cannot be exposed to any of this either. He is my only grandson and his protection is paramount. I'll have a private jet waiting when we arrive at the airport."

"I'm going with you to San Diego?" Jenna looked genuinely confused.

"Private jet?" So did Deni.

27

IT TOOK ALL OF THREE HOURS TO GET ORGANIZED, PACKED, and onto the parked plane at Charleston International Airport. The executive area for private jets was segregated from the major carrier area, though it did share runways since the entire airport had just two of them. They were chauffeured to the parked jet in an area near what looked like a hangar used by the United States Air force; which it may have, since they owned and operated the airport.

The silver Land Rover pulled up to a gold 2007 Embraer Legacy *600 SN 1002* executive jet, currently worth between fourteen and fifteen million dollars, which was significantly less than when it was new. They were led from the SUV, up the stairs, and inside the luxurious aircraft. Everything on the inside was white leather, gold trim, and varnished wood. The pillows on the jet sofa were nicer than Deni's actual sofa in his home.

"Jesus Olivia, how rich are you? You have this thing in case you want a quick flight? No *Travelocity* for you huh? I don't think I could afford the fuel."

"It is not my personal jet, Warren. I simply have access to it whenever I should need a flight."

"If by access you mean your friends, I gotta get myself some better friends."

Fortunately for him, Deni did not have to unload the luggage from the SUV and load it into wherever the stuff was being stored on the jet, as they prepared for takeoff. There was a crew for that. He was unsure if these people required a tip, nor how much the going-rate was, but he knew it was likely to be more than he had in his wallet, especially after what he'd already spent on the trip down from Boston. Olivia would have to take care of that as well. Besides, she was the one who had packed like she was leaving forever. She had Jenna do some shopping for Brady, so he would have things to wear and play with on the return. Olivia seemed to be more optimistic than he was.

Warren had what he had on his body, which is what he had bought at the overpriced marketplace that morning. He had shoved his clothes he'd worn on the red-eye down to Charleston into the back of his rented Dodge Charger, which was still parked in the metered spot by the water. He had remembered about the car once they were in the air, mentioning the dilemma to Olivia. With one phone call, she said that it was taken care of. He had alluded to his clothing situation while telling the rental car story, and she had said that would be taken care of as well. *I really do need to get better friends*, he thought.

He had never traveled in such luxury. Olivia, as always, was elegant and nonplussed. It was as if she hailed a cab, one that would take her twenty-five hundred miles. A very expensive cab ride indeed.

The captain and crew could not have been more affable, nor more accommodating. With the kind of money being shelled out for this little excursion, he thought, why shouldn't they be. No question was too trivial, no food or beverage request off-limits. He wondered who was really paying the bill for it. She said access, which meant friend or friends. He wondered if for rich people, asking to borrow their super-fancy jet was like a normal person asking to borrow their friend's row-boat for the weekend.

The novelty of the idea that the three of them were off to San Diego, on a private jet, to confront and convince Anna, had worn off. Warren thought it stupid to bring the woman whom Anna believed was sleeping with the husband she tried to kill along for the ride. Not to mention the mother she had thrown into exile. If their company was supposed to bring tranquility, he felt that they were going about it the wrong way. When he broached the subject with Olivia, she justified the decision by saying that she would be able to talk some sense into her daughter and that Jennifer would calm Brady, as she had never met the boy and was a grandmother that he probably didn't know existed. Those may have been fair points if there was any chance in hell that Anna would listen to a woman she hated, and if they would be able to get anywhere near Brady. Anna was bound to put up a fight. And that fight was going to be an all-out war, which was Deni's big fear. Separating that momma from her cub would mean the claws would be out. And teeth.

He was, without question, exhausted. He had virtually no sleep on the red-eye to get down to South Carolina, and hadn't any sleep since. The plush seats were wide and comfortable, easily able to recline if so inclined. But he had calls to make. He needed to call Ryan, only Olivia was across the aisle. He moved toward the sofa with the nice pillows, but Jenna was lounging there. So he made his phone calls from the confines and privacy of the toilet. A fancy toilet, but he was calling from a toilet nonetheless.

Ryan began the thousand-mile conversation by giving Deni the riot act. Things like, "What in the name of Christ are you doing, Deni?" and "You're going where?" and "Unless she confesses, how does this help us?" were all screamed out of the phone, heard even over the dull hissing of the plane.

It took a while to calm Ryan down. Deni told him that this *did* help JG because they were going to bring back Brady before Anna realized the jig was up and took off again. That if Anna did take off, justice for the victim may never be done. They would attempt to get a confession, but even without one, anything she said might be helpful to JG. He wasn't a cop any longer, and didn't play by nor subscribe to many rules, but Anna had gotten his Irish up. His mission was to bring her down, and nothing short of that would suffice.

His next phone call was to a contact in Boston, who gave him the phone number of a retired ex-cop in San Diego he could reach out to. Nobody who lived in San Diego was originally from San Diego, his contact had said. He was also told that if he needed a liaison with the police out there, he should contact the fellow in San Diego who was originally from the Boston suburb of Mattapan. Deni wanted a weapon not a liaison, but that wasn't being offered, so he wouldn't have one. He was also unsure if Anna would come in peace or if police would be needed, but he was thankful for the information all the same. They may have to extradite her, if she was unwilling to come back to New Hampshire. He also hoped that the plane would be able to be borrowed for the flight back to New England. He was ruined for commercial flying ever again.

The rest of the four hour and forty-five minute flight was uneventful. Warren slept, trying to catch up from close to forty hours without it. With the three-hour time difference, they just made the 11:00 PM curfew for what they consider a stage three aircraft. The planes land so close to downtown and the residential homes in San Diego, that a curfew was put into place in 1989. No planes, other than emergency aircraft, were allowed to takeoff or land before 6:00 AM or after 11:00 PM, unless the aircraft falls below the designated decibel level. Microphones were put into place and fines were assessed. When one lives in paradise, it cannot be noisy.

Another chauffeured car, this time a Mercedes *M-class,* picked them up at Lindbergh Field. They drove on North Harbor Drive, hugging the ocean toward downtown San Diego. It was late and they were going to deal with Anna in the morning. They took the left onto 5th Avenue and were dropped off at the *Taj,* a super luxury hotel that jetted up from the asphalt, past the palm trees, toward the sky. The enormous convention center, made famous by Comic-Con, was across the street and would have blocked their view of the ocean had they not been in the penthouse suite. Warren was too tired to comment on the extravagance, Olivia too unfazed to care, and Jenna said nothing in either case. They all retired to their respective rooms in the suite. It had been a long day, they would need their rest for the trying day to follow.

The five-star hotel would have gotten seven stars if the ratings went that high. Part of the reason for the high rating were the amenities, for sure, but their service was superfluous. The wake-up calls were not executed with a callous phone call from the lobby or a concierge, they were done in person. At least they were for guests in the penthouse suite. Warren hadn't asked or expected one, but he received one anyway. He forgot to thank Olivia. The nice, young man who entered the suite the following morning, who had knocked on Warren's individual door inside the suite, was almost punched in the throat. This was not the young man's first wake-up call, or he had been warned, and so he was fortified with coffee and breakfast. Warren let him live.

The city of Poway, California, is a posh community spread out in the center of San Diego County. Because the various neighborhoods are sprinkled about the mountainous area, upper middle-class communities abutted the grossly affluent. Poway is consistently in the top twenty-five most expensive places to live in the United States, and it doesn't have a beach. One traveling through the 'City in the Country' can determine with ease which community is which by the existence of a very large forbidding gate. Or lack thereof.

The journey out of downtown toward the Poway address was a relatively short one, if one could fly there. The California Freeway system didn't allow for an easy hop or a direct route. Instead, the wide 15 north was a long stretch of freeway that should have been called a parkway. No matter how many lanes, they were always congested and slow-moving. Part of the 'sun-tax' was to put up with traffic. Paradise at any cost.

One hour and twenty-five minutes after departure, still stuck in traffic, Warren was ready to kill something. He would soon get the chance.

Olivia's desperation to calm her travel companion became more desperate with each slowly passing mile. Jenna was keen to help for a while, but as his Irish went into full swing, she backed off. She bee apprised of Deni's physical abilities when he didn't want to hurt someone, the amount of potential violence concerned her when he was actually angry, like now. Olivia was not backing down, however, her daughter and grandson were on the other end of this trip. She needed a calm and collected Warren Dennihan.

The final arrival at their destination necessitated a celebration. What they did instead was stare at yet another seemingly insurmountable gate.

"Ah, another fuckin' gate. What's this world comin' to when you can't stalk someone, or sneak up on someone easily?"

"You're language, Warren. Please. I thought you were able to circumvent these types of obstacles."

"If you mean, can I get around the gate? Then yes, it's just a pain in the …. Well, it's a pain. And it eliminates the element of surprise. Usually." He got out of the Mercedes, going around the front of the vehicle, in order to confer with the chauffeur. Once the conference was over, the SUV backed into an inconspicuous parking spot a couple of hundred yards down the road, but still in view. Warren hid in the manicured shrubbery which lined the massive gate.

The wait was a long one. The sun was getting hotter and the sweat dripped from places on his body he was not sure could sweat. They were well inland of the Pacific Ocean and there was a noticeable lack of a coastal breeze. The sun continued to beat down on the mountainous desert-like region, which heated even the shade. His iPhone rang. He removed it from the pocket of his new cargo shorts to find that sweat had saturated his screen.

"Olivia?" At least the phone still worked.

"Warren, what exactly are we waiting for? Let's just alert them to our presence and discuss this like adults."

"At least you're in air conditioning. I'm sweating my — "

The timing was perfect, albeit a little late, for the gate began to recess sideways into itself. He was not sure how much longer he would be able to hold off Olivia, but he was thankful not to have to find out. The gate was opening for the vehicle that was departing from the premises. The Jaguar F-type *V8 S* jetted away from the drive in the opposite direction from the Mercedes on a stakeout. The top was down on the salsa red convertible sports car, music loud, and the woman behind the wheel was gone with the same quickness in which she had arrived.

" — We're in Olivia," Deni said into his cell. "Hold on."

Warren slipped out of the shrubs and through the closing gate before it re-locked.

"Was that Anna in that car? I couldn't tell," Olivia said.

"I don't think so, but who knows?"

"So how was that helpful? We don't know if she's in the house, and Jennifer and I are still out here while you are in there. I will not sit idly by while you — "

" —Easy, easy. You think I'm impatient. Brady wasn't in the car, that's definite. So either way we're leaving with him. Just have your guy pull up to the gate," he said before turning off his phone and returning it to his wet pocket.

The chauffeur pulled the car up to the gate, spying Warren on the other side of it, doing jumping-jacks, waving, and running from side to side in the driveway. The motion detector finally did its job, sensing the flailing and reopening the gate for the others. The driver pulled up to where Warren was; allowed him to crawl into the air-conditioned backseat, but the ride was not long enough to cool him down. The Spanish-influenced stucco building ahead of them had many front-facing windows. If anyone was watching from any of those windows, his jumping jacks and sweat-soaked clothing were for nothing.

Jenna took a jab at him. "That was cute, but what's the rest of your plan?"

"I'm wingin' it. I'm kinda surprised it's worked out this well so far, truth be told."

"This is trespassing, I'm sure you are aware of that Warren. You are drenched with sweat and I don't know which is worse, your sight or smell. Maybe I should go to the door and discuss things with Anna," Olivia offered.

"Yeah, that'd be piss-ah. The banished mother travels cross-country to confront her daughter and grab her grandkid. What could go wrong? Besides, we don't even know for sure if she's even in there."

"Your sarcasm is unappreciated, I am simply trying to help."

"Just stay in the car, both of you. Please. Just give me a sec and we'll see what happens." He got out of the car, back into the heat. He made his way to the front door along the stone walkway.

The first set of knocks on the door with a doorbell follow-up went unanswered. As did the second set. Deni was beginning to wonder if anybody was home at all.

When the door did open, just prior to his third attempt, a house opened the door to the house. The mammoth man stood in the doorway, filling it. He wasn't mammoth in terms of fat, he was over three hundred pounds of pure muscle.

"Oh shit."

"Who are you and how did you get in here?" He was as unfriendly as he was intimidating.

"I'm with the Jehovah's Witnesses. Is the lady of the house available to discuss the coming of our Lord and Savior? I'm here to save her from eternal damnation." Deni then realized with whom he was speaking.

"Hey, aren't you Vinny Mahlrhone? The Tackle from the Chargers? Fancy meetin' you here. I'm a big fan, we could use you on the Patriots," he continued

"Yeah, thanks. Who the hell are you, again? Reporters aren't allowed here."

"Holy shit! Get rid of him." Deni heard the female voice shout from behind the giant. She then sounded like she took off in a full run after her command.

If he hadn't been able to be a professional football player, Vinny would have made a phenomenal goalie. Deni couldn't see a thing past him in the doorway, so he didn't know for sure whom had yelled from inside the house, but he had a very good guess.

"Ah - ha. There's the lady of the house." His move to get past the All-Pro Tackle was unsuccessful, the gigantic mass that was Vinny didn't budge an inch. Instead, Deni was grabbed by the collar like a football dummy and pushed back onto the middle of the lawn with ease.

"You have to go now." Vinny wasn't asking.

When he was set down on the lawn and given the ability to gather himself, Deni brushed the wrinkles out of his shirt. He was trying to be as non-threatening as possible when he spoke.

"I gotta talk to Anna, the lady of the house. I'd rather do this the easy way, Vin. You're still in good shape after the Chargers terrible season, by the way. You don't spend too many marches at Disneyland though, do you?"

"So this isn't random. What do you want?"

"It's between me and her. You're caught in a bad situation, and so am I. I just wanna talk with her."

"She just said that she don't want company, bro. Whatever this is, you aren't welcome here. Please leave."

"I get that. But we came a very long way, and we aren't gonna leave without speaking with her. So maybe you could help convince her. What are you, her bodyguard? Kinda a big fall from professional football player to personal protection isn't it?"

"Fuck you buddy. I asked nicely. This is my house, and now *I* want you to leave. I don't want to hurt you, I don't need the headache, but I will if I have to, bro. You're trespassing."

"I don't wanna do this the hard way either, Vin. But I will warn you, you might beat the shit outta me, but you are definitely gonna know you've been in a fight. Nobody is *that* big. Think of your career. Just let me just talk to her."

Meanwhile, Olivia and Jenna had already exited the SUV with stealth and entered the house behind the preoccupied football tackle. His back was still to his home, as he was ridding himself of the trash that was now on his front lawn. Warren had seen their sneaky entrance and was finished stalling. He continued before Vinny could respond.

"I'm going in there Vin. Neither of us want the trouble a fight will cause. I'm not gonna hurt her, I'm just gonna talk."

"Not happening, bro."

Deni made a move to get passed him, but getting past a professional football player was all but impossible. Vincent made a move to grab him, with the same collar grab he'd used two minutes prior, but failed as his elbows were pushed together in a clean sweep. With his right foot, Deni used the exposed right side of his aggressor, in order for him to step on the big right knee. This last made an audible cracking sound that made exactly as much damage as the horrifying sound indicated. The hyperextended knee looked like it belonged on an ostrich instead of a human. At the same time as Vinny's knee was being shattered, using his left fist, Deni punched Vinny's adam's apple in the center of the man's huge neck. He was able to achieve a downward motion from his perch on the man's knee, further forcing Vinny toward the lawn.

Mahlrhone may have been choking and have a permanently destroyed knee but he was not finished, and managed to snatch Deni's right leg with his long, muscular arm. He was used to working through intense pain during games, his hold on the much smaller leg was like a vice-grip. Deni was being pulled into the huge chest for a crushing bear-hug. He went to work on the man's face with his elbows on his way toward the behemoth. Left, right, left, right. Elbow after elbow was drawing blood from the increasingly mangled face. Blood was gushing from what was left of the nose, eyes and mouth. Pain was making the powerful tackle squeeze his prey with more pressure rather than less. Deni was being squeezed like a rodent wrapped in a serpent.

The sound of crushed bone was now emanating from Deni, as his ribs were snapping like pretzel rods. This made the continued elbows to his attacker's face excruciating but he continued as it was necessary for his survival.

Warren was able to find purchase on the lawn, as Vinny was kneeling on his only good knee. He tried to leverage away from the Tackle, but elbow after elbow he remained unsuccessful. The bloody meat that was once a face, remained very determined to squeeze the life from him. Both falling to the ground, Deni using his position on top to lean on Vinny's massive neck.

At last, the hold on Deni was released and they both laid on the front lawn, bleeding and gurgling. Both trying to attain oxygen. The entire fight was over in a little more than a minute, but the damage would last much longer.

"It's a good thing you're not on the Pats, now that I think on it Vin. You're not that tough." He said this through the pain of his broken ribs, which made the pain worse. He struggled to get up to go into the house as Vinny continued to lie on the lush, green lawn now sprayed with blood and broken teeth. "I'm goin' inside, you just stay right here big-boy."

Vinny didn't respond.

Inside the house, Olivia and Jenna spread out, moving about the house looking for Anna. They were on opposing ends of the large home calling after her. "Anna? We just want to talk to you." Each of them getting no response at first, and not hearing each other either. Jenna had gone around to the back side of the house, spying the nonplussed yellow Lab in the back yard, chewing on a toy. Olivia had taken the front part of the house. As they circled around one another, they heard from a distant part of the house not yet covered by either woman, "Get the fuck out, I'm calling the police."

Olivia said, "I don't think that would be a good idea, dear." She knew her daughter's voice and knew she was just ahead of her in one of the rooms to come. What she didn't know was what she was going to do about it. Or if her grandson was here. "We know what's happened, Anna, and we know your part in it. Let's not make this any worse than it already is. It's very upsetting to everyone, but think of Brady. Just come out so we can have the lawyers sort it out." She slowly moved up a small flight of stairs, large windows to her left looking out onto the front lawn. The massive man was on his back on the front lawn. Ahead, several rooms were to her right.

"I don't want anything from you. Just get the fuck out," Anna said from one of the rooms. Olivia was close. Jenna was somewhere else in the house, of no use at the moment.

"Where is Brady? He doesn't need to be exposed to any of this."

Anna didn't respond but Olivia had narrowed the search to the room in front of her as the shouting seemed to come from behind that door. She turned the doorknob with caution, opening the door. It was a weight room, and the mirrored room appeared to be devoid of humans though filled with exercise equipment. Olivia was wrong, nobody was in the large room, as she heard mumbled voices, one being a child's, deeper into the house to her left, further down the hall. She closed the door and continued in that direction.

"This is ridiculous, Anna. Just come out so we can speak like adults. Nobody needs to be hurt any more than they already have been."

"I already killed one woman, what makes you think I won't kill you?" The voice was still closer and could only be in one of two rooms remaining down that hall.

"You would kill your own mother, Anna? I cannot believe that. I'm sure you didn't kill her on purpose, accidents happen. Let's not make this any worse."

"Keep coming closer, bitch, and you'll see just how fucking bad it can get." The shout was on the other side of the door that Olivia was now in front of. Again, she cautiously turned the knob and opened the door. The mechanism was silent, as were the hinges, as the door slowly creeped open. Olivia peered into the room with apprehension as the door moved open inch by slow inch. The back wall was painted like a football gridiron, a small boy sat on the floor in front of it visibly frightened.

The Taylor Made *R1* driver swung out of nowhere, on a bearing toward the right side of Olivia's skull. Anna was on the other side of the door, swinging the golf club like a Louisville Slugger baseball bat. The swing and the eventual contact with the club face to Olivia's temple would shatter any chance at life beyond that moment.

In that last millisecond before coming into contact with Olivia's skull, the door swung completely open. Warren had come rushing through, taking the full impact of the club on his left shoulder which dislocated it in all of an instant. The thud made from the contact simultaneously fractured the humeral head and vibrated the club out of Anna's grip. The sound that howled out of Deni's mouth was as awful as the sound of the impact itself. He fell to his knees in yet more agony.

The vibrating club flew away and the utter shock on Anna's face did not last long. She dove across the room to her son, now crying in a ball on the floor. Jenna was now behind Olivia and Deni, she had somehow made her way to the large room that was getting rather crowded. Anna, seeing all of these people before her, clutched the sobbing child, putting him between her and the intruders.

"Just leave us the fuck alone." It was clearly a last and final effort. One that was in vain and everyone knew it. She knew everyone in the room. Deni was like a relentless dog. There was no way he was going to be 'live and let live' about this situation, injured or not.

"You busted my arm Anna. Was that really necessary?" He was trying to keep both his temper and his language in check. The child was upset and could easily be more so if the circumstances were to degenerate further. "Olivia, talk some sense into your daughter before I really lose my temper." He was plainly in the throes of immense physical pain.

Olivia was almost catatonic. She was looking at Deni in horror, seeing that while his pain was debilitating, the blow from her daughter was meant to, and would have, put an end to her life. She too sat down harshly on the floor.

Jenna took the reins. "Brady, do you remember me? It's Jenna. I don't know if you remember Warren, he is kinda like your uncle. And this is your Grandma. You've never met her, but she loves you very much. We are here to bring you back to see your Dad. Do you want to go see your Dad?"

"Just leave us alone. Haven't you done enough damage?" Anna was a mess. What was once a beautiful woman was now a psychotic, angry, sobbing mess.

"I didn't do anything wrong, you just think I did. If you would have had a conversation with me, maybe ask a few questions, none of this would have happened."

"What was I supposed to do? Just sit quietly by while you, you fucking cunt, you come in and ruin my family? And her. Look, even now she won't say anything. Look at 'poor old mom the martyr'. Never. I would never let him get away with it."

"No matter what you think of me, your husband doesn't deserve to rot in prison for the rest of his life. He didn't do anything wrong."

"When he dove into bed with a whore, he deserved to die. I wanted him to suffer. I still want him to suffer. It's too bad the monkey-woman had to die, but better her than me."

Deni seemed to be reading between the lines while suffering from his injuries. How he was able to concentrate on anything else was a mystery, but he interjected.

"Anna, if you didn't try to kill JG, then what happened that night?"

"And everybody thinks you're the clever one, Deni. JG *was* supposed to die. When he didn't, by some fucking miracle, I was happy to watch him suffer. To live with the fact that he killed someone. He killed me Deni. He killed our family. We could have had a great life."

"He didn't do anything, Anna. You can keep saying it as many times as you want, but he didn't cheat. You did all of this for nothing. *You* ruined what could have been a great life. And that woman, the monkey-woman you called her, what did she do to you?"

"This twat and my husband have you all fooled huh? Well not me. The dead woman may have been innocent, she may have been my half-sister. Who knows. That was just a lucky bonus I guess. It could have been anybody coming down that road that night, but all the people of quality were at the charity event."

"How did you get outta there, Anna?"

"Chamille covered for me. Nobody knew the difference. How'd you know I wasn't there?"

"There are cameras everywhere these days. Saw you buy the burner phone, saw you drop the drugs into JG's beer, and saw you pick up Brady." While she was talking he wanted to put the last piece of the puzzle together, the presets on the twin Volvos. "And you forgot to reset the presets on the Volvos."

"Can't think of everything I guess. The drugs didn't work as fast as I had thought but they worked enough. He didn't realize he was in the wrong car, dumb shit."

"So if we get his keys out of property at the prison, is it going to be your key on his ring?"

"I switched them back when I dropped off Brady. I'm not an idiot."

"That's debatable."

"Hey Deni? Go fuck yourself!"

Brady had eased his way away from his mother, hiding by his bed next to Olivia. Anna, with all the chaos and interrogation and confessing, was unaware that her son was no longer in front of her.

"So he made it home safely in your SUV, while you put a dinger in his. You really sold the story, Anna. Too bad you did it all for nothing. No matter what you think, JG didn't cheat. The more you thought it, the more you stayed away. The more you stayed away, the more time he spent with Jenna, here. And around and around it went."

"We're friends, Anna, that's it. There's nothing else going on," Jenna said.

"You moved in on my fucking family, I should have killed you too. I should have cut off your fucking head."

"Well, I don't think there is anything more to say to you." She turned to Brady and Olivia. "We should get him out of here, the rest of this is going to get even uglier." Olivia was in agreement and they made their way out into the hallway.

Now alone, it was just Anna and Deni. Anna suddenly realized that she no longer had Brady and began to freak out. Deni hoped his attempts to subdue her would not be physical. He was in no condition to move, let alone get into another physical confrontation. The police were on their way, maybe they had arrived. He hoped for the latter.

"We have some things for you in the car, Brady. It's going to be a long trip back to see your Dad." Jenna was trying to ease the young boy through the next set of hurdles, as this was a traumatic day, indeed.

"Is Uncle Deni going to hurt Mommy?"

"No, no. They just need to talk about some things while we go see your Dad."

"Mommy says that Daddy's gone." He looked over Jenna's shoulder at Olivia and said, "She said my Gramma was in heaven too."

Olivia's tears began to gently roll down her cheeks. She squatted down in front of him, grabbing his little hands as they had stopped at the top of the stairs.

"Well, I finally get to meet you, sweetheart. For me this is very much like heaven." She pulled him into her chest to hug him and he didn't resist. His little arms wrapped around her neck in a tight hug.

When the embrace was finished, he held on to his Grandmother's hand while they descended the stairs. "Mommy said some bad words."

"Yes honey. Your Mommy has been a bad girl."

28

THE FLIGHT BACK HOME WAS THANKFULLY QUIET. Warren was unaccustomed to babysitting, nor was he used to traveling with a child. He was becoming very fond of private jets, however. How he would fly commercial again in the future was beyond him. His pain was being steadily diminished, however slight, by the unlimited amount of alcohol that was being supplied to him by the helpful flight attendants. He was falling in love with one of them, more so by the drink.

Olivia had stayed behind in Poway. She wanted to be there to help sort out her daughter, though she was told without equivocation, and on repeated occasion, that she was not wanted there. Anna had killed a woman by staging it to look like a deadly OUI crash. Premeditated murder was going to be a great deal of work to sort out. He thought if he were in Anna's situation, he would take any help offered to him.

Arranging for Brady to go back to Wayland with Deni and Jenna also took some doing. Anna was losing everything in one fell swoop, her freedom was bad, but losing her child was the backbreaker. In the end, the Poway police left her with no choice, but that did not stop her from trying.

Olivia had finally met the Grandson she so desperately longed to hold. She hugged him repeatedly and at length, commenting on how good his hugs felt. Letting him out of her sight so quickly after meeting him was almost as torturous for her as it was for her daughter. But duty called, as it had so many times before.

Deni and Jenna had been chauffeured off of the property shortly after the police had arrived. He had communicated with his contact from Mattapan on the trip toward downtown. Deni was notified then that he would do his best to clean up the mess he'd made, but it sounded like this Anna Grantes was in a lot of trouble. Deni didn't mention the mess his body was in because of Anna and a golf club, nor the amount of excruciating pain he was in. Anna was in enough trouble already.

The questions posed to 'Uncle Deni' were fielded by Jenna on the ride back to the San Diego International Airport because he was in too much pain to deal with the youngster. But only when all of Brady's questions were satisfied did he board the plane. He was a smart kid, smarter at his young age than people gave him credit for.

Mercifully, the long flight into Manchester, New Hampshire was all but silent. Brady and Jenna slept while Deni drank away the pain. They were flying into Manchester because it was closer to Wayland than Logan Airport in Boston. It was a small airport, Southwest Airlines was the only major carrier out of it, but they had a private jet, so they could fly into almost any airport they wanted.

Olivia had arranged for a driver to pick them up as they didn't have a vehicle in Manchester to drive. They could have rented one, but Jenna was preoccupied with Brady. And Warren was in no condition to drive. To say that he was hammered would have been an understatement. He needed more help out of the plane and into the car than Brady, who was still half asleep. Jenna was left to babysit two children. Luckily she was used to it.

It was almost midnight, eastern standard time, but Warren called Ryan anyway. He could have called from the plane, which would have made more sense, but he was too busy getting drunk. It was technically Sunday, the day before the trial. It was fortuitous for them that Ryan was not asleep, as he was unable as of late.

"Deni, what's going on? Where are you?"

"In the car."

"Wonderful, where is the car? I'm kind of losing it here."

"Almost at your place. Jenna and Me. And Brady." The slurring speech, added to his already thick Boston accent, was almost undecipherable.

"You're in New Hampshire? You sound hammered."

"That's cuz I am."

"That's terrific. You're not driving are you? Please tell me after all that has happened that you are not driving."

"I'm not driving. Ha ha. Be there in a couple 'a minutes."

"I'll put some coffee on."

"Coffee ain't gonna help, Ry."

"That's what I'm afraid of."

Ryan was not prepared for what poured through his door. What was planned to be a long day of preparation became an even longer day of interrogation and nursing. Jenna was not able to help carry Deni, as she was carrying a comatose Brady into a guest bedroom. It took both the driver and Ryan to carry a drunk, war-beaten Warren into the house. The jarring of his wounded body roused him in brief, intermittently, the pain cutting through the inebriation.

In one of the brief bits of coherence, he was able to articulate that he needed to vomit. Or urinate. Or maybe both. It was far too mumbled to interpret. Ryan asked the driver how he had gotten to this level of intoxication. To which he was told that he needed to ask the other woman in the car, but his guess was the mini bar in the back of the car. They propped him up as close to the toilet as they could in the downstairs bathroom.

Angie slept through all of the commotion.

After some time, Jenna came downstairs, she was tucking the boy in. The driver had been tipped and coffee poured but Deni had still not resurfaced from his bodily functions in the bathroom.

"What the hell happened, Jenna?"

"He's drunk, isn't it obvious? He should go to the hospital, which he has been told repeatedly. He's killing his pain with alcohol."

"What's wrong with him?"

"We don't know for sure, because he won't seek medical attention, but I think he has some broken ribs and his shoulder is shattered in all probability."

"Again I'll ask, what the hell happened? I'm supposed to go to trial in a little over thirty hours and nobody has called to tell me what's going on."

Jenna spent the next hour explaining everything that had happened in Charleston, which he knew from Deni's call while he was on the plane to California. He waited patiently and without interruption until she started explaining what had happened in San Diego. She was stopped only a few times to answer some of Ryan's questions. The big questions were toward the end; asking if any of the conversation was recorded, or if the Poway Police had a statement from Anna. Both went largely unanswered.

"I don't know, Ryan. I don't think it was recorded, but she did admit to killing that woman. She switched vehicles and because they were the same and the fact that Jake was drugged, he didn't notice. She switched the cars back to their correct parking spots in the garage when she went home to put Brady to bed. Not resetting the presets was a mistake."

"Well, do we have a contact person at the police department?"

"Deni does. In San Diego, I think. He had one all set up before we even got out there."

"Speaking of Deni, it's been over an hour. I've been so wrapped up in the story I forgot he's in the bathroom. I gotta go check on him."

When he opened the door, Warren was face down on the tile floor. Ryan panicked, thinking he choked on his own vomit or worse. Had he given himself alcohol poisoning? He lifted his friend's head, the tile marks lined his cheeks. He had a pulse but a faint one. He called out to Jenna.

"Jenna call 911. He needs to go to the hospital."

"He won't go quietly."

"He's passed out, if he is going to go, this is the time. You go with him, I need to work and be here to explain when my wife gets up."

******

When Deni woke up at the hospital, he was pissed off. He was pissed at Anna, pissed at Mahlrhone, and pissed at his nurses who woke him up every hour on the hour. Jenna was allowed to go into his room to visit him, but only after a long wait and some cockamamie story she told about being his sister. He was in a foul mood and in a lot of pain. His head hurt but not as much as his ribs and shoulder.

She was told exactly what she expected to hear, that he had broken three ribs, bruised others, and that the ball in his shoulder was fractured. Debris had to be removed from the arm socket and fluid removed. It was going to be a long recovery for her 'brother'.

She asked him who the police contact was in San Diego, because Ryan desperately needed to speak with him in an offer proof of Anna's guilt to the Wayland prosecutor. Extradition would not take place in the time that they needed, so he was going to need an official statement. Deni told her, but only after a rambling complaint about his morphine drip dosage being 'bullsh'. Which she interpreted as not being enough.

After leaving Deni in his room, he then called Ryan from the hospital. The sound on the other end of the phone when she relayed the information, was as if she had just told him that he had won the lottery.

29

THE REMAINDER OF SUNDAY WAS LIKE A FAST-MOVING YET foggy dream. Ryan was making phone calls to San Diego County and City of Poway Police to acquire statements and possible extradition dates, and to La Fontagne who was not happy to have his Sunday ruined. The day flew by. Angie was a Godsend looking after Brady, and she was even good about asking him some questions. Brady would never take the stand, but a statement could be used to broker a deal. A plan was formed and documents created. Ryan had one shot at avoiding a trial, which he still wanted to avoid, even with the mounting evidence, because trials were always a gamble. He needed to convince the ADA that they had the wrong man and to drop the charges.

Ryan arrived at the courthouse fifty-five minutes prior to first call on Monday, which was ten minutes before he was supposed to meet Jabba. La Fontagne was aware of the new developments, but Ryan still had a dog and pony show that he needed to present in one of the conference rooms. He and the ADA didn't exactly get along with one another. He needed a presentation that moved beyond personalities and forced the prosecutor's hand. He was also aware that La Fontagne could continue on with a trial simply out of spite.

It wasn't long before the enormous prosecutor was spotted in the building, and not much longer after that, he was in the conference room.

"Okay Wells, what do you want to do here?"

"Hi, how are you? I'm fine, thank you. Nice manners."

"You called this meeting, I'm still happy to go to trial. You are long on supposition and little on evidence, unless something has changed since you phoned yesterday. Most of what you have cannot be authenticated."

"Well, a lot has changed, actually. I am sorry for having bothered you on a Sunday, but I didn't want to ambush you in front of the judge today, who hates you by the way. "

"You called this meeting, I don't have to sit here and take your abuse."

"I told you what happened yesterday, but today I have a statement from a San Diego Police Sargent, and three arresting officers from the City of Poway, California. I also have a signed statement from your boss, the District Attorney, stating that he intends to extradite her back, at the very minimum, for questioning. It's probable that formal charges will be made. I also have a statement from their son, who's only four years old. I would like to keep him from testifying in court if possible, but I will put him on the stand if I have to. She did it. Premeditated. That, added to all the video footage that I emailed over to you, the receipt from the bar which you already have with only two beers on it, and my client is never going back to WCHOC. He never should have been remanded to begin with."

"Nice speech."

"And your response?"

"Nothing you have said proves he wasn't drunk. Two beers may have put him over 0.08 BAC."

"Are you fucking kidding Jab, er, Pierce? What do you have against Jacob Grantes? He has been incarcerated for six months for crimes he didn't commit, now you want to move forward on a crime that he may have been guilty of, but you can't prove? It's not illegal to drink and then drive. It is illegal to drink *over the legal limit* then drive. You would have to prove he was over the limit with evidence to support the contrary."

"I need a win out of this. He pleads to OUI - first offense, he gets time served with no after care or treatment. He pleads but he is free and clear. This has been sitting on the books for six months, I need something here."

"OUI is a felony. He'd lose his license to practice law. Now way. And you're going to get his wife, Anna, after she is shipped back. *THAT'S* your win."

"Uh huh. And do you think that she is going to be convicted? She's rich with all sorts of contacts and influence in this area. Who is going to convict her?"

"You thought you were going to convict JG, my client. It's the same family, same influence."

"You think that you were the only phone call I received about this case yesterday? 'Olivia Craig and friends' are on the case."

"Look, that's up to you. I thought no special favors and that? You can't make my client pay for the fact that the right one might go free."

"Are you going to bring the offer to your client or not?"

"Drop it to careless and negligent operation, misdemeanor. No fine, time served. That is my counteroffer," Ryan said.

"Grossly negligent operation, first offense, which is still a misdemeanor. He keeps his ability to practice law. No fine, time served. Final. Green sheet it right now or we go to trial. We're out of time."

"Fine, deal. Now if we can get the judge to accept it."

"That's a big if, Mister Wells."

※※※※※※

JG had been moved from the Wayland County House of Corrections over to the courthouse for his trial. He was sitting in the large holding tank in the bowels of the building in shackles, and impatient in his waiting for his friend and lawyer. He knew Judge McCaglia, he also knew that she held her court punctually. There wasn't a clock in the tank, and therefore didn't know the exact time. But 9:00 AM had come and gone, of that he was sure.

At 11:00 AM on Monday morning, he was cooling his heels in the basement of the courthouse he was supposed to be in two hours prior. Something was wrong. The cacophony of irritating noises and conversation from the myriad other inmates or prospects were beyond aggravating. He called to the CO keeping watch over them over and over again, but the guard was very good at ignoring Grantes and the others. No word. No notion as to what the holdup was.

By lunch break, JG was nearly out of his mind. Had he not been shackled, he may have assaulted one of the ignorant wretches he was housed with, just to get one or more of the COs to pay attention to him.

The lunch that they were fed consisted of; a half-full (or half empty depending on one's outlook on things) paper cup of Gatorade, and a soggy, paper-thin hamburger from the less-than-a-dollar menu, from a less-than-good fast food joint.

Grantes immediately threw the burger-like food substance back at the CO who gave it to him. The food bounced off the solid jail door and onto the floor which had a strong odor of urine. Now that he had the man's attention, he wanted to use it to his advantage.

"I wanna see my lawyer."

"Join the club," the CO said. He turned and walked the other direction like nothing happened.

A hungry inmate picked the burger wrapped in paper off the urine-soaked, concrete floor, inspecting the outside of the packaging. Normally, it would be beyond belief that nobody was disgusted by the action. Nor were they when he ate it after unwrapping it. But Grantes hadn't even noticed, he shuffled back to the bench and sat back down.

Midway through their makeshift picnic in the holding tank, Ryan came down to the solid jail door. He looked into the large cell, spotted his client and waited until he looked his way. They were unable to hear one another until the port in the door was unlocked and opened. Ryan was lucky to have not heard what was shouted back at him by his friend. The CO that was so gifted at ignoring everyone on the planet, brought a chair over for Ryan to be more comfortable. The porthole was at face level for Ryan when he was seated. Grantes, of course, was not as fortunate and had to manage bending at the waist, contorting his face upward to see his lawyer, as squatting was not an option in the shackles. Privacy was not an option either.

"What the fuck, Ry?"

"Nice to see you too, pal. You look like shit, what's your secret?" He was smiling and joking which should have calmed JG down, but it didn't. In fact, it only made him more angry.

"Pardon me for not making tea, asshole, but down here niceties are a little hard to come by. Besides the fact that I was expecting you fucking hours ago — "

" — Hey, hey, hey. Take it easy. No trial. Not today, not ever for you. That's what's taken so long. We are finalizing the paperwork to get you out of here. Give me another hour at the most and you are a free man."

219

"Oh thank God. Jesus Christ, tell me I'm not dreaming. What happened? How? Get me out of here, then."

"Listen, I'll explain everything in a little bit. You just have to hang in there for just a little while longer. It's been a long couple of days."

"It's been a very long six months, Ry. I wanna get the fuck out of here and piece my family back together."

"That's part of what I have to explain to you in a little while."

"Did something happen to Brady?"

"He has been through some shit, but he's fine. He's gonna be fine."

"He's all I really need."

30

THE WELCOME HOME GATHERING WAS IMPROMPTU AND WASN'T at Jacob's home, for what seemed to be obvious reasons. JG didn't want to go home for all his six months worth of wishes to be there. Too many memories and now nothing left in it. But what a glorious homecoming it was. JG rode with Ryan to his friend's house, where Anna, Jenna, and Brady were anxiously awaiting their arrival. Deni was out of the hospital and present as well. Heavily medicated but present. Physically. He was not supposed to be mixing alcohol with painkillers but he was not-so-big on rules.

It was a warm, sunny day for March. The snow was beginning to melt but still present. They decided to eat in the sunroom but grill the food on the attached deck. It was perfect. Everyone was excited to be able to see him, make contact with him, but they were also cautious and gave him space. There were plenty of hugs to go around, some more important to him than others.

Jacob could not stop hugging his son, who's main interest after giving his Dad one of his own, was to play Uncle Ryan's Playstation. Angie and Ryan's main objective was to get JG back in the office and help with the heavy workload, but they knew it would take some time. JG was not interested in that at all. Jenna's goals were to help Jake and Brady get settled back in. Deni was interested in partying, which the others were doing with much more moderation, save for JG. His favorite, Stone IPA, was ice cold in the cooler and went untouched. Nobody said a word about it, and nobody asked why.

Instead, they grilled steak tenderloins and Maine lobsters while filling him in on all the recent events. Everyone chiming in on their perspective of a truly fantastic story. How well the plan had almost worked was the big elephant in the room that nobody would touch or recognize. They did make quite clear who deserved the majority of the credit, at least Ryan did.

"None of it would have been possible without Olivia and Jenna. They were your guardian angels pretty much the entire time," Ryan said. "Although in exhile, Olivia managed to keep track of you through her connections. Jenna was just one of her sources of information, but she was most valuable to her in the weeks leading up to the crash."

"I think I did my part." Warren was half in the bag.

"All of you did, and I can't thank you enough," JG said. "I'll spend the rest of my life trying to repay you for saving it." JG was getting misty-eyed. He wasn't drinking so he could not use that as an excuse, not that any of them would make him give one.

They all hugged him again, letting him know that they would do it again if asked. And they knew he would do the same for them, if the situation was reversed. It wasn't said outright, but it didn't need to be. It was an emotional time for all but Deni, it seemed.

Warren always tried to portray a rough exterior, never one to get too emotional. Handshakes were all he could muster from his calloused soul. But while he was all but numb, inside and out, his beat-up heart was glad.

"You're welcome, but I'll just take the cash," he said.

They all laughed because they knew what he meant.

EPILOGUE

GETTING RE-ACCLIMATED TO CIVILIAN LIFE TOOK SOME TIME. Six months doesn't seem like a long time to most, under normal circumstances it flies by like a football season. But six months in prison can and did change Jacob Grantes. Large spaces and being outside was unsettling after being in confinement for all of that time. Making decisions became a daunting task, for he was not allowed to make many in prison. He didn't like being approached from behind or have his back to a door. Moving fast in a car was disconcerting, and he consumed his meals incredibly fast as if someone was going to take his food away. He could not go back to his house, the house he and Anna had lived in. He could not go back to work.

Ryan and Angie pressed often, if not daily, to get him to come back to the office.

"It will feel so good for you to sit behind your desk," they said. "Just take some baby steps, or just come by and check it out for a couple of hours," they said other times. Anything to get him back, but none of it happened. He preferred to spend all of his waking hours with his son.

Six weeks went by. His house was on the market for about a minute, it was purchased by the third couple that inspected it. The closing on the house was still a few weeks away. He and Brady were living in a rented home in the meantime. Nothing fancy, just enough room for the two of them. The phone would ring, he wouldn't answer it. Not unless it was Deni, but he didn't call often. Or Jenna. She'd gone back to Charleston but checked in every day.

He thought about Anna, and how they had gone so wrong from something that had started out so right. They were in love back then. Or

223

did he imagine that? It had seemed so real. Maybe it was his drinking. Maybe he was drinking so often because she wasn't around very much in the last year or so that they were together. And around and around his mind went. Another bad habit that would be hard to break. Why was she living with Vincent Mahlrhone out in San Diego? Was she seeing him before he went to jail. How long after he went there? He was depressed when he wasn't hanging out with Brady. Was that healthy? And what happened to Chamille Destrier? She was most likely naked on a beach with some poor cabana boy.

Ryan tracked JG and Brady down one day at the park. Like time hadn't passed, Brady was trying to play on the swings with the bigger kids, while the two adults talked. Ryan told JG about the latest with Anna, that she was finally back in New Hampshire after being extradited. That she refused any and all legal help that came from her mother. She would have a long, hard road ahead of her, and she was determined to do it without the help of Olivia Craig. Ryan said that he had made some inquiries to see how she was doing and she was not good. She didn't want to see him, nor anyone else for that matter. She didn't even want to see her own son.

Ryan said that Olivia contacted him because she had made so many attempts to phone Jacob, but there was never an answer. Ryan said that he told her that he wasn't answering many phone calls, including his. She said that she would send some letters, but Ryan told her that he wasn't opening those either, but not to take offense. He said to JG that Olivia was desperate for a relationship and reminded him of her role in his freedom. He said that he understood and would contact her.

Ryan was concerned with his best friend's solitude. He was worried that he would not bounce back from the depression that he was obviously in. He and his wife had discussed an intervention, but decided to wait a few more weeks to see if the situation would correct itself.

Another week had passed, JG and Brady just happened to come by Ryan and Angie's house uninvited after supper. He said he needed to talk with Ryan, his partner. Angie was desperate in wanting to be apart of the discussion, but she took Brady which gave the two friends their privacy.

"I'm giving you the practice." JG just blurted it out.

"What? Just take your time, you'll — "

" — I'm done. I'm done here anyway. Too many memories. People look at me differently, they talk to me differently. I drive by the crash site every day." He paused while trying to gather himself. "I've repaired my finances after Anna. This is very hard, Ry, and I'm not sure where we will end up, but it's not going to be here in Wayland."

"You're scaring me. Maybe some counseling will help."

"I've had my fill of counseling in prison. Listen, I've thought about this and the practice is yours free and clear. Get another attorney if you want, get five. It's all up to you. I just need one favor."

"Anything. You know that."

"I know. You too, believe me. After all you've done, it's even hard for me to ask for another favor."

"Anything. Just ask."

"The money from the sale of my house, can you get it to the family of the woman who died?"

"What? All of it? It wasn't your fault. You didn't kill her."

"I've got some money, with Anna's situation being what it is, I will probably have access to more. She siphoned off a fortune in our assets that I will be getting back. I don't want the house or the money from it. That Brazilian woman is dead and I feel horrible about it. Have Deni find her family, take out his fee or whatever, and send the proceeds to them. Please. It will make me feel better. Will you do it for me?"

"Of course." Ryan gave his friend a very tight hug, not the one or two pat, manly hug which was their normal exchange. "This is kind of all-of-a-sudden. You have time."

"It's not sudden for me, I've had plenty of time." They were still embraced, as if this was the last time that they would see each other. "Thank you both again. For your friendship."

They silently embraced each other for a time. All that they had shared, all that they had been through since they had known each other, was now being washed over them.

"Speaking of Deni, are you going to say goodbye to him?" They separated at last, Ryan looking into his friend's eyes.

"I tried but I can't get in touch with him. He hasn't called or answered for weeks. He's not at his place in Barstone, either."

"Yeah there seems to be a lot of that going around. Last I knew he was being nursed back to health by this woman named Althea." They both laughed a much needed laugh.

"That sounds about right. Hey, listen. I'm not dying, so I'm sure we will be in touch. I need my son, and I need to say goodbye to Angie."

❋❋❋❋❋❋

The next morning, after the car was packed, the new Volvo (some things never change) departed the driveway of the rental house for the last time. They didn't stop in Wayland at all. Not for gas, not to go to the park, not for coffee nor breakfast. They would do all of those things, for they were in no rush. They would not do them anywhere near their former home. They were leaving and they were leaving for good. JG sincerely hoped that Brady would never remember any of the events that took place here. At least the bad ones.

"Where are we going Dad?" Brady asked from his child seat in the back of the car.

He considered the question for a moment before responding.

"To Grandma's house. And to see a friend."

AUTHOR'S NOTES AND ACKNOWLEDGEMENTS

The previous work is one of fiction, any resemblance to specific and true incidents is purely coincidental. Some of the places, laws, crimes, procedures and the prison experiences are based upon real places and real research, however. This novel could not have been accomplished without that vast research and help from many people.

There is no town of Wayland, New Hampshire, nor County that I can find. The prison facility doesn't exist in this fictitious town either, obviously. While there are many places that are real in this novel, towns and businesses, I made a conscious decision to invent that prison facility. I did so because I felt after many interviews, with many different people who have been convicted of many different crimes, I found that all jails and prisons are virtually the same. To isolate one in the entire penal system is like trying to pick one burning piece of lumber from an entire burning building. That is to say that in my humble opinion, the system is broken.

I have a ton of people to thank. Some for their considerable help, some of the people are in this book, but in essence only. Thank you to JT, Marino, Joe, Millie and Wanda, your insights were invaluable. Kate, your legal expertise was essential in making this story believable. You also showed me that there are plenty of good people who are locked up, they are just paying for their deeds, while some people never do.

For my friends and acquaintances, you are all represented in spirit, and in some cases outright. These characters would not be as rich and dynamic if it weren't for you. To my family and friends, I am lost without your support.

Finally, much of this book takes place in New England, a place where I grew up. I have nothing but love for the people of the Northeast. I was born and educated there, I miss it, and I don't get to spend enough time there. Some of the novel takes place in California and South Carolina, I love these places as much or more, but for different reasons. Beautiful places and beautiful people are in both. Because of my travels, I don't spend enough time in these places either.

Hospitality could learn a lesson from the people of Charleston, South Carolina. The definition of Sunny California is San Diego. To my friends there, I love and miss you.

Brazil is an amazing place. To say that I have seen the entire Country would be a gross falsehood. But each new place in that vast land is a new place that I adore. If I have offended any of you or misrepresented your culture in any way, I apologize. Você é verdadeiramente um pessoa bonito de uma terra bonita.

To everyone in all corners, I have endeavored to craft a unique perspective on a crime that is truly unfortunate and an all-too-often occurrence. Please don't drink and drive.

Thanks for your time and I hope you enjoyed the read.

-SW-

ABOUT THE AUTHOR

Photo ©2014 WWPGroup, Inc.
www.WWPGroupInc.com

Scott Wellinger is a well-traveled writer and novelist. He has written many novels, articles, scripts, musical lyrics, and essays under pseudonames. His more popular novels feature, among others, the fictitious private investigations of Warren Dennihan. A native of New England, he was born in Vermont and was educated in Boston, Massachusetts. He holds a Master's Degree in Applied Economics and when he is not traveling, writing, playing music, cooking or painting, he is on a golf course.

For more author information: www.WWPGroupInc.com

Also by scott wellinger:

Use It Up (2015)

The Season for Moths (2016)

Other novels in the Warren Dennihan crime-fiction series:

Venom (book 2)

Sinn (book 3 - prequel)

Ebb (book 4)

Juror (book 5)

Flight (book 6)

COMING SOON:

The stand-alone legal thriller

The Deposition

These novels can be purchased in Ebook and print wherever books are sold.

Thank You for Reading!

If you enjoyed reading this novel, please help others appreciate it as well.

Recommend it. Please help other readers find it by recommending it to friends, reader groups, discussion boards, or wherever you purchased the book.

Review it.   You can add your thoughts to Amazon, GooglePlay, iBooks, kobo, Barnes & Noble, at the publisher website (WWPGroup.com), reader clubs like goodreads or LibraryThing, etc., etc. If you do write a review, please share it with either my publisher at WWPGroupInc@mail.com or me directly at scottwellinger@gmail.com (or both) so that I can thank you personally.

Follow me on twitter and Instagram for updates and special offers. @wellinger_scott , and @SCOTT_WELLINGER , respectively.

Best Wishes,

~SW~

The following is a sample of Venom, the follow-up novel in the Warren Dennihan series. The novel is available in ebook and print wherever books are sold.

PROLOGUE

THE RED AND BLUE LIGHTS COULD BE SEEN LONG BEFORE reaching the building, or entering the complex for that matter. The road past the main gate leading up to the enormous pharmaceutical research facility was lined with trees and signage which enabled workers and visitors alike to navigate to the appropriate building within the compound. All of which were reflecting the flashing emergency lights from deep within facility.

The property took up nearly one thousand acres just outside of Downtown Charleston, South Carolina. The various buildings which held various research data were dropped sporadically about the premises. The half-blind could have found the building being sought because of all of the lights and commotion in the early morning darkness of 2:00 AM. No signage nor a GPS was needed. A vehicle was approaching the epicenter of activity at triple the posted speed limit of twenty-five miles per hour, as the driver was late to the party.

The sedan made the right turn hardly slowing down, as if it were on rails. The blaring music of Miranda Lambert's *Crazy Ex-girlfriend* could be heard, muffled from outside of the racing vehicle, which ricocheted through the corner. The car raced through the turn and the large parking lot toward the building to the very edge of the cordoned area designated as such with yellow police tape. The illuminated sign above on the glass and brick building which read 'BIOGENESIS Pharmaceuticals Toxicology and Herpetology laboratories' was lost in the flashing lights of the Charleston Police cruisers, unmarked Homicide Detective sedans, the Coroner's van, CSU vehicles, and BIOGENESIS security SUVs. The scene was a rave, only previously without music.

The lissome and attractive Homicide Detective, Carina Fischer, exited her air-conditioned sedan as quickly as she had driven onto the site.   She pulled aside the bottom, left, front corner of her blazer, revealing her Charleston homicide detective badge to the sweaty, flat-footed patrolman who was maintaining the perimeter.   He lifted the yellow police tape for her.

She nodded to him and said in her Southern drawl, "BIOGENESIS. Isn't that the steroid company that — "

The officer interrupted her, which she hated.   " — Totally unrelated. I thought the same thing. Somebody's dead but it isn't A-Rod, unfortunately."

She paused on the other side of the police tape, staring the patrolman in the eye. It was hot and humid even without the sun, she wanted to go into the building, into air-conditioning. But not before setting the patrolman straight.

"Bless your heart.   Your Momma never taught you not to interrupt people when they were talkin'?"

The Patrolman got red-faced. He clearly didn't like to be dressed-down, and by the way he looked her up and down, she guessed especially by woman. Even if she was his superior.

"Aren't you a little late? Probably nothing left to investigate at this point. I'm sure you'll take all the credit though."

"What y'all doing here anyway? Issuin' parkin' tickets?"

She was in no mood for the usual red-neck, sexist crap that was dished out to her regularly. She was promoted because she was good at her job, if the lesser-achieving males have a problem with that then they can just get over it. At thirty-four, she had already accomplished more than the forty-something uniformed cop who was currently razzing her.

If he had a snappy comeback, he either didn't say it or she didn't hear it a she quickly moved toward the entrance to the building where more personnel were milling about. Their conversations were abruptly halted as she approached them, obviously preferring to gossip and theorize about what transpired inside privately. Once she reached the main lobby, she was informed that they were waiting for her on the third floor laboratory. The loiterers didn't say who 'they' were, but she didn't need them to. She knew who was waiting because she'd taken the late-night phone call from the people requesting her presence.

The ornate yet understated lobby was surrounded by glass, a waterfall fell from the top floor down into the center of the reception area. The falling water hid the side-by-side elevators behind it on the back wall. All of the appointments were made of glass, wood, stone and to a lesser extent steel, creating a very natural-looking environment. The tall trees added to the organic effect.

Both of the semi-hidden elevators were being held on higher floors, so Carina decided to take the stairs after pushing the elevator call button. Her long legs allowed her to ascend the stairs two at a time despite being in heels. She reached the third floor long before either of the elevators made a bid to drop to the lobby to collect her. The exposed stairs deposited her in the small reception area of the lab on the third floor which was decorated with the same muted, natural colors used in the lobby. A crush of people occupied this area, including her boss, the man whom had called her cell at her home. The Captain of the Charleston, South Carolina Homicide Division, Bryan Simms did not look happy.

"Captain Simms, I got here as soon as I could. I wasn't aware that I was on rotation. My desk is full, Sir."

"I called you because it looks like the case on your desk and this homicide are related. We have ourselves a very serious situation."

"Isn't murder always serious, Sir."

He broke free of his entourage, drawing Detective Carina Fischer out of the crowd with him.

"You can lay on that Southern charm can't you? What I'm saying is that we unofficially have a serial killer here in Charleston."

"This is related to my poison cases? Here?"

"I think it will make more sense once we go inside. But before we do, I need for you to know that we are trying to keep this out of the public for as long as we can. At least until we have an arrest. The last thing we need right now is to destroy our prime tourism season with a panic."

"Y'all know this is goin' to go viral, if it hadn't already. All the people millin' about? I had to get through a half-dozen news crews 'fore I could even get through the main gate." Her Southern drawl was thick.

"They know there was an incident and that a third-shift lab worker is dead because of it, but they know nothing else."

"Then they already know more 'n me."

"Always a wise-ass, Detective. Why can't you act like a lady? You certainly look like one. I must let you walk all over me because of your close-rate."

"You wanna show me the scene, Sir?" She was tired. Tired after having worked all day and then being dragged out of her much needed rest. Tired of the same conversation with her boss. She wasn't a lady, and if she attempted to act the way she thought he wanted her too, she was cussed out for that too.

Captain Simms had overcome some of the same obstacles that Carina had to overcome on her way up the ladder. He gave her a wide berth for that and other reasons but constantly felt the need to tell her that she was playing it wrong. That she wasn't going to move up the ladder with her current attitude. She had already surpassed what everyone said would be her ceiling.

Simms shook his head and guided her into the secure lab where an ID badge had to be used no less than three times to get into the main part of the lab. Simms had been fortified with a magnetized security card, which he needed to slide through the electronic reader. Each time Carina and her boss stopped at another electronic gate-keeper, she noticed that in addition to needing a badge, the entrances were being surveilled by Closed Circuit Television cameras.

"Before you ask, the system that records the security footage for this floor has been disabled and the card that was used to access the lab was assigned to a member of the night cleaning crew. Only that cleaner hasn't worked here in three years."

"They can't all be easy I s'pose. How'd you know I was fixin' to ask you?"

"I can read your mind."

They entered the lab which was filled with wall-to-wall laboratory machines. Other than the trays with test tubes resting on the large machine that presumably filled them, Carina hadn't a clue as to what all the equipment did. Along the perimeter of the lab were glass walls with doors leading to an assortment of desks and computers. They made their way to the back of the room where under the counter of a workstation, a slight man was dead on the floor. The amount of blood that was pooled on the floor could have filled a gallon milk jug. The man's lifeless eyes stared at their shoes, his arms folded in a way which indicated he was dead when he hit the floor. There was obviously no way that he could have been comfortable or tried to move once he'd landed there. The Medical Examiner, Spencer, approached behind them to restate the facts that had already been relayed to Captain Simms.

"You cannot see from this angle, but this guy was hit rather hard on the back of the head. He was a tiny man. Judging by the damage, he was hit harder than what was needed to kill him." The ME Squatted down under the counter and turned the victim's head so Carina could see the matted, blood-soaked hair. The victim had been struck with such force that the hair and skin on his head had been pulled away from his skull.

"Wow. The little guy really pissed somebody off."

"But that's not the best part. It gets weird."

He set the victim's head back on the cold linoleum floor, which was now red from the pooled blood, and pointed to the lumbar portion of the small dead man's back. He lifted the wet lab coat with tweezers the size of salad tongs which revealed what was once a white Oxford shirt. It had already been untucked and lifted, the ME pulled it up again for Carina.

"Same bite marks as my other two vics," Carina said.

"Exactly the same from what I can see. I'll remeasure and confirm when we get him back to the lab, but it seems pretty clear that he was bitten just like the others. I'm just not sure which came first, the chicken or the egg. Either one would have done the trick."

"So he could have gotten bit, which would have made him bleed out, then slipped and hit his head on the counter or something, which would have made him bleed out. But either way he never had a chance?"

Spencer shook his head. "Yes and no. There are no clues or marks to indicate that he struck his head on this counter, or any other counter in this lab. All the blood is right here." He pulled a pen out of his shirt pocket and pointed to the bite on the victim's back. The two holes were swollen and purple, still slowly leaking blood. "These are classic snake bites, just like your other two victims, Detective. I'm no reptile expert, so it's impossible for me to pinpoint the exact species of snake, especially without finding it, but the bleed-out suggests it is in the Viper family. The colleague that I consulted with on your other two cases said that there are several types of Vipers who's venom has a vicious anti-coagulant component. Meaning that if you get bit, you don't stop bleeding until your dead. Like your victims."

"Makes it hard to nail the bastard, darlin'," she said to the ME. "If I don't know when he was here, alibis are pretty loose."

"Just like the others, Detective, I will narrow it down the best I can. But it seems pretty clear that your killer likes to use his pet snake to do his dirty-work."

"Thanks a bunch." She turned to her Captain. "Who else was here in the lab tonight?"

"Nobody. There was another technician working in another lab on the floor directly below this one. The blood got under the linoleum, soaked through, and started dripping on the lab below. His ID card doesn't allow access to the lab on this floor, so he had to call security. The rent-a-cop saw this mess and called us."

"We have someone on the loose who over the last five weeks has killed three people, that we know of, by unleashin' a snake. You say that the ID used to get in here has a high clearance status but hasn't been used in three years?"

"Correct."

"Ain't that lovely."

"It gets even weirder Fish," Simms said as he waved off Spencer, relieving him of his duties with them for the moment. "Carina, take a guess at what they research here."

She shrugged.

"Venom."

1

THERE ARE SOME THINGS IN LIFE THAT YOU'LL NEVER forget.   Certain people, certain events, are stuck in your mind no matter how much time passes. A smell or a word can trigger those memories to come rushing back like they happened yesterday.   I wonder if when I'm eighty, if I make it to eighty, I'll still have the ability to recall with such clarity the events that have transpired over the course of my forty years on this planet.

As I sit here with a cup of coffee steaming in my hand, the smell takes me back to the not-so-distant past.   The case wasn't closed yesterday, nor the day before. In fact, it hasn't yet been six months, but this one will be burned into my brain for while. It ripped the heart out of me for good measure. It's not like I live a boring life. So the story that I am about to share with you sticks with me, not because it was one odd-ball story in an otherwise dreary existence. Nope, I have a very colorful past.

I was born in Boston, and raised in Southie. For those that've never watched one of the many Boston movies that have been recently made and become hugely popular, Southie is South Boston. It was, and still is to a lesser extent, a rough Irish neighborhood. Where the Irish mob that Irish cops don't want to mess with live and do business. Whitey Bulger was from here.

I made my way through it by boosting car radios. Sometimes the occasional car. I can admit that now because I was a kid when I did it, a long time ago. I still stay in contact with all of my old acquaintances, but most of them have been gentrified out of Southie. But that's another story.

I became a Massachusetts State Police Trooper, which was very boring, but it happened so I'm giving you context. Sitting on the Mass Pike watching the daily commuters struggle through gridlock was like watching grass grow and plucking the odd weed. It sucked. But the powers-that-be had originally sent me through the Police Academy, after my juvie record was expunged, *because* of my questionable past. Meaning they wanted me to rat on my neighbors. They got pissed when they finally realized that it wasn't going to happen. But I'd already been through the Academy at that point and passed with flying colors. So they stuck me on the Goddamned Pike.

My memory isn't the only long one, as it turned out. It took forever, but I finally made detective. I don't know what you do for a living, or what your daily life entails, but I can tell you that it probably involves exponentially less bullsh than what I had to deal with. Politics is not my thing. I grew up in a very tough and very poor neighborhood, where you call a spade a spade. Mind games and alliances a-la-*Survivor* would earn you a beatin'. Again, I wouldn't play ball, so everybody in the department knew I was never going to be promoted. I would retire a Detective Junior Grade, which would just be fuckin' sad.

So I took on some odd-jobs to keep life exciting. One of which was MMA fighting. I was only an amateur, but I had offers to go pro. Technically I was a welterweight (170 pounds), and a lean one at that, but I would always cut weight and fight the lightweights. I won more fights than I lost by far. That's not braggin', that's just true. I grew up fightin'. That's just what you did in Southie. Even the fags fought, they would just scratch the shit outta ya. Problems were a lot easier to solve back then. Anyway, I learned Brazilian Jiu-Jitsu while in the academy and went on to train with Kenny Florian after. No, I'm not name-dropping. Again, I'm just giving you context. I still practice five or six days a week, as time permits. I don't get into the cage anymore, not unless the pay is really good, but the skills come in handy for my current career.

While with the Staties, I also took side jobs helping out some friends in Southern New Hampshire with investigations. This would not have gone over well with my superiors, but everybody saw the writing on the wall and anything to grease the wheels of my departure was looked at kindly. I helped out my friends so often that I ended up going into business for myself. I was a licensed Private Investigator in both New Hampshire and Massachusetts. I still am. Life is good now.

I helped out one of those friends in New Hampshire, a lawyer with his own firm, regularly. I saved his life at one point. He had an entirely new perspective on the prison experience, let me tell ya.

We don't talk about that though. Not anymore. That was a humdinger too. The past is the past. We don't really talk at all anymore, he and I, since he moved to South Carolina.

Everybody always says that they'll keep in touch when friends move away, but they never do. JG and I were no different. Out of sight, out of mind. Life happens. We get busy and one day leads into a week, which leads into 'holy shit has it been that long?'.

I don't have that many true friends. I have a ton of contacts, acquaintances, people to whom I owe favors, people who owe me. But true friends that you can call on when the feces hits the proverbial fan, no matter how much time has passed? No. I ain't got many of them. So I was shocked and stunned when Jacob Grantes called me. JG.

Happy to hear from the guy, don't get me wrong, but I knew there was a reason. He needed a favor. Again.

It wasn't JG's ass in a sling this time, but he needed help nonetheless. He needed my help, specifically. My name is Warren Dennihan, but everybody calls me Deni.

As I sit here drinking my Starbuck's Costa Rican blend, I'm reminded about this case. In retrospect, I'm not sure I should'a gone down to Charleston. Hindsight is twenty-twenty though right? You know who your friends are when they drop everything and come to your aid. So I went. But sometimes a friend in need is a pest. Especially when you don't get all of the facts right away.

"Deni! It's JG. Jacob. Long time, no see. How are you?"

"Hey. How are you? How's Charleston? You're still in Charleston, right?"

"Yes, of course. I was trying to think of the last time that we spoke. It must have been when Olivia passed."

Olivia Craig was Jacob Grantes' mother-in-law. Ex-mother-in-law, to be precise. She was very wealthy in life, both when she was married to the financial mogul Norman Craig, of CIG fame, and kept her station after he passed of esophageal cancer. Jacob and his wife, Anna, the only daughter of Norman and Olivia Craig, were married for many years and had one child together. But in the end the marriage didn't work out and he now has custody of their boy, moving them and his law practice to Charleston, SC, from Wayland, New Hampshire.

Olivia and Jacob stayed very close, especially since they lived in the same city, and when she passed, she left him a windfall. Deni helped her out on a case several years ago, the same case that freed JG from a lengthy prison sentence in New Hampshire. For that reason, she left Warren a significant sum of money as well. Olivia Craig never forgot who her friends were.

"Yeah, must be. Sorry I couldn't make it down there for the funeral. I kinda felt like a heel, especially since she left me money."

"No worries. There were so many people at the funeral that I would have felt bad for not being able to spend much time with you anyway. It was a little chaotic and awkward for me, being that she was my ex-mother-in-law. But it's not like Anna could be there, so what was I going to do? Nothing? Hey look, I'd love to catch up but I have some time constraints."

Here it comes, Deni thought.

"I need to speak with you in person. I need your help with something that's going on down here. What does your caseload look like?"

"I've got some things going. I can't just book a flight and pop down to Charleston on a whim."

"Look, I know it's terrible to just call you after so much time, especially needing a favor. But it's important. I have a case that is an absolute mess. I was hoping that I could talk it over with you. I Just need you take a quick look. I need you buddy. Name your fee."

Now that JG's rich, Deni thought, *he's coming off like some of the people that I can't stand.* Money buys rich people whatever they want. 'NO' doesn't mean 'NO' because everybody can be bought. Some just have a higher price than others.

As he listened to JG on the other end of the phone, he wondered what it said about him that he didn't hang up the phone. *I must be a high-priced whore.* "Are you in trouble?" he asked instead.

"Me personally? No. But I have a colleague and friend down here that is being charged as a serial killer. Falsely."

"Jesus, a *serial killer*? That's not usually a label that gets put on someone falsely. Anyway, how long have you been down there? You don't have an investigator by now?"

"I have a few that I use. But none of them are as good as you."

He was playing to Deni's ego. It was working.

"I can have a private jet waiting at Logan Airport in two hours. Fly down here and listen to the situation. If you don't want to take a look at that point, I'll understand. What do you say?"

Deni headed to Logan Airport two hours later.

2

I CAN TELL YOU FROM PAST EXPERIENCE THAT THE
only way to fly is on a private jet. Security, jet-lag, and ears popping
from the elevation changes cannot be avoided. But you don't have to
deal with things like the four hundred pounder that tries to squeeze
into a coach seat with the same gumby-like approach that he would
use to get into a Yugo. They always pick the middle seat too, have you
ever noticed that? Anyway, you don't have to deal with all of the
screaming children, lines at the tiny bathroom, rude flight attendants,
baggage claims, and believe me I could go on. None of that shit.
You're now free to roam about the cabin. Drink your fill. And for an
Irish cat like myself, that is *the* perk. It also may have been my
downfall.

When I landed in Charleston, I was buzzed and feeling good. I
seemed to be getting on well with the super-hot flight attendant.
There was no mile-high club involved, not even a good make-out
session, but I still felt the vibe.

I deplaned and JG had a car waiting for me. I'm not usually
impressed by such things, but he had a Mercedes Benz *S63 AMG*
parked with the door open and a driver waiting. Between the booze,
the flight attendant and the pampering, I felt like a million bucks.

The last time I was in Charleston, South Carolina, I didn't have
such a great time. I was on a case and chasing a runaway suspect. I
was in no mood to truly appreciate how beautiful the area is. You

can't help but notice, but I didn't have the time to really take it all in. The suspect that I chased lived on the coast, which is also where JG lived. He lived in his ex-mother-in-law's house, a huge and historic in the district known as Rainbow Row. These four-storied mansions-turned-condos were juxtaposed along East Bay Street and were varying shades and colors in pastels, which is why it has the nickname. I didn't know what to expect in terms of their living arrangement, probably not a condo, but definitely not this. They owned the whole building, which ran one-block deep. Brady had to be the richest seven year old ever.

The ride from the airport didn't take long. None of it really took long when you stop and think about it. I was sitting in his home on Rainbow Row on the same day that he had reached out to me, a relatively few number of hours within that same day to be more accurate.

"Deni, thanks for coming down. I wanted to meet here rather than at the firm. It's a little less formal."

I was happy about that. I didn't want to be around a ton of stiffs because I had added to my buzz by having another drink in the car. Which was stupid.

"Thanks."

"Uncle Deni!"

I turned and saw his son, Brady, running toward me for a hug. He seemed genuinely happy to see me. How he remembered me was a mystery. The kid was always smart, but my gut told me that he had been coached. 'Make the long lost guy I'm trying to persuade to help your dad feel warm and fuzzy, Brady' JG probably said to him before I arrived. Joke is on them, though, I already felt very warm and fuzzy.

"Hey kiddo. How ya doin'?"

"Great. Will you be around later? I've got to go for my guitar lesson now."

"I'm not sure. I might be. Your dad and I have to discuss some stuff."

"Okay. Hope to see you when I get back."

I'll bet, I thought but didn't say.

"Can I get you anything before we sit down?" JG was smiling. Everything was to plan for him thus far, I would imagine.

"You got any Irish Whiskey?" Stupid.

"Of course. Right this way."

We went into a room that could have been an upscale pub. Only it was in my friend's house. Oversized leather seats, dark oak, old looking books that lined shelves, library-style. The bar was long and the shelves behind it were stocked with everything one could imaging, and I have a pretty big imagination. None of the stuff was Well. All of the various bottles of booze were high-end brands.

"You like Redbreast right?"

"You've got a good memory." I also noticed that he had only one lowball glass out on the bar. "Aren't you havin' any?"

"I don't really drink anymore."

"You have a bar in your house, but you don't drink anymore?"

"Not often. The bar is for entertaining. Besides, I need to be sharp to go over this case with you."

Buzzkill.

"But Deni, feel free," he continued as he handed me my three fingers of the expensive twelve year old whiskey that I loved but didn't need. I felt silly drinking in front of my friend who was abstaining. But I drank it anyway. Partly out of nervousness. Partly because 'why stop now?'. We sat in our respective plush, riveted, leather sofa-chairs. JG began spelling it out for me.

"Deni, it's been a while so let me catch you up on what I've been doing, it will give you some perspective."

I nodded but said nothing. What was there to say?

"When I came down here after the fiasco in New Hampshire, I wasn't sure that I wanted to practice law anymore. I was able to, I just needed to register with Bar Association down here. Jenna and I played house for a while, but my being home all the time was too much. She went back to school and she continually urged me to get out of my funk and do something with my life. I had no idea what to do, so I went through the motions and got myself set-up to practice law. Are you with me? You look bored."

"I'm here." *Just get to the point.*

"So anyway, I started and expanded a practice with the money with Olivia's financial support, before she passed. It's now the largest law firm in South Carolina. But I was bored. Jenna used to spend a lot of time at the University Library, as you can imagine, while she finished up her degree. I met her there from time to time and it kindled a passion for teaching. So I met a few contacts and now I teach law at South Carolina University, School of Law. In my practice, I'm really just a figurehead and take only the cases that truly intrigue me. I use them in my classes as case studies. This is one of those cases."

"Must be nice to have that option. Why am I here? You're obviously super-rich and can get anybody you want to investigate whatever it is you need to investigate. Why me?"

"I'm getting there. So South Carolina University at Charleston has an enormous campus. It actually started as a medical school in 1824, which is now the South Carolina Medical University and

Research Institute. The Law School and the Medical University are on the same campus. I met somebody there and became very good friends with her. After Jenna and I didn't work out. This person that I met, she's the one who's been charged as a serial killer."

"*Her? She?* Here we go, JG. Again? What is it about you that's attracted to crazy killer psycho chicks? Haven't we been down this road?"

"It's not what you're thinking, and she didn't kill anybody."

"What am I thinking?"

"That I cheated on my wife with Jenna and then on her with a women who is, as you call her, a psycho."

"So where is Jenna in all of this?"

"She's no longer in 'all of this'. I just told you that. Because of Sierra. The woman I'm seeing."

Is this guy for real? That's all I kept thinking. Clearly my friend had changed, and not for the better. If I were to show the man before me to the JG I knew in New Hampshire, I don't think he would even recognize himself. I knew then that my impromptu decision to go down there was not a good one either. I need to drink less.

"I've had a few adult beverages, so please interrupt me if I have this wrong. Your life in New Hampshire was very close to being ruined partly because you were suspected of cheating on your ex-wife. You get out of that mess and move down here. You miraculously get beyond all that, start a new life and *actually do* cheat on the woman who you were suspected of having an affair with up in New Hampshire? This new woman, the woman you met after coming down here to be with Jenna, is the one who is presumably incarcerated after being charged as a serial killer? What the fuck, Jacob?"

"Like I said, it's not what you think. My relationship with the accused, Sierra Byrne, was not .... consummated .... until after Jenna

251

and I both realized that our relationship wasn't going anywhere. There wasn't any cheating going on, not on my part anyway. Jenna was left with quite a sum of money from Olivia, she is and will continue to be just fine.

"As far as Doctor Sierra Byrne, even if we weren't together she needs a proper defense. She's innocent. There have been three murders affiliated with the same research facility and/or university where she works. The first death was originally designated an accident. The second was suspicious, so they reopened the first case because the deaths were similar. The third was ruled a homicide, no doubt. Three individual deaths with a cool-off period between, in this case over a five week span, is classified as 'serial'. They needed someone to pin down and quick. A serial killer on the loose in the beginning of summer, prime tourism season, would be another murder on the entire city, if you'll excuse the pun. Sierra has ties with both SCMU and the research facility funded by BIOGENESIS Pharmaceuticals. They have some circumstantial evidence that they're going to try to make stick."

"So why me?"

"It's getting political down here. Big Pharma, serial killer, government officials trying to save their precious city and tourism .... You aren't part of any of that. I need someone that I can completely trust. Someone who doesn't give a sweet shit about anything and someone without fear. I need to save the woman I love. I need you, buddy. The incomparable Warren Dennihan."

"Yeah, okay. Need, need, need. Want, want, want. It's all you do. Nice speech though. How long did it take you to practice that?"

He smiled. "A good-long while. Did it work?"

Shit.

3

THE FOLLOWING DAY WAS A REAL TREAT. I was hungover and in desperate need of a toothbrush before needing a change of clothes, which I didn't bring. I really did think that I was going to be able to go back to Boston, even if I did look into the case. At least that is what I kept telling myself before going to Logan Airport. So I didn't bring a bag. I called my ad hoc business associate who was working a case in the Financial District of Boston so he would know where I was, and told him that I was generating three times my usual rate down in Charleston. South Carolina not Charlestown, the bureau under the new Zaxim Bridge, home of the Bunker Hill Monument. He was as unenthused as I was, apart from the money.

I then called Ryan Wells, JG's former law partner. I needed to let him know that I was going to be out of pocket for the duration of this fiasco. He was fine with it as long as I hurried back. He had a few things that could wait but would need my attention when I returned.

My wealthy friend gave me a credit card for my expenses. An Amex Centurion Card. The black one with no limit. I'd heard of one, but had never seen one before then. JG said that I could blow it up if I wanted, he would pay my inflated fee and expenses. I wondered if I bought a Mercedes like the one that I rode from the airport to his place in was considered an expense? I needed transportation. I needed clothes more.

For the second time in my life, I went shopping for clothes in Charleston. And for the second time in my life I was taken to the pee-patch. I don't really see the appeal for designer clothes. I'm a t-shirt and jeans kind of guy. Nothing fancy. Designer clothes are for women and fags, in my opinion, but whatever floats your boat. Anyway, my search for basic jeans, a few t-shirts and maybe a sport coat in case I need to look presentable turned into a fleecing. My new non-skinny jeans were over $300. Each pair. What happened to t-shirts under $20? I was looking in the wrong places, because there weren't any. The sport jacket was as expensive as my first car. The one I didn't steal.

After purchasing my new wardrobe and had finally caffeinated away my hangover, JG and I were ready to go over to Leath Correctional Institution for Women. This is the Level Three facility that currently housed Dr. Sierra Byrne. She had been denied bail, which was no shocker. After all, it's not like she was accused of breaking into a piggy bank. This lady was labeled a serial killer and put into protective custody. The ride was a long one. Apparently the posh don't like to have their societal refuse too close them. Or to their tourists. I found that ironical because the same tourists spend hard-earned money on the Haunted Jail Tour of Charleston by the hundreds and thousands, but are forbidden to see an actual prisoner. But what the hell do I know?

After going through the various gates inside the prison and my new wardrobe being patted down by the butch she-man Correctional Officer, we were led to a private meeting room. It was drab and concrete, but it was private.

Two different female COs tugged a woman into the room who I presumed and later was introduced to as Sierra. The officers took off her ankle chains; the cuffs on her wrists, however, remained in place. She sat down only after the officers left the room, and they only left after informing us that they would be waiting outside if they were needed.

Sierra was a stunner. Very sinuous. Very tan. Or maybe she was milatto or milano or whatever you call those gorgeous women who have the natural perma-tan. Perfect skin. Her brown eyes were currently wearing the weight of the world in them, but still stunning. I could see why JG had given up on what was, at the time, the most beautiful girl I'd ever seen face-to-face.

His new girl looked happy to see him. I could tell she wanted to make physical contact, but that's a no-no. "Jay, I am so glad to see you. It's only been a week and I have no idea how I'm going to survive it any longer."

"This is Warren Dennihan. The man I told you about. Everybody calls him Deni. He's going to investigate your case. I wanted you to meet and maybe you can fill him in."

"Nice to meet you Deni. I wish it was under different circumstances. I have heard so much about you. I am not sure how much Jay has told you."

"I haven't told him much," JG interjected. "The information is privileged and I wanted to make sure that everybody was on-board before we delved into it too far."

"Well, there really isn't very far to go. I have no idea who did this, but I know it wasn't me."

My turn. "So why do *you* think, that *they* think, that it *is* you?"

"You're accent is thick. Where are you from? New York?"

"Not a fuckin' chance. Boston. Southie, actually. But back to the point, why are you gettin' blamed?"

"Because I knew all of the victims in this case. The first was a doctoral candidate that was working directly under me. The second was a lead researcher at our lab at SCMU and the most recent victim was a lab worker at the BIOGENESIS lab. He ran tests at the pharmaceutical lab. All of us at SCMU worked closely with them. I worked particularly close with all three of them."

"BIOGENESIS? Isn't that the steroid company that — "

" — No, Deni. It's the same name, but no. I could see how you would be confused but steroids are not what we do."

"I'm a little behind. Maybe we can share with me what it is you do, exactly."

"I apologize. I thought that Jay might have covered that. I hold three PHDs in Toxin/Toxicology, Herpetology, and Bioengineering. I am also one of the leading experts in Venomology."

I had no idea what any of that meant except that this chick was fuckin' smart. How does one person get all that? Looks and brains? God is cruel.

"Yeah, let's pretend I am not as smart as you and just tell me what you do with all of them degrees and what-not."

"Of course. I teach Bioengineering, among other things, at SCMU. My erudite grad students actually do most of the teaching these days, as my workload is very rigorous. My doctoral candidates assist in the research that I oversee, which takes up most of my time. They benefit from cutting-edge research to complete their respective dissertations, while we attract top minds to assist in the work."

"Pardon for interrupting, but did you say what that work is yet? Lots of big words and really just the one question I need answered."

She gave JG a look that I didn't like. I make my living at being able to read people and she just shot a look that told her lawyer and boyfriend that she was afraid that I'm not smart enough to investigate a missing dog, let alone her case. Lets face it, I ain't no genius. I barely graduated high school, but there is book smart and regular smart. I'm in the latter category. I'm smarter than I let on, though, and I do that on purpose. People underestimate me, which puts me at an advantage. I may not be the best speaker, have the biggest vocabulary, or even a fancy degree; but I'm not dumb.

I let the look slide and let her continue. "Simply put, we create drugs. There are many chemicals found in nature that have a very specific purpose. We study those chemicals and develop synthetic drugs to cure illnesses that align with the original purpose. For example, have you heard of the Nano-bee?"

"Nano-bee? No, I don't think so."

"Ok, well, the Nano-bee—just like other bees—sting people to protect their hive. Every bee sting injects a venom, but the Nano-bee is named such because their venom contains nano-particles which carry a toxin that, like all venoms, have a specific purpose. That purpose is to effect the immune system of the recipient, which has been shown to attach itself to HIV. HIV, as I'm sure you know is the Human Immunodeficiency Virus which causes AIDS. A synthetic drug is currently being tested which was derived from Nano-bee venom that has very few side effects. That drug will be the cure of AIDS."

The excitement was back in her eyes. I could see that she loved her work. Curing AIDS. Pretty cool. I couldn't imagine ever dating this chick. I'd come home and ask, 'What'd you do today honey?' She'd say, 'oh, nothin'. Just cured AIDS'. What did I do? I took pictures of a cheating wife last week. She's out of my league.

"So you think that these murders are bee-related?"

"No. Not specifically. That was just an example. We have many projects. I say *we*. The university is funded by a huge pharmaceutical company that has many projects. SCMU, the research institute,

BIOGENESIS, and the World Toxin Bank work closely together because the work is mutually beneficial."

"Did we go over what the Toxin Bank place is yet?"

"No, probably not. The World Toxin Bank houses the largest collection of natural toxins on the globe. It's the only one of its kind. Think of it like a semi-public spice rack. Or a toxin library. When researchers are looking to analyze a specific toxin, they can obtain a sample from the WTB instead of having to obtain a live specimen from the field."

"Semi-public?"

"Yes. It can get a bit political. Those that contribute to the WTB supply get first priority, along with the largest financial contributors. There isn't an infinite supply, so it has to be parceled out fairly. And while the WTB has over 10,000 known toxins on hand, there are an estimated 20,000,000 other toxins on the planet. Of those 10,000 that we have access to, only about 1,000 are actually being studied at present. The goal is to eventually have a blueprint of every toxin. It's a lofty goal because animals adapt, toxins mutate. So it's a far-reaching and likely never-ending goal, as you can see. In the meantime, the arrangement with the WTB is the best we can do to accommodate everyone who is researching toxins."

"Obviously not everyone is pleased with the arrangement. Have the police looked into this World Toxin Bank?"

JG chimed in while fumbling through his files. "The investigating detective's name is Carina Fischer. I had another investigator, Eric Stubbs, look into her. She is a tenacious thing. She looks clean and is very good at her job. Except this time. Sierra was her one and only suspect."

"So our alternate theory is that someone doesn't like this research or WTB arrangement. Who might that be?"

"Take a number. I get threats every day, Jay will tell you. We get some at home …. "

I let it slide that she said *we* and *home* in the same sentence. Clearly JG and Brady were not the only ones shacking up on Rainbow Row. I pondered it for a moment while she was speaking.

" …. PETA, other research facilities, other universities, other big drug companies and— "

"—Walk me through that."

"PETA? People for Ethical Treatment of Animals are—"

"—Yeah, I know. They think bees are *pets*?"

She looked at JG again. I couldn't quite read what that particular look meant, but it wasn't good. She probably just continued to think about how stupid I am.

"No. No, they don't think that bees are pets. Bees populations are dwindling, and colony collapse will ultimately end life on earth as we know it. Which is true, but frankly they don't really know what they're talking about.   They think that we kill the bees and other animals, conduct drug testing on them. PETA is against all of what we do, some of which they claim exacerbates the decline in bee population, for example. We have no interest in hurting animals, in fact we want their populations to flourish so we can use their natural gifts to solve the ills of the human population. They make a big noise despite not having any facts."

"OK. What about other universities?"

"This research is very competitive. Drugs are big business and everyone tries to get a piece of the pie. Research brings in dollars. Universities love dollars. The quicker and better the research, the quicker the patents. The patents mean that only those drug companies can produce that drug for the length of the patent. When the patents run their course, generic companies get involved."

"So we have no shortage of people who could have killed these people. All we really know is that it has to be research related, and somebody who had access to all three of the victims."

"That's what makes the most sense and why they quickly arrested me. I fit. But I didn't do it."

What had I gotten myself into? This was going to be like trying to find a needle in a stack of needles. As it turns out, I *am* dumb.

I really should have asked more questions.

4

I NEEDED TO LEARN SPECIFIC DETAILS ABOUT THE
murders. The latest crime scene would be the easiest to glean
information from. Which, according to the reports I had attained from
Jacob Grantes, meant that I needed to go to the third lab, the location
of the third murder. JG made some calls and arranged it for the
following day. The lab was on hold until day three. It seemed
appropriate.

The rest of my night was free until then. The house was big
enough where all of the occupants could be present but not seen or
felt. If Brady came home that night, he didn't come to see me. He
must have forgotten. Or he was tied up with his friends and stayed
wherever he was. It seems like the last was a long-shot though, he was
only seven. But I'm no parent and have no earthly idea how to raise a
child in this day and age. So what do I know about kids and curfews?

With the night free, I wanted to look up Jenna. JG's old girlfriend
was a smoke-show. She used to work at this bar, Sully's, in Barstone,
New Hampshire. It's conveniently located across the street from Ryan
Wells' practice. I still work with Ryan, who now runs the practice with
his wife Angie, and I still go into Sully's but with less occasion because
it's just not the same without Jenna. I used to flirt with her, and she
used to rebuff me. And so we danced.

Now that she and JG were on the outs, maybe I had a shot. So I
wanted to get in-touch with Jenna. It's against 'guy code' to go out

with a friend's ex. That is axiomatic. A steadfast rule. But I'm not much for rules. And whoever made that rule hadn't laid eyes on Jennifer, Jenna, Beaumont. So a guy's gotta do what a guy's gotta do. Odd for a former Mass State Police Detective to break rules all willy-nilly, but I'm paradoxical I'm told. Whatever that means.

I am not going to say that I didn't try to find her. That would be a big fat lie. I called the old cell number I had for her. Disconnected. I hit up six dining establishments and bars looking for her. I asked everyone who paused to talk to me, and showed just as many people the picture that I had of her on my phone. Only one person said that she looked familiar. I knew the guy was full of shit, because let me tell ya — if you saw Jenna, you'd damn-sure remember. She wouldn't just 'look familiar'. I suspected her of some shenanigans a while back, she knew it and tried to disappear on me, and I found her down here. Now that she was through with JG, she'd vanished for good.

Could she have been behind this? Jenna might have felt tossed aside for another attractive and wicked smart woman, which was a strong motive to frame said attractive and wicked smart woman. I had suspected her of some shady shit in the past, could she be involved in this mess? I would keep it in mind. Or maybe I just had her in my mind and I came up with any excuse to find her.

Don't judge.

In any case, I failed in the one attempt I was afforded and didn't have the time to continue my trace on her.

The following day, day three, I went out to BIOGENESIS Pharmaceuticals to check out the lab. I had an appointment with the Director of Operations, the top dog over there. JG had classes that day, so I was on my own. I'm not sure if the driver had the day off, but the Mercedes *S63 AMG* was available for use. I put it through it's paces.

That car was as fast as greased-lightning. German engineering at it's finest.

The GPS told me it was going to take 27 minutes to get to the compound. Over the Ashley River, onto Route 17, and North a few exits on Interstate 95, I weaved in and out of traffic. I made it just over fifteen minutes. It would have been faster but I sped past my exit and had to turn around.

The rent-a-cop at the main gate was busy with all of the commotion outside, so it took an extra few minutes to get to me. News crews and protesters were congesting the entire entrance. Once I made it past them without running someone over, which is what I wanted to do, I was told to park in the parking lot off to the left and one Jarod Lynde, the Director of Operations himself, would be there shortly to transport me to the appropriate lab. Despite the delays I was early for my 10:00 AM appointment, so there was another wait. I spent the time playing with the buttons and what-not in the *AMG*. I also found a cool music channel on SiriusXM, called *Lithium*. Old-school Seattle bands. Nobody makes Grunge anymore.

Jarod Lynde showed up in a golf cart. After introductions, he drove me about ten football fields over to the Toxicology and Herpetology Lab. The building was still cordoned off, but from whom I had no idea. The parking lot was empty.

"You will have to excuse the mess," Lynde said. "CPD has cleared us to clean it up but with the entire lab having been shutdown, it hasn't been the top priority, as you might imagine."

"You aren't getting back to business as usual?"

"Unfortunately no. We have some other .... Internal issues that have occurred which has further disrupted what you would call, 'business as usual'."

"Like what?"

"I am afraid that is confidential information."

"I am trying to help you find out who killed one of yours. Help me help you, guy."

"BIOGENESIS is a publicly held company under the umbrella of a much larger conglomerate. I simply enforce what has been directed from above me, who report to the Board of Directors, who report to a Fortune 100 Corporation. Stock Prices are volatile, I am only allowed to say so much without lawyers present."

"Then what am I doing here? If you aren't going to answer any of my questions, why did you agree to meet with me? Jacob Grantes, the attorney that I work for, had this all set up like we would be able to work together."

"I'll do the best I can within certain confines," Lynde said as he parked the golf cart, then ushering me inside the building. He used a magnetic ID card to unlock the door. Lynde then led me into a conference room on the second floor, not a laboratory. He waved his hand indicating that he wanted me to sit in one of the chairs surrounding the conference table. "We can chat here for a bit, where I will give you what information I am able. You will have to sign some waivers and confidentiality agreements before I can let you see our Lab. Then, and only then, will you be able to tour the third or any other floor."

"Pretty cloak and dagger, wouldn't you say?"

"As I said, we have a very large company to protect."

"Can you elaborate? I'm a bit confused by that."

"What I am about to tell you is public record, so I can. BIOGENESIS is one of the top Pharmaceutical Research Corporations in the world, yet only a small fraction of our umbrella company. We have thousands of projects in which we design and manufacture innovative drugs for human illnesses. All of which are in various phases of the process by which a drug is available for sale by prescription. Our revenues alone last year were close to $100 million US dollars. We are but a cog in the wheel of our umbrella company, PROXER, which is currently *the* number one Pharmaceutical Company on the planet. With revenues of just under half a trillion US dollars last year, we are in the top 100 of *any* company on the planet. Bigger than Apple or Google."

"Did you say *trillion*? Maybe medication could be a little more affordable if you greedy fucks would settle for making half-*billions*."

"I said revenue, not profits. Everybody thinks it is easy to generate these medications."

"You just drove me over here in a golf cart wearing a designer suit that would probably cost me a years salary, and you claim to be a low-level Director of Operations. Don't cry poverty, guy. Especially after you just said trillion. You'll make me cry."

"Your quips aside, do you have any idea how much money and research goes into creating a drug?"

"No, not really. But I'm guessing that's what you're gonna share with me, instead of the information I came here for."

He ignored the slam, and went on with the *School House Rock* version of how research becomes a drug.

"There are currently forty-nine umbrella companies in the pharmaceutical and biotech industries that each generate as low as tens of millions of US dollars per year. Everybody from Bayer to Proctor & Gamble to AstraZeneca and many, many more are all competing for the next miracle drug. BIOGENESIS is just the underling of one of these companies. They are all trying to hire the best researchers in the field, from the best universities, to advise them in their research and testing of potential drugs. I say potential drugs because there are millions of dollars that go into a potential medicine before it even gets to a beta phase.

"A lab, like ourselves, generates promising data off of a theory. We then submit an Investigational New Drug, or IND application, to the Center for Drug Evaluation and Research. The CDER. Once the application takes effect, clinical trials can then begin. But that application can be stalled by the FDA on a 'clinical hold' for virtually any reason, which is usually political. Kickbacks usually take place to spin the wheels of progress. Clinical trials can last years depending upon the side effects, and the FDA is basically up our ass the entire time about; rules on reporting, specs, methods of analysis .... Everything from packaging to distribution. These formulae are patented, but the trials could outlast the term of the patent, which makes the research free game for competitors. Any of these forty-nine huge companies, never mind the smaller ones like us, could swoop in and generate the same medicine with comparatively no research money shelled out. That is *if* the drug even makes it to that point. I can't tell you the number of 'promising data' theories that never make it to the local pharmacy. Millions and millions of dollars are spent with no return.

"We haven't even mentioned pilfering researchers from competing companies to steal research. It's highly illegal, but it's done. It's easier and more cost beneficial to pay a Piracy or Infringement settlement than shell out money for research. By the time our lawsuit gets into the Civil Courts, this lab will have been vacant for years."

Ah-ha. There was the slip.

"So that's what you meant by 'internal issues'? Somebody defected? Stole research?"

"Oh. No. I was speaking hypothetically. We do need you to sign those confidentiality documents now, if you please."

He handed me a stack of papers with little adhesive arrow tabs pointing to where I needed to put my John Hancock. I didn't even read them, I just signed while I pressed Mr. Lynde.

"OK, so let's speak in hypotheticals. Hypothetically, if some people were to be eliminated from the equation and other key people were to be enticed to bring their expertise to a competing company, that would put and end to the research?"

"Hypothetically, yes. At a minimum it would set the research back decades. By that time the patent would expire, the drug could be released by a competitor, or never get made at all. Millions of dollars lost."

"And millions of people don't get a cure for what ails them. You were studying a cure for AIDS correct?"

"No, that is not correct. Who told you that? We are well beyond hypotheticals now aren't we?"

"I must have been misinformed. I thought you were studying bee venom or something to cure AIDS."

"You have been misinformed. But even if you were correct, I couldn't say," Lynde said. He was visibly uncomfortable.

"So whatever it was that you *were* researching, who would want to kill it? Or kill for it?"

"Are you kidding? We have thirteen buildings with independent projects all working simultaneously—"

" —I'm not askin' about twelve other buildings, I'm askin' about this one. Unless there were murders in the other labs, I don't give a shit about 'em."

"Get in line. Did you see the crowd outside the main gate?"

"The news crews? They have somethin' to do with this?"

"Yes, Mister Dennihan.   The news crews.   The news affiliates killed a lab worker and are barricading the complex. Are you mad?"

"Are you tryin' to piss me off? 'Cuz I'll beat the life outta ya in your designer suit." When I stood up, he backed down.

"I apologize. It's a trying time and I'm on edge, as I'm sure you can imagine. The crowd outside would be there whether there was a legal incident or not.   PETA is upset about animal cruelty, religious organizations are incensed about snake venom being the seed of Satan, Unions about outsourcing, fair wages and benefits. Doctors. Political nut-jobs. And God knows who else are outside those gates every day trying to interfere with our work."

"Did you say *snake venom*?"

That's not good.

The tour of the lab was fruitless. The body was gone but the outline of the lake of blood was still present. I didn't see any animals in the lab, and Lynde said that they never have any animals in the labs with the exception of lab mice on certain projects. He would not elaborate on what was going on in that lab, or what was being developed. With all of the equipment in that glass fortress, it could have been microprocessors for all I knew.

For every question I asked, he would respond with statements of confidentiality, me not being a cop, and the fact that I didn't have a subpoena. I love the classics, but every once in a while some new material is nice. I was getting nowhere and I was getting there slowly.

Since I was being chaperoned, there was no way to get into one of the other buildings to interview other people who may have known what was going on in the now defunct one. Especially cleaning crews. The report JG had given me said that the last ID card that was used to enter the lab belonged to a member of the cleaning crew three years prior.

I asked for a list of employees and that went over like a fart in church. Square one. The only thing that Lynde said to me, that was of any interest, was about a defector. More accurately, he hinted at one. I needed to know who that was. He also had a glancing comment about snakes. I was desperate to get that out of my mind. I have no interest in snakes whatsoever.

Outside the gate, I parked the *AMG* in line with all of the news vans. I decided to canvas the crowd. See what I could learn. The reporters and cameras were doing their own interviews and coverage, which gave me an idea of how to approach the protestors. Amidst the crowd was a tall female in a blazer that I spotted as a detective a mile away. She could not be in many crowds and go unnoticed. The lady had a Natalie Portman thing going on, only taller. She was five-nine or ten. Maybe eleven, she had heals on which made it tough to tell for certain. The interview pad she was writing on, the badge, and bulge for her weapon was what made me add 'detective' to the other things that I was thinking about her. The closer I got, the more I liked.

I started doing interviews of my own, but kept her in the corner of my eye. *Let her come to me.* She eventually did.

What I learned in those interviews wasn't much. PETA went on about the rights of animals, but had no specific information about the case or the specific lab. A religious group prattled on endlessly about the facility being an anathema of God, an abhorrence in the eyes of Christ that will bring about Armageddon. The End of Days were upon us and I should get my affairs in order.

Good, I thought at the time. I'm more of a night guy anyway.

There was also a unionized group or something that disliked that BIOGENESIS used cheap labor and college students instead of paying a fair wage, but their hearts didn't seem into it. There was a small faction of them that supervised the picketing, while the minions apathetically went through the motions. I found that to be hypocritical, but about right.

"Are y'all at the eighty?"

Here she was. Just a matter of time. When I turned to face her, she was even more beautiful than from afar. Not like high-def TV where the closer the camera gets to the celebrity, the less attractive they become. Her Auburn hair had the slightest of red highlights, which accented the green in her hazel eyes. And that Southern drawl melted my soul. She was hell on heels.

"Uh. Excuse me?" And apparently my brain.

"Eighty Broad. Crimes Against Persons?"

"Oh. No. I'm with myself."

"Not a cop? Y'all a reporter?"

"No. Investigator. I'm Warren Dennihan. You can call me Deni. And you are?"

"Ah, Lord Almighty. Let me see some ID, hun."

I didn't remember that all Southern women say *hun, honey, darlin', handsome, sweetie* and the like. Even if they can't stand you. I thought she was keen on me. When I see a pretty girl, I do what I always do. I flirt.

"You can see anything you want."

"Just your ID 'll be fine." The way she said 'fine'? I was in lust. I broke out my driver's license and my Private Security and Investigation licenses for both Massachusetts and New Hampshire. I handed all three pieces of identification to her.

"You didn't say who you are." My Boston accent is strong. Wicked strong. As strong as her Southern drawl. She picked up on the accent, I'm sure. She definitely did when I said *are*, because they sound like *ah*. Like all born-and-bred Bostonians, I don't pronounce *r*'s in words, and I add one where they have no earthly business. But my licenses proved what she already knew.

"Missin' a State in here aren't ya there loverboy? I knew y'all were a Yankee. That accent gives you away, darlin'. I'm Detective Fischer, and we've got a problem."

"You're damned right we do. I hate the Yankees. I'm a Red Sox fan."

"Great. Follow me." She handed me back my IDs, along with her business card and guided me to her unmarked sedan. With her perfectly shaped buttocks in front of me, I would have followed her anywhere. She stopped at her car and turned around to face me. An even better view.

"Just what are y'all doin' so far from home?"

"I'm looking into the death that occurred here. I work for the attorney Jacob Grantes. He's defending the accused, Sierra Byrne. I'm helping with the investigation."

"Bless your heart." She said it in a way that left little doubt that she was telling me to fuck myself. "Hun, you're not helpin' me or anybody else. Not even yerself. You can't investigate a damned thing down here. So unless you are down here buyin' souvenirs, you should pack yer shit and head on back to your Red Sox."

Hot as a two-dollar pistol, curses, sarcasm, and feisty. I was ready to propose.

"Not a baseball fan, huh?"

"This is football country down here. Real men play contact sports."

She was killing me.

"But that's got nothin' to do with it," she said. "Things are different down here. I'm gonna cut you a break. Today. I'm gonna help you out and tell you somethin' that your fancy lawyer-boss should have told you. You need to be licensed in South Carolina. These out-of-state PSI licenses don't mean shit down here. Even if they did, PI's in my fine State do background checks, insurance scams, security, infidelity cases and such. No crimes. Cold cases maybe, but only if they're no longer bein' investigated. This one *is* being investigated. By me. Which means it sure as shit ain't cold. South Carolina Title 40, chapter 18. Might be good readin' on your plane ride home, darlin'."

"So maybe I'll just get a license down here, beautiful."

"Typical. Yer cute but you don't listen for shit. You can't be anywhere near this case. I see you again anywhere but on one of our beaches, and I'll see you get locked up and fined ten grand. Am I gettin' through that perdy little head of yours now?"

OK. Maybe she didn't dig me.

5

I HAD, FOR ALL INTENTS AND PURPOSES, BEEN KICKED IN the gift-bag. Detective Carina Fischer intrigued me. Lets face it, we're all friends here, she gave me chest pains. Read into that what you will. But I licked my wounds and headed to SMCU instead of following her around like a puppy, which is what I wanted to do. At any rate, I needed a word with my employer. I raced over there and made it in thirteen minutes, or three songs and a news report on the Rock Station, 98.1 FM. God, I loved that car.

Finding your way around a campus that size is a nightmare. Whoever was in charge of the look and feel of that university was far more interested in beauty than function. Flowers and cobblestones everywhere, but find a fucking sign? Never gonna happen. It took me longer to get to JG once I reached the campus than it did to get over to the campus from BIOGENESIS. I eventually had to call him back and have him talk me through it. SCMU and the law school within the university were considered the same campus but did not occupy the same buildings. I was turned around and lost three times, even with JG on the phone explaining where I was and where I had to go. Freshman must never get to class at that school.

JG was in his office. He was supposed to be having his office hours, where students with issues could go in and talk about what they weren't understanding, but I put an end to that. The two cute undergrads and the nerdy kid had to screw. And after a few words from me, they did.

"Deni, you can't talk to people like that down here. Southerners already think of Yankees as brash, abusing people doesn't help the cause. These students pay tuition and have the right to come see me during posted office hours. You can't just run them off like that."

"Listen, I've had a tough morning because you've been less than forthcoming about what I'm able to do down here as an investigator. Lynde was useless and the hot-as-hell detective chick who caught your case dressed me down for all to see. I'm down here doing you a favor and you feed me to the fuckin' wolves."

"I don't know what you mean by 'feed you to the wolves', but I thought that doors would open up for you, yes. When I spoke with this Lynde, he gave me no indication that he would be uncooperative. I kinda of knew Detective Fischer was a ball-buster, from her reputation, but I had no way of knowing that she would even be there. You're a big-boy, I've never heard you whine like this."

"Yeah well, it doesn't matter. According to her, legally I can't do anything anyway. Neither of my licenses work down here."

"That's not *exactly* true. I have a fix for that."

The door opened without a knock and a tall, blonde, mountain of a man came in through it. I've never been one to be intimidated by anybody. The bigger they are the harder they fall kinda thing. The fights that I've been in, I might not have won them all, but the sons-of-a-bitches knew they'd been in a fight. I have literally gone toe to toe with a linebacker and have the scars to prove it. Most fights end up on the ground anyway, so it doesn't matter how tall they are.

But this guy was diesel. Huge and muscular. I'm six feet tall, and he stood over me by three or four inches. Imagine if he had a neck? He would have been seven feet tall. We won't even get into how much wider than me he was. His nose had been broken a few times, so he looked the part. He stuck out his hand as he made his way toward me in the mid-sized office. I was thankful and apprehensive at the same time. Thankful that he was only trying to shake my hand, apprehensive because his hand was the size of an Easter ham. And his grip on my hand crushed like a vice.

"Deni, this is Eric Stubbs. He's an investigator at my law firm," JG said.

Eric had the softest voice I have ever heard. "Nice to meet you. I've heard quite a lot about you. It will be an honor to work with you, Sir."

"Sir? Excuse me? Work with me?" *What the fuck just happened?*

Eric obviously read the shock on my face, because he immediately removed his hand and looked to JG for guidance.

"Ah, yes. We were just getting to that, weren't we Deni? Have a seat gents." We both did.

How Eric fit in his chair is still a mystery.

"Deni, Eric is licensed in the state of South Carolina and has formed relationships with many people in Charleston. He is down here what you are to New England. Eric is from Charleston and almost played professional football, which makes him a celebrity. He will be able to—"

"—OK, well then. You don't need me." I stood to leave but that big ham was back, this time on my shoulder strongly encouraging me to remain seated. Apparently this ride had not yet come to a complete stop.

"I'm sure you don't like to work with other people," Eric said. "I don't like partners much myself. But from what I have heard, I could learn a lot from you. I can help you with the locals." I could not get over his voice. It was soft and tranquil. This guy had the look of an enormous polar bear, but sounded more meek than a teddy bear. Winnie-the-Pooh has a more grisly voice. I wonder what it took to make him mad. I would eventually find out.

"Listen Eric—"

"—Call me Stubbs."

"Really? You *want* to be called Stubbs?" *Is this guy for real?*

"Deni," JG said, "it takes a minimum of thirty days for you to get your PSI license down here. You have to take an oath with the Attorney General or SLED. But you can be made a temporary employee of someone who is licensed without having to be registered. That would also get you your Conceal and Carry permit. It normally takes ten days but I greased the wheels and can have one for you tomorrow, once they determine that you have no outstanding warrants. They have a much more tolerant approach to guns down here."

"So I would work for Eri .... I mean Stubbs? Technically."

"Correct. Technically."

"But why go through all of the trouble? I'm telling you Detective Fischer was as serious as a heart attack when she told me to back off. Not that I am a big stickler for rules, but you seem to have a capable investigator. Why pay me, uh, what you're paying me when I'm not really going to be able to do shit?" I was not sure what Stubbs was being paid, but I would bet it was less than me.

"Because I need a result. And more importantly, Sierra needs that result. I need you on this, Deni. You have not failed in the past, at least not with me. No offense, Eric, because I need you on this also, but you aren't Deni. Not yet anyway."

"None taken," he whispered. If he was offended in any way, he didn't show it.

"All right. With that settled, lets move forward with the real meeting."

He didn't wait for me to orally agree to the new terms of the arrangement. But he didn't really have to, I suppose. He knew what he needed to say to get me to stay, and he said it. Like I said, sometimes a friend in need is a pest.

Stubbs unzipped his shoulder bag, which I didn't even realize he was carrying until that point. He retrieved a shoulder harness with a handgun holstered in it.

"I wasn't sure if you had a preference in your pistols, but I like the stopping power of a .45 caliber. You?"

"You're speakin' my language big-boy. Whatta we got?"

"Taurus *PT1911 stainless*. The key lock has been taken off the hammer but other than that it's out of the box."

The gun was beautiful. And loaded. Eight in the magazine and one in the chamber. I liked the guy's style.

"Just make sure you keep a low profile with it until your Carry Permit comes tomorrow. My gift to you as a way of saying thanks for working with me. JG can handle the paperwork to make it all legit. It will be registered to you here in the State of South Carolina."

Correction. I loved the guy. Full-on man-crush.

But it was time to get down to business.

"Deni, why don't you fill us in on what you found out over at the lab," JG said.

"Not much really. I now know the process by which a drug comes on the market. Whether that's beneficial in our investigation or not, I don't know. It does mean that there are a ton of people along the way that could halt the process if they had a problem with the drug or the company."

"Right," Stubbs said. "So why not do what you can to stop that part of the process if the end goal is to eliminate the drug? No need to kill anybody."

"Good point. And I don't even know what drug they were making over there. Very hush-hush. It seems Sierra's AIDS theory isn't what they were cookin' up over there though. Lynde may have been lyin' to me, but how are we gonna know for sure?"

"She may have been using that as an example, Deni. That was probably one example of what bioengineers do. Or maybe that was just one drug among the many that they're researching. She has a confidentiality agreement in place, so she's not likely to divulge her actual projects. Nor will Lynde. But I'll see if I can find out the exact nature of what was being tested at BIOGENESIS."

"It doesn't matter anymore, I don't think. Whatever it was, the game is over. That lab is as deserted as the Sahara. I guess they had a defector or two, so that really put the kibosh on it."

"That's where I might be able to help." It was Stubb's turn. He was studying his notes which he had also removed from his bag. "The number two guy over there Enrique Estabados, excuse me *Doctor* Enrique Estabados, went over to Nahash Pharmaceuticals, which is a subsidiary of Wyatt, the number two pharmaceutical company in the world. Anybody want to venture a guess as to the number one?"

"Ooh, ooh, pick me." I raised my hand like I was in a classroom. Seemed fitting considering I was in the office of a professor at a prestigious university.

"You …. in the corner." I loved that he played along.

"Ummmmmm, would that be PROXER?"

"Give the man a prize. And we all know that BIOGENESIS works under PROXER," he continued. He was coming out of his shell.

Still soft-spoken but at least he had some personality in that immense body of his.

"Lynde said that they had some internal turmoil over there."

JG chimed in. "So he murders and sabotages to bring down BIOGENESIS as a way of getting at PROXER because he's a mole for Wyatt? You almost need a scorecard."

"I can help. Wyatt is winning." I was a quick study.

"By killing three people? Seems a bit strong doesn't it? I could see taking all of their trade secrets and giving them to Wyatt, but murder?"

"Stubbs, I just spoke with Lynde and he told me that these umbrella companies generate a half-trillion dollars in revenue. Each. I would kill for a burger right now, never mind a trillion bucks. Just sayin'."

"Let's go talk to Estabados then. I'll fill you in on the rest and buy you a burger on the way."

We would get along just fine.

6

I WASN'T SURE IF THE AMG WAS GOING TO BE SAFE IN the parking lot at SCMU, so we took it instead of Stubb's ride over to Nahash Pharmaceuticals, a division of Wyatt. We needed to have a word with Dr. Enrique Estabados. Route 52 north runs out toward the 17 and Summerville, where Nahash was situated. I offered to let Stubbs drive since he was technically my boss, but he declined because he wanted to reference his notes when he was filling me in on the other details of the case. It suited me fine, because driving that car was a blast. That is, of course, until I got my speeding ticket.

I was half-tempted to see if I could outrun the pig, the car was under two tons and had 451 horses, so my thinking was that I had a shot. But I didn't know the roads that well and you can't outrun radio. I didn't give a shit about the ticket anyway, JG would pay the fine even if he didn't know it yet. And since I was out-of-state, no points were attached to my driver's license. My fear in not wanting the ticket was that two unfriendly interactions with the local law in the same day might get noticed. And not in a good way.

Stubbs dropped the big bomb on me after we were through with the speeding ticket, thankfully. Because if I'd heard the news before being messed with by the Charleston County Sheriff, I may have been charged with murder myself.

The first death in the three serial murders was a doctoral candidate that worked under Sierra. That much I knew. But I didn't know that she died in her home, having bled to death from a snake bite. *Snake - there it was again.* She kept a pet snake, so it was originally labeled an accidental death. Only later, upon further investigation, the lovely Carina Fischer and the ME determined that the snake bite wasn't consistent with *her* snake. But it wasn't until after the second murder, seventeen days later, that it was officially deemed a homicide.

Stubbs enlightened me on the second victim as well. He was one of the lead researchers at SCMU, which again I knew from the report. He was penultimately killed at a lab on campus, again by a fucking snake. Which I didn't know. He too bled to death, but he had a nasty whack to the side of the head to go along with it. It ripped the flesh, tearing the ear off completely. Again, it was originally labeled as accidental but this time suspicions were up. They had an entire lab full of snakes, spiders and the like, but all were accounted for in their cages. Add to those facts that the shattered orbital bone and ear that they couldn't pair with any other surface or instrument in the lab, was leading to the scratching the collective heads of the investigators. Detective Carina Fischer first and foremost. It was then considered suspicious and coupled with the first victim.

Lastly, the death of the skinny lad at BIOGENESIS. It didn't take much to kill this poor prick, according to my new friend. He had his source or sources but I didn't ask him to share them with me because if the situation was reversed, I wouldn't want him asking. Anyway, this kid was a third shift lab worker. All he did was run tests for a living. Like the other victim, he had a massive head trauma, sending shards of cranial bone into his brain, the skin and hair were torn off the back of his skull. That alone would have done the trick, but the signature snake bite marks were present. He also bled out. Only there were no snakes in the lab. No snakes in that building.

Snakes. I fucking hate snakes.

We arrived at the main gate of Nahash at 3:30 PM. The guard working the booth was unimpressed. He was not about to let two private investigators into the facility to question anybody. But we got in.

Apparently the way to get what you want in the South isn't to be sneaky, snarky, or threaten with beatings. Which sucks because that's what I'm good at. Stubbs could have choked the life out of the guy without delaying another bite of his burger. His size alone would raise some pulses. But he didn't.

No rent-a-cop wants to be doing what they were doing for work. They all take on-line classes or go to Kaplan to study Criminology or some such thing. And they end up here, or places just like it. They don't show that on the commercials.   The guards want to be investigators, they want to be cops, they want to be anything other than a babysitter to a security gate. At $12 an hour, they could give two shits about a $12 billion patent. Which was probably the catch twenty-two of why he wasn't promoted and why he was still a security guard, but I digress.

Stubbs offered him a way out. He gave him his business card and told him if he let us in, that we wouldn't cause any trouble and he would see about a position as an Investigator with JG's firm. He also asked him politely to refrain from calling anybody inside to warn of our presence. We needed the element of surprise, he said, which is a key element of investigating, which he was sure the guard knew.

No shit, it worked.

For the second time that day, I was inside a pharmaceutical research complex, which looked almost identical to the first.   I wondered if inside all of the buildings were projected drugs for illnesses that people suffered from. And if so, how many of them were redundant? There were forty-nine parent companies with who knows how many sub-companies like the two I was in that day. There had to be two separate entities working diligently on curing the same illness.

Was it a function of keeping up with the GlaxoSmithKlines, or have we invented illnesses? I also wondered if we needed to invent new drugs to counteract the side effects of the drugs that were being invented in these buildings. I still wonder that, because I never received an answer.

We had no idea which building Dr. Enrique Estabados worked in. It wasn't like the Mall of America where we could just look at a directory. I think the guard who hoped to have another job the following Monday might have told us where to go, but we never told him who we were looking for.

We eventually found the Administrative Building. It was completely by accident because we were lost and had to turn around. But we stumbled upon it and thought it a logical place to start, even if it did ruin the element of surprise.

I must have been looking incredibly 'Metro' that day. I don't know if it was the designer clothes that I was forced to buy; or that I'm lean; or my dirty-blonde hair with a touch of gray; but I was definitely the receptionist's type. The gay male receptionist's type.

He was not into gargantuan muscles and rugged good looks, which was my new friend Stubb's look. It would have been my preference for him to be attracted to Stubbs. Nope, he was into the heavily tattoo'd and athletic type. All of my tattoos are covered as long as I am wearing a t-shirt and shorts, that was on purpose in case I needed to look respectable. I had taken my sport jacket off because it gets hot in the South during the summer months. The super-expensive designer t-shirt that I had on fit smaller than any other shirt I'd ever purchased. The short sleeves fell high on my arm, just off the shoulder, exposing my tattoos. He liked what he saw. I know this because that's what he commented on before we'd reached his desk. He cat-called me from across the lobby.

"Hello, handsome. Those tattoos are crying out for me to see them. How are you, delicious?"

Yep. Full-on Liberace, ballerina, pirouette, butterflies and rainbows gay. So I played the role. I'm a total whore, what can I say?

"Better now."

"What can I do you for? That accent of yours is so sexy, you just made my month." Two words. I said two words and everyone in a five mile radius knew that I was a foreigner. Well, Boston. Which in the South means that I'm a foreigner.

"I'm looking for someone, I was hoping you might be able to help."

"Get rid of that slab of meat next to you and I think you found him." I am pretty sure that he was referring to Stubbs, because he was sending him looks like daggers through his eyeballs. I was sincerely hoping that I wouldn't have to promise this guy anything. I wouldn't have lived up to any promise that I made, but I was still hoping I wouldn't have to make one just the same.

"Flattering. But I was looking for, excuse me, *we* were looking for Doctor Enrique Estabados. I lost track of which building he's in."

"Oh he isn't your type, honey. He might swing from both sides of the plate, if you take my meaning, but there's something about him that I just don't like."

"Unfortunately, we have to do some business with him, so there isn't much of a choice. I'll keep your comment about him our little secret though. Which building did you say he was in?"

285

"I didn't muffin, because he isn't here. He's out of town on business. Are you sure you have an appointment with him? Maybe I should just call—"

"—No reason to get other people involved. I don't want to disturb anyone. I lost the piece of paper with his address on it, I probably got the date wrong too." And that was the comment that sent his little pink antennae up. I never recovered. He must have hit a silent alarm or something because the storm troopers walked toward us calmly from several rooms on the periphery. We were surrounded by Secret Service looking dudes.

Stubbs and I had hoped to have the element of surprise, and we turned out to be the ones surprised.

Our first instinct, mine at least, was to go a couple of rounds with the security boys, just to see what was up. Stubbs looked at me for guidance as they slowly approached us. I think they were wondering what the giant was capable of just as much as I was. But it was neither the time nor the place. Dr. Estabados was our only real lead, and he was out of town. We weren't going to find out where he was hiding by causing a scene, or getting beaten up, or arrested, or any of the above.

These well-dressed security personnel weren't cops. Not even close. While they may have looked like FBI or Secret Service, they were not well-trained. They didn't cuff us, nor did they take either one of our weapons. I was happy about that, because I had just received my *PT1911* and hadn't even had the chance to test it out yet. They also put us in the same room to question us. Rank amateurs.

The guy in charge tried to play the bad-cop role, but he was the only person in the room besides us. No good-cop. And nobody was backing him up. With two guys that individually could give the guy a viscous beating, that was a stupid move. I know what I was thinking of doing to the guy, and I'm nowhere near as big as Stubbs.

He kept asking us where we were from, what we wanted, what business we had there and why we wanted to see Dr. Estabados? Neither of us said a word. It's not like we were in Guantánamo Bay and being water-boarded. This guy put on a scowl and changed his voice from soft to ear-drum shattering loud, and he would occasionally hit the table with his open palm, but he was pretty harmless. The last time he smacked the table I think he hurt his hand, because he winced and never did it again.

I didn't look anywhere but straight ahead. Not at Stubbs, and not at my watch. So I can only guess that it was about a half-hour to forty minutes of that nonsense before the guy left the room. Maybe to bandage his hand. I don't know that either because he never came back. Someone else did and led us to an elevator and then a non-numbered floor that needed an ID badge to get to.

We then were guided into an office. And when I say 'an office', I mean the mother of all offices. You could have played hoops in that thing if you took out all of the furniture. It was a corner office facing

Northeast, two of the adjoining walls were floor-to-ceiling windows. Those windows overlooked the trees of the Francis Marion National Forest to the right and Lake Moultrie to the left. We were well above the tree-line, so I would guess that we were at least ten floors up. I don't know what a space like that costs in Summerville, South Carolina, but you cannot buy a view like that in Somerville, Massachusetts.

The office was filled with fine furniture and fine books and fine knickknacks, but was void of humans other than me and Stubbs after our guide deposited us therein. We tried reopening the door but we were locked inside. I could think of worse places to be locked up, but trapped is not really my thing. I made my way over to the expansive desk to play with stuff but was thwarted by the man who was coming out of his private bathroom.

He wiped his hands on a towel and tossed it onto the floor of the bathroom from whence he came.

"Good evening gentlemen. It's almost five o'clock and I was planning on leaving for the day, then you two showed up."

"I think this is called prevening. Not evening." I looked to Stubbs who was trying not to laugh, then back at the mystery man. "Do you know what hour officially starts evening? I know it's not afternoon anymore. Happy Hour. Yeah, it's happy hour. Prevening or happy hour I believe is the preferred nomenclature. Either way, you must have a bar in this office."

"Very funny, Mister ....?"

" — Abbott. Bud Abbott and this is my friend Lou Costello. We're a comedy team. You might have heard of us."

Stubbs looked at me and said in his sheepish voice, "But I wanna be Abbott. He was the tall one right?"

"I am not amused gentlemen. You're both trespassing on a secure facility — "

" — It's really not that secure, guy. You should really look into that. As you can see anybody can just walk right in here and meet some hot-shot in a big corner office. What are you the President of the company?" I was fishing, and the guy seemed to know it, but he bit anyway. My guess is that he thought he had to give a little information to get a little.

"Whomever you are, this is not a laughing matter. We have a great relationship with the Charleston Sheriff's Department, and both the Summerville and Charleston Police Departments. A simple phone call can make both of your lives fairly miserable, I presume. I'm sure you don't want that, and I don't need the headache." *Yeah, I'm sure that's why you haven't already called the cops pal.* "My name is Rueben Feinstein. I am President and CEO of Nahash Pharmaceuticals."

"A subsidiary to Wyatt Pharmaceuticals," Stubbs said.

"Pharmaceuticals?" I said, "You must have something for my headache then, Rueb. Something without side effects though please. I don't want any anal leakage or anything."

"Yes, yes. Very drole. So I see that this is not an accident, you both being here. What can I do for you gentlemen?"

"You can tell us what you were stealing from BIOGENESIS, and where Doctor Estabados is. Yeah, let's start with those two things," I said.

"I think I need to know who you are before I get into denying any of your ridiculous accusations."

"My name is Warren Dennihan and this is Eric Stubbs. You can deny anything you want, but we know that Estabados was a double agent or mole or whatever. We can prove that he was on the books as an employee of BIOGENESIS, and your fabulous little friend at the front desk confirmed that he works here. I'm certainly no genius but it seems to me that something is askew. I wonder what the media would think? Whattaya think, Stubbs? Stuff like this goes very public, very quickly right?"

Stubbs didn't have a chance to answer.

"I don't believe you know half of what you think you do." He sat behind his desk and straightened out something on his pants, he was definitely picking at something while he thought about what to do or say. "I will only say that Nahash and BIOGENESIS compete rather vigorously in different areas because we are after some of the same things."

"How politically correct, Rueb. What the hell does that mean? What are you both after? And why did you have to kill three people to get it?"

What the hell? He was talking, so why not go for broke. In for a penny, in for a pound.

He was lost in thought for a few moments. Again, I can only assume that he was looking at damage control. Because what he told us was far more than what he should have.

Everyone around this case so far was talking about confidentiality this, and trade secrets that. This Estabados was all about stealing trade secrets and research. In terms of sound business decisions, telling two people who stormed into his offices, whom he had not vetted, was just stupid.

"Do you know what Nahash means?"

"Enlighten me. My vocab ain't what it used to be."

"It's Hebrew for serpent."

I shit you not, I looked at Stubbs and thought, *is this guy going to confess to ordering the murders of the victims*? Instead I said, "A pharmaceutical company named after a snake in a religious language. No separation of Church and State for you guys, huh?"

"Did you know that snake venom is already being used as a drug for people with heart conditions?"

Stubbs and I looked at each other and we both shook our heads.

"We hold the patent, and Wyatt currently has in distribution, a drug in pill form for those with high cholesterol and who are at risk of a heart attack. You may have heard of it."

"Fluxir? Flexor? Something like that right?" Stubbs asked.

"Yes. We—"

"—Did *you* know that all three victims of the serial killer were either bitten by, or made to look like they were bitten by, snakes?" I interrupted.

"I assumed. The news coverage had been extensive. The accidental death that has now been linked to all three was originally blamed on an unruly sna—"

"—So why isn't anybody beat'n down your door?" I interrupted again in an effort to keep him off balance.

"I'm sure it is just a matter of time before they do. But I can assure you that we have nothing to do with these victims."

"So you're saying the snake thing is just a huge coincidence?"

"We don't keep snakes here at the lab or in any of our buildings. We hired Doctor Estabados because of his expertise and connections at the World Toxin Bank."

"Refresh my memory on what that is again." I was playing stupid to keep him talking.

"SCMU campus houses a library which holds the most complete collection of samples of natural toxins in the world. Frogs, lizards, scorpions, eels, spiders, bees, pufferfish, snails, insects, even some mammals all secrete venom for a myriad of reasons."

"And snakes." The second victim died at a lab at SCMU. This guy was an idiot.

"Yes, and snakes. We're only interested in snakes. BIOGENESIS studies snake venom to create synthetic compounds, just as we do. They also have theories on other types of toxins found in nature, which is why they have sponsored the World Toxin Bank at SCMU."

"If everything is so confidential, how do you know that? Estabados?"

"The WTB is available to researchers all over the world. For a price. We have been unable to attain the access that we need. For reasons of self-incrimination, let's just say that it is my job to know what my competitors, such as BIOGENESIS, do on a daily basis and leave it at that."

"So why try to get them out of the way? If only part of what they do is what your company is focused on, why not merge or something?"

"This is cutting edge science. There's room at the table for everyone. I don't want them out of the picture. What I want is access to the World Toxin Bank and to beat them to the cure of very specific ailments. There are over 100,000 animals on this planet that have evolved to produce venom, and every few generations, they mutate. Some venom changes with either the prey's or the secreting animal's diet. So you see, there are an infinite number of combinations, and an almost unlimited amount of research that can be executed."

"Executed. That's a good word, the appropriate one. You're basically saying that you have unlimited resources for poison," I said.

"You have no idea what you are talking about. There is an enormous difference between a toxin and poison. Venom is a toxin. If venom were a poison, the secreting animal wouldn't be able to then eat their prey after they inject it. Venom is injected, a poison is ingested—"

"—You say tomato, I say—"

"—If you would stop interrupting and let me finish, sir ..... Venom contains toxic proteins and short strings of amino acids called peptides. Because of the ever-changing mutations and diets, we can only estimate that there are about 20 million venom toxins. That we know of, or can fathom. The World Toxin Bank, which my competitor has in its hip pocket, so far has only about 10 thousand samples. So you do the math, who would have easier access to a toxin?"

"Estabados. How's my math?"

He looked away from us and fixed his gaze on the bank of windows in the corner of the room. He was lost in thought again. Probably trying to help me and the silent Stubbs understand what the hell he was talking about. I was starting to get lost. All I knew is what I had already known when I was marched into this room, that Estabados was up to his neck in this. My only reason for finishing the conversation was to see if Rueben was involved also.

He started talking again, but didn't bother to look at us.

"Those toxic proteins and peptides that I just told you are found in venom? Each one has a very specific purpose, and that is what makes venom such a wonderful substance." He turned to face us again, to bring home his point. "They all have varying molecules with varying targets, which is what makes the science so cutting edge. Don't you see? While one venom might target the nervous system which paralyzes the messages from nerves to muscles, another might eat cells, which makes tissues collapse. Yet another might clot blood which makes it thick so blood cannot move and stops the heart, while its counterpart in yet another strain can prevent blood from clotting. Depending on what you want to target, you can use venom to cure

Multiple Sclerosis, Arthritis, Diabetes, Cancer, Alzheimer's, Parkinson's, Heart Disease .... You could isolate the target to the point of curing everything from Depression to Nicotine Addiction. The possibilities are endless."

"And you wanted all of those possibilities to yourself."

"NO. NO. NO. You are not understanding what I am telling you. Compared to BIOGENESIS, we are small potatoes. All of those facilities out there, that you passed on your way into my building, are *waiting* for samples of venom so we can begin to create these miracle drugs. We have created only one so far, and the rest are on the drawing board. It will be years before any of what we do gets to a pharmacy, if the FDA lets us get there at all. Estabados is to help us with that. BIOGENESIS has access to the World Toxin Bank, we don't. BIOGENESIS is on the verge of some major breakthroughs; but as I told you, those comparatively comprise one cell, off of one fingernail, off an entire human being."

"So where is Estabados?"

"You *still* think Doctor Estabados had something to do with these deaths?"

"I think, from what you just told us, that your good doctor was number two in a huge machine. And now he gets to be number one and in on the ground floor of what could be another huge machine. You just said he has ties to the World Toxin Bank. We have three deaths and somebody wrongly accused for them. He had motive, he had access, and now part of BIOGENESIS is shut down because of it. Estabados works for you as well, which benefits you in two ways; BIOGENESIS failing and access to the WTB. If you would like me to get the police involved, or the media, I would be happy to do so. Otherwise, tell me where Estabados is."

I knew he didn't want the police to be involved, otherwise they would have already been there to arrest us for trespassing. There was more to this than meets the eye, and the doctor was the key to it. Of that I was sure.

He turned back to face the windows. The long, early summer day was coming to a close and sun was fading into sunset on the other side of the building. The forest trees were reflecting the reds and oranges, while the stars were trying to wake up for the night.

"Costa Rica. He is taking venom samples in Costa Rica."

7

THE TWO INVESTIGATORS HAD NO SOONER LEFT THE office of Rueben Feinstein and the CEO was on his phone. While the two gentlemen could do nothing to him legally, they could still pose quite a threat to his enterprise if they followed through with the threat to go to the media. Or the police.

The President and CEO of Nahash Pharmaceuticals had underlings still in the building that were at his beck and call. It was late, and most of the employees that worked at one or more of the buildings had gone home for the day. A cleaning crew or two may have been lingering but for the most part the entire complex was empty. Rueben, some security personnel, and Jeffery his assistant were all that remained in the Administrative Building.

Feinstein picked up the receiver of his office phone and pushed the intercom button. "Jeffery, get me connected with Enrique on the secure satellite phone please."

"Is this with regard to the gentleman who was flirting with me earlier?"

"Jefferey, I don't have time for your nonsense. Just get Enrique on the line right now."

"Yes sir."

He returned the phone receiver to the cradle and sat in quiet thought while his minion worked his request.

Rueben had always been fascinated with snakes. He'd spent his first seven years in this world living with his parents in Brooklyn, New York. He grew up in a Jewish community, not devout, but they went to Temple every week. His father paid for good seats, until he was laid-off. The garment factory could not keep up with the rising costs of doing business in the city in the 1950s. What was once a thriving business that paid its workers well, was the shell of a building being sold for the real estate value. His father's building was now apartments. After the sale of the factory went through, Rueben's father had a line on a textile job in South Carolina, so he relocated his family.

Generally speaking, people in the South did't like New Yorkers in the late 50s. That is still somewhat true today. South Carolinians didn't like Yankee accents or their sense of superiority, even if it was just a perception. Maybe it was just the remnants of the ideals that the 'South Will Rise Again!'. Or maybe it was that not many people from New York were Baptist or even Christian. Or that the Yankees were moving south to take jobs from those that were born and bred in the South. The Feinsteins moved to take a job and they were definitely not Baptist.

Rueben had no friends. Not people anyway. He found a pet snake within his first week in his new home. It wasn't difficult, South Carolina was rife with them. Especially in the country. Going from Brooklyn, New York to the back woods of western South Carolina was a culture shock to say the least. Nobody liked him, and he didn't like them or their 'Sweet Jesus' ways. All Rueben had were his snakes.

"Doctor Estabados is on the secure line, Sir. The signal is five by five," Jeffery said through the speaker on Rueben's desk phone.

"Thank you Jeffery. You may go home for the night now."

"Thank you, Sir. Should we alert the security at the main gate about our earlier visitors?"

"I'll take care of that, thank you."

Rueben picked up his Iridium *9555* satellite phone to connect to the one just like it in another time zone. The hand-held device looked like an expensive walkie talkie but had the capability of securely speaking to anyone on the planet via satellite orbiting in outer space versus utilizing a cell tower. The secure line could also send and retrieve data by connecting the Iridium phone to laptops and other gear via those same satellites.

"Enrique. How is the field?"

"I have collaborated with the locals and we have a team here. The lab is rudimentary but we can make do," he responded with a hint of a latin accent. The connection wasn't crystal clear, nor was it difficult to hear one another.

"Excellent. When do we start sampling and when can we get molecular data to our researchers here? I have ten buildings full of people with their thumbs up their asses."

"I have some more people that I need to hire in order to ease the process. These people are very touchy about their natural resources. Any time the locals, especially the Costa Rican Government, thinks that we are going to damage their ecosystem, they come out with riot gear. Literally.

"I have the skeleton of a security team made up of Costa Rican mercenaries, but should have a full compliment that is fully operational by tomorrow. Two days, maybe three, and we can start analyzing samples."

"Have there been any problems with the locals so far?"

"No. That is why we must use the security team, in the event our purpose comes to light. We have been covert, but there is another, more urgent problem that I must confess to you, Sir."

Ruben closed his eyes and pinched the bridge of his nose with right thumb and forefinger. "What is it?"

"The other entities down here. We are not the only ones. I am working as quickly as I can to, how shall I say? …. Eradicate them and relieve them of their data. But there are at least five universities down here at the behest of other companies that are sponsoring them. New Colorado State and the University of Florida have been eliminated from the competition as of today. But we still have the University of Delaware, University of Utah, and the University of Chicago that are still an issue. Not to mention the Clodomiro Picado Research Institute and the religio—"

"—What have they learned?"

"I cannot say what the others have learned, but New Colorado and Florida have made significant strides in analyzing, among others, the Bothrops Asper. I was going over all of their data after gaining access to it; and it seems that not only are the aspers excitable unpredictable, and unbelievably dangerous, but they reproduce faster than any other in their genus. Which makes their venom mutations occur exponentially faster. Their venom is a virtual kaleidoscope of peptides with ever-changing attack sites. We just need to fix the other problem that I was about to mention before it's too late."

"More problems? Other than the Goddamned researchers? Just get rid of them and clean it up. Accidents happen. It's the rainforest for Christ's sake."

"I told you, I would take care of them. It's not just the researches, however. It's those religious nuts again. They are very well funded and very well organized. They've taken to air-dropping toxic mice into the field. I have no idea how they get through the very tight Government controls down here, but they're doing it."

"Air-dropping toxic mice? What the hell are talking about, Enrique?"

"I inspected one of the mice today. It's rather ingenious actually. They give the mice Acetaminophen, which is harmless to them, but is poisonous to the snakes. The Aspers eat the laced mice and die. They're killing off the snakes here like genocide."

"*What*? *HOW*?" Feinstein was now on his feet, pacing about his office, listening to Estabados explain their growing troubles on speakerphone.

"As I was saying, they give the mice Tylenol and attach little parachutes to them. They drop them out of a plane or something. The little parachutes get caught in the trees, which makes them easy prey and an easy meal for our precious material. Once the aspers are dead, their venom is rendered useless to us. But at least they won't have headaches, Sir."

"This is not funny! Get on it Estabados! We cannot let them do this! I will not let religious zealots be our downfall. Do whatever it is you have to do, but make sure you take care of it. And I mean quickly."

"Yes, Sir."

"Oh, and I almost forgot. The reason I called. Two investigators came looking for you today. They seemed fixated on the three murders here in Charleston. One of them, the smaller one, seemed very tenacious. The other one was a monster but he was quiet and probably harmless. If I were a betting man, I would say that they are coming down there to pay you a visit."

"Pay *me* a visit? How do they know that I am down here, Sir?"

"I'm not sure. They might be aligned with BIOGENESIS. Be on the look out. I will forward you the pictures from the security footage. If you see them, take care of them."

"I'm not sure I am going to be able to contain all of this …. Collateral damage," Estabados said.

"Just take care of it." Rueben terminated the transmission before Enrique could respond. He then turned around to look out his windows, but there was no view. Night had befallen the forested backdrop. Everything was pitch black. He needed to think things through.

You wanted to be the number one guy? He thought with regard to Estabados. *Well, welcome to the big leagues, son.*

8

AFTER THE MEETING WITH RUEBEN FEINSTEIN, WE HEADED back into downtown Charleston. Which, oddly, they call uptown. I again drove because Stubbs said that he wanted to jot down the conversation we had just had with the President and CEO of Nahash while it was still fresh in his mind. I was beginning to think that he didn't like to drive, because he seemed to have repeated excuses for not wanting to.

When he was finished, we called JG using the bluetooth interface technology of the *AMG*. He could hear both of us and we definitely heard him in perfect Dolby Digital 5.1 surround sound that was generated from the Harman Kardon *LOGIC7* entertainment system. Man, that car was sweet.

Stubbs informed JG that the Doctor that had defected over to Nahash was a prime suspect. Like his girlfriend and client, he too had access to the three victims. He also had the means, just like the accused. But he had a motive, whereas Sierra Byrne did not.

Dr. Estabados had been an undercover spy, if you will. Informing Nahash on trade secrets, stealing information, maybe even samples from the World Toxin Bank which he had access to. Not only did he not want to get caught, he wanted to get rich. Getting in on the ground floor of Nahash while taking down the competition and current employer, BIOGENESIS, could be billions of dollars was good for his wallet.

Dr. Byrne had no such interest. JG, our boss and her boyfriend, was filthy rich. She was the lead consultant or whatever to BIOGENESIS, and I was sure that she made a pretty penny as a tenured professor at SCMU. What possible reason would she have to kill colleagues that were working toward modern medical breakthroughs? None that we could think of. But that didn't stop Detective Fischer now did it?

Dr. Enrique Estabados was in Costa Rica, however, which made putting his feet to the fire all but impossible.

Or was it? JG told us that he would make the jet available to us. Stubbs was virtually dusting off his passport, but mine was back in Boston. Who brings a passport to South Carolina? It's definitely another world, but it's still in the same Country.

JG, of course, had a fix for that too. He had a company that he'd used in the past that could get me a replacement passport within 24 hours. He would let us know in the morning what time the flight left.

I had never been to Costa Rica before. I didn't really have a deep desire to either, if I was being honest. At the time, I wasn't sure why.

I dropped Stubbs off at SCMU, where we left his ride in favor of the *AMG*. He really was the Southern version of me. He drove the same Escalade that I drove back in Boston. I mentioned that I had the same ride back home. I also asked him why he didn't like to drive. He did love to drive, he said, but he found that sports sedans were a bit too confining for a man his size. He preferred his truck.

After a short conversation about the day to come, we bid each other a fond adieu. I think he might have wanted to go get a drink or something but I had other designs on the evening.

The night before, I tried to seek and destroy an old acquaintance of mine in Jennifer Beaumont. Jenna. I had failed. I couldn't even find her. At the time, she was the most beautiful woman I had ever met, in person. Inside and out. But that changed the following day, that day, when I met Detective Carina Fischer.

She told me to stay away from the case, but I felt that it was the right thing to do to inform her that she had arrested the wrong suspect. The wrong would-be serial killer. I insinuated as much earlier that day, but this time I had proof. Well, kinda. Plus I wanted to see about getting into her pants.

She hated me. Which meant that I wanted her all the more. She was hot, fiery, and confident. She knew sports and was not afraid to speak her piece. I was intrigued and I wanted her in the worst way.

When men really want something, they will go to great lengths to get it. Search everywhere to find it, even the dark recesses of their brain. I'm no different, slave to my desires. She had asked me earlier if I was with the 'eighty broad'. Which meant 80 Broad Street. I was on my way to pay her a visit. I didn't care that she told me to stay away from the case. Insinuating that I should also stay away from her.

I arrived at the Crimes Against Persons building of the Charleston Police Department on 80 Broad Street at about 9:00 PM. The old guy at the reception desk paid me no mind as he was much more interested in his *National Rifle Association* periodical. Which was fine by me. I was happy about the fact that he was preoccupied, I could not have cared less what he reads.

The vestibule on the way in told me where the Homicide Division was located, so I shuffled on past the man at the front desk that probably should have been retired. There was a man in shirtsleeves and a loosened necktie in an office off the left, and at one of the sea of desks in the middle of the room was Detective Fischer. She was slumped with her back to me under a desk lamp. I walked through the long room, weaving through the desk farm, approaching her from behind. In retrospect, it is unwise to approach someone that is armed from behind.

"Wanna get a cup of coffee or a late supper?"

Her head shot up as she saw me come around to the right side of her desk from behind her. She had an empty chair there, so I occupied it.

"You." She paused and looked behind her and around the room. "It's a little late in the day for coffee and I don't know what a *supp-ah* is. What is that, some kinda sissy drink?"

"What? No. It's a meal. Sup - per," I exaggerated.

"What'er y'all doin' here? And how did you know where to find me?"

"I came to see if I could have a chat with you. Maybe a meal."

"What, like a date? I don't date possible suspects."

"Suspect? What am I suspected of?"

"Nothin' yet, darlin'. But I told you to stay out of my way and here you are. I'm bettin' you will be."

"C'mon. What harm is it in having a friendly conversation? Think of the positive reviews your Board of Tourism will have."

"How do you know I'm not married?"

"No ring. And the way you were eye-fuckin' me earlier today, I just know. Plus if you were happy, you'd be home in bed with the guy. It's after nine."

"Yer pretty cocky, ain't ch'a? Whattaya wanna talk to me about anyhow?"

"You'll have to buy me a drink first. I'm not that easy."

"Yeah, I'll bet."

She took me to what she called a 'honky tonk'. I think that's what she calls a bar, because that's what it was. They had whiskey, so I was happy.

To my surprise she had one too. We settled into a relatively quiet corner where I started the conversation and made my first mistake of the evening.

"A pretty girl like you should be a model or somethin'. How are you a cop?"

"If I had a nickel for every piece a shit with a red neck and a small dick that asked me that? I'd be a rich girl."

"I didn't mean anything by it. I was just thinkin' that it might be tough to be taken seriously, looking the way you do."

"In the beauty lies the struggle."

"What is that, Shakespeare?"

"Is playin' stupid an act, or are you really not very bright?"

"I make up for it in other ways. But back to you. People probably give you a hard time. More than they give other cops. Men."

"I can handle myself, darlin'. It doesn't take-'em long to figure out that you don't have to mess with a bull to get hurt with a horn. You Yankees all think that pretty Southern girls are fragile and lookin' for a man to take care of 'em. This is gonna be a short conversation if you don't get over that notion and right quick. Now enough about my looks, and lets get on with why you wanna talk to me."

She may have said to ignore her looks, but I just couldn't. Her hazel eyes and pouty lips were not to be ignored. She had pulled back her auburn hair into a pony tail which displayed her long neck. She was tall and athletic, made taller by her high-heeled boots. Victoria's Secret models could eat their collective heart out.

"Have you ever heard of Nahash Pharmaceuticals, Carina?"

"My name is Carina. Not Carin-er, or whatever you just said."

"It's my accent, I know what your name is. Your accent is pretty thick also. Do you know of them or not?"

"Yes. They're an outfit out in Summerville. How have *you* heard of 'em?"

"Listen, I know you told me to stay away from this case, but there are things that you should know. Things that I am very sure that you don't."

"My end of the case is closed. I have my suspect locked up. The DA always wants more, but you can't bleed a stone. Hell, he'd love it we could get a confession out of 'em all, but life ain't perfect. Your lawyer-friend may have gone to Harvard and all, but he's puttin' the wood to the suspect. So pardon me if I don't rush on over to side of innocent just yet."

"He went to BU."

"What?"

"You said Harvard, but he didn't go to Harvard."

"In that case never mind. Let me just call the DA and see about gettin' the good doctor released. How could I have been so careless?"

"You're a ball-buster. I like it. But there's more that you don't know. And if this case is closed on your end, why were you interviewing the protestors?"

"You've got plenty a balls to bust, I'll give ya that. You come down here and think you can just muscle your way into this. That's why we don't like you Northerners, you think you're better'n us. You think you're smarter than us too. But you don't know shit about shit."

She paused to take a sip of her whiskey. By sip I mean she slung it back.

"Did you know that your doctor, Sierra Byrne, has a juvenile record. This ain't her first rodeo. People think that juvenile records are sealed, well not when you're suspected of a Class A Felony. That thing flies open for all to read, even if it was expunged.

"And has she come up with an alibi yet? Cuz she didn't have one when we arrested her. She wasn't where she claimed to be. She said that she was with her attorney, your boss, on campus. But she wasn't. In fact, nobody could place Attorney Grantes where he said he was either. He has a verifiable alibi for the first two, so he gets a pass. For murder, not for bein' a bad judge of character. I'm guessin' from the expression on your face that you didn't know any of that."

I didn't.

Carina continued. "So I looked to see if our suspect was on campus at all. That ID badge of hers kinda makes it hard to say you were in a lab when you weren't. All of those facilities are secure, you need one of her ID badges to get into her offices or any of the labs. They weren't used, which means she wasn't there.

Well that definitely complicates getting Dr. Byrne off the hook quickly, I thought. Where had she been for all three murders? And why hadn't JG mentioned that fact?

I ordered us another round of drinks and told Carina what transpired the rest of my day after seeing her. I told her about how competitive Big Pharma is. How they all beg, borrow, and steal to get their hands into the best universities. The best researchers. The best possible data.

I told her about our visit with Rueben Feinstein and his obvious reluctance to contact the police even when his security had been breached. About Dr. Enrique Estabados, who was essentially a double agent working for Nahash, and how he had set BIOGENESIS back decades according to Jarod Lynde. That the lab was shut down.

"My heart bleeds for 'em. But what does that have to do with the price of tea 'n China?" She slung back the rest of her second whiskey and winked at the nearby male bartender who had been eyeing her since the minute she walked in the joint. He didn't need to be told to pour another round. He probably spit in mine.

"What that has to do with China, is that Nahash needs access to the World Toxin Bank, which they wouldn't have access to without Estabados and won't if Estabados is found out to be playing both ends against the middle. Nahash is struggling while SCMU and BIOGENESIS are getting rich. PROXER stock prices are already a car payment per share, so investing in them is pointless. But if he tanks BIOGENESIS and gets in on the ground floor with Nahash, which is backed by Wyatt Pharmaceuticals, Estabados could be a rich man. These three murders are worth billions. And that, girl, is a lot of tea."

"You're a little short on proof though, Warren."

"Deni. Call me Deni. And Estabados fled the Country. He's hiding in Costa Rica. Besides, you must have a serial killer psychological profiler or something in your department. Does Sierra Byrnes as a mass murderer fly?"

"You watch too much CSI. We don't make psychological profiles on every suspect, we certainly can't afford one on staff full-time. A female serial killer is rare, which is different from mass murder. Your Boston Marathon asshole was a mass murderer. He did a lot of damage at one time. A serial killer kills outta anger, for the thrill, for attention, or for money."

"Exactly. Money. Sierra Banks doesn't need money, she's already well-off and dating my friend. My boss. He is stupid rich," I explained.

"That was just one of the motivations. We have to study all the psychological modeling published by the FBI, its part of my job. But they all don't fall neatly into place. For every profile that fits dead on the nose, there are the outliers. Did you know the first female serial killer ever recorded was right here in Charleston?"

"No shit?"

"None. It was back in the early 1800s. Her name was Fisher, but spelled different from mine. Anyways, her and her husband owned a hotel here, poisoned their guests and snuck the bodies out through trap doors. I think there might even be a tour if your interested."

That was an interesting side note. I wasn't sure if she was getting drunk or what the point of telling me that was. She flagged the bartender with her beautiful eyes again, but the drinks were already made and on their way over to us on our server's tray. I know I was getting drunk.

"Are you drunk, or what's your point? You still haven't said why you were conducting interviews on a closed case."

"I was dottin' my eyes, sorta thang," she said.

"And?"

"Try and keep up with me, darlin'. What I'm sayin' is that sometimes there's just a black widow. She gets messed up as a child and does shit where she gets a taste for killin'. Like your Doctor Byrne. Serial killers are always perceived to have a high IQ, but they are usually about average. Unlike the movies, most villains don't have advanced degrees. Ninety-three IQ I think is the average figure. And serial killers usually ain't female, though they don't always fit the mold. But of all female serial killers, over half of 'em use poison and are organized. That sound like anybody you know?"

Organized, used poison, and smart? Yeah. It sounded familiar.

I woke up the next morning with a huge hangover and a kitten had crawled into my mouth. It may have died in there. The bright light glared in from a window that I knew was not the one from my room at JG's house. It was on the wrong side of the bed for starters. I quickly realized that I was not alone in bed, either. I would recognize that head of hair anywhere.

Carina had her back to me sleeping, lightly snoring in fact, on the other side of the bed. She slept in the fetal position, which if I hadn't been so hung-over I would have found adorable. I lifted the covers enough to realize that I was naked, and let my hands do some reconnaissance to find that she was also. But my hands were cold.

"Aaaah. Warm your hands up first." She turned to face me. How was it possible that she was just as hot the morning after a night of drinking as she was during the day, roaming the streets looking for criminals?

"What happened last night?"

"You don't remember? It was a hoot'n a half."

"I'm a little hazy."

"Lightweight."

"What do you weight, like a hundred pounds? How were you not blitzed?"

"You handled yourself all-right."

311

"Oh yeah?"

"I did most of the work, but you can make that up to me right now."

I didn't mind that job one bit.

I had managed to have sex before my morning coffee. Which was rare. This woman was not bashful or reserved, which for me was also rare. When she was through with me, she left the bed as naked as the day she was born. She didn't cover herself in a sheet or tell me to look away, she just got out of bed and let me watch her go into her bathroom. She didn't even close the door when she got into the shower.

I guess when you look like she does, you get used to people staring at you. She was by far the most beautiful and most interesting woman I had ever been with. She didn't care what people thought, which is also unlike any woman I had ever been with. Her slender and perfect body is forever burned into my brain.

My iPhone rang while Carina was showering. It was JG. He told me that because he didn't know until too late in the day yesterday that we had to go to Costa Rica, my passport wouldn't be ready today, but we would fly out at oh-dark-thirty the following morning. I told him that was good, because we needed to talk. Today. That he needed to make time for me. He told me to meet him at 1:00 PM at a cafe on campus, and that he would call Stubbs to make sure he was there also. I liked Stubbs, but if he knew about Dr. Byrne's past and didn't tell me, we were going to have problems. I don't care how big he is.

When she returned from the shower and dressed, she was all questions.

"Are you sick? Do you have Alopecia?"

"No. I was drunk but my memory is fine. Mostly."

"Alopecia not Amnesia. The not having any body-hair thang."

"Oh. That. It didn't seem to bother you too much."

"So are you trying to show off all of those tattoos or all of your scars?"

"Being hairless isn't a choice, it's a lifestyle."

"You don't have to tell me, darlin', I'm a woman. I spend half my life shavin' my legs. Between ladyscapin', sleep, and the job, my day is pretty full. I'm askin' why *you do* it."

"You have very long legs, I'm sure it takes a while."

"Are you gonna answer me or not?"

"It's not just one reason. I have many. I don't understand why all women don't like it. Who wants a mouth full of hair? Can we get off of this subject now, please? I have a headache."

"Sure. So what are y'all plannin' on doin' today? It better be nothin' to do with this case. Don't let last night and this mornin' fool ya. I will bust you for obstruction if I have to."

I thought it was oddly sexy that she was a ball-breaker, but not that early in the morning and not with a hangover. At that moment it was irritating.

"I'm going to talk to the boys about what you told me last night. About Byrne's past."

"The boys?"

"JG and Stubbs. Eric Stubbs."

"Oh Eric! Now he's a sweetheart."

"You know him?"

"Everybody knows him. He's like a local celebrity. He only had two minutes of fame with the Atlanta Falcons, but he will always be famous in our hearts. Big 'ol teddy bear that one. Just don't make him mad. That boy'll make a mess you get him mad."

"So you *really* know him."

"Not like that, but sure. We went on one date. But I never called him back. Poor thang. Since we're gettin' into pasts sorta after-the-fact, you got a girl back home?"

"Not really. I have an on and off kinda *thang* with this chick who is crazy about me."

Althea was her name but I didn't get into it with Carina. She loved me right, but loved me wrong at the same time. Every once in a while I would run into Althea while on a case. Or I made sure to seek her out so that she could help me on a case. There was nobody on earth that could handle a computer better. Not that I knew personally anyway. We would always end up in the sack, which would lead us down the same old path. She is needy and I need space.

"Girl. Or woman. Not chick. We don't like to be called chicks. It comes from the word 'shiksa'. Which essentially means an outcast woman. It ain't nice."

"Well, get over it. Because you are a very hot chick. And that's a compliment."

"Very funny. I gotta go to work, so you gotta go. But I'll give you my number in case you wanna call me sometime."

"How about tonight?"

"Smotherin' me already? When do you go home?"

"When this case is over."

"I'll pretend that I didn't hear that."

9

I'VE HAD DRUNKEN SEX ON THE FIRST DATE BEFORE, but I really liked it this time. It wasn't just because she was super-model hot. It wasn't that she was smart and obviously had a wealth of useless knowledge. It wasn't that she was superbly confident in herself and what she wanted. Or maybe it was. But there was something about that woman that I can't put into words that drove be me bat-shit crazy. Maybe it was her foul mouth. I know my language could use some cleaning.

I had to find my car. Well, not my car but the one that I was using. The *AMG* had been left on the street overnight and I had hoped that it would be all right. The application was automatically downloaded onto my iPhone when it was synched to the *AMG*, thankfully, because I am not tech-savvy at all. Fortunately, is was right where I had last parked it. The map appearing on my iPhone allowed me to walk directly to the car, which surprisingly didn't take long. It turns out that if you leave your car in front of a police station overnight, nobody tows it or even touches it. I was relieved.

By the time I got back to JG's house, had some coffee and freshened up, it was about time to find the cafe. I remembered that nothing on that campus was marked, so it was going to take some time to find the place where I was supposed to meet JG and Stubbs. And it did take a long time. Even the map on my phone had a difficult time. Plenty of time to get there turned into I was late.

JG and Stubbs were already out at an outdoor table on the patio of the cafe when I arrived. They didn't have any drinks or food yet, so I wasn't *that* late. Or the service was terrible.

I made my way over to them, but I was made to go through the cafe first from the inside instead of just going over or through the outside gate.

"Hey guys, sorry I'm late. JG, why is nothing on this campus marked? How does anybody find anything? How do these kids make it to class?"

"We figure it out. Let's get going because I don't have a lot of time, even less now."

He was testy today. The early summer sun was bright and beautiful. Most of the other tables were utilizing their umbrellas for shade, but we were not. I could feel my Irish skin getting sunburned. The campus and the cafe were not busy, I assumed because it was summer and fewer students were taking classes this time of year. Either way we were out of earshot and eavesdroppers.

"I found out some things last night, and we have a lot to discuss. You two have been holdin' out on me. You might need to clear your calendars," I said.

"I'm not sure I like your tone, Warren."

"And I don't like being kept in the dark, Jacob."

"Fellas. Why don't we calm down and chat like civil people," Stubbs said. Odd that the big brawler was the voice of reason in this trio, but he was.

"I met with Carina last night and she told me that you provided an alibi for Doctor Byrne . An alibi which proved to be false. She said that nobody can account for her whereabouts on any of the nights the victims were murdered. She said that you weren't where you said you were, but they *can prove* that you were nowhere near the murders.

Which then leaves me to wonder two things. One, you aren't guilty of murder, but you are covering them up, which is a crime. And if so, why?"

JG sat in silence for a moment.

I filled in the silence with another question. "Did you have any part or know about this Stubbs?"

"No. What's going on JG?"

"She's Carina now huh?" JG said to me.

"I think that you're fixated on the wrong point here, kid."

"Listen, it's not what you think. I didn't kill anybody. Deni, you of all people should know that I would not risk my freedom unless absolutely necessary. I have Brady to think about here."

"I'm listening," I said.

"I was with Jenna the night of the third murder."

"Who?" Stubbs asked.

"His ex. Girlfriend not wife. It's a long story. I'll fill you in later."

"We had to discuss logistics. She has money and assets that were left to her from my ex-mother-in-law, and money and possessions from when we lived together. Our breakup was too painful for her, so she was moving out of Charleston. To Savannah, I think. Sierra is very smart and level-headed, but spending time at night with Jenna, my ex-girlfriend whom she was jealous of, would not have been good. I knew that she was incapable of the heinous murders, so I covered for her. It was impulsive."

"Why was she jealous of your ex-girlfriend, JG?" Stubbs asked.

"Jenna has the type of conventional beauty that stops traffic," he explained to us, though I already knew. "While Sierra is incredibly smart and stunningly beautiful, she was not able to get past Jenna's looks. It bothers her that her jealousy isn't rational, but deep-down she knows that things are over between Jenna and I. It would have upset her to know that I met with her that night."

JG had a point. I don't care how level-headed you are, Jenna incites attention and jealousy. It wasn't her goal or intent, but when you look like she does, it just happens. Flaxen hair and jade eyes on a body like that of Sophia Vergara. She gets noticed.

Dr. Sierra Byrne was also strikingly beautiful, albeit in less of an in-your-face kind of way. I have never succumbed to the whole jealousy thing, but in my business I have seen enough about the damage it does. Unfortunately some people lie and cheat. Spending your every waking moment of everyday wondering if your partner is one of those people, may just drive them to do so.

"Well she obviously knows that you were lyin', JG. She knows you weren't with her on the nights of the murders, and you told the police that she was with you on the night of the last one. Like you said, she's smart. Your credibility is takin' a bit of a beat'n here, kid."

"Another reason that we need to prove her innocence. In order to save my reputation, and my relationship with her, we need to extricate her from her current predicament."

"Did she say where she was on all of those nights? You covered for her — "

" — I covered for her on only *one* of the nights. My thinking was that if she had an alibi for one, she couldn't be a plausible suspect in all three. She said that she was doing research in the labs those nights. She teaches, has projects at SCMU, the World Toxin Bank, and at BIOGENESIS. She's very busy."

"Only the police looked into her schedule and calendars. All of those facilities are secure, you need one of her ID badges to get into her offices or any of the labs. They weren't used, which means unless she passed through without using an ID, she wasn't where she said that she was on any of the nights when she said that she was there," I explained. The looks around the table were all blank so I continued. "And what is the likelihood that she was able to access any of those facilities without an ID, Stubbs?" I already sorta knew that answer but I was driving a point home to my boss. The other one, not Stubbs.

"Nearly impossible. The murderer at BIOGENESIS used an ID badge from a former cleaning crew employee. I say former, because the person hadn't worked there in over three years. But they took out the CCTV footage. But that employee ID wouldn't be able to get into the SCMU lab or the first victim's house," he explained.

"Lets walk through this one more time shall we?" I asked. "The widely respected Doctor Sierra Byrne is a busy woman. She teaches at SCMU, where she had undergrads and doctoral students. Where she also heads the research for biotoxins, herpetology and venomology for that university. Her school also houses the World Toxin Bank, which is the authority on live samples of toxins, including snake venom. That university and the bank therein are funded, in large part, by BIOGENESIS, which is a subsidiary of PROXER Pharmaceuticals, whom she consults with on several projects. How am I doin' so far?"

All nods.

"So, the number two Big Pharma company is Wyatt, which owns Nahash. Nahash has their own doctor, Estabados, working covertly under Byrne in order to steal the research. Three deaths happen, all related to SCMU. All fingers point to Sierra because she worked with these victims, is really the only person who has unique access to two of the three crime scenes and can circumnavigate those security procedures. She really has no motive, but she doesn't have an alibi either.

"Meanwhile this prick Estabados is the number one guy over at Nahash Pharmaceuticals while still working under BIOGENESIS. He realizes this is not the best time to be in town, so he gets outta dodge and goes to Costa Rica in order to attain their own samples to start their own library of toxins."

"You missed the part where Doctor Enrique Estabados also had the same access privileges *and* he had motive," Stubbs said.

"Right. Thank you. Does he have an alibi? Was he investigated and cleared?"

"I don't know. Maybe you can ask Carina," JG said.

"Was that a dig? 'Cuz it ain't funny. I wouldn't know half of what I know about this case it wasn't for her, and I work for *YOU*."

JG didn't respond so I went on. "We also have to discuss, speaking of information that I got from Detective Fischer, the fact that your girl has a juvenile record."

Stunned silence infected the table. I waited for the weight of my words to settle in the brains of my two bosses. The fact that the famous Dr. Byrne had a record was obviously news to both of these men.

"Not possible," JG said. "She would have never cleared the background checks necessary for either the university or BIOGENESIS. What did Detective Fischer say that she did?"

"Juvenile record probably didn't show up on a background check. So you didn't know about it?"

"No, but that doesn't mean that she's a serial killer. What did she do?"

"I don't know, but it has to be pretty bad. We're going to need to ask her."

"I will ask her, Deni. Not we," JG said.

"Fair enough. You have anything else for me? Stubbs, no? You, JG?"

JG didn't answer. He was likely lost in thought about hearing for the first time that his beloved had a juvenile record that was severe enough to be re-examined and inserted into this case.

"No, but I did research Costa Rica a little bit last night while you were busy with Detective Fischer," Stubbs said after another awkward silence that was palpable.

What did he mean by busy? What did he know? Those thoughts ran through my mind along with *I gotta remember to ask Carina if she is going to look into Estabados after our chat last night.* Which is why I was only half-listening to Stubbs. Which meant that in all likelihood, nobody was fully listening to Stubbs.

" .... Costa Rica is a big Country, we can't just take a flight over there and hope to stumble into Estabados. But there is one central but large area where many universities and research projects go because of the diverse animal populations and the rainforest."

"Wait, what did you say? Are we are going into a rainforest? Like with the wildlife and shit?"

"Yes. Exactly. Where did you think we were going? The rainforest is located in the Tilaran Mountains which has an active volcano." Stubbs shuffled through some papers and read while continuing, "The Reserva Biologica Bosque Nuboso Monteverde, in the province of Puntarenas, is a tourist mecca for the wildlife and flora. But the research universities are permitted by the government to set up camps high up in the hills and rainforest, away from the tourists and modern comforts. That is where we are likely to find Estabados."

"Yeah, fuck that. Have fun. Keep me posted and let me know what I can do for you back here."

"You're not afraid are you? From what JG's told me, you're not afraid of anything."

"I don't have a passport." That was the only thing I could come up with at that moment.

JG was out of his funk and corrected me," you do in less than twenty hours. You leave at 9:00 AM tomorrow."

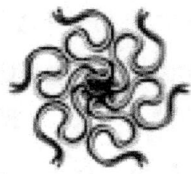

I wanted to call Carina once I was finished with the meeting at the cafe. I say meeting instead of lunch, because once I was informed of my impending trip, I was no longer hungry. I just needed to calm down first. I was nearly at the point of a panic attack.

I really don't like flying. I should clarify, I don't mind flying now that I was getting used to private jets. What I didn't like was the probability of crashing. You never hear of anybody surviving a plane crash. 'The odds are better of getting in a car crash' people say. And the way I drive it's more than likely, but I can and have survived a car crash. My thinking is that with every flight I keep pushing the probability that something will go wrong on the flight, and you cannot survive that shit.

Aside from the flying, I really don't like going to foreign countries. I don't speak the languages, I don't know the customs, and from my experience the food always sucks. I went to Ireland some time ago on a case. It's my homeland and I had been meaning to check it out anyway, so my thinking was that it would be great. But apparently I don't speak the same language they speak, the weather was horrible, and the food was worse. That shit they serve you on St. Patty's is not what they eat in Ireland. I did love the whiskey though

But the big reason I didn't want to go on this trip was the real likelihood that I would be around snakes. I cannot express into words my hatred and fear of snakes. I am afraid of an aggressive worm. People have tried to reason with me; tried to explain that not all snakes are dangerous; but when something can move faster than me without arms, legs, or wings; I scream like a girl at a Justin Bieber show. Only not because I'm over-the-moon happy. With snakes there was the very real prospect of me soiling myself. I was going to have to bring extra underwear.

"Carina. You got a minute?" I called her from my cell phone. I added her number to my phone that morning. The picture that I used for her contact was not one that she would appreciate, as I took it that morning while she was walking around naked.

"For you? Maybe one."

"Can we meet?"

"Sorry sweetie, but I don't have time for that kinda meetin'."

"That's not really what I was thinking but I like where your heads at. Have you looked into Estabados?"

"I told you that this case is off my desk. Why would I look into a case that has a suspect in lock-up? And why are you looking into him? This is all fun and games but if you go harassin' good citizens we're gonna have a problem."

"I spoke with Grantes about what you said last night. While Byrne may not have an alibi, she doesn't have motive either. Nobody but you thinks she did this. She may have been doin' somethin' shady but she ain't a serial killer. Estabados had the same access and he had a motive. Does he have an alibi?"

"Your attorney-boss lied to me, he's lucky I am not charging him with obstruction. I still might, along with you for interferin' if you don't knock it off."

"Do you know if he has an alibi or not?"

"No. Once we settled on Byrne, we stopped lookin'."

"I'm asking you to look. Please. For me," I begged.

"Why don't you do it, sense you're so hell-bent on breakin' the rules."

"Since."

"What, darlin'?"

"Since, not sense. Since I like to break the rules, not sense."

"I know how to speak, you ass. It's my accent. Yours is pretty hard to understand, we've been through this."

"Good point. Are you going to look into this or not? I would do this myself but I'm flyin' to Costa Rica in the morning. Me 'n Stubbs are gonna find Estabados."

"Is that really smart? If, and I do mean if, in the unlikely event that he is your serial killer, which I'm not concedin' that he is, isn't it kinda dangerous to be huntin' him down in a foreign country? Besides, even if you do find him, it's gonna take more 'n a lick and a promise to get him back here."

"I've got Stubbs. Besides I can take care of myself."

"And *I've* seen your scars."

"I'll be back in a couple of days, can you help me or not?"

"We can talk about it tonight. You are comin' over to see me tonight, correct?"

"With an invitation like that, how can I refuse?"

"Pick me up at the station around nine," she said.

"I'll wear somethin' clingy."

That night was magic. I was not drunk and able to focus on what I was doing. I couldn't keep my hands off of her. She seemed to be having the same struggle.

If our sex was compared to a boxing match, we were in a title fight. Round after sweaty round we went. And not just toe-to-toe.

We broke for food at one point. And some water. I had never felt so good in my life.

I had to get up at 3:00 AM in order to get home, change, and pack a bag for my flight. By get up I mean that I had to get up out of bed, because I was definitely already awake.

So was Carina.

"Hey Irish. Are y'all gonna come back and see me?"

"That's the plan. Are you gonna help me out? Look into Estabados?"

"You sure know how to ruin a moment."

"We've just had about fifty moments."

"Speak for yourself."

"Really? All that moanin' and grindin' and you didn't have a good time?"

"I was fakin'," she said with a shit-eating grin on her face.

"Yeah right. Ball-buster." *Sexiest ball-buster on the planet,* I thought.

"I'll see what I can do. Off the record. Just make sure you bring that dick back here. I kinda like it. My toys just ain't gonna cut it like they used to."

She was nasty and I loved every minute of it.

"I'll do my best."

Venom and other Scott Wellinger novels are available in print and ebook wherever books are sold.

GooglePlay

amazon.com

iBooks

WWPGroup.webs.com

nook.com

BarnesandNoble.com

kobo.com

and other fine retailers.

www.ingramcontent.com/pod-product-compliance
Lightning Source LLC
Chambersburg PA
CBHW080821250626
47160CB00008B/2819